Dmitry's Closet

Latrivia S. Nelson

Dmitry's Closet

First published by RiverHouse 01/08/2010

ISBN: **978-1-61658-745-1** *(sc)*

Printed in the United States
Memphis, Tennessee

This book is printed on acid-free paper.

For Adam,
My brave Viking

Acknowledgments

Thanks to Laura Sitterson for indulging me with hours upon hours of drafted material. Thanks to Markum Todd Lenowski for your invaluable insight and guidance into a new world. To my professor, Kevin Beaver, thanks for sparking my interest in organized crime. Thanks to my dear friends at Pa Pa Pia's, the local Italian restaurant hangout and watering hole, for jolly good afternoons and evenings. Thanks to Felicia & Robert Gray for helping me maintain my family and my sanity.

Special thanks to Kandace Tuggle for your help in my newest project. The cover looks great. Thanks to The Carter Malone Group and Deidre D. Malone for giving me the support and resources to finish this before I went crazy. Deidre, I hope to call you Madame Mayor before 2010 ends.

Eternal thanks goes to GOD for my dear family (Adam, Jordan and Tierra) who put up with me when I flocked to the cave. I couldn't have done it without you.

A special, juicy thank you goes to my loving husband, who fed me, held me, loved me and shoved me throughout this tedious process. *Tusen takk.*

To all of my fans, I love you so much. I hope that you enjoy this. It's all for you.

Chapter 1

Graduation was less than a week away, and Royal had no idea what she was going to do about living arrangements. The job that she had secured fell through two days before with a short phone call to inform her that the offer was off the table due to cut backs. So, she was about to be living in a hotel off of her small and meaningless savings unless she found a job.

Determined, Royal was now walking the hot pavement of downtown Memphis in a pair of worn black stilettos and an awkward, black borrowed dress suit going from interview to interview trying to close a deal that would promise her the ability to sign a lease to a one-bedroom apartment by month's end.

The economy was a mess. Over three million people had lost their jobs in the last few months; the unemployment lines were unbearable; banks were being bailed out by the bus loads. They were in the middle of a presidential primary election with no sure way to know who would win. And still, she was out trying to find gainful employment.

In her mind, there had to be hope. All it took was one manager to see her potential and give her a chance. She would do the rest. However, the odds for such an event happening today were not looking good.

The sun had baked completely through Royal's rayon getup causing the icky clothes to stick to her body. She was sweating from the outside in and holding back a heat stroke with a bottle of tap water.

Adjusting her worn out, black leather satchel on her aching arm, she stopped for a moment at an inviting, old wooden bench under the cool shade of a lonely tree.

She sat down, slumped over and took off her pumps. Wow, did her feet hurt! They were red from irritation, and a nasty little bruise had started to form on her baby toe.

Exhaling her last bit of hope, she massaged her heels and prayed for strength. Really prayed. Meditated as the waves of smoldering heat consumed her. For a moment, all was silent. The heat didn't burn, and the sweat stopped. The millisecond of peace gave her just enough clarity to not lose it right then and there by a homeless man, who stood a few feet from her talking to himself about the aliens coming on Thursday. She finally opened her eyes and focused.

Slipping back on her shoes, a small tear crept from behind her pride and tried to fall down her burning face, but she wiped it quickly. Like a stretching seam, she could feel her strength giving away under the stress, but she had to push on until she met her objective. She was capable of that…wasn't she?

The Memphis heat was ridiculously relentless. With not one cloud in the sky, the rays beamed down on the concrete and cooked the aching bones of her body like meat in a steamer. Salty sweat started again to pour down her face and neck into the collar of her shirt, making her feel sticky and leaving an unattractive and unmistakable stain. Her stomach growled. Rubbing it, she thought about the last time that she had eaten – many, many hours ago.

"Screw it," Royal huffed, taking off her jacket.

She could feel the humidity wrap around her skin as she unbuttoned the top notches of her shirt and curled up her sleeves to her elbows.

Desperate for a meal, she pulled a ten-dollar bill from her purse and wondered down Main Street looking for something to eat.

She would resume her job hunt after she had fed her growling stomach. Maybe then she would be able to think straight.

It was mid-afternoon and all the lunch dwellers had rushed back up into their high-rise buildings and their important business meetings. Now only shopkeepers, vagabonds and tourists walked the streets, monitored by police officers on bikes and in beaten up patrol cars.

Royal slowly inched down the cobblestone lane along the trolley line clutching her money and trying not to further agitate her pulsating toe. A hot wind blew down the street and brushed through her long, damp hair. She moved the wild strands from her face and yawned.

Feet swollen and stomach growling, she followed the beautiful smell of cooked apples and mangos to a small shop covered with large crimson awnings and smoke-tinted bay windows. She inhaled again, feeling her stomach growl louder in response to the prospect of a hot meal. Grasping the elaborate, hot gold handles, she pulled opened the large black, embroidered wooden doors and walked into the dark restaurant.

From the outside, the restaurant appeared very simple and adequate, but to her surprise inside the beautiful two-story building was decorated in decadent colors, gold textures and brilliant hues of crimson. It reminded her of a setting that she had seen on an old movie. She looked around curiously, wondering what new world that she had accidentally stepped into and grateful for it.

The winter breeze coming from the air conditioner cooled her hot cheeks instantly as the door closed behind her.

Gratified by the change, she sighed thankful for some relief. She would owe them strictly for the ability to not breathe fire.

Remarkably, the place was empty. No waiters or waitresses came out to help her. Standing alone in the middle of the floor, she looked around confused and cleared her throat.

"Hello?" Her voice cracked.

There was no answer.

She walked on.

"Um...helloooo?" she called again, this time louder.

There was an intoxicating aroma coming from the kitchen, indicating the place was still open. But where were all the people? Where was one person? Anyone would do. All she heard was music playing from the back of the room.

Instinctively, she followed the sound of a lonely violin weeping its melody from small stage near the bar in the back of the restaurant. She walked slowly on the wooden floors, feet still aching, to the edge of a staircase, where below a man sat playing the instrument.

The musician was perched flawlessly on a long, black piano stool. His wing-like arms were perfectly formed around the small instrument with his left arm protectively cupping the hollow wooden frame and his right hand gracefully guiding his bow. While his fingers plucked the strings, his eyes tightened as if the music was a continuation of his own emotions. Somber. Magnificent. Resilient.

Royal stood entranced by the beauty of the harmony, by the smell of the food, the stunning translucent glow of the foreign restaurant and the welcoming crisp air. Alas, she had found a safe haven in the eye of Memphis' hell storm of heat.

She listened on gratefully as he played, trying not to interrupt his apparent concentration. However, the melody that he played was so sweet and so alive that it nearly brought tears to her eyes. It sounded very much like her own life, full of high peaks and such low, intricate valleys. It was controlled by the men who had touched her, played like the man who now played his violin, made to cry out – to weep. Her little life.

The music swept through her, creating small goose bumps over her body. She sighed deeply with her eyes closed for a moment, trapped in his lovely tune.

Oblivious to his audience, the man played passionately with his eyes closed for a while, until he felt her presence. When the slits of his ice cold blue eyes opened, the grip on his bow loosened and his perfect chin dropped. He stopped, looked curiously at her for a moment and then set his violin down on the polished Fazioli grand piano.

Royal's breath was suddenly shallow. She didn't mean to spy on the man. She didn't mean to disturb him, but she could not help it. Without saying a word, he had imprisoned her with his fiddle.

There was a moment of utter silence as the exchange was processed. The two locked eyes and captured each other in a blank space in time, strangely enough with Royal still hearing his now silent violin. She looked on not knowing what to say.

At a loss for words, she swallowed hard and blinked. Only, the man did not move; his body was like a statue. He had no expression on his face, no surprise in his movements. He was merely there.

Finally breaking away from the moment, jolted out of his shock, the man stood up, exposing the full height of his monstrous enormity, and began to walk towards her.

His black, Italian dress shoes clicked on the wooden floor as he moved. Click. Click. Click.

Royal's eyes widened in awe. He had to be nearly seven feet tall. He was a giant; a very beautiful Zeus-like creature commanding in all of his presence. His golden blonde hair caught the sun in the reflection from the mirrors behind him and casted a luminous glow as he came to her, making it even harder to take her eyes off of him. He was absolutely mesmerizing.

Royal tried to move but was stuck. Maybe it was his sheer height or his liquid blue eyes or his chiseled, high cheek bones, or maybe it was just someone to serve her a meal, but Royal felt an indescribable urgency. Unable to move, her posture horrible, she was planted concretely at the top of the steps as he approached her.

In long, leisurely strides that equally matched his very graceful body, he moved down the aisle. She barely blinked as he stopped at the bottom of the short steps at eye level with her. He looked dead into her wide brown eyes, paralyzing her more.

While the shock was over, Royal still did not speak. Her mouth would not move. She only hoped that her eyes would speak for her.

The man stood stone faced for a moment then smiled at her nervousness. He instantly recognized her discomfort, sensed her attraction. Perfect, white pearly teeth were revealed under his shapely rose-color lips. A long dimple exploded in his left cheek and his eyes sparkled like diamonds. It only made Royal weaker, more lost in his spell.

"Is someone helping you?" he asked in a thick foreign accent. His cologne floated up to her nostrils, and she took in the scent of extremely expensive cologne.

"No," she said, voice pitched high. She cleared her throat. "Excuse me. No. No one is helping me."

She opened her sweaty hand and showed him the money to validate her reason for intruding on him.

He made his way up the polished wooden steps past her. She looked up at him as he did so, still in wonder of his giant build.

"Do you want to pay me for music or for food cooking in kitchen, my dear?" His deep voice reverberated throughout the empty restaurant as he talked.

"Just the food," Royal swallowed again.

He chuckled a little. "This is polite way to tell me not to quit day job, *dah*?"

Royal smiled. "I enjoyed it, actually." Her eyes told him that she loved it.

"Er…enjoyed it? Well, good. Now, come with me, my little spy," he said reading her.

She followed him obediently to the front of the restaurant, where he pulled a single seat from a table near the bay windows.

"Anatoly, bring me a plate of duck you are cooking," he ordered towards the kitchen door. He looked back over at Royal and motioned towards the seat. "Please, love, sit down. I have made you wait long enough."

"Thank you," she said sitting. His hospitality and warmness was most appreciated. It almost made her blush.

"You're welcome." He pushed her up to the table and bent down to her ear. "Do you like duck?" he asked, tickling her nose with his minty perfumed breath.

"I…I've never had it," she answered, feeling slightly embarrassed and completely controlled by the situation.

"Never?" the strange man asked, amused. His eyebrows arched.

She nodded no.

"Well, you will try my duck today. It is best in all of Memphis, recipe straight from Russia." He stood back up.

She nodded yes, frustrated at her sudden lapse in verbal communication. Struggling, she tried to make herself spit out her words and stop acting like a school girl.

"Thank you," she said again, forcefully this time. "I'd like that very much."

"It is my pleasure," he said, bowing out like a trained waiter.

"One question though?" she asked before he could get away.

"Yes?" He stopped and looked over at her curiously.

"I only have ten dollars. How much does the Russian duck cost?" Her eyes were wide. Maybe the man had mistaken her second-hand business suit for something valuable? She was in no position to pay for an expensive dinner.

"It will cost you *conversation* with me." He looked at her sweat-stained white oxford, run over pumps and exhausted state and felt instantly responsible for feeding the woman. It was the least that he could do.

"Now, if you'll excuse me for just a minute."

"Okay. Thanks," Royal said, watching his long, muscular body disappear into the restaurant.

A duck recipe straight from Russia? So he was from Russia? She looked around the restaurant again. Yes, unmistakably Russian. So unmistakable, she found the whole setting to be slightly stereotypical; all that was missing was a framed photo of Putin and the national flag. She looked over in the far corner, saw both and giggled to herself.

The day had most certainly turned around. She was about to have free duck in a plush restaurant with a hot man out of the hot sun. And that was completely fine by her. She needed a break. She's been job hunting all day. And if she heard, *we'll be contacting you*, one more time, she would lose her mind. What they really meant was that the economy was in a complete downward spiral, and she had a degree in business and no real experience outside of working her butt off doing odd jobs to pay for school, so she would never hear from them again.

However, she wouldn't focus on all of that now. This man had given her a millisecond break. She would just take it and forget for a while that her life truly sucked. Happily, she slipped her feet halfway out of her shoes, wiggled her toes and sighed. *Ahh.* Freedom at last.

Minutes later, the man whom Royal guessed was Anatoly came walking towards her lonely table with a two plates. The young dirty blonde moved quickly. His stocky frame was covered in tattoos, and he wore dark blue jeans and a black t-shirt covered by a white apron. His hooded eyes never looked up from the ground. He sat the food down and walked away. Then an even shorter redhead woman came out with two shot glasses and a bottle of vodka, two red crystal glasses and a bottle of wine and set it on the table in the same manner. She also never spoke a word.

"I was hoping that you'd still be here," the man said returning.

He pulled his seat away from the table and sat directly across from her. She watched him carefully while he inspected the presentation of his meal. His long, muscular arms rested beside him, reaching nearly the length of the table.

"Shall we toast?" he asked, picking up his glass once he was satisfied.

"Sure. What to?"

He thought for a minute then smiled. "To prosperous futures."

"I like that."

She toasted his glass and drank the potent contents. The burn rushed down her throat to her empty belly and caused a shiver through her body. Maybe it would do exactly what she wanted it to do - numb the awkward exhilaration of being across the table from the giant man.

"You took good drink," he smirked, sipping from his glass. "But it's vodka that I would recommend taking straight to the head, not the wine." He lifted his glass for her to observe.

"Well that depends on what kind of day you've had," Royal said, coyly. "If you've had a day like mine, then you take everything to the head."

"Oh, I see," Dmitry grinned, utterly fascinated.

Leering back, she poured herself a shot of the Jewel of Russia vodka. Boldly, she took the shot and set the glass softly on the table. With her index finger, she pushed it farther away from her. Instantly, she feels the magic burn rush through her body. She wanted to cough but held it in – defiant until the end. Her watery eyes told on her as she tried not to gag.

The stranger looked at the empty glass, at the strange woman and laughed aloud.

"You look like flower and drink like weed." His dimple deepened.

Following her direction like a good host, he set his wine glass down and poured himself a shot of the expensive vodka. He toasted her again and drank it quickly. The contents went down smooth and with no tingle.

His Adam's apple barely moved. Then, he set his shot glass softly beside hers and smiled back.

"I like your attitude," he said leaning over. "Tell me, what is your name?" His eyes sparkled like diamonds.

"It's Royal," she said, placing her napkin on her lap.

"Excuse me?"

"My name is Royal Stone." She looked up at him under long dark eyelashes.

"Where did you get a name like that?"

"I don't know." Royal poured another shot of vodka. She started to feel a little more relaxed and maybe even a little buzz. "Don't know my parents. I lived with a foster family until I was 18, and then I went to college. I graduate next week, and the company that I had landed a job with went under this week," she explained.

"Oh, so, you're out job hunting?" the man asked, more intrigued.

"Exactly," she said, taking another shot.

Dmitry eyed her. "Try the duck. I think you'll like it even more than the vodka." His silky eyebrow arched again.

"Oh, sorry." Royal smiled with more ease, putting her hand over her mouth. The alcohol gave her the edge that she needed. Plus, she liked how sometimes the strange man missed words when he spoke. English was definitely not his first language.

Dmitry smiled. "So, you're looking for a job doing what?" He continued.

"Is this an interview?"

He shrugged his large shoulders. "It could be." He sat back in his chair relaxed.

"Shouldn't I at least no your name then?" She was mildly sarcastic.

"Wait. You don't know my name?" The stranger winked his eye at her. "Everyone knows who I am."

His voice was now a low whisper as if he were telling her a huge secret.

"I don't know who you are," she replied, whispering as well. She tasted the duck. Absolutely delicious.

"It caught you by surprise, did it not?" He looked at her plate, forgetting their conversation for a minute. "I told you. The best duck in Mid-South. This dish was featured in…Memphis Magazine one month ago." He slapped his large hand on his equally large thigh in satisfaction. He was always pleased with a happy customer, even if she was not paying.

Royal nodded in satisfaction and at his enthusiasm. "Yes, it is very good," she confirmed. "The best duck I've *ever* had."

"Yes, after this, everything else will be all downhill." He looked at her for a moment, then shifted back to their conversation with a large smile on his angelic face. "My name is Dmitry Medlov." He stuck his hand out across the table and offered it to Royal.

She wiped her hands on her crimson-colored napkin and shook his hand gingerly, feeling his large fingers wrap around her entire hand.

"Nice to meet you. *Like I said*, I'm Royal Stone." After a few drinks, she was starting to feel a little better.

"Nice to meet you too, Royal." His eyes locked on hers, lingering. "Tell me what subject are you getting your baccalaureate degree in?"

"Business. Umm…would you like to see my resume?"

"You have it with you?" he asked, watching her as she quickly turned to her little tattered bag. His head tilted as he watched her every move.

Her long thin fingers rummaged through the well organized folders and pulled out an off-white cotton sheet of paper. It was the most pristine thing in her disheveled little existence.

Proudly, she reached out and passed it to him. Her resume. Her life on one miserable page. He pulled his glasses from his jacket and placed them on. She was surprised for a minute. Although, they did make him look even more distinguished, he didn't look like the type that would wear glasses. The silver wire rimmed frames sat perfectly on his chiseled narrow nose, across his suntanned face and his over his dreamlike eyes.

"Is this your restaurant?" she asked, interrupting his attention as she looked around.

"*Dah*." He nodded but did not look up from the paper.

"Does that word mean yes?" Another interruption. She looked back at him.

He glanced up at her, "*Dah*." His voice was silky smooth. He looked at her with a strange gaze then looked back down her resume. Royal was finally quiet, giving him a moment to digest her unworthiness.

Dmitry read her resume carefully with no expression on his face. She could not tell if he was impressed or like many of her other interviewers - unmoved, indifferent and ready to see her out of the door.

"And you graduate in one week?" he finally asked, placing the resume beside him on the table and taking off his glasses.

"Yes. I graduate next Tuesday." She sat up a little straighter.

"Tell me, Royal. Are you particular about what job you would like?" He put his glasses back inside of his coat jacket and focused in on her, a hint of interest on his face.

"I'd like a job with the potential to move up in the organization, but I'm willing to start anywhere."

Dmitry smiled. "That is sign of hard worker," he said pointing at her. "You've never been given anything. And so, you know how to work hard to get it or take it."

"If I need to, *dah*." She smiled.

Dmitry's eye twitched. She was quick and spunky, and he was completely paralyzed by her natural beauty. He had been struck since the moment he opened his eyes, and she was standing in front of him while he played the violin.

She had appeared like a dream, standing there like she had just fallen out of the sky. He had to blink when he saw her. He blinked hard to make sure that she was real and not some figment of his imagination, some illusion due to his aching loneliness. He knew that she was real when he saw the sweat glistening from her body. It was the only sign that God had given him to let him know his angel was human.

Her long, shapely figure was concealed under her baggy clothes. Her gaze spoke of trust, not deceit. She was refreshingly innocent. Her bright eyes told her entire story. She was what he was playing for and praying for…a sign.

"So what do you think?" she asked finally.

"You've done good work," he said, realizing that he had zoned out far too long. "I'd like to make you a proposal." He smirked at how fluid that statement was for him.

"Okay," Royal said, putting down her knife and fork. She listened on attentively.

"I'm opening new business not far from here. Really just couple blocks over. I need someone who is willing to give it their all. It's a new clothing store. I call it *Dmitry's Closet*. It's full of nicest clothes for women. However, I need young shop keeper for this one. Do you have kids, husband, something like this?"

"No," Royal said, clearly seeing that this guy knew nothing about HR. One was never supposed to ask those types of personal questions on an interview, but she didn't care, *as long as he gave her the job.*

"Good. This is just what I want to hear," he said, slyly. "The person that runs my shop will have nice apartment just above the store. You see, I own entire building. You have the degree, the professionalism, the drive I need to make *Dmitry's Closet* into Memphis' next big boutique."

"So, you want me to manage your store and in exchange you'll give me an apartment?" She was suddenly unimpressed. It was only half of what she needed.

"No…I want to offer you much more," Dmitry said, excited about her ability to bargain.

"How much more?" Royal asked, leaning into him in anticipation.

"As long you work for me, you have this and to start off sixty grand. You have to hire part-time staff, do inventory, and keep books. But I see from your resume that you have experience with this." He knew in this economy, he was offering her a lot more than he had to, but he wanted to keep her, even though her experience was actually very limited.

"$60,000?" Royal sucked in her own breath.

"Are you starting to be interested now, Royal Stone?" he smiled.

"Of course. Since it is close, can we go there and see it?" Suddenly, the duck was not at the top of her list. She could eat later, after she had secured this job.

Dmitry smiled a little smile of success. She had taken the bait. He would have easily paid her $80,000 to take the job, to keep her near. Now, he was simply saving twenty grand.

"Yes. After you finish your meal, I'll take you over."

Dmitry smiled at her. He could see the passion in her eyes. She was a young businesswoman. Her ambition would drive his newest investment, and if she wasn't careful she would drive him to give her much more.

"Anatoly, get my car to the front. I want to take Ms. Stone to my new shop," he ordered, absently. His eyes were still fixed on hers.

Chapter 2

When Royal finished her late lunch with Dmitry, he escorted her back out to the front of the restaurant, where his silver SRL McLaren Mercedes-Benz was parked waiting for them. He opened the door for her and waited as she hesitantly loaded herself and her little bag inside. He slid on his shades as he closed the door behind her and made his way to the driver's seat.

Royal watched him carefully. She was young, barely 23, but she knew money when she saw it. And if his car was any indication, Dmitry was very wealthy.

Dmitry drove calmly through the streets, not caring for theatrics. He did not have to prove himself. And his confidence was apparent, probably because he was driving a four-hundred thousand dollar car and wearing a suit that cost more than her tuition. His long body fit perfectly into the gray leather chairs. His curly blonde hair shined like spun gold in the sunshine.

He looks perfect, Royal thought to herself as she glimpsed over at him.

Dmitry looked over and smiled softly at her.

As quickly as they had pulled onto the streets of downtown Memphis, they were pulling off into the back alley of a renovated building. Dmitry parked and helped Royal out of the car.

"I want you to get full effect," he said, taking her hand. "So, we must go around to front."

The building sat across from the fire department and the National Civil Rights Museum only entries away from the popular boutique Muse. His place was swank and modern. A real attention getter. The architect had paid extra close attention to the detail of the brick masonry and custom limestone design. The boutique screamed money, even before she saw the inside.

"You believe in facing the competition head on," Royal observed, looking at the customers pile into the neighboring store.

"This is healthy, yes? The customers now have true variety." He took the keys and opened the huge wooden double doors that mildly reminded her of his restaurant.

"These doors are beautiful," she noted.

"I had them flown in from Moscow," he said proudly. "Well, here it is."

As the doors opened, the light shined in on the dark boutique. It was clean and empty, awaiting clothes to fill its hollow shell. *Dmitry's Closet* had massive potential. The floors were a shiny alabaster wood. The mirrors were over exaggerated and designed with beautiful gold frames. Crystal chandeliers hung from the tall ceilings illuminating the room with sparkling light as the sun shined in from the front door. The large windows were covered in beautiful stain glass and the walls were painted in Dmitry's signature crimson.

Royal shook her head. "It's so…beautiful." She touched the mirrors and looked around in awe. "This whole place is like a dream."

"This is what I want. When women come in to buy best in clothing, I want them to feel as though they are in best that Memphis has to offer. I, of course, had to give it a little old time Russian flare."

"Yeah, like the restaurant," Royal chimed in delighted.

"This is what you business majors call *buying into the vision.* Yes?"

"Exactly," she giggled.

Dmitry looked down at her and bit his lip, as he captured a glimpse of the beauty mole on her neck – ever so feminine, ever so inviting. Her bright brown eyes gazed up at him oblivious to his thoughts. In her mind, she just wanted a job. However, he wanted to reach down, grab her soft, caramel face and kiss her satin pink lips. But he could see she would resist him. He stepped away, removing himself from the close proximity of her body and the heat that she naturally radiated.

"I think that I've definitely bought in, and I haven't even seen the apartment."

"It's upstairs," Dmitry said quietly, bringing himself back from his trance. "And there is surprise for you. Well, not you specifically, but for whomever, I choose for job."

Royal followed him out the shop into a beautiful back office with a dark cherry wood credenza, continued Russian elegance and expensive furniture.

"This is where you will keep inventory," he said, barely stopping so that she could see the office.

She followed carefully, felling a little weary of where she was going. What if Dmitry had only one intention – to get her upstairs and rape her?

Her heart fluttered at the thought. No one knew where she was or what she was doing. As quickly as all of this had happened, it could end. She stopped on the first step and looked up.

"What is the matter?" he turned and looked at her staring at him like a deer in headlights.

Royal did not speak.

"Strange man, strange place?" he asked, realizing her concern.

"Something like that," she answered, sighing in relief that he understood.

"Do you have cell phone?"

"No."

"Here, use mine." He pulled his Blackberry from his coat jacket and offered it to her. "Call someone. *Anyone.* Tell them where you are. And that way, you have peace of mind."

Royal took the phone and looked at it. She really didn't have anyone to call. The thought mildly angered her. No best friends. No sisters. No brothers. Her adopted parents would not be at their apartment this early in the afternoon. She shook off her pain and looked back up.

"Whatever, just show it to me," she snapped and walked past him on the stairs.

"This is what I'm trying to do." He put the phone away, realizing that this must be a very touchy subject for her.

There was only one door on the second level of the entire building. It was a sprawling creation with the same wooden cherubs that were carved on the front of the restaurant doors at *Mother Russia*. Again, he took a key and opened the large oak double doors to an airy, romantic loft.

As the doors swung open, a fresh cinnamon aroma drifted out to greet her. He walked in first, and Royal soon followed absently. Her mind was still wrapped around her lonely existence until she saw the luxurious space.

Expecting to see white walls and simple fixtures, instead she was greeted with elegant luxury that rivaled anything she had ever witnessed firsthand, and she had worked in a four-star hotel. In amazement, she wondered around the airy place engulfed by its exquisiteness and imagining what it would be like to live there.

"Do you see my surprise? It's fully furnished." He hit the lights and the large living room lit up. Leisurely, he sat down on the plush leather couch and checked his cell phone.

"Dmitry, this is gorgeous. I can't believe it." She paused for a moment. Walking aimlessly through the loft, she marveled at the endless, intricate beauty of the magnificent baby palace.

From one room to the next she wondered until she arrived at the master bedroom. "Oh my God!" she exclaimed, standing beside the king size canopy bed, draped in fine fabrics under the wooden vaulted ceiling and dimming lights of her future bedroom.

Dmitry finished sending his text messages and met her at the door of the bedroom, where he found her sitting on the side of the bed rubbing the comforter. He leaned against the door but refused to cross into the room.

"My thought was that if woman who runs my shop feels what it's like to live in luxury, she might better understand what quality of *Dmitry's Closet* must be." He smiled cleverly. His wide pink mouth showed signs of age. "You are very impressed, yes? I can tell. You have…sparkle in your eyes."

"Very impressed," she repeated, getting off of the bed.

She stood in the room tapping her foot with her arms crossed and smiling. An overwhelming sensation of accomplishment consumed her. This all could be hers.

"So, you want me to run the shop and live here?" she squeaked, shaking her head in astonishment. Placing her hand over her throat, she smiled and cleared her throat again. Why did she keep choking up around him?!

"No, I want much more from you than that. I want you to transform my vision of *Dmitry's Closet* from fantasy into reality. I have clothes being flown in from every stretch of the United States, Europe, Asia, Africa and mother Russia. I want this to be international house of style for southern belles of Memphis, and I want *you* to make them feel as though they cannot get this experience anywhere else in city."

Royal felt a little tipsy from the wine and vodka that she had earlier, so she sat back on the bed as she listened quietly. Dmitry went on like a professor in a lecture series about his marvelous ideas for the store and what he expected from her. During which time, he barely looked at her or took a breath, rather he looked towards the ceiling and around the room, as though he was envisioning the tasks that he was laying before her come to fruition before his very eyes.

When he finished, he zoned back in and realized that Royal was still sitting there.

"Did you get all of that?" he asked with a half-smirk on this face.

"It's a grand plan, Dmitry," she sighed and shook her head. "But as much as I want it, why would you pick me? I don't know anything about rich people, rich women, or expensive designer clothes. I mean, Jeez. I'm poor. Have you checked out my suit?" She pointed at her clothes and sneered.

Dmitry stood listening to her quietly berate herself with his hands folded against his large chest and his eyes glued to her mouth, not only listening to what she was saying but how she said it. Such doubt. He finally spoke, cocking his eyebrows as he did so.

"You are not rich. Okay, but you are beautiful, and you are mysterious and what you do not have, you must learn to fake, until you can obtain it. Trust me. I know little something about this."

Dmitry was mildly entertained by the humble creature. She was so beautiful, it was hard to look at her, yet one did so with ease because of her constant humility. She was a marvelous spectacle to him, only she did not know that she was a spectacle at all.

"I don't want to let you down," Royal professed, feeling a little overwhelmed. "This is a lot to offer any one person. It's a great opportunity." She sighed.

"May I come in?" Dmitry asked, still behind the threshold of her bedroom. He looked down at the doorstep menacingly but never let his large leather shoe cross it.

"I'll come out," she said, very happy to keep the barriers intact. Quickly, she walked out of the bedroom and followed him down the long corridor through the large living room to the breathtaking dining room, where they both sat at the elegant wooden dinner table.

Dmitry sat down across from her with ease. His long body sprawled out in the plush velvet-bottom seats as he crossed his legs. His swagger was almost too much for Royal. Did he intentionally try to seduce her?

His ice cold blue eyes were fixed on her as he began to talk. His baritone treble was silky smooth and crystal clear. It shook his Adam's apple and the words that twisted menacingly around his accent. Yet, he talked with ease and his voice soothed a lonely, dark spot in her heart.

"When I first came to this country, I was just a little younger than you. I was not poor, but I was not rich like I dreamed of becoming. So, I faked it until I got where I wanted to be. It's not easy, you understand, but it is not hard, if you think of other option."

"What is the other option?" Royal asked, sitting across from him with her hand on her face listening carefully.

He sighed and smiled. "The other option is to fail – to go back to your family with your tail tucked between your legs and pray that someone has mercy on you." He leaned forward pulling her deeper into their conversation.

"I don't have a family that will take me back. And I don't have a tail to tuck." She did not blink.

Royal's game face emerged. While she did not always master a thing, she did not believe in quitting. And to assume or presume that she would, hit a nerve that created a faint sense of offense in her tone.

Dmitry instantly picked up on it and enjoyed the frustration and desire that boiled in her stomach.

She breathed heavily as she listened, her cat-like eyes burned through him, and the veins in her neck pulsated. He watched her – nostrils flared – make her case. Royal was a fighter. He could tell.

"Well, now's the time. Tell me what you think that you have to offer. I think that I know, but it means nothing if you don't know yourself," he lectured.

"Well, I may not have the best grades, but I don't have the worst. I may not have two dimes to rub together, but I have pride. If you want me to do this job, and you trust me to give it my all, I will, because I'm no coward. If I do it, I'll do it right and face every challenge head on. I just want you to know up front that I'm no glamour queen. I'm not part of the *in-crowd*, and I don't come from money."

"Well, good. Because neither do I. We're just couple of people chasing the American dream." Dmitry smiled.

She was incensed that he had insinuated that she could not perform.

He liked that. He liked her.

Royal smiled, eased by his observation. "Okay then, if you're okay with that, I'll do it. I'll run your shop."

"I have great confidence that you will," Dmitry said.

He reached in his pocket and pulled out a key. He stopped as she reached out.

"Has man ever given you apartment on first date?" he asked playfully.

"No," Royal said as she reached out and took the key from him.

"Well," he hunched his shoulders. "There is first time for everything."

Chapter 3

The airstrip stunk of burned rubber and jet fuel when the latch snapped open to Dmitry's private jet. Hot winds blew through his hair and singed his cheeks as soon as he ducked out of the plane. He took a deep breath and smiled. Home. He and his party unloaded quickly, perspiring instantly as their feet hit the steel stairwell.

Dmitry was glad to be back from his short trip to Manhattan. The grueling meetings had all but exhausted him, and he longed for the slower, simpler life of Memphis. Plus, he was eager to get back to see the progress of the new shop and Royal.

Feeling the high-noon rays beaming down on him, he quickly threw shades over his Arctic eyes and ducked into the back of his limo. As his driver loaded his luggage into the back of the black Mercedes, he checked his voicemails and text messages. Two texts from Anatoly. Nothing from Royal. That was not hard to believe. She worked like a scared horse, bucking at anyone who got in the way of her progress.

A tall, breathtaking woman got in on the other side of the limo adorning gold jewelry, a short white silk dress and gold stilettos. She instantly reached for the bottle of water in the side compartment. Hot and frustrated, she looked over at him typing away on his Blackberry and scoffed.

"Why do you stay in this hell hole?" she asked incensed by the heat. Her Russian accent was as thick as his, only she was far more arrogant.

Dmitry looked over at her and then sat back in his seat.

"Anatoly, take me to Royal. I want to see what she is up to," he ordered, ignoring the woman.

"Who is *Royal?*"

"She is shopkeeper for my newest store. It's coming all together, perfectly. We'll be ready to open in two weeks."

He looked over at her to see if what he assumed was correct. It was. His companion had cut him off already. Whenever he began to talk about anything other than her, she tuned him out. With her long porcelain legs crossed, she rested back on the leather seat massaging her temples.

"What time is show tonight?" she asked, changing the subject.

"Nine."

"Well, I don't want to go hang out in closed store while you work."

Dmitry looked over at her again, this time slightly annoyed. Dahlia was no rocket scientist, but she was remarkably beautiful. Only a few inches shorter than Dmitry in her stiletto heels, she was six feet two and stunning. Her eyes were a shade of deep blue that reminded him of the Baltic Sea, her hair naturally platinum blonde and her bone structure rivaled the Heidi Klums of the world. She was a perfect muse, great for runways and billboards – slim, tall but shockingly empty. Unfortunately, outside of sleeping with her, he found her completely dull, even if she was a grand show piece.

"I will have Anatoly take you to hotel after he drops me by my store."

Feeling that he had given her far too much attention, Dmitry turned his focus back to his Blackberry and remained engrossed in his business the remainder of their drive.

∞♥∞

Dmitry's Closet was closed to the public and the many downtown dwellers that had pushed their faces up to the glass to see into the intriguing building, but inside it was alive with music, lights and boxes, all being animated by Royal, who had the stereo blasting as she worked.

Alone in the large building, she fell over mannequins, wooden hangers and plastic bags, as she tried to wrap up the first part of her day to go have a late lunch upstairs in her bedroom. All she could think about was a nice quick power nap and a hot shower.

She looked around the boutique at how far it had come in such a little time and sighed in wonderment. All the things that Dmitry had spoken of were coming to fruition right before her very eyes. It had become more than a job to Royal; it had become her passion. He had fed it into her daily with his constant support and his ever trusting guidance.

Dmitry was equally inspired, constantly bringing over his friends and colleagues to see his newest project, and from what little she had learned about Dmitry, he had quite a few of them. Everyone who was able to sneak a peak of the place left in awe and gave him nothing but good reviews on the shop and her.

According to her boss, she was dependable, on schedule and under budget. So in his eyes, she was on point. A little smile crept from the sides of her mouth as she relished in her accomplishment.

Plus, she always liked pleasing Dmitry. It was the way that he conveyed his appreciation that was so special, always with an endearing kiss on the forehead, a gift of precious stones and a look that swallowed her whole. His eyes would capture her in the middle of all of their conversations. They would burn through her thoughts like lasers before he drowned her with his silky voice and his cool demeanor. That was Dmitry. She was sure that he had that affect on everyone. She brushed it off now. After all, what was she to him? An employee.

Needing motivation, she grabbed the remote, turned off the stereo and turned on the large 72" plasma television mounted against the back wall. CNN's *Black in America 2* was showing. Seen it. Twice. But it would do. She just needed something to keep her going.

"Let's do this," she said slapping her hands together.

"Yes…let's," Dmitry replied standing in the back of the shop watching her.

"Dmitry!" she turned and exclaimed both happy to see him and shocked that he was back so soon. "I thought that your business in New York would keep you longer?"

"I closed the deal and moved on," he said, shrugging his shoulders. His smile was smug and confident, but his eyes were happy to see her. They sparkled in exhilaration.

She set down her hangers on the wooden floor and bounced over to greet him. Dmitry watched in complete satisfaction. Royal wore a pair of denim skinny-legged jeans, a grey tank top that showed the round melon-like shape of her breasts and her hair in a ponytail. She was such a simplistic beauty, a refreshing contrast from Dahlia. He smiled wider, this time more appreciative to be in her presence.

"Sorry, I look a mess," she said, noticing his stare but misinterpreting it. "However, I've gotten tons done since you left." She ran her fingers down her long, bo-legs and turned to look at the store. "It's really coming along." She sighed proudly and turned back around to him. Her long ponytail danced behind her.

"You're doing a great job." He moved her long mane from her shoulders affectionately.

"Thanks. It's just that we are getting closer and closer to opening, and I'm getting so nervous." They walked as she talked. "I want you to look over the numbers again. I don't know how you're doing it, but the purchase of these clothes at these prices has saved us a bundle. We are nearly twenty-five percent under budget right now." Her eyes were bright with enthusiasm.

"Due largely to you," Dmitry added, lightly touching her arms. He could never keep his hands to himself around her. "I'm very, very proud of you, Royal. You have exceeded all my expectations."

"Wow, Dmitry," Royal said, a little choked up. "Thanks. That…means a lot."

"You're welcome," he sighed, remembering to pull himself from her trance. He blinked hard. "I've got something for you."

He reached into his pocket but didn't take his eyes off of her.

"What's this?" she asked.

"Thank-you gift," he said, leaning over her body to give her his present.

"Another one?"

"Open it now," he urged.

Royal was never uncomfortable to be close to him. Dmitry found that odd. She was so close until he could smell her sweet perfume and the sweat of a long day's work. But she did not back away. She stood there as if to say that this was her space and if he felt uncomfortable, he should step away. But he did not; he stood closer – as close as he could.

She looked up at him with huge, cat eyes and smiled, recognizing the teal blue box wrapped in a white ribbon. Tiffany's.

Dmitry constantly showered her with gifts, and she let him. However, he wasn't sure if she allowed him to because she felt that she deserved it, *which she did,* or if was because she understood his growing attraction to her and felt the same. Either way, he was glad that she accepted his gifts, and he looked forward to giving her something that they both could enjoy in the very near future. He smiled devilishly at the thought.

"This is beautiful," she said, looking at the diamond earrings. They sparkled like his eyes. She liked that most. Constant reminders of him.

"They are two carats. You should wear them out on town, on date." He winked at her.

"A date with who, Dmitry?" She chuckled. "My job is my life."

There it was – a window of opportunity to pry into Royal's life. She was a closed book to him, never referencing family or friends. All that she ever did was work. When she was not working, she was…well, he did not know what she did when she was not working. He doubted that she did very much.

"You are beautiful woman, Royal. Why is it there is no one to love you?" He stood behind her as she looked in the mirror and put on the earrings. Carefully, he pulled her long black strands of hair up so that she could better see the diamonds. Her back rested against his chest, breathing synchronously with him.

The touch of his strong hands to her warm skin sent chills down her body. She caught herself gasping a little. Dmitry mouth watered. As short as she was, he could easily bend down and kiss her wet lips now. All he needed was one kiss. He had been longing for a month to see what beautiful actually tasted like.

"I don't have time to date," Royal said, barely looking up. Her skinned turned red as she blushed. "I don't want to make time either." Her eyebrows spiked at him, hinting that the conversation was over, but there was a curious part of Dmitry that died to know more.

He continued. "Don't you ever want to go out?"

"I do. Just the other day, I caught a movie."

"I mean with other people, with man?"

Royal sighed. Dmitry was so nosy. She folded her arms and perched her mouth. "I don't have time to fall in love. I'm busy trying to form a life for myself here. I'm young. There will be plenty of time for all of that later."

Dmitry laughed. His deep voiced vibrated throughout the back of the store. He leaned his long, sexy body against the counter and looked at her. Her innocence reminded him of why he desired her so much, why she constantly set him ablaze.

"What's so funny, Dmitry?" Royal asked, giving him an evil eye.

"*You* are funny." He reached out for her arm and pulled her closer to him. "But you don't fool me. You need man in your life. Someone to make that beautiful brown skin of yours glow. You try to be tough, but your needs are no different from any other woman's." He rubbed his large hand across her cheek.

"A man, huh? Oil of Olay makes your skin glow, not men. Besides, how can you talk? I haven't seen you with a woman the entire time that I've been here, and I know that you're not gay. So evidently, you don't have time either."

Royal marveled at his arrogant grace. He was dressed in a tailored black Armani suit, looking and smelling like a million dollars.

His hair curled in golden locks around his tanned skin. And his eyes – they were the same burning prisms ever day – torturing her with horrible thoughts. His look was full of lust and fire. It was trying to consume her now, but she fought him. She could smell his cologne floating around her nose. She stepped away, careful not to fall into him.

He chuckled and walked closer to her. "That is where you are wrong. I make time. And no, I am not gay. If I were, the gay community would be extremely lucky," Dmitry said quickly. "As matter of fact, a female friend of mine is here in town now for dinner, a show and some personal time."

"Okay…maybe you're not gay or too busy, but I am," Royal said half-laughing.

She was close to having him all figured out. He was swaggering around Memphis with a walk that somehow tooted that his big feet may be a definite sign that he was somehow more than blessed in all the right departments. Women probably threw themselves under buses to get to him. Not her. She liked him tremendously, but not enough to jump in the bed with him. She reminded herself of that fact daily to keep her focus and her fleeting sanity.

He backtracked. "No, Royal. I am not gay. Perhaps, I should have made that clearer to you before. In there lies the problem, eh?"

Royal brushed off his statement. "Poor little woman. She doesn't know what she's getting into then." She picked up a couple of hangers off the ground and placed them on the rack.

Dmitry watched on quietly. His thoughts multiplied too fast to process. "You know, you should come too."

"What?" Royal stopped. "Your accent got in the way that time."

"You should come to dinner with us. You need to get *out* of house."

"I thought that's what you said. The answer is no," Royal said, shaking her head.

"But why, I don't understand."

"So you can look like a pimp with a white girl and black girl on your arm for dinner? No." Royal put her hands on her hips and rolled her eyes. "If you want to take me out for dinner, cool. But it won't be with your girlfriend, because I don't get down like that. One woman at a time, Dmitry."

"Who said that she was my girlfriend, and who said that she was white? You southern Americans are so ridiculous about race," he scoffed.

"Whatever. It wouldn't matter if she was *the* Mother Teresa, I'm not going."

"Because it would be with me?"

"No, because I wouldn't be the center of attention."

"Oh, you'd like to be the center of my attention?" his interest sparked.

"Who wouldn't?"

"Huh," Dmitry puzzled. He bit his lips to prevent himself from uttering one more word.

"So, do you want to look over the numbers again?" she changed the subject.

"No." Dmitry stood up and kissed her on her forehead. "Since you won't have dinner with me, I'll leave you here to make love to your boxes," he rubbed her back. "Good night."

"Stop pouting," she yelled as he walked out of the room. "And enjoy your date." She giggled at his frustration.

Chapter 4

By eleven o'clock that evening, Royal had retired upstairs to her apartment. Rain tattered at the windows and thunder shook the foundation outside, but inside she was so very comfortable that she barely paid attention to the bad weather. After showering, she crawled in her bed to watch reruns of the *Family Guy* and eat Ben & Jerry's ice cream out of the box.

The diamonds Dmitry had given her that afternoon inspired her to also purchase a pair of French lace panties and bra that a year ago would have paid for her tuition. She lay in bed now wearing them and enjoying the very exciting, uneventful life that she had only recently acquired.

During a quick commercial break, she jumped up and dashed out to the kitchen to grab a bottle of water, when the doorbell rang. She stopped in her tracks and looked at the large wooden doors.

In the last month that she had lived there, the doorbell had never once rang. Now, when it was not supposed to be ringing for any reason, it was. She looked down at her lack of clothing and sighed.

"Who is it?" Royal asked. Agitated, she peered out of her peep hole.

"It's Dmitry," Dmitry said, leaning against the door. "Who else would it be?"

Royal wondered if Dmitry ever stood all the way up. Every time that she saw him, he was leaning on something, like the weight of the world was on his shoulders.

Slowly, she opened the door just enough to see his face. He looked down at her and smiled softly. "Hello, Royal." His minty breath floated down to her.

"What do you want, Dmitry?" she asked, looking him up and down. He was soaking wet. His blonde tendrils were trenched in rain and his body made a small pool of water under him.

"I'm here to take you out," he reasoned, trying to catch a glimpse of whatever she was hiding behind the door.

"What?"

"Your exact words earlier today were that I could take you out, *but not with my girlfriend*," he smacked his lips and raised his eyebrows. His accent was even heavier now that he had been drinking. It was almost impossible to understand what he was saying when he spoke quickly. Finally, he stopped his rambling. "Hey, what are you wearing in there?" His train of thought jumped when he saw bare skin.

"None of your damned business," Royal said, moving away from the door. "Well, I meant that you could take me out at a decent hour, not now."

"What's wrong with now? You don't look busy," he leaned down further to her and smiled. "There had better not be anyone in there." His voice was deep.

"Of course not. Stop being stupid."

"Only you would think that was stupid," he shook his head. "Okay, then why won't you go out with me now?"

"It's too late at night," she said in a matter-of-fact tone.

"For whom?"

"Me." Royal tried to keep from laughing. "What happened? Did your girlfriend get tired of you?"

Dmitry rolled his eyes. "No, I got tired of her. I sent her away, and she is not my girlfriend for the *umpteenth* time." Dmitry sighed. "Royal, I want to come inside and sit down. I'm drunk. This hallway is not…"

"Not what?" She pushed the door up a little more.

"Accommodating." He wiped his tired eyes.

"No," Royal said, watching him as he walked to the stairwell and slid down the opposite wall to sit on the floor.

"Fine. I'll sit out here and sleep at your doorstep like dog," he yawned.

"Fine with me," Royal said, as she closed the door and locked it, but from her peep hole, she could see that Dmitry did not move.

She snickered. He was so pitiful and so dramatic. He deserved an Oscar for his performance. She started to leave him there until morning but decided to slip on a pair of jeans and t-shirt.

When she was fully dressed, she opened the door to find him snoring lightly.

"Wake up, sleepyhead. I thought that you said that you wanted to go out?" She locked her door behind her.

"Yeah," he wiped his watering eyes. "I'm up...ready."

Getting up off the ground, he stretched his long body and moved out the way so that she could get to the stairs. He followed her down to the back door, where she found Anatoly standing out in the rain with a large black umbrella waiting for them.

"You've been waiting here the whole time?" she asked horrified.

Anatoly did not speak to her or blink. He simply raised the umbrella to cover her body from the rain and escorted the two of them to Dmitry's limousine.

It really did not bother Royal that Anatoly would not answer her. He rarely spoke. At first, she thought him to be a mute, until once she heard him speaking in Russian on his cell phone. After that, she decided that he simply didn't speak English.

Once they were inside the limo, Royal sat across from Dmitry, curiously looking at his outfit. He was in a tailored black-tuxedo. She was in jeans. Where could they go as mismatched as they were?

"So, tell me what happened," she demanded, reaching over into the distinctively expensive French silver-plated bronze & brass champagne bucket to open the unopened bottle of Louis Roederer Champagne Cristal Brut Rose. She looked down at the bottle impressed. This was at least at $500 bottle, yet he kept it stocked like it was Red Bull.

"Night ended early," Dmitry said, smiling at her. His dimples were not deep but long and showed only when he smiled. His face was covered in a fine five o'clock shadow of dirty blonde stubble, but it only caused him to look more rugged and sexy.

"Did you not tell her who you were? And how happy she should be to be with you?" Royal mocked him.

"She knows who I am; I sent her away," he said slowly, over articulating his words. "I was bored, and I wanted to be with you."

"You're so full of yourself," Royal said, shaking her head.

"It's true," he rested his arm on the armrest and rubbed his stubbly beard.

"I bet," she scoffed.

"You think I'm harmless, don't you?" Dmitry leaned forward soaking wet from the rain. His long legs stretched across the limo like a black spider.

"No." Royal poured them both a glass of champagne, unmoved by his question. "I'm sure that you're trouble," she said, offering him the glass.

"If you only knew," he said, sitting back after he had taken the crystal flute from her. "*Spasiba.*" He thanked her in Russian.

"Enough about you, Dmitry. Where are you going to take me?" Her long body sat relaxed in the black leather seat opposite him, mirroring his own entitled demeanor.

"Where do you want to go?" He took a sip of the champagne.

"It's pouring rain." She tapped her finger on the door as she thought. "Ummm, how about to the movies?"

"What is with you and movie theatre? Is this the only thing you enjoy?"

"Yeah, it's *the* thing that I enjoy," she said, mildly excited. "There's nothing like a good movie."

Dmitry gave a curious stare, but Royal could not tell what he was thinking. "Anatoly, take us to my house. I need to get dressed for Royal's movie," he said finally.

"Uh uh," Royal protested. "You can wear what you have on. I'm not going to your house," she said, shifting in her seat a little, suddenly uncomfortable.

"You don't really expect me to go to movies soaking wet, do you?"

Royal thought for a minute, tapping her foot as she debated. "Fine. I'll wait out in the car while you go change."

"Who said that you were invited in? I don't need help dressing." Dmitry shot her a stare. "Someone that thinks very highly of themselves in this car tonight."

"Call it what you want to Dmitry, but I don't go to strange men houses in the middle of the night so they can get dressed or undressed."

Dmitry laughed at Royal's inability to control her complete discomfort with the thought of him. He pealed out of his wet tuxedo jacket and unbuttoned the top of his collar. The cold clothes stuck to his body and wet white shirt showed the defined muscles under his many layers of fine dressing along with a plethora of tattoos that Royal would have never guessed were there.

"Я должен иметь секс с вами теперь," he said raising his eyebrow at Royal.

"What did you say…speak English," she snapped.

Dmitry smiled. "I should get naked right now, just to see how you react to what grown man looks like." His eyes twinkled in the darkness.

"That's not what you said. I tell you what. You will be out of this car, Dmitry, if you take off one more thing," Royal said, in a matter-of-fact tone, pointing her finger at him.

"You know, Royal. You are very sexually frustrated. I can tell. You're always scared that someone will steal your precious gift." He looked in between her legs and licked his lips.

"Ooh. Uh uh. Not an appropriate conversation," Royal said, closing her legs. "I'm gonna need you to stop worrying about my sex." She rolled her eyes and tried to repress a broad smile.

Dmitry was funny and arrogant. It was a preposterous mix, but it made being around him constantly exciting.

"It's just that I'm worried about your overall happiness," he whined sarcastically. "Happy employee is productive employee."

Royal leaned forward, taking the power from Dmitry and using his same mannerisms to drive her point home. "Poor Dmitry. Do you consider sex to be happiness?"

"Do you?" Dmitry asked, finally having fun with Royal. He waited on baited breath for her to liven up; now here was a glimpse of it. The woman hiding inside of the shrew.

"No. I don't consider sex to equal happiness," she said curtly.

"Nyet?"

Royal smirked. "No. Happiness cannot be defined by such a physical pleasure when happiness itself is so abstract – so intangible."

"Well now. Look at little philosopher. I never said that I considered sex to be happiness, I asked if you did." Dmitry chuckled.

"What do you consider to be happiness?" Royal was finally curious.

"Control." His tone was sincere.

"Control?"

"Did I stutter? Such a thing is also intangible." He half chuckled.

"That's just such an S&M answer."

Dmitry laughed. "Your choice of words amuses me. Okay, maybe it's the loss of control. Either way, the control is going to land in someone else's lap."

He leaned further into her, close enough to smell the sweetness coming from her breath and the heat eradiating from her body. He wanted to suck her scent into his nostrils and grab her, rip her clothes from her limbs and take her in the back of the limo, but he settled for thumping her nose.

"What do you know about anything, eh? You're girl…and barely that," he whispered.

Royal's smile quickly crooked, and she snatched back in the corner of the seat. Dmitry could see it. She was incensed. She wanted to tear him limb from limb for mocking her, and he really didn't care. Anger was closer to sex than glib calmness.

"I'm not a girl," she said, defensively.

"Of course, you are," he said, patronizing her and enjoying every minute of it.

"I am a grown woman!" she protested.

Her ponytail and the soft hair flirting around the nape of her neck and the front of her ears caused her to look more like a teenager than a woman in her twenties, but the excitement that caused her blood pressure to rise and her nipples to harden seemed more sinister to Dmitry than child's play. He licked his lips.

"Calm down, Royal. I'm just fucking with you," he said, sitting back, happy to have gotten a rise out of her.

He stopped smiling. His face was like wet ice, glistening and chiseled. He rubbed his hands through his blonde wavy curls and raised his eyebrow at her. "But you don't like to be fucked with, do you?" He breathed calmly.

There was complete silence for a moment.

"No," Royal said finally, realizing that there was something off about Dmitry. "I don't."

The car stopped, and Royal found herself in front of large white Plantation-style home. Anatoly parked quickly, jumped out of the car and opened the door for Dmitry with the umbrella eagerly awaiting his demanding boss.

"Are you sure that you want to stay in car?" Dmitry asked, before he got out.

"Positive," Royal said, looking at Anatoly curiously, wondering if he did everything that Dmitry told him.

"Well, I'll only be minute." He stepped out of the car and stopped. Leaning back in, he smiled cleverly. "Should I wear jeans for your movie, Royal?"

"If you'd like," Royal said absently.

"See, the control thing isn't so bad is it?"

Royal smiled but didn't say anything. Anatoly closed the door softly, and she sat back in the car feeling sleep overtake her. She wished now that she had stayed in the bed.

She listened to the storm rock the city with wind, heavy rains and lightening as she waited. Curiously, she looked out the window across large gated lawn undisturbed by the late night rumblings. Security guards with dogs walked the perimeter of his property even in the rain, while Anatoly stood on the porch watching her and waiting for Dmitry. Rich people, she thought as she sat back in her seat. They are so freaking dramatic.

She closed her eyes finally and relaxed her head on the leather, feeling the warm seats caress her body. She had nearly gone to sleep when Dmitry arrived back. As the door opened for him, rain quickly rushed inside, dampening her face. He jumped in with a pair of dark jeans and a blue v-neck top, looking the most casual that Royal had ever seen him.

"Hope I wasn't long," he said, taking a swig of the Foster's beer that he carried with him.

"Actually, I dosed off there for a minute." Royal sat up in the chair. "You look...great. Like a walking Ralph Lauren advertisement." She nodded.

"A compliment? It seems that we are making progress, Royal," Dmitry said as he tapped her knee. "Anatoly, let's go," Dmitry instructed keeping his eye on Royal. The car started, and they pulled off.

Royal watched Dmitry curiously but did not speak.

"I've called in favor to have Paradiso movie theatre all to ourselves tonight. It closes in hour. I was hoping that we could have dinner at restaurant first and go over there for late showing of whatever you want to see," he offered checking his Blackberry.

"After it's closed? Are you serious?" She grabbed the phone from him and put it into the side compartment of her seat. "Stop with that phone. It's weird a.m. hours. Can't whomever it is wait? You are the boss, remember?"

"Fine, but only if you take off tomorrow. You work too hard anyway. People probably think it's me working you, but it feels like the other way around. Just…just hang out with me tonight and spend tomorrow in the bed or doing whatever introverts like you do."

"Alright," she sighed, giving in. "I haven't been to your restaurant since I was hired. I'm excited. And I never have had a movie theatre stay open just for me. That's pretty cool."

"You should come over to restaurant more and have lunch or dinner. It will save you money."

"Okay," Royal said, moving her long hair from her face.

Dmitry smiled deviously. "You should sit over here with me and let me kiss your lips too," Dmitry said scooting over. He rubbed the leather seat.

"What?"

"Just kidding," Dmitry said quickly. "Hey, you were saying okay to everything… had to try."

They both laughed, but Royal did not move from her seat. In fact, she sat with her eyes directly on Dmitry watching his every move.

They arrived at the restaurant soon after. Dmitry had arranged for his staff to stay late and cook a huge Russian meal for Royal. The two of them ran out of the rain from the car, while Anatoly pulled the limo to the back.

They were met at the front door by two red-headed young waitresses, barely in their twenties, dressed in all black and holding menus. As Royal ran in, she stopped amazed at the romantic transformation.

Dmitry had a single, intimate table set up in the back with a beautiful golden candelabra full of blood-red candles, golden table settings and a large bouquet of red roses. The rest of the restaurant was covered in candles as well.

Royal turned to Dmitry for an explanation, but he only smiled and escorted her to her seat with his large hand placed carefully at the base of her small back. He sat her down in the seat, pushed her up to the table and kissed her forehead.

The staff scurried about ensuring that everything was perfect, while Dmitry went behind the bar and brought back two glasses and a bottle of champagne.

"More Cristal?" he asked, raising the bottle.

"Dmitry, what is this about? Why could this date not have waited? It's raining cats and dogs out tonight, and you're frolicking around like its noon and sunny."

"First of all, I do not frolic. I thought that we had this discussion. Secondly, time waits for no man – not even me. This afternoon you agreed to go out. I thought about it all day after. I couldn't even focus on my evening. So, I cancelled. I…didn't want opportunity to pass, and so I came for you. End of discussion."

"All this for your shop girl?" Royal asked, impressed.

"My shop girl is best girl that I know."

Royal appreciated that. Her smiled showed it.

"What are you thinking about?" Dmitry finally asked.

"I wonder… how old you are?"

He laughed. "How old do I look?" He stared in her eyes as he sat across from her.

"I don't know. I want to say that you're in your thirties."

"Barely. I'm thirty-nine," Dmitry informed her.

"That old?"

"I don't consider that old."

"Of course, you wouldn't," Royal said, smirking. "So let's flip the script, shall we? Tell me. Why don't you have a family?"

"I have my reasons – most of them deal with my life-style," he looked up at her and paused, stopping his sentence in mid thought. "You and I. We are very much a like, eh?"

"No, we're not." Royal continued. She could clearly see he was hiding something. "You never talk about a mother, father, sister, brother. No one. I never see you around anyone except Anatoly and the men from the shop. You have no wife, no steady girlfriend…"

"It's funny that you don't have any of these important people either."

"Yeah, but I was an orphan for most of my life. Then a family adopted me, mostly because they need a babysitter. When I turned eighteen, I went to college, and I only call them now once a month to check on them, because I think that is what family is suppose to do. Otherwise, I have no one. I'm alone in this world. Now, why don't you?"

"Same story, really, different time. Well, I grew up in Moscow on streets. The people there became my only family. When I came to America as young man, I was a lot like you. I had no time for anything that was not delivering immediate profit."

"You never knew your mother, either?" The rest of Dmitry's statement was lost on Royal.

"Barely, she died when I was very young. Then, I went to prison very young."

"Oh, I'm sorry," Royal said, realizing his story was as pathetic as hers. "You know, I've never had either, but I'm willing to bet that it's harder to grow up with out a mom than a dad?"

Dmitry didn't answer. It was if as such a thought had not crossed his mind either way.

Royal continued. "What about your father?"

"I only know what I was told about him by men in prison and on streets. From what they say, he wasn't worth talking about."

"What did you go to prison for?"

"I was thief. Moscow gets cold in winter. I had to make life for myself at first. Besides I only spent a few years inside. Not so bad."

"Not a thief by choice, then. You had to survive."

"I moved passed simply surviving by the time that I was 15. I'm afraid that I just enjoyed it. What about you? Have you ever been to jail, Royal?"

"No. I've been close." Royal bit her lip. "It was a petty domestic dispute when I was a teenager. My foster mom's boyfriend tried to feel me up in bathroom one night, so I cut his ear off."

"Petty?" Dmitry laughed. "Rape is hardly a petty crime." The thought of Royal being raped infuriated him, but he tried hard to conceal it.

"What was worse was that I had to get the damn cops to believe that it was actually attempted rape and assault. He said that I wanted it." She shook her head. "He was such a jerk. I had to show them the choke marks around my neck to prove that I wasn't lying."

"He choked you?"

"In truth, he was kicking my ass, but I got a hold of the scissors and managed to cut him." She formed her fingers together like a pair of scissors and smiled.

"What was his name?"

"Woodrow Conners," she chuckled. "Such a lame name."

"Here in Memphis?"

"Yeah."

Dmitry was silent for a minute.

"Really, I'm okay. I've got thick skin," she continued.

"What did your foster mother say about you nearly being raped by her boyfriend?" he asked, intrigued.

"Not much in my defense. She had me removed. I finally ended up with the Stones. They were just a family that needed someone to help them with their four biological children- all under the age of ten."

"So, you went from sex toy to nanny." He sighed.

"Oh, I never was raped," Royal quickly added. "I protected myself always from that at all costs. I'm still a virgin to this day." She was proud of that fact.

"Excuse me?" Dmitry's eyes bucked. His mouth hit the ground.

"I'm still a virgin. I just haven't met the right guy, and I'll be damned if I give it to the wrong guy."

"Yes. That would be crime. Well, I'm...amazed and shocked." Dmitry shook his head. "It explains a lot, and yet...nothing makes sense."

"Well, I wouldn't spend too much time thinking about it, if I were you. It's not going to change anytime soon."

"Of course not." Dmitry smiled innocently, but inwardly a raging fire boiled inside of him. Royal was a virgin. The words caused a small stir. The thought of taking her would be ever present in his head now, he was sure of it.

Royal felt as though she had said far too much. Dmitry became quiet, thinking probably about how much of a girl she was - so very young and inexperienced. But as far as she was concerned, that was not at all true.

"Enough with that," Royal gawked, dismissing his new fascination with her sexual status.

"Alright, alright." His voice became softer.

Stepping closer to her, Dmitry reached out and pulled her by her small waist into his body. His large hands caressed her warm body and searched for bare skin. She looked up at him and wrapped her arms around his lower back, then closed her eyes.

Tenderly, Dmitry leaned over and kissed Royal on the top of her forehead. Ever so softly his full lips caressed her caramel skin. He breathed in, taking in the scent of her body. It took everything in him not to lift her up, carry her across her threshold and make love to her. Having never been told no or wait, he was no good at being obedient. He desired her more than anything; he wanted her so badly until it was physically painful for him to release her. Soon, he thought to himself.

Evidently, even she was expecting much more. She opened her wide eyes, surprised by his choice and exhaled. Royal could nearly read his eyes. It was if he was telling her that he had to stop. She understood but didn't want him to…so she thought.

With a nod, he headed back down the stairwell quietly, leaving her unspoiled and in the safety of her home. He owed her that since Woodrow Conners had tried to take it from her.

In a daze, Royal leaned against the door flabbergasted. Just when she suspected that he would strike like a villain, he behaved like a gentleman.

When Dmitry heard the door, he smiled and shook his head. "Royal is virgin," he sang aloud, smiling to himself, happy that he had discovered such a treasure.

The only thing that kept her from carrying the title of woman in a lot of people's eyes was the fact that she was yet a virgin.

To her, that made her more of a woman. Self-control was not an easy beast to tame, but she did so, even if sometimes begrudgingly.

Royal's virginity had been the topic of many conversations before Dmitry, but her status had never changed. Every man seemed to have one thing on his mind. To take it, but not to keep her. She did not want to end up unloved again, only this time with nothing to show for it. And it seemed that every time that she exposed her secret, she felt like she was a leper.

People had looked at her like something was wrong with her her entire life, jealous that they had given theirs away and had chosen poorly. She had lost so many opportunities with young college men because of her fear of going all the way. She was not afraid of the act, just the aftermath. She knew very well what it felt like to be all alone and rejected, she didn't need to amplify it. The thought infuriated her now. She bit her lip and grunted slightly.

"Ugh. This silence is going to make me sick at the stomach," she said finally. "I didn't tell you that I had AIDS, Dmitry. Please don't act like that."

"Act like what?" He looked up at her oblivious of her mood change.

"Like I'm not normal," Royal sighed.

Dmitry put down his fork and smiled. "But you're not normal. You are better," he said trying to focus. "Alright. Alright. We'll talk about something else."

∞♥∞

It was nearly four in the morning when Dmitry's car pulled behind Royal's building beside her little red Honda Accord. He had chosen to drive her home himself after the movie.

Anatoly was finally allowed to go home and get some rest. The rain had stopped and the skies were clear, allowing the stars and moon to shine brightly down on them. Crickets chirped and dew fell on the grass. The wind blew through the night, refreshing and full of force. Royal yawned and sat up in the seat, hitting the button to let up her window as she did so.

"I had fun," she said rubbing her eyes. "Did you?" She looked over at him, relaxed in his seat and looking over at her curiously.

"It was *theeee* most civilized date that I've been on in many years," he said, opening the door of his car, but not answering the question.

He walked around to her side and helped her out carefully. She stood up in front of him and smiled. Dmitry's height continued to leave her in awe as well as the enormous size of his well-sculpted body, but what was most amazing to her was that in the dead of summer, he wore long shirts.

He looked down at her, gazing into her bright brown eyes.

"So you were bored out of your mind?" she asked. "Or did you have fun."

"*Dah, dah*, I had fun with you, shop girl," he said, finally. He moved in closer to her body.

"You've got a five o'clock shadow," she said, touching his stubby beard, and only inches from his bulging chest. She had to say something to break the ever-growing desire to kiss him.

"I've been up since day before yesterday. Guess I should get some sleep." Reaching behind her body, he closed the door and grabbed her hand, escorting her up the back steps of the building.

Exhausted, Royal fumbled for a minute, then opened the door with her key. Its jingling chain echoed throughout the small parking lot. Dmitry walked in after her, checking the place as he heard her small feet creep up the back staircase to her suite. When he was sure that they were alone, he walked up behind her. She was standing in the doorway of her apartment waiting for him with a soft smile and an innocent glow.

He swaggered over to her, stopped at the doorway, leaned liked normal against the threshold.

"Promise me that you won't work tomorrow. I want you to rest," he said, looking down at her breasts. It odd to him that they had never been suckled as succulent they seemed. He found that his mouth watered just thought of what they must taste like. He looked back at her with a grin. He knew that she could tell what thinking.

"I'll rest. Promise." She sighed, then yawned happy at the moment. She knew now that he would kiss her, and she braced herself for it, hoping to through.

"This is the part of date where you invite me your home, and I rip you apart under the sh whispered jokingly. His icy eyes looked directly causing a funny thump of her heart.

"Sorry, I'll have to pass." Royal's voice wa sweet. She pivoted on her feet a little, trying to on her tip toes.

"I'm not surprised, now that I know your s

Chapter 5

The grand opening of the *Dmitry's Closet* was an undeniable success. Nearly two hundred of Memphis' affluent women came to the opening. The event was complete with the cutting of a splendid red ribbon, a few words from the area councilman and tons of champagne, strawberries, great cheeses and caviar beluga for the guests. And best of all despite the warnings from the local meteorologist, it did not rain giving everyone a clear, not-so-hot August day.

Royal had used all of her textbook skills to attract the local newspapers and reporters by giving them gift bags full of free but expensive gifts all hand picked by her and her new staff of two. Dmitry was also extremely impressed with the entire event, receiving constant praise from his new patrons, who not only loved the selection but the presentation.

By seven o'clock when the doors closed, they had made thousands of dollars and a big splash with the new boutique. After counting down the drawer and giving the money to Anatoly as previously discussed, Royal and her team cleaned up the boutique and prepared to head over to the *Mother Russia* restaurant, where Dmitry had arranged for a celebratory dinner.

It had been an excruciating month for Royal, full of last-minute details to work through, promotions to pull together and fine clothing to inventory, but things had worked out better than her wildest dreams. She was a success. Her hard work had paid off literally. And most of all Dmitry was happy with her.

"The limo is here to pick us up, Royal," her assistant, Renée said, grabbing her purse. "I can't believe he is sending over a freaking limo!"

"Yeah, that's pretty sweet," Royal said hurrying.

Renée was a young, energetic neo soul sister from Atlanta, who rocked a large, very pro-black afro and large gold hoop earrings. She was a dark, short, petite woman with tons of retail experience and new to the city. Royal hired her on the spot during their interview, feeling a strangely familiar kinship with the woman. Her other assistant Cory was young man who had come highly recommended by the councilman, Mr. Avers, who had also spoken at their grand opening.

Cory was a clean cut, attractive young white man with a very small, but muscular frame. Dmitry had questioned her choice for him, but she knew that it was only because he was a man. Cory was extremely professional and kind and his ultimate goal was to one day own his own shop. She thought his ambitions to be admirable and decided after several days and a few conversations with Dmitry to hire him as well.

The three of them loaded into the limo quickly and were escorted a few streets over to the restaurant, where a small group of Dmitry's friends and colleagues waited. When they arrived at the restaurant, a traditional Russian band was playing and the entire place was covered in festive crimson decorations. There were tons of expensive wine, fine Russian vodka, traditional Russian food and of course, caviar.

Once, Royal had inquired why caviar was a staple in Dmitry's life. He explained that he was part-owner of a caviar company near the Caspian Sea.

Naturally, she said shaking her head when he had informed her of yet another business he owned.

"Ah, there is my little shop girl," Dmitry said, picking Royal up and whirling her around.

His festive spirit made Royal light up. She hugged him as tightly as she could, relishing in the moment.

"Wasn't today, great? I...I couldn't believe it. So many people came to the opening," Royal said as Dmitry sat her down. There eyes were glued to each other. His hands were glued to her tiny waist.

He finally spoke, breaking out of her spell. "*Dah...dah* today was great...was reflection of you, eh?" He waved at the waiter. "Bring her a big glass of wine. I want to get her as drunk as possible." He gave a wide grin then took Royal to the head table.

"Did you do all of this for us?" She looked around in amazement.

"No, I did all of this for you," he whispered in her ear, as he pulled a seat out for her.

Dmitry had flirted with Royal many times but ultimately kept his sexual ambitions at bay after their date. Royal thought it was because he felt that she was too inexperienced for him, but Dmitry was a business man. He had left her alone to ensure that she would focus on his shop first. He knew that there would plenty of time for his other plans.

However, they still continued to spend many days and evenings together planning for the grand opening, which Dmitry enjoyed immensely. It gave him an opportunity to get to know her on many levels, something that he found quite refreshing in a woman after many years of dealing with empty vessels.

Every day, she would always reveal something newer, something brighter to him. He found himself impatient to get to the boutique, to hear her voice and see her face. Royal was fascinating to him in every way that a woman could be fascinating to a man. A hard worker. Honest. Loyal. Pure. He could never have asked for more in whatever she had grown to be to him.

Royal had also been enslaved by Dmitry. He was not only beautiful but incredibly wise. He gave her so much advice on how to run the business and how to be savvy about all her negotiations with vendors. He explained the market to her and how to stay on top of it. She was his ever-faithful pupil.

"Could I have your attention, please?" he asked, standing at the head of the long, decorated wooden table. He clinked the gold knife on the crystal glass and cleared his throat.

As he raised his glass, the room quieted to a dead silence. All the chatter stopped, and the band put down their instruments. Royal looked around, astonished at how people snapped to his command. All eyes were glued to him and his eyes were glued to her. The attention made Royal incredibly self-conscious. She fidgeted a little as she tried to look at him and not at all the people who were now focused on the two of them.

His voice reverberated throughout the large restaurant like a microphone had been placed below him. Eyes sparkling under the romantic lighting, he turned to Royal. If she had believed in Prince Charming, she would have sworn that he was him.

"I would like to make toast to Royal Stone and the hard work that she and her team have put into making my newest shop a great success. I am very proud of her and my own decision to keep her so very close. She has truly become...asset," he paused and smiled at Royal. "So, tonight we celebrate a new part of my vision and welcome Royal to the family. She has my blessings, and I'm sure all of yours. *Budem* everyone!"

"Budem!" everyone replied at once, toasting Royal and her staff.

Instantly, the music began again and the ginger chatter resumed. Royal was happy in that fact. Now all eyes were not on her, but she could still feel a few burning through her back. She turned slightly to observe. Around them sat several men that she had never met before but who were most definitely Russian and wealthy. All of them were adorned in expensive suits, shoes and polished accessories. With them were women of the finest breed – beautiful, exotic beneficiaries of fine living.

Near the end of the table were Renée and Cory eating and laughing, both enjoying each other's company and their new found success. Royal observed everyone while she sipped on her wine, feeling a small buzz as she neared the bottom of the glass. She smiled to herself feeling more apart of something than she had ever felt before. Suddenly, a warm hand crept across hers, and she looked over to find Dmitry. His bright eyes were fixed on her.

"Are you alright?" he asked, concerned.

"I'm wonderful," she said, holding back tears. She clinched his hand tightly. "Thanks for all of this. It's beautiful. I've never had anything like this done for me before." Her voice was nearly a whisper.

"Get used to it." He waved over the waiter for more wine. He could see her wide brown eyes start to relax. Her long lashes flopped lazily and the tension had started to come out of her erect posture.

"You feel relaxed yet?" He ran his large hand over her shoulder and massaged her back.

"Umm, yes," she said empting her glass. She wiped her lips gently with her finger tips. The wine perfumed her breath and hazed her thoughts.

Dmitry watched her, still smitten by her small perfect movements. He looked away for a moment and smiled to himself.

Royal looked over and caught his smirk. She raised her brow and set down her glass. Used to his idiosyncrasies, she knew sex was on his mind.

"Can you manage to keep that mind of yours out of the gutter, Dmitry?" she asked slurring her words a little but still in control of her thoughts.

"You've now gone from shop girl to mind reader?" Dmitry laid his long arm around her chair and her exposed back like a boa constrictor and let his thumb rub against the bare skin of her back.

"It doesn't take much to read your mind." His movements aroused her.

"If that were true, I'd be out of business." He smirked again showing his long dimples.

"It's not that. I've just had more time to know how to read you."

She met his eyes and swallowed hard as he leaned in.

"What am I thinking right now? Tell me exactly. Each and every word."

"You're thinking you want to give me a raise," she said smiling.

He grinned. Her humor continuously renewed him. "You have proven yourself to be quite the remarkable woman," he said softly. "I have watched you transform from this diamond in the rough to…Hope diamond. Irreplaceable. Irresistible. Irritating." He smiled.

She laughed.

"Jeez, don't set the bar so high," she whispered.

The band played in the background, hand organs bellowing out beautiful Russian music. He smiled. "Dance with me?" he asked, urging her from her seat. His hand caressed her back.

"Alright." Royal stood, placed her napkin in the chair and followed Dmitry to the quaint, candlelit dance floor. Again she could feel the many eyes burning through her. They all watched her like spectacle she was. It would have driven her crazy if Dmitry had not continued to steal her thoughts.

He turned to her and bowed gracefully.

"May I have this dance and every other there after?" He winked at her.

"Yes, but I have to warn you, I tend to lead."

"So you've danced with many seven foot men, huh?"

"A couple," she grinned. "Okay. You're the first, but don't let it go to your head."

"Too late," he hummed. "If I was foolish enough to omit observation earlier…you look absolutely beautiful tonight."

"Thank you." Royal smiled. "You do too."

Dmitry looked regal in his black tailored suit, cut for his large lion frame. As normal, there was nothing out of place. His hair was just the right shade of blonde, his tan just the right shade of bronze, his eyes just the right shade of blue and his lips just the right shade of pink. Even more was his intoxicating cologne – a signature fragrance that she had never smelled before meeting him, but could not forget.

He dipped his head to greet her, ever so gentle and refined in all of his movements. As he took her small manicured hand in his own, he pulled her close into his towering body. She slipped her hand in between the tailored shirt and satin on the inside of his jacket; gripping his marble body and feeling the heat come from under his clothes. Their bodies fused together.

Seeing Dmitry swaying softly, the band instantly stopped their upbeat tune and started a more romantic melody. The violins harmonized, tickling her ears with delicious sounds. She smiled at him as he looked down at her.

"What are you thinking now, Royal?" he asked as they swayed.

"They don't sound nearly as good as you do, when you play."

Dmitry grinned.

Softly, she laid her head against his body and felt his arm tighten around her waist. The guests looked on as the two danced, somehow moving with every step further into their own world, where no one else existed. Her eyes closed as she danced dizzily with the harmony of the music. He nearly hid her from the others with his massive frame. She felt safe in his embrace, protected by his presence.

The other guests soon began to move to the dance floor as well, partnering up to join in the beautiful moment. Without words, the room spoke in volumes. There was love in the air, contagious, crazy love-even if it was just for as long as the band played.

"I don't ever want this moment to end," Royal finally said, unsure of how Dmitry would react.

"Umm....me either, shop girl," Dmitry hummed, holding her tighter.

Minutes later, Anatoly appeared from the back room, dressed in his normal dark boot cut jeans, black boots and a black t-shirt. Obviously, he had not been invited or not accepted an invitation to the event. His hooded, brooding eyes were menacing and his walk forceful, each pace gaining momentum. Dmitry saw him from a far and stopped dancing. Royal looked over, sensing urgency as Anatoly approached. Her heart sank.

Not now, she thought.

"Excuse me for just a moment," Dmitry said, walking away, giving her no time to respond. She stood on the dance floor alone as the others danced. The mood changed quickly. Like a king at court, all eyes followed him as he left the floor, but it was Royal who truly felt like the jester.

Anatoly spoke to Dmitry under a calm but urgent voice, gesturing something violent with his hands. Dmitry looked towards the front window and then back at the men on the floor and at the table. They all stopped talking and dancing and migrated collectively from their dates to circle around Dmitry and Anatoly.

Dmitry said something to them, then they quickly dispersed out of the front door without bothering to inform their guests of their departure, then he walked back over to Royal, who stood clueless.

"I'm so sorry, Royal. It appears that I must excuse myself for just a while," he said, escorting her back to the table. His hand caressed the small of her back. "You should finish your dinner, and I'll return shortly, if I can." He pulled out the seat for her again. She sat down with a dumbfounded look on her face. Was he serious? He would just leave like this?

"What's wrong?" Royal asked, concerned. "I don't understand…"

Dmitry interrupted. "A small problem with another business that I own," he said, a little irritated by her inquiry. He bit his lip and humbled himself.

"How many businesses do you own?" There was no reply for her question. He simply pushed up her chair to the table.

"I am sorry, Royal. Stay and wait for me as long you can." He kneeled down to make eye contact with her. "I'll return later. Enjoy the meal that I've prepared for you and your guests." He rubbed the tip of her nose with his index finger and stood back up. He could clearly see the disappointment in her eyes.

With an apology, he left the now nearly empty restaurant. His heavy footsteps echoed across the hardwood floor as he walked out without turning around. She watched his body disappear beyond the gilded glow of the decadent room through the front door that Anatoly held open for him.

"And he's gone just like that," she said, absently.

∞♥∞

Royal had managed to stay and wait, despite her bewildered embarrassment. She was like a birthday girl at a party with no guests. All dressed up and no where to go, she sat in the same seat that Dmitry had placed her in before he left and waited faithfully, obediently and most of all perplexed.

As she sat talking to an old man, more than likely in his eighties about the various types of caviar and its history in Russia with royal families, the front doors to the restaurant opened suddenly, and Dmitry and his large entourage of men flooded into the building. They came in by the droves, filling the place back to capacity. They came in like nothing had happened, like there had been no interruption.

Royal sat up and watched on like everyone else who was left behind. Each man found his date and settled down to talk and smile.

Anatoly immediately disappeared into the back again, and Dmitry came in and locked eyes on Royal. As he passed them, the women, who were left behind in the whirlwind of urgency only hours before, looked up at him like hungry wolves each pining for his attention. But he did not look their way. His eyes were fixed on Royal, glad that she had stayed and waited for him. He zoomed in on her with an irate scowl on his face. His furrowed brow straightened as he approached the table. Royal noted the transformation, giving him a curious frown. What had he been up to?

"I'm sorry that I was taken from you for so long," he said, seriously. His voice was distant. He tried to regain his composure and get back the moment that he had clearly lost with her on the dance floor.

"It's okay." Royal's smiled lacked all enthusiasm. "I'm going to get out of here in just a minute, anyway. Have to get ready for tomorrow. I…can just walk over," she said, trying to hide her sadness. "Cory and Renée are going back with me. I just didn't want to leave before you returned considering all that you've done for us."

"Nonsense. I'll have you driven back over. Anatoly will take you."

"Oh, I don't want to bother him."

"There is no bother. As a matter of fact, Anatoly will stay at the store from now on, down in basement. It's not safe for you to be there alone. People know there are large sums of money at the shop now. I wouldn't want anyone to think they can take advantage. Someone has to be on the premises to protect you."

"I didn't know that the place had a basement."

"A very nice one," he said, tasting the caviar.

"How does Anatoly feel about this?" She watched him eat, frustrated at his quick commands and the fact that he was ignoring her discomfort. "I don't like this. *Now*, he has to uproot himself to stay with me. I don't want to be a bother. Maybe we can just get a security system or..."

"Anatoly does as he's told. And he's been told to stay in basement and make sure that no one disturbs you after or before hours." He wiped his face and looked at her sternly, the full strength of his prominent bone structure obvious as he gritted his teeth. He picked up his wine and took a big gulp, most unlike him.

"It looks like everyone around here does what they are told," she huffed. "Does anyone ever ask why? Because I'm not the *go fetch dog* type."

Dmitry noted her anger and possible hurt. He calmed. "I told you why," his voice was softer. "It's not safe."

"You seem...*different*, Dmitry. Strange." She looked down at the table to control her own growing resentment and distress.

Dmitry sighed. "I seem, because I am." He tried to lighten his forceful tongue. "Just... listen to me, Royal. Anatoly does not mind at all." He reasoned softly with her, smiling to make his point more agreeable for her. "The basement is nice enough. He'll be fine. You'll barely know he's there." He lifted her chin to see her face.

Royal rested her case, realizing that Dmitry had come to his final decision. She nodded to him in agreement and gathered her things.

"Well, thanks again for everything," she said, understanding that something else was bothering Dmitry. "I'll see you later."

"*Dah*, you will," he said, making eye contact with her. Royal didn't respond. Dmitry stood up as she stood and escorted her quietly to the door.

She stopped at the threshold of the restaurant with her jacket in her hands and her purse under her arm waiting for the to limo pull up to the front of the restaurant. It was amazing to her how in a couple of months, she had completely gotten used to having a driver, a limo and a staff of people.

Renée and Cory stood behind them intrigued by the oddly-matched couple.

"I'm very proud of you, Royal," he reiterated with conviction. His large hands rested on her bare shoulders. He gazed at her for moment then motioned for Anatoly, who waited just outside of the door with the car. "You'd better get out of the night air."

"Is he my bodyguard now? I don't need a slave, you know." She rolled her eyes.

"Think of him as your *unofficial assistant*." He ran his index finger down the side of her neck. "I will see you later to make up for having to depart from you so abruptly."

Royal still did not respond. She just touched the softness of his face and walked away.

Watching her and her staff into the car, Dmitry closed the doors of the restaurant behind him as they drove off.

Renée and Cory watched on as Royal sat beside Anatoly in dead silence. She was broken hearted and completely incapable of hiding it. Ignoring them all, she sat in her v-neck, satin black Bagley Mischa dress, spoiled by the night's events. She had worked so hard to get dressed, to make him see her tonight. It was all in vain.

Her diamonds earrings sparkled in the darkness, weighing down her small lobes. Beautiful canary yellow diamonds laid close to her neck dangling from the gold necklace and created a spectrum of beautiful light every time a reflection hit them just right.

Her newest diamond gift had come only days before and had been the largest so far in celebration of her recent accomplishments. In his normal fashion, Dmitry had kissed her only on the forehead and in return was allowed to place the necklace on her himself.

She wore only the jewelry he had given her tonight. She wanted him to know how much she appreciated him. But how could she show him when he was barely there?

Her smoky eyes were adverted to the window staring past tinted glass into the clear, dark night. Her glossy, pouty lips were pierced together, clinched by perfect white teeth. She was a picture of true beauty and true agony.

While Royal sank into the leather drowning in her thoughts, Anatoly looked at her staff with a sort of disdain, never uttering a word, but making them very uncomfortable.

Unsure if he was provoked by direct eye contact, Cory shifted in his seat and tried to keep from staring the husky brut in his pupils. They were always worried that perhaps Royal had forgotten to hook him to his chain.

However, Royal had learned over the past couple of months to simply ignore Anatoly.

He was like a permanent prop in her life. She was only inches from him, but they were miles away only connected only through Dmitry. His close proximity to her body did not bother her at all. She leaned against him as she pouted, absorbing his body heat and sulking profusely. He was like the *personal assistant* that she had grown accustomed to having around. It was a good thing too, especially now that he would be living in her *hidden basement*.

Cory looked over at Renee with unspoken suspicion of Royal's relationship with the rich and powerful Dmitry Medlov. They had watched as he embraced her not only with his physical touch but his pulsating eyes every time he was around her.

The mysterious couple was the constant subject of endless conversations when Royal was not around. Everyone marveled at the infinite number of expensive gifts that he showered upon her; the quiet conversations between them in the back office that would erupt into sudden laughter and the sexual tension that wrapped the store like a hungry fog.

"Thanks for today," Royal said, trying to change the silent subject. A faint smiled came across her face, but she continued to pierce her lips, visibly worried. Moving the soft wisps of her hair from her face, she focused in. "Remember to be here tomorrow by nine. We open at ten. I want to spend some time meeting about today and ensuring that we have it all together for the rest of the week. It's all up hill from here." She gave a fake, almost disturbing smile.

"Sure thing," Renée said, cocking her brow.

When the limo pulled into to the back parking lot of the shop, Cory and Renee jumped out and headed to their respective cars before the chauffer could properly open the door. Each was trying desperately to get away from the glaring pit bull Anatoly.

Ignoring them both, Anatoly got out of the limo before Royal and helped her inside of the empty shop.

"Thank you," she said, not expecting a response. He did not. Anatoly was always quiet, not bothering to respond to any of her constant gestures of kindness.

He walked in front of her to check the shop as he had been instructed, while Royal stopped and looked over her office to make sure that she had left nothing out of place or unlocked. She was looking at a business card left by one of the women who had visited her earlier when Anatoly appeared in the doorway.

He looked at her for a minute before he sighed. "I'll be downstairs, if you need me," he said, giving her the same icy stare as Dmitry. His eyes were a riveting cobalt blue shaded by layers of thick lash. His voice was a deep, silky baritone.

Royal was startled. She had never heard him speak in English. His accent was even stronger than Dmitry's. She tried to suppress her sudden urge to ask him one hundred questions about their boss. Instead, she kept it simple.

"Where is the basement?" she asked, trying not to look as shocked as she actually was.

Anatoly walked pass her to the bookshelf, grabbed the large wooden furniture by its ends, grunted a little as he shifted the heavy oak and moved it further down the wall. There, as plain as day, was a door. He hit a code on the security system and opened the vault-like contraption.

"You can buzz me from your place on the security system. Just hit 22#. I won't be here when you open or when you close. Just at night and early mornings."

Royal shook her head in amazement. As normal, Anatoly showed no emotion and with a nod he disappeared behind the door and left her alone.

"Well, I'll be damned. What else don't I know about this place?" she asked, taking her shoes off her aching feet.

Letting her long hair down from its bundle, she slowly made her way upstairs to recover from a very tedious day.

Chapter 6

Steam billowed up creating a marvelous and aromatic fog throughout Royal's marble bathroom. To set the mood for a more relaxing late evening, she had taken some of the candles Dmitry had given her a few weeks ago and lit them around the bathroom and her bedroom. The luminous glow made her feel pretty or at least relaxed.

To purge her thoughts, she connected her IPod and let the music blast throughout the apartment. Chris Cornell sang his heart out on his Euphoria Morning CD, and Royal hummed along.

The hot water cascaded over her body, relaxing her aching muscles and drowning some of her more disturbing thoughts. Unfortunately, there were many of them tonight. She drifted into the haze for a while thinking of Dmitry – trying to figure him out. Her infinite questions consumed her.

Did he really care about her at all? What if she was reading too much into their friendship all along? Dmitry was a millionaire with homes and businesses all over the world. He was beautiful and brilliant. And she was a broke, orphaned virgin with nothing to offer. Did he really take her seriously or was she just something to do for the moment?

The steam curled her long hair dangling down her back and over her long caramel shoulders, cooking through her skin and interrupting her thoughts. She couldn't tell if it was the heat or her heart, but she suddenly felt claustrophobic. She wiped the water from her face and took a deep breath.

"Ugh, I need to get out of here," she said, turning off the violent water rushing from the showerhead.

Wrapping a large terrycloth towel around her body, she opened the door to the congested bathroom and allowed the cloud to drift into her bedroom. Shivering, she dropped the fluffy towel and slipped on her short, black silk robe quickly, trying to minimize her exposure to the cold air blasting through the vents.

Royal sat on the side of the bed for a moment, as still as could be in a daze. Her mind began to drift again, back to Dmitry. It had been so thoughtful to put on such a grand affair for her. However, she was pained by his unexpected interruption. And she was even more pained by his return.

With Dmitry, she could never tell what was next. He was a *spur of the moment* type of man, something that was not always a good thing. What bothered her more was her growing connection to him. Was it possible that she was the only one who felt the strong, red emotions? Were all the smiles, kisses and compliments simply kind gestures of a seasoned man who felt sympathy for an underprivileged youth? Had she romanticized their friendship into something more because of her lack of intimate relationships? Her questions were endless.

Blinking fast to push back the tears, she thought about the work that was still left to do and grabbed her notepad off the nightstand. There were other things to occupy her time with besides sulking. Things that had to be done. Feeling sorry for herself would do her no good. Dmitry was probably having drinks with his real friends at that very moment – not thinking about her.

To change her dismal mood, she would make herself a cup of hot tea, sit in front of the fireplace in the living room and tweak her marketing plan.

The thought comforted her. Work. It was the one thing that she could depend on to numb her senses and to remind her that there were things more important than silly, overrated emotions, like not starving to death or having a place to stay.

Remembering what it felt like for her stomach to growl with no end, to have stomach cramps due to lack of food snapped her out of her thoughts of Dmitry. Grateful for evident and more importantly current blessings, she got up and headed to the kitchen.

As she entered out of her bedroom, she looked across the large living room in its darkness to see Dmitry quietly sitting by the fireplace on the couch sipping out of a crystal goblet with his long legs crossed. He stared into the fire. Thinking. Brooding. Stunned, she stopped in her footsteps. Her heart pounded in her chest. She caught her fleeting breath and cleared her voice.

"Dmitry?" she whispered softly.

"Royal." He looked up from his glass but didn't move. His eyes focused on her.

"What are you doing here?" she asked.

Dmitry chose his words carefully, visibly fighting with himself over what to say.

"Remember in restaurant, I said that I would see you later. Well, it's *later*," he said, putting down his glass.

"Yeah, it is," she looked over at the clock. A quarter past midnight.

He followed her gaze to the grandfather clock and sighed.

"Sorry to come so late. It couldn't be helped."

"What was so urgent that you had to come tonight?"

"Don't you already know?"

"If I did, would I ask?"

There was complete silence. The fireplace crackled.

"You know that you have money to burn when you have the air on and fireplace," he said, redirecting his sudden discomfort. "It is just like you, you know. To have two forces working in the same room at the same time to satisfy you, and you never even notice." A smile crept across his face as he looked over at the fire.

"Did you come over to tell me to turn off my fireplace?" Royal snapped.

"No." Dmitry looked over at her and sighed. "I know that messed up with you tonight. And I wanted to come to you before it was too late to mend." He smirked. "Tonight was supposed to be special. I wanted to talk to you about us now that shop is out of the way."

"Us?" Royal's voice was barely above a whisper.

"*Dah*, I want there to be an *us*. You can't tell me you don't know how I feel about you. Everyone knows. It's grown to be too difficult for me to hide."

Royal bit her lip. So he did care. She was relieved, even without clarification.

"I know how I feel about you, but I'm clueless about how you feel about me," she confessed, voice quivering. "I haven't had much training in this. So, I'm really confused. I don't know if you give me all this stuff and all this attention because you think of me as your pet or if you really like me or if you really, really like me."

The darkness cloaked her face and the range of emotion that flashed over it, but Dmitry could detect her guard down without visibly seeing it. He stood up and walked over to her, towering over her. Taking her chin under his finger, he lifted her head where he could see her face under the moonlight shining in through the blinds.

"Royal, I don't like you. I love you. There is big difference between the two."

She looked up, tears in her eyes. Swallowing hard, she tried to control her beating heart. Dmitry's words sounded like an angel playing his harp.

"Do you know how impossible that is to believe," she asked, blinking fast to push back her salty calamity.

Dmitry was confused. Why would she not believe him? What had he done? Were the gifts and attention not a reflection of his growing admiration? He tried to simplify his thoughts, focusing on the primaries of their relationship.

"Why is it so impossible for me to love a woman who is so innocent, so beautiful?"

"Because I have nothing to offer you. And the one thing that I do have, I'm so damned reluctant to give up...even though I want to." She made sure to clarify her desire. "Men like you are hard to read, Dmitry. You've said it yourself. I don't want to sound like I don't have self esteem, but it's pretty hard to battle my shortcomings when everything comes up *short* against you."

Dmitry was shocked and humbled.

"But you are worth more than all of my possessions. I will trade everything for you. I mean, don't you love me even just little bit?" He had to know. His voice ached.

"It would be impossible not to love you, Dmitry."

"Oh...because of my money."

"No," Royal shook her head adamantly. "Not at all. It's because you make me feel...special, like I'm the only woman in the room. No one has ever made me feel like that."

"You *are* the only woman in the room." He spoke softly. "Do you love me?" He wanted to hear her say it again.

"Yes, I love you," she confessed with tears in her eyes.

Dmitry smiled like a new born seeing his mother for the first time. His suspicions had been correct. His timing was not off. It had been hard to come to her for fear of possible rejection and how it would affect their working relationship, but she had made is easier for him now. She loved him.

"Would it be absurd to see yourself dating a man like me? I mean, I know I am older than you, nearly old enough in some countries to be your father, but…"

"It wouldn't be absurd. I'm just not fully sure what type of man you are, Dmitry?"

Dmitry's eye twitched as if the answer was far too complex to explain, even to her.

She shifted her weight to one side and put her hand on her hip. As she took a deep breath, Dmitry watched the swell of her breasts under her robe. In the sudden outpour of emotion, she had forgotten that she was naked with the exception of a small slip of silk fabric, but he had not.

"I want you so bad it hurts," he whispered running his fingers over her collarbone. He watched her breaths quicken. She looked up at him wantonly, lips formed for a kiss. He could not resist her or the throbbing below controlling him, pushing him to have her. His fingers caressed her soft silk. Pulling her to him, he leaned down and grabbed her by the waist. He picked her firm, voluptuous body up in his arms and held her at eye level.

She smiled at him.

"So you've broken in my house; we've confessed that we love each other; you've picked me up; I guess I know what's next."

"Umm…are you afraid?" he asked, carrying her to her bedroom.

"Yes," she nodded. She wasn't expecting for him to ask for her now. His sudden assumption, however, prevented her from backing down. In fact, she wanted to make love to him. That in itself was a foreign emotion to her. She had never desired someone the way that she desired him.

"Don't be afraid. I make sure that you enjoy."

Dmitry had never seen her hair down before and enjoyed very much how naturally beautiful she was. Smelling of vanilla extract, its mass fell down her back and around her shoulders in an inky, full mane. She wrapped her arms around his neck and laid her head on his shoulders while he carried her. The trip was short.

The candles had created a beautiful aroma of sandalwood and jasmine and the large bedroom casted a romantic glow over Royal's body.

"Are you sure that you didn't know that I was coming?" he asked amused.

"This wasn't for you."

"It is now."

Dmitry sat her down on the bed carefully, marveling at the contrast of her dark skin and the monochromatic comforter. His liquid eyes looked almost silver in the dark; they barely blinked. Taking off his suit jacket, he kept his gaze on her. She lay in bed waiting for him, still covered by the silk robe, clinging to it nervously. Watching his every move, her eyes became bigger as he approached. Clothes still on, he crawled in between her long, shapely brown legs and rested his elbows beside her.

"This is our first kiss," she said, voice quivering.

"Umm…among other things." He raised his brow at her.

Slowly, Royal lifted her head as she felt Dmitry's massive arms swaddling her like a blanket. She rested back in his hands and wrapped her arms around his neck. Like when they first met, they caught each other in a mesmerizing gaze – happy to have finally arrived at this moment.

Still smiling, Dmitry dipped his head and carefully, slowly kissed the fullness of Royal's sweet lips. He met her wet mouth with a gentle greeting, tasting of wine and chocolate. She barely responded at first, but the more she smelled his cologne and felt his hard body between her thighs, the more her lips parted and her own body came alive.

They wrapped themselves in a passionate embrace, synchronizing their kiss to move with the ebb and flow of the moment. Angelic. Erotic. Beautiful. She felt herself drifting away in a sweet euphoria of her own. Kissing him was like floating, like the first high of some dangerous and illicit drug. The inviting shape of his full pink lips drew her in more, and she moved past the initial shock of being there with him and began to kiss him deeper, stronger.

He moaned a little as she opened up, exciting him more by the moment.

Inhaling his cologne as he ran his hand down her stomach, she felt the robe open. His hands brushed against her hot skin causing her to gasp. A new tingling sensation ran through her.

He caught her lips and kissed them again, releasing her only to push closer to her body. Her long thin fingers glided through his fragrant hair as she tasted his kiss, curling her fingers in his large blonde tendrils. It felt like cotton.

"We'll go very slowly," Dmitry whispered, cupping her breasts in his large hands.

Royal eyes opened wide. Excitement and urgency mixed like a strange medicine in her blood. Her heart raced, beating against his own like a drum.

"Wait," she stopped. Planting her elbows in the bed, she glared up at him.

Dmitry stopped and sat up. His eyes focused in on her, their diamond prisms flickering in the darkness.

Royal took a deep breath, trying to calm herself. She swallowed hard.

"I...need a minute," she panted, pulling her long tendrils from her face.

Moving from in between her legs, Dmitry ran his hands through his own hair, trying to calm the beast that had been nearly released in him. "Okay, baby," he said, allowing her to crawl out of the bed.

"Just a minute," she said, lifting her index finger. "I'll be right back."

"Alright," Dmitry said, watching her run into her bathroom and close the door behind her.

Leaning against the wall, Royal looked at herself in the mirror. She wiped his kiss from her mouth and went to the sink. Running water over her face, she tried to stop her shaking hands. She was in complete shock. Peering at her reflection, she took the towel and wiped her face. Her cheeks were fire red.

The weight of her actions consumed her. Twenty-three years of waiting and here she was about to do *it*. Her heart started to race again. The sound clearly audible through her chest. *Twenty three years.*

God, please let me be making the right decision, she prayed silently. I hold on to it for twenty three years, but I meet this guy and in less than three months it's thrown all away because of some diamonds and money.

She berated herself, but inwardly she knew that he had given her much more than material gain. He had given her true and utter happiness.

What if I do it wrong, she continued as she grabbed her toothbrush. What if I'm just horrible at this? She opened the medicine cabinet and grabbed her toothpaste and deodorant.

The climate was much different outside of the bathroom. Dmitry sat back on her pillows with his hands behind his head listening to her rattle through the cabinets and the water running. He yawned and pulled himself out of the bed.

Pealing out of his clothes one slow layer at a time, he watched the door, waiting for her to finish her unneeded beauty regiment. Once he had pulled the covers back and put his clothes on her dresser, he heard the racket stop.

The door slowly opened, illuminating the bedroom as she walked back out. She stopped at the entryway with the robe tightly tied around her waist. Perfume floated out and tickled his nose.

Dmitry sighed when he saw her. She was absolutely breath taking. Her long hair was pulled up in a pony tail. Her caramel-colored skin while only slightly revealed, glowed in the darkness.

She eyed him curiously as he stood up and walked to her.

Royal didn't speak. She could not. Her eyes were stuck to his colossal naked body. Muscles rippled through his tanned skin from his neck down his long muscular torso pulsating with little intricate muscles in his stomach through his large shaped legs to his giant calves. Besides the perfection of his muscular frame, there were also many tattoos. There were stars, crosses, butterflies, words in Cyrillic. What did it all mean? She took his body in through her eyes and was now more nervous than ever.

Realizing her inexperience, Dmitry gave her a reassuring smile. With a tender kiss on the forehead, he ran his fingers down her arms and grabbed her hands to pull her to him. Leaning down, he kissed her again, holding her face in his large hands. His sweet passion relaxed her. She felt herself melting into his embrace again, forgetting about everything including the large member that poked at her ribcage.

Still kissing her, Dmitry pulled at her robe again. The soft fabric hit the floor and exposed her long perfect temple. Feeling vulnerable, she curved into his body and wrapped her arms around his neck. Her skin felt like the silk against him. He picked her up quickly and carried her back to the bed.

"Are you ready *now?*" he asked, laying her down again.

Royal sighed and touched her head. "I think so." She had a nervous smile on her face.

Dmitry crawled into the bed, in between her shaking long legs and bent down to kiss the delicate crease between her hip and thigh. He ran his fingers down the length of her flat stomach, caressing her skin. Complete perfection. He marveled at her softness, the muse-like form of all her limbs.

The scent of vanilla masked her skin and transferred to his lips. He tasted it, allowing his tongue to massage her gently. He could hear deep breaths as Royal watched. The bewilderment of his actions were visible in her bright eyes. He smirked. If she only knew how his excitement rivaled hers, it might have frightened her. It had been torture to see her and not have her for so long. Now that he did, his only hope was to control all of his desires – to be careful not to treat her like an experienced lover.

Royal closed her eyes and laid back in the comfort of the pillow. She could hear his kisses as he made his way up to her breasts. His hot breath was like electric shock to her skin. She arched her back and reached out for him. As her fingertips touched his hard chest, he could feel her trembling, aching and afraid.

Her large melon-shaped breasts sat up invitingly. They were soft and full, matching the wonderful curves of her exotic body. Dmitry looked at her, amazed at her perfect splendor. Hungry for all of her, he circled the tip her nipples with his lips then sucked her slowly. Royal moaned, biting her lip and gripping his skin.

Cupping her breast in his hand as he kissed her lips, he nestled his hardness in between her legs. He growled a little as he felt her move under him, moving towards the mysterious phallic form. Instinctively, she opened her legs wider.

It was amazing to her how statue-like his hard body was against her own skin. His stomach pushed against her as he kissed her passionately. The intimacy of the act created a wave of excitement that rushed through her when she felt him raise her left leg. He bent and kissed her knee and slipped his hand down between her legs. She tensed up immediately, gripping his back tighter.

His eyes were fixed on hers, watching her every inexperienced move, basking in her enjoyment. His thumb rested at her maidenhead. Unable to take the exhilaration, she let out another moan and shifted her body as she planted her feet on the bed.

Dmitry put his free hand on her stomach and pushed her back down against the mattress. His finger now inside of her, she sucked in a deep, low breath. She moaned a throaty whimper . He snaked his lips with his tongue. Suddenly, he was hungry. His mouth watered.

Rolling her hips under him rhythmically, she placed her hand on his, enjoying the pressure. She breathed faster. He pushed deeper.

The candles illuminated the room and his murals of tattoos, one of a large cross, two oddly designed stars on each side of his chest near his shoulders, many more up and down both arms and on his neck. Inquisitively, she ran her long, slim fingers down his chest, tracing the inky art.

"Dmitry." Her words were nearly in a whisper.

She looked into his eyes because they were soothing, not like as his monstrous body, that was extremely intimidating to her now. There were muscles everywhere, protruding out of his skin and framing him like armor; his body was long and wide, full of valleys, deep creases and ink. Even his knees where tattooed with the same funny large star. He looked like a deviant. A beautiful, dangerous deviant.

She had not noticed that in the process of their interaction, he had kissed the rose lipstick off her lips, slipped the earrings and necklace from her ears and had her spread her body in the bed. He wanted to see her in completely natural form – no man-made additions to confuse God-given beauty. Watching her long hair fall down around her was the final step.

"We'll see just how long you can take it," he said.

"How long I can take what?" she whispered finally, feeling carnal exhilaration.

Dmitry bent to the curves of her body and kissed her from neck to breast to stomach, to…the feeling of his mouth on her tiny secret caused her back to spasm. He kneeled before her. The black stars on his knees now pointing directly at her.

Grabbing her calves, he pulled her hips off the mattress to his face and planted his head in between her thighs. All she could see was his curly blonde hair. Devastated, she reached for it and grabbed it as he kissed the inside of her body. Her moans became screams, and she grabbed at the covers. It was so amazing! It was so wonderful!

Chills ran through her body as she felt his curious tongue. In and out, he moved, carefully until she finally called his name.

"Oh my God, Dmitry! I can't take anymore," she screamed, panting and teary eyed. Her body convulsed on its own, pulsating with a new and vivid reaction.

He released her as soon as she said the words. Her body drifted back down to earth, on to the comforter. She lay before him defeated. Her long hair danced about her body and created a crown for him to lay his large hands in as he lay on top of her. His manhood resting in between her steaming highs.

She was ready. She wanted him inside of her. She pawed at him, pushing herself against him, opening wider.

Dmitry was crazed with desire. The blood pumped through his protruding veins at a painful pace. He looked at her like a wild animal waiting for the perfect moment to strike.

"While you are still virgin, I'll tell you my only stipulation of taking you," he said suddenly.

"What?" Royal moaned. Her long legs were wide open and her back arched.

He sat in between her legs looking at her with a strange desperation.

"I don't want anyone ever make love to you except me," he whispered. "Do you hear what I'm saying to you?"

"Yes," she promised sincerely. "No one. I promise." Her eyes rolled, much too weak to truly open.

"Are you sure? What I'm asking is not fair or practical, but it's my stipulation, just the same."

She finally looked up at him. "No one, Dmitry."

Between deep breaths, she felt him reach down with his hand and slowly slip a finger inside of her again. It was an aching but enjoyable pain, deeper than before. She closed her eyes and wrapped her arms around his neck.

"Open your eyes," he said, kissing her lips. "Look at me, while I make you mine."

"I don't know if I can," she said, scared of what she knew that he was preparing to do. "Don't hurt me," she begged as she felt his long member hard against her belly. Her request was not just protection from physical pain but also emotional.

"I'll try not to, love," he said, lifting her leg a little, understanding the totality of her plea. He looked at her strangely, throbbing to be inside of her. Bending down, he kissed her mouth again. "Hold on to me," he instructed softly.

She locked eyes with him as he gripped her behind in his hands.

Slowly with every kiss and every maneuver, he moved closer to her center. He was diverting her way from what she feared. He was trying to take her attention away from what he was about to do to her.

"This is the painful part?" she asked with signs of fear in her face. She was both excited and afraid. Locking her legs around him, she held close to his hot marble-like body.

Dmitry did not reply.

The sensation that she felt as his blunt tip rested at the door of her maiden head was unexplainable to Royal. She felt him rubbing against her, causing more excitement with every brush. The sensation caused her to breathe heavily and pull at his curly locks as he continued to kiss her lips.

Finally, when she thought that the enjoyment would never end, she felt his long wide back arch and pull away. Then there was a monstrous rush into her body, and the completion of the powerful surge that knocked over her weakened temple like an army pushing against a weak front.

Her mouth opened, but he quickly covered it with another kiss. She gasped, winced, screamed. He pulled back again and pushed deeper into her, this time allowing her mouth to be free as she screamed.

"Oh my God!" Dmitry exclaimed in a strained and un-recognizable voice.

It did hurt. It was a painful, painful sharp stabbing of her body that paralyzed her and shocked her senses.

"Dmitry!" she exclaimed, looking at him with her eyes full of fear.

"I know, love, but I have to complete it," he said push-ing all the way down into her body with a third, slow erotic surge.

"Complete, what?" she panted, pulling the hair from her face and holding on to him tightly.

"The covenant," he moaned, kissing her again, feeling himself in very bottom of her love. He pulled back and made slow advances that recoiled the pain into some strange and indescribable pressure.

She pulled at the sheets as he made her his, unable to run from the sheer magnitude of his 270 lbs force.

In her own pain, she did not realize how reverse the spectrum was for him. He fought the pleasure of her unspoiled body with fierce intensity. With every stroke he longed to end his battle. Instead, he had to stay and make sure that she was completely pleased, a task that caused his entire body to tremble as he tried to concentrate on not concentrating on her beautiful body, amidst her sexy screams and the constant fact that he was so deep inside of her.

She held on to his massive back as he pushed deep inside of her, leaving a trail of blood on the sheets. Her nails dug into his tanned back and left welts and marks of a battered lover, but Dmitry ignored the pain or welcomed it. She could not believe the throbbing pleasure all wrapped in one large stroke.

Tears formed in the corners of her eyes as he destroyed what she was to build what she would be. Realizing that she the *old* Royal no more, she was suddenly afraid. Dmitry recognized the strange bewilderment in her face and bent down to kiss her gently, carefully rocking her body.

"It's better now, baby?" he asked, moving slowly.

"Yes," she said breathless. "So much better."

She moved along with him, her body spread to its capacity as his body shadowing over her. The pain had left her now, and there was a new feeling. Something that she quite enjoyed. It caused her body to shake and shiver, clamor in his hands like clay.

He adjusted her long body slightly under his strong grip, moving her to a position where she could only feel the pleasure of his strokes. A sensual moan escaped her lips. Where had he learned to do that? She thought as she floated beside him.

"I love you," he confessed again as he made love to her.

"I love you too," Royal whispered softly.

Chapter 7

The night air swept in through the open window and flirted with the soft curtains floating in its breeze. The soiled comforter had been placed by the door for Dmitry to discard in the morning, and their sweaty sheets lay in a pile by the bed on the floor. Exhausted, Royal lay beside Dmitry quietly watching the fan circle above her while Dmitry ran his large hands through her hair. Neither one of them had said anything for nearly an hour. There was a peace between them now that their bodies had done battle.

Royal was in awe of Dmitry's skill in lovemaking, and Dmitry was awe that he finally had her. It had not been an easy task for him. No woman had ever made him wait more than a week before being intimate. Royal had finally broken three months into their pseudo-courtship, but it had taken much coercion. The deliberate wining and dining and thousands and thousands of dollars in gifts had been the easy part, developing trust had been the key. Royal required trust. It was a staple in their friendship. He laughed a little as he thought about her and then glanced over at her long body still glistening with sweat. Who was he kidding? The wait had been well worth it.

Every once in a while, Royal would take her eyes off the fan and look over at Dmitry. To see him naked was quite amazing. While he looked absolutely devastating in clothes, he was even more lethal in nothing at all. As normal, his body was relaxed, maybe even lazy. His long limbs completely covered his side of the bed. The intricate muscles and tattoos danced over his tanned skin in harmony. And while Royal had never seen him workout, she was certain that he had to do so often. His body was a testament to a dedicated weight-lifting regiment.

"What are you thinking about?" Dmitry asked, propping himself up on one arm to face her. His bicep bulged.

Royal smiled. "I'm thinking that I couldn't have picked a better man," she said, nearly hoarse. "I was sort of scared about that at first...I mean, to wait so long and pick the wrong person. That would suck."

Dmitry lifted his brow.

"But I didn't," she assured him.

He ran his finger down the side of her nude frame and sighed. He was horny again – aching to be inside of her one more time.

"I'm sure that you could've picked someone...*anyone* better, but I would not have been happy about it," he said, pulling her closer to his large chest.

She nuzzled into him comfortably.

"Change of subject." Royal said, abruptly. She looked up into his eyes. "What do the tattoos mean, man?" She had been waiting since he disrobed to get an answer.

"Well, each of them means something different. Pick one, and I'll tell you."

"What do the stars mean?"

Dmitry rubbed his hand across his chest. "It means that I'm apart of very elite organization. In my country, it takes a lot to get these stars across your chest. The ones on my knees mean I kneel before no man."

"What about a woman?" she snickered suggestively. "You *kneeled* before me."

"What I do in the bedroom does not count. And if I recall, you kneeled before me as well." His eyes glimmered. He was rock hard again.

Royal nodded. "Point well taken. What does the Madonna mean?"

"That I've been a thief since I was child, and the crucifix means that I've mastered the art of thievery."

Royal smirked. "Dmitry, you don't steal."

"Oh, I used to. Now, I just take what I want."

"And the beautiful butterfly?" She traced her finger around the wings.

"That I can maneuver very easily in many complicated situations."

"Maneuver? "

"It's how I got out of prison as young man."

"I don't even want to know," she said, laughing.

"Enough about me." Dmitry pulled her up on the pillow and snuggled his head in her breasts. He closed his eyes and sighed. "What about you?"

"What about me?"

"Tell me something that no one else knows?"

"Only if you do."

"You first."

"Umm. I keep empty picture frames in my dresser drawers, hoping to put family pictures in them one day."

"Tell me something important," he said, scoffing at her light response. "There has to be a secret that you keep from everyone, something dark that you don't want anyone in the world to know." Dmitry spoke as if he had many.

"Okay, okay," she sighed and looked up at the soft linen above her in the canopy swaying under the force of the ceiling fan. Her carefree smile turned into a frown. "Some secrets are meant to be kept though."

"What could you have done? You're just a girl. I'm sure it couldn't have been too bad."

"Don't be so sure," she replied solemnly, forgetting to sneer at the *girl* statement.

"Well, I would hope that if you gave me something as precious as your virginity, you could trust me with a secret – no matter how big it is."

"It's really awful, actually," she said, wiping her face quickly. "Horrible, in fact."

"If you tell me that you were born a man or that you were once a whore, then it'll be horrible, because I'll be forced to kill you."

"Of course, I was born a girl." She laughed a little in between the sudden sorrow. "And the proof my virginity is by the door." She motioned over at the comforter.

Dmitry looked over at the comforter. "Speaking of which, are you hurting still?" He rubbed face. "I could give you hot bath. It would make the aching go away."

"No," Royal yawned. "I'm just tired."

"Well then, back to your secret then."

Royal hesitated. "I've never told anyone."

"Then, I should be the one to know. Go on," he said, urging her.

"Fine. I…shot a man once." She held her breath as the words fell clumsily out of her mouth. It was strange for her to hear, even after years of living with it. She waited for him to say something, anything.

Dmitry's eyes opened. Shifting his long body a little, he looked up at her. "You'd better explain that one to me," he said in a deep raspy voice. His crystal blue eyes beamed through her, waiting. A small smile crept across his full lips. Could it be that he was amused?

"When I was fourteen, one of my foster parents' friends used to come over a lot. He was a truck driver, and when he was in town, he would always stay at their house. He was a real...funky looking guy, wiry beard and looked like he never washed. My foster parents would let him sleep in the den on the couch. He'd watch porno while everyone was sleep. He was a real dirt bag.

"One night when it was really late, while I was gone with some of my friends, he snuck in my sister's room and raped her. She was real quiet, you know. Plus, she was super skinny. It wouldn't have been hard for him to overpower her. She didn't tell anyone – probably thought no one would believe her. Then the signs started to show. You know...more weight, sick all the time, sleeping all the time. I got nosy and suspicious.

"When she finally confessed to me what was going on, I was...on fire. You see, he would have never gone after me. I was the loud mouth, the bad kid. I would have fought. I always did," she smiled. "So I waited for him and the next time that he was in town, I followed him up to the truck stop and when nightfall came, I snuck into his cabin, seduced him and shot him to death with his own gun. I wanted to stab him; I even brought my own kitchen knife, but the gun was there. In a rage, I just grabbed it, when he had his pants down." She let the tears fall. "I donno. I wish that I could take it back sometimes."

"Damn," Dmitry sighed. "I didn't know that you had any family." It seemed that the murder was not very exciting to Dmitry. He brushed it off. "What happened to her? Your sister?"

"She killed herself a day after I killed him. She was pregnant at 12. We were only teenagers – barely that. She didn't know any better. The cops couldn't link me to it, but they did suspect my dead sister. Either way, I felt that I had avenged her."

"And you did. Sometimes, what we do in this world is right but not legal and other times legal but not right. Plus, you will do anything for family, even when it makes no sense," he reasoned, justifying her actions and secretely his.

"It doesn't change that sometimes, I feel hollow inside. What I did won't bring her back."

"But your vengeance probably protected some other poor girl."

"I miss her. My sister's name was Chloe." She said the name and for the first time felt the reminiscent feeling of family.

"I am truly sorry for you, Royal. If I could change it, I would. Unfortunately, death is sometimes a part of life – whether it comes fairly or unfairly is often not left for us to decide."

"You sound like a fortune cookie," she said wryly, trying to cut her emotions off. Royal didn't want to talk anymore about her sister, not tonight during something so important in her life. She tried to move on. "What about you? What's your secret?"

Dmitry smiled a mischievous smile, one of deceit and enjoyable trickery. "Anatoly is my biological son."

There was a long silence before Royal replied. She continued rubbing through his hair and looking at the top of the canopy. "I get that. It's his eyes, you know. They're like ice, like yours."

"You *get* that, huh?" Dmitry expected her to be more shocked.

"Yep…sure do," Royal said without looking at him.

"Well, besides the blonde hair, he looks just like his mother. So damned short," he continued.

"He's not short at all. You're just *too* tall. How old is he, anyway. He looks thirty?"

"From hard life, I suppose. He's only twenty. He'll be twenty-one this year."

"You had him early."

"Yeah. I was on my way out of the country and stopped to see an old girl that I used to mess around with. He showed up in America three years ago. He was looking for work and new start. His mother had told him about me, and he used his last dime to get here."

"No one knows?"

"Not a soul. And no one can ever know."

"Don't worry. Your secret is safe with me."

"Everything that I tell you is secret, Royal. You can never repeat one word," he said, closing his eyes again.

Royal bit her lip, thinking about what he was demanding of her. Who would she tell? She didn't know anyone.

"Just promise to always be as honest with me. I can handle a lot of things, especially considering the things that I've done and where I come from, but I can't stomach a liar," she said sternly. "That's my stipulation to you *before I take you.*"

They both smiled.

"Lying is for people with no authority. I don't lie. I can't say that I'll ever tell you everything, but what I do tell you will be the truth," Dmitry said.

"So, it doesn't bother you that I killed a man?"

"No," Dmitry yawned. "You were just protective of what little family that you had, I suppose. I can understand that. Look at where I came from. I'm a gutter rat in nice clothing."

"No, you're far from that," she said conversely. "You're the best man that I've ever known."

He laughed. "You don't get out much, my love."

"One more question, and then I'm going to bed?" Royal continued.

"What?"

"What did you mean by making a covenant?"

"When I was boy, my mother was whore. The only good thing good I had in my entire life was church down the street from our shitty little apartment. The priest was like my father. I learned to play violin there, and he taught me about sacred bonds between man and woman, a marriage of sorts through a woman's virginity. It is covenant between her, the man and God. The hymen is sacred – only to be broken by husband. It's ironclad. What we did is ironclad. No man or woman can take it away."

"So, I have you forever then?" She asked smiling.

"Yes…forever."

"Like we're married without the papers."

"For now, it is all that I can give you."

"Wait. Are you saying that you can't marry?" The thought disturbed her. "But I want to get married one day. I don't want to stay single or shacked up my whole life. It's so *incomplete*."

Dmitry could hear the sudden worry in her voice. He didn't want to ruin their night together by explaining all the complications in his life. It was clear that she would not understand.

"There is no other woman involved, if that's what you mean. It's just not as easy for me as it is for most. We'll save that conversation for another time, when you're sure that you want to marry me in the first place."

Royal sat back in the bed quietly. She did know.

"But it doesn't mean that I don't love you. I do…love you." Dmitry pulled her hair from her face and kissed her. "Let me show you how much I love you, now."

∞♥∞

Nine o'clock had passed, and Royal lay in Dmitry's dress shirt slumbering in the comfort of her bed. She had been permitted to rest only a few hours, because Dmitry, in his cunning manner, had smuggled one more love session out of her, before he rocked her to sleep. She had gone to bed a little frantic of the hour, scared that she would oversleep. But Dmitry had assured her that he would take care of everything.

The staff arrived just a few minutes before nine and was greeted by Dmitry. When they came in the back of the store, he was sitting behind the credenza reading *The New York Times*. While Royal suffered from wine and sex, he was a veteran of such affairs and had risen early in the morning to shower and have Anatoly run over to his home and bring back a fresh suit and his daily newspapers.

In the month that both had worked for Dmitry and Royal, neither Renée nor Cory had ever seen Dmitry at the office early in the morning. He sipped on coffee now and talked to Anatoly, who stood listening attentively across the room and sending text messages.

The two unsuspecting employees walked in chatting and laughing, but they stopped as soon as they saw Dmitry. He looked up from his coffee and set his newspaper down. A large smile came across his face, showing his pearly white teeth and long dimples. His cold, ice eyes were bright this morning.

"Hello," he said, watching the two slip past him.

"Hi. Is Royal alright?" Renée asked, setting down her lunch bag in the adjoining kitchenette.

"She's fine, just resting upstairs. She'll be down soon enough," he said, crossing his hands together. "She said that you two would be here at nine, and here you are. This is good. I'm sure that she's given you a list of things to do."

"Yeah, she gave us a few things," Renee said, looking at Cory.

"Well, I'll start to set up everything." Cory excused himself from the small room.

"I'll help." Renée followed anxiously.

They both scurried up to the front of the shop and left Dmitry and Anatoly alone, where they resumed their conversation in Russian.

Renée ran her long nails across the remote and turned the television on, while snickering to Cory. "I told you that they were sleeping together," she said in a half-whisper.

"We still don't know for sure," Cory said, giving Royal the benefit of the doubt. "She could be sick."

"Whatever. You saw the same thing that I did last night. You and I both know that a man doesn't look at a woman like he looks at her, unless it's something there."

"I don't look at women like that at all, Renée. I'm gay, remember?"

"You know what I mean," Renée said laughing. "Bless her soul, that big man probably wore her out with his fine ass."

They both snickered again.

∞♥∞

Royal finally rolled over and realized that not only was Dmitry gone, but the sun was up and the clock said eleven! She jumped up, terribly sore and ran to the bathroom. She was late, really late. She knew that Dmitry had told her that he would take care of everything, but it was her shop, her deal. She never meant to sleep so long. Jumping in the shower, she let the hot water cascade over her body, drench her hair and soothe those aching parts that had been excessively used in the last day.

By 11:30, Royal was locking her front door and headed downstairs. In a comfortable pair of blue linen slacks, a canary yellow Chanel tank top, and blue wedge-healed Bottega Veneta patent leather shoes, she inched downstairs with her hair pulled up in a careful pony tail.

Forced to take short, choppy steps, it was painfully apparent to Royal that it wasn't easy to walk as she was still aching from the pain of being a new lover. It was a sensation unlike any that she had ever known. On one hand she felt like she was glowing and could sing like a bird, but on the other hand, her body felt like it had recently suffered the business end of a Billy club.

As her feet hit the bottom step, she quickly turned and ran out into the store. She could feel Dmitry behind her, watching her, but if she stopped and dared look at him, she might end up back upstairs in his embrace – naked and panting like a dog in heat.

Dmitry smirked as he watched her shimmy out of the back office away from him. He also noted her soreness, and the fact that he should have soaked her in a hot bath, even against her will.

Anatoly uttered something to him in Russian and gave a smug smile.

"Enough of that," Dmitry replied abruptly.

Hoping not to be terribly missed or noticed, Royal quietly announced herself and quickly made her way around glass and marble countertop, where Renée was checking someone out. A few early morning patrons looked through the new dresses and talked to each other, ignoring her all together. Royal was thankful for that.

"Hey, boss," Renée said, turning to look at her visibly exhausted friend.

"Hey," Royal said, moving her bangs out of her face. "Sorry that I'm late. I didn't get much sleep." She yawned.

Cory laughed, most unexpectedly. He tried to repress it, but it shot up from his diaphragm. He grabbed his mouth, trying to muffle the sounds, but they crept across the boutique. Renée smirked and turned away.

"What is so funny?" Royal asked, flinging her head to look at Cory, her long pony tail trailing around her shoulder like a black python.

"Nothing," Renée said, touching Royal's neck. "You've got a little bruise action going on there."

Royal touched her neck and looked in the mirror. Damn it! How could she have missed that? It was a huge passion mark that was deep red and completely visible – undeniable in fact.

There was a whistling tune that rang from the back of the store as Dmitry made his way through the boutique. With his newspaper tucked under his arm, he walked casually over to Royal, who stood looking in the mirror at her neck and ignoring him all together. As usual, the patrons stopped shopping and gawked at both his size and his haunting beauty. And as usual, Dmitry kept his eyes on Royal. She was always his target.

"What are you staring at in that mirror," he asked, looking down her shirt.

"Evidence," she said, showing him the passion mark.

"Dear, I'm afraid those are all over your body. Besides that, how are you?"

"Fine," she said, forced to smile at the sight of him. Her eyes brightened. "I'm perfect."

"You should have rested longer. You are only as competent as your weakest employee. And I think you have strong employees, eh?"

"I should have been up two hours ago." She felt a flutter in her stomach, remembering his masculine smell all over her. She'd hated to wash it off.

"Well, you look great. Actually, I wish that I had more time. I'd let you know exactly how beautiful you look."

With his long arm, Dmitry reached across the fine jewelry to the back of her neck and pulled her in to his embrace. Slowly, he kissed her right in front of Cory, Renée, the customers and God Almighty. Tasting the sweetness of her lip gloss, he released her and licked his lips. He was fighting a hungry erection again.

"Umm...you still taste delicious," he noted.

Royal opened her eyes and knew instantly that all eyes were on her. She stood back up straight and smiled.

"Thank you...for that. Have a good day," she said blushing.

"You, too," he said, rubbing her arm. He looked at Renee, who was standing dumbfounded with her mouth gaped wide open. Quietly, he turned and walked out just as he had come in -with all eyes on him.

Royal could feel the chaotic energy in the room, but for once she didn't care. They were in love, and if he didn't mind that the world knew, neither did she.

"Don't say a word," Royal said to Renée as she grabbed a yellow button down to slip on to hide her bruises. "You either, Cory."

"Oh, we are way past words," Cory said, turning to help a customer.

"I need to grab the fire extinguisher. It's hot as hell in here," Renee joked.

Chapter 8

The basement of *Mother Russia* restaurant was basic and unattractive, quite the opposite of its upstairs luxury. It was illuminated by industrial halogen lights, painted in pewter black paint, covered in black linoleum floors and highlighted by one very large wooden table sent from Russian with seating for the divine 16.

No windows gave the large space a depressing, dungeon-like feeling. It reminded Dmitry of the rainy nights he had spent in prison. It was such a constant reminder until he absolutely hated going downstairs in the basement and would only conduct business there when it was most necessary.

Today, unfortunately, was one of those necessary days. Dmitry had just left the springtime of Royal's presence and had abruptly entered the hell that he called his private life.

Anatoly followed closely behind him as he walked down the steps of the hidden space, where a small group of men sat around a long table awaiting him. His feet made an echo through the concrete staircase as he made his way down. Each step made him nervous. The winding stairs were in a tight place, perfect for ambush. When his foot met the last step, the entryway expanded into a very large opening. Dmitry took a deep breath, glad to get rid of the claustrophobic feeling.

Two men with automatic weapons stood at a double door's entry. When they saw Dmitry, they opened the doors quickly and moved quietly out of his way.

He walked in the room and sighed. "Gentlemen," he said, bidding them a good morning.

They all spoke collectively and watched as he sat at the
head of the table. It was after all his rightful spot. He was
the head of the Medlov Russian Organized Crime Family, a
faction of the feared and revered Vory v Zakone that had
migrated from Russia to southern London to New York to
Memphis.

Dmitry ended up in Memphis due to the growing distribution hub in the city and the convenience of the ever
useful Mississippi River. When he first arrived, he had only
a team of three, but his expansion required the recruitment
of old friends from around the globe.

The men had come obediently through the years to
serve the Vory and their fearless leader, Dmitry. He had
spent ten long years working to build his empire, and in one
decade he had amassed more wealth and power than anyone
had in his position before him.

However well-known he was in the dangerous under-
ground circles, Dmitry hid in plain sight well, behind
lucrative and very upstanding investments both in safe
stocks and real estate, starting new businesses and pretending to be an upstanding citizen working hard in his restaurant because of his passion for food and his desire to be
around people.

However, everyone in this room knew that he was the
coldest, strongest, and most astringent of them all. A true
member of the obocheck. He had slaughtered anyone who
dared stand in his way, purchased both politicians and
police alike, intimidated and followed through on the most
unthinkable threats. And never truly worked a day in his
life. He was Boss Dmitry Medlov.

The other fifteen men around him had been allowed to
live within a modified code of the Thieves-in-law. They had
been permitted wives, children, the ability to intermingle

with the society and the denial, so far, of the penalty of death for their transgressions against the code.

However, Dmitry had stayed true to the old ways. He had watched over them, rightfully chosen as their leader because of his denial of all things that went against the code. He had not taken a woman as anything more than a lover; he had no children bearing his name; although he had businesses, he had never worked a day in his life – lived on only what he made through the code; and he loathed the government and all of its criminal justice departments. He had a file within every federal agency in the U.S., several in UK, was on watch by Interpol and still feared in Russia, the Ukraine and Georgia.

Only no one could touch him, because he was so skilled at covering his tracks.

"You know the drill, Anatoly. Check the room before we begin," Dmitry said, looking through a file that had been placed in front of him.

Not only did Dmitry run all of their secret gatherings like corporate board meetings, but he also had paid an FBI agent to train Anatoly to check the room for bugs and the phone for taps.

"It's clear," Anatoly said, standing in the back of the room, two Glocks visible in the leather holsters under his arms.

"Good. Now, I'll make this quick, mostly because I just don't want to be here today," Dmitry huffed, irritated. "While I am your leader, I've always considered us to be brothers. I have been fair with you. Where I have prospered, so have you. But the knife cuts both ways. Where I have suffered, so shall you, *if you are the cause*. Would you not agree that this is wise?"

They all agreed that it was not only wise but generous.

"Then why would one of you desecrate the most scared of our laws by talking to the police?"

The men looked around urgently, all surprised, at least one scared of what he knew the consequence would be. Death. It was part of the code. No Vor cooperated with the government. It had been the one code that was unbreakable, and so far in all the years they had been in Memphis, it had gone unbroken.

"Which one of you is it?" He pointed down the table as he talked. "I'll make things much easier for you, if you *just* tell me the truth, now. But if you force me to tell you who you are, it will be most unfortunate for you." His voice never raised but his demeanor was cold and sinister. His long finger fell behind the force of his stare. He sat back in his chair and sighed, waiting for a response. There was none.

The room was silent. Some of the older counterparts grumbled under their breath, angry at the leak, anxious to know who the snitch was. How dare someone talk! The outrage overflowed.

Dmitry looked down at his watch. The long ivory dial made its way around the circumference of the golden plated watch face.

"I'll give you another thirty seconds. I'll even count it down for you. One, two, three, four…"

As Dmitry counted down the death sentence, Anatoly moved from the back of the room out of the darkness of the shadows with the shiny, chrome nine millimeter in his hand. Each person looked at the other while watching Dmitry's face for some indication of who the traitor was. But he gave no sign, he simply kept counting. "Thirty," he said finally.

There was an unmistakable click as Anatoly pulled the trigger. The shot was quick and accurate. A man's body on the far end of the table flew forward, blood spewing out of his disfigured head in ulterior-spray red on the others. There was no gasp or shock. They all looked on bemused, horrified that their friend had been a traitor. His death was insignificant because of his treachery.

Dmitry looked down at the brain matter on the folder that had projected across the room and cringed. Even in the man's death, Kirill had made a mess of things.

He took the handkerchief from his side pocket and wiped the folder off. Then, he carefully passed the folder with the leaked transcripts of conversations about each of them along with pictures of the traitor meeting with the police to the man on his immediate right.

"It's sad day when we cannot trust our own. This man has been my friend for many years. He was one of the original settlers. I know his wife, his children, *his mistress*, his life. It pains me to have to have done this, but you all know the rules that we live by. I have granted you the ability, unlike many of our brothers across the world, to marry, to have more than we would have in Russia, but one thing will not change. We do not cooperate with police; they cooperate with us. We do not roll over on each other. It has always and will always be punishable by death."

The men agreed silently, looking on for their leader's direction.

"What was he speaking to the police about," Khalid asked, a mid-fifties, balding Russian man. Putting on his glasses as the file arrived in front of him; he clinched the paper with his bony, slender fingers and squinted as he read the sobering transcripts.

"The police are forming a strong investigation against us. They want to find out who is the leader. They think that if they cut head off, organization dies."

"We have evolved much since the old days," Khalid smirked.

"Sometimes I fear to our own detriment," Dmitry replied.

"How did you find out?" another man asked perplexed.

"I am not without my own contacts in most agencies. I will not, however, reveal my source."

"For how long has this gone on?" another man chimed in, disgusted by the betrayal.

"He was arrested the other night by a local. Subsequently, he was questioned by feds because of his knowledge. One of *mine* inside got the information to me." Dmitry sighed.

Frustrated, he clinched his teeth, but did not raise his voice. "With every choice, there is a consequence. So, enough about him. We move forward."

The men were dead silent but in agreement with Dmitry. He focused in, past the fury and hurt in his heart.

"In the next few weeks, we have much to do. If we are going to successfully take over the northern territory, we have to get new reinforcements from New York. I've already met with them. We have about ten new guys coming in soon. Plus, I have sent to our friends in New York for a seasoned leader for *his* place. I have asked that they send someone with impeccable skills in nuclear trafficking," Dmitry said, daring not to ever utter his dead friend's name again.

"The northern territory has always been crap shoot. It's time to organize it and utilize the roadways to transport. It's cheaper, and if you lose one shipment, you've got hundreds more behind it and before it. Now, this won't be easy. State troopers are doubling in number up the I-40 highway, but its prime real estate. I've already purchased a few houses up and down the highway as far up as Knoxville. We'll use them as safe houses to push the product out to the east coast safely."

"These men. Are they going to secure the way up to Knoxville?"

"Yes," Dmitry said calmly. "That is their singular purpose."

"When?" one of the men asked, looking at the file.

"As soon they arrive, we'll begin sending them out in shifts," Dmitry said, walking to the door. "This group of ten that they are sending will be our newest muscle. They're all professionals with military, drug trafficking, munitions trafficking experience. They didn't come cheap, but New York has loaned them out to us for a while. So, go home and spend time with your families. We should not be concerned about all of this. We have capable men handling it all, and we can go home to our families and spend time with them in peace."

We was a term that was never used by Dmitry. They looked up at him curiously. *We?* Who was *we?* Dmitry had no family. He had sworn when he became the boss of to uphold all codes of the Vory v Zakone ensuring purity at the highest level for the organization.

He had never so much as even hinted at a lover being a significant other. He treated women like jewelry, discarding them on a whim. Now he spoke of family? Everyone automatically thought of the beautiful black girl that he had thrown the party for the night before. Could it be the Boss Medlov had softened over the years? Had his tyrannical reign over Memphis started to come to a slow end?

They also thought of how kind he had been to their now dead friend. One bullet, no torture. Dmitry had to be in love. This was a man who would have walked into the meeting with a steak knife and cut out the man's entrails.

However intrigued, no one dared say a word to Dmitry; to ask him about his personal life might mean that they would join their departed friend. Instead they nodded in agreement and saw him quietly out followed by his faithful henchman Anatoly. He left the room silently, almost remorseful for the loss. It was strange to see a reaction of any sort coming from a man who had never shown remorse for anything before.

As the door closed, they looked at each other with raised eyebrows but still did not utter one word. Conversations would take place far from this place, far from the corpse lying before them bent over the table in a blood pool.

Chapter 9

The calming change of autumn was welcomed in Memphis. The city needed a break from the heat. September was a transition month, mixed with days of smoldering sun and cool breezes.

Royal had adjusted accordingly. Sale pieces were moving fast and being replaced by sweaters and scarves, darker colors and more layers. Also, the clientele for *Dmitry's Closet* was starting to really pick up. Royal had over 2,000 names on her VIP list for special showings of the new diamond collection, special trunk shows and private parties. She had women coming from all over the mid-south to shop and to be seen in the newest prêt-a-porte clothing from the finest French, Russian, Italian, Chinese, English and American designers.

She even had a new billboard on Poplar Avenue that was creating a wave of new inquiries about the shop and the owner. Several local magazines had requested interviews with Dmitry, but he had deferred all media to Royal and insisted that she be the official face of the boutique.

"Royal's been so much different since that morning she was late for work," Renée said, hanging the new Diane von Furstenberg dresses that had arrived only hours before on the front display.

"I know. I've been watching her," Cory said, looking out for Royal, who stepped out to grab lunch for the trio.

"I wonder what's it's like to try to have a relationship with a man like Dmitry?"

"Petrifying, I suppose," Cory answered absently.

"I mean, he's beautiful, rich, powerful and sexy. What could be bad about that?"

"Trying to figure out how he got to be so rich and po-werful."

"What do you think it really is?" Renée asked, setting down the dress. "I think its drugs."

"I think it's a combination of all sorts of organized crime," Cory said, checking his hair in the mirror.

"Do you think that she knows what he really does?"

"No." Cory turned to her. "But we should tell her. Don't you think? I mean, we're supposed to be her friends for goodness sake." His southern accent came out more when he tried to be so flamboyantly gay.

"How in the hell do you broach a subject like that?" Renée huffed. "This woman is still our boss and our friend. What are you trying to do…hurt her?"

"Save her," Cory said, over emphasizing the "s" sound. "Royal's a great girl. It'd be a damned shame to watch her go up in the smoke of Dmitry's fire."

"It'd be a shame to watch us walked out the front door of this place if we crossed the line with her too."

"Royal would never fire us," Cory said sternly.

"Get real. She'd make one comment to Dmitry, and we'd both be gone."

"You think she'd talk to Dmitry about something that we've said to her?"

"Of course. You white boys are so freaking territorial; as soon as she said something he'd give us the boot."

Cory ignored her snide remark. "He does look territori-al."

"All of you do."

"Please don't tell me you're one of those *black* women who think all *white* men look alike."

"I know that they all don't look alike. You don't look at damn thing like Dmitry. He's sort of dreamy, while you're sort of... I don't know. Peculiar. You could be cute if you wanted to, but the jeans are so tight, I can't focus on your face."

"Dreamy, huh? No, I don't get that from him. He seems, dark and sadistic to me. Maybe it's the creepy bodyguards, the obscene amounts of money he spends or the trace of Anatoly's gun in all of his jeans, but I would never want to get on Dmitry's bad side," Cory said, turning around in the mirror to examine his butt. "And my pants are not tight."

"Shut up," Renée said quickly. "Here comes the prom queen."

Royal walked inside of the boutique with lunch from the Arcade, the oldest restaurant in Memphis, in white oily bags full of fried treats. She entered beaming brightly as usual and wearing a gold silk Dolce and Gabbana sundress, a denim jacket, white D&G shades with Swarovski crystals and cultured pearl accents, a matching yellow leather and white purse and flip flops. All together, she was wearing about ten thousand dollars worth of clothing and accessories. The thought made her blush. Dmitry spoiled her beyond belief now, surprising her with diamonds, pearls, expensive and exotic gifts all the time.

"Sorry it took so long," she said, taking off her shades.

"It's okay. No one has come in since you left," Cory said, helping her with the bags.

They all made their way to the back office to eat lunch and watch out for any clients who might pop up. Sitting around the credenza, they opened the oily bags and set the table for a hearty meal.

"Did we get anymore calls for the VIP showing of the Cyrille Gassiline collection?" Royal asked, stuffing her face with a large juicy hamburger. She wiped the excess grease from her mouth with a wad of napkins.

"No, but so far, we are at 150 people with a 175 max capacity," Cory answered, wolfing down a hand full of French fries. "Man, a beer would be great with this," he said belching.

"It's barely noon, lush," Renee snapped at Cory. "I thought gay men were supposed to be refined."

"Stereotypes coming from a black woman? Really?" Cory raised his eyebrow.

"Enough you two," Royal interjected between the catty couple. "We only have 25 more people to place before we close the event. This is a good sign." The thought was comforting.

It had been hell to bring the trunk show to Memphis. Royal had desperately wanted to bring the popular Russian designer Gassiline's designs to her shop for months, but she had been turned down due to tight scheduling. Then, after a call from Dmitry, things were worked out, and she was able to bring the hottest trends in Moscow to the Southern belles of Memphis for fall. When her VIP list of clients received the invitation, they went mad calling to reserve seating for them and their friends and family, who would be flying region-wide to get her shop on October 1st.

Dmitry laughed the night last month when Royal got the call from Gassiline's American contact in the middle of the night. When the phone rang, they were in her bed watching reruns of *Criminal Minds*. She reached over and answered it, then screamed so loud when she hung up; he had to cover his ears. "Thank you!" she exclaimed as she kissed him over and over again on his full mouth. For a woman who was not at first even a decent dresser, Royal had blossomed into quite the connoisseur of fine clothing.

Dmitry had been pleased to help her, pleased to see her pleased and pleased that in her excitement she would please him. He quickly seized the opportunity to strip her naked and turn his attention from the make believe FBI agents to his real Royal Flush.

"Someone's coming in." Renée wiped her mouth with the napkin.

"Oh, I'll get it," Royal said, jumping up from her seat. "Really. You guys finish eating."

A tall man, nearly the size of her Dmitry stood with his back turned to her looking at a rack of Chanel dresses as she approached him. Her footsteps tapped on the hardwood floors and echoed throughout the empty shop as she made her entrance, but the stranger did not turn around. Royal eyed his frame curiously, wandering if he was one of the NBA locals picking up a something special for a girlfriend or wife, which had become quite typical since she opened.

"Can I help you?" Royal finally asked, her voice pleasant and soft.

"Yes, I'm looking for Dmitry Medlov," the man said, turning around to face her. His voice was deep, baritone and strangely familiar.

"He's not here. May I help you with…something?" Royal's eye twitched.

"Ah. You must be Royal," he said, fixing his eyes on her.

Royal stood stunned for a minute with a waded up napkin in her hand unable to say anything. She was struck by his features and his accent. All Russian. All familiar. He wore the same type Armani black tailor-made suit Dmitry wore. His face was perfectly chiseled; every line faultless, free of blemish and full of beauty like Michelangelo himself had carved it from marble stone. He was nearly as tall and definitely as muscular as Dmitry.

However the contrast in the men was undeniable in their hair, their complexion and their polarized demeanors. Where Dmitry had heavenly golden locks, this man had inky black waves that were cut low and highlighted by his naturally arched black menacing eyebrows and high cheeks bones. His skin was milky white and completely free of a tan. He had a faint, stubby beard that etched his breathtaking features, giving him a rogue quality. But his eyes were what truly captured her. They were even more intense than Dmitry's. Liquid blue, bold and bright like a clear sky on a Sunday morning. He looked at her now with a threatening stare.

"How do you know my name?" she asked, stepping away. As beautiful as he was, there was something about him that scared her speechless.

"The magazine article," he said, raising the *Memphis Magazine* in his large right hand. He walked towards her slowly, his long strides closing the distance between them.

"Right. What can I do for you?" she asked, walking quickly behind the counter to ensure her space.

He chuckled. "If I told you, would you do it?" He licked his lips.

Royal scoffed and narrowed her eyes at him. "No, I don't think that I would, *sir*."

"Pity," he said, smiling. "I'd heard about you, but I had no idea just how beautiful..."

"Heard about me?" Royal interrupted.

Even in the stranger's smile, there was something evil in his eyes. He propped his large hands on the marble-top of the counter showing Cyrillic writing tattooed on each of his fingers and his sprawling frame stretched out like wings as it shadowed her entire body. He looked her up and down before he spoke again, enjoying how she fidgeted in discomfort at the sight of him.

"Yes, heard about you," he replied, biting his bottom lip. "I'm afraid that they didn't do you justice. Probably too fucking jealous." He laughed.

"I'm afraid I still don't know why you're here or who *they* are," Royal scowled.

"Well, I just recently got to this hell hole. Dmitry knows why I'm here. In his own way, because of his nasty little temper, I guess that he sent for me."

Royal raised her brow at him.

"Anyway, Royal, I just want you to tell him that I stopped by to see his new property. Trust me, he'll appreciate the irony." He smiled again and looked at her breasts. The lustful thoughts were evident in his furrowed, black brows. He looked back up into her eyes again and took a deep breath as he crooked his head a little. "I can see now why he broke his pitiful little monk code. You are absolutely devastating."

Royal sneered at his advance. "His *what* code?"

"Nothing." He looked around curiously.

Royal followed his glance then eyed him. "Well, if he knows why you're here, then he'll know how to find you." She wanted him out of the shop right then.

"Well, one thing is for sure. At least I know that he'll never be too far here. So, I now know where to find him." He winked at her. "Take for instance now. I bet he's only a few blocks away. I know Dmitry. He likes to keep his possessions very, very close to him. He's a greedy fuck that way. Hoarding everything."

"Do I look like a possession to you?" she snapped.

"Yes, you do actually. The big question is how much does a woman like you cost?"

"Is that a racist comment? You actually had the balls to walk into a shop and speak to a black woman about how much she costs?"

The man smiled, revealing deep dimples. "That was not racist comment. I was giving you compliment. Would you like to hear a racist comment? I have many."

"Only if at the end, you go screw yourself." Royal snapped.

"Oh, I'd rather fuck you." A smile crossed his lips. "And I'm sure that I could do a better job than that anal nut job of a boyfriend you've got."

She looked into his eyes and saw a stir of something dangerous. That had hit a nerve. He was a typical chauvinist, unable to deal with the directness of a confident woman.

He watched her like a vampire as her blood pressure boiled. The veins in her neck protruded out. The pulsating rhythm of her body could be seen through deep breaths that she took making her breasts rise and fall under the golden silk.

Royal reached below the counter and hit the panic button. Just in case he was a psychotic as he seemed, she would need help. Her heart beat so loud and fast; she could hear it in her ears and feel it pushing out the confines of her chest. Calmly, she looked back up at him and rolled her eyes.

Exceedingly grateful when Renée and Cory came out from the back, she literally belted out a sigh of relief. The man looked over at her and smirked. Her fear was like some loud perfume sprayed all around him. Hard to ignore or escape. He took a deep breath, trying to inhale it all.

To Royal, his eyes looked liked they belonged to a wolf. That's what he reminded her of, a predator. He looked at her like he wanted to eat her alive. He turned his stare from Royal to Cory, who nearly halted in his tracks when they made eye contact. Renée quickly inched up beside Royal and stood behind the counter.

"Who is this?" Renée asked, equally intimidated.

"This is... I didn't get your name," Royal said, stepping back from the counter.

"Ivan Medlov. I'm Kirill's replacement," he said menacingly as he looked over and sized up Cory. "Who's the fag?" he asked.

Royal looked at Ivan in shock. A Medlov? Really? The similarity was evident, but Dmitry had never mentioned him. Why? She divulged something as precious as her sister's memory to him, the murder of a perfectly dreadful man by her own hand, and he failed to admit to having a living, breathing blood relative outside of Anatoly? She found his secret cruel. Regardless of how absolutely revolting Ivan was she still felt betrayed by his careless omission.

Ivan turned around and caught her curious frown. It wasn't the same angry scowl from a minute ago. He instantly put the pieces of her puzzle together and smiled.

"You didn't know about me, did you?" he asked enjoying watching her realize his connection.

Royal did not respond.

"You know, if you'd like to know more...about the Medlov men, I can take you out for drink. Get us room and show you ..."

"I'm not interested," she interrupted.

"You sure?" he raised his brow.

Cory walked over to the counter and stood with Royal. Grabbing her hand, he smiled. "If we can't help you with anything else, then we're going to have to ask you to leave."

"Aren't you cute," Ivan said sarcastically to Cory. "Where's your little leash?"

Cory's eye twitched a little, but he didn't move. "And if you need to get in touch with Mr. Medlov, you can leave your number here, and we can pass it on to him."

"A number?" Ivan asked.

"Yes," Cory answered irritated.

"Oh. Okay," Ivan smirked, digging into his pocket. "I've got a...business card with me somewhere."

Reaching into his pocket, he pulled out a silver-plated Glock and laid it on the counter while he dug in his pockets.

"I know it's here somewhere?" he continued, sticking his hands into his back pockets, where he pulled out a knife and laid it on the counter. "Just give me one minute." Reaching into the holsters under his arm he pulled out two more guns and laid them on the counter as well.

Royal stepped back as she looked at her counter, cluttered with guns. Her heart skipped a beat. Suddenly his bite appeared worse than his bark.

"There is no need to threaten anyone," Cory said, unmoved. "I have a pen right here. I can just write your number down. And you can put your guns away." Cory's voice was even and still, so much so that it calmed the women visibly shaken beside him.

"No, no. I have one." Ivan pulled out a shiny silver pen and smiled at Royal. "Told you." He took the paper and wrote down his number, then slowly put the guns away.

The clock seemed to slow, drawing out every second. It felt like a millennium before Anatoly walked into the store from the backroom, but it had only taken him five minutes.

Five minutes to get from the *Mother Russia* to the *Dmitry's Closet*, and he hadn't come alone. Three men were with him, all wearing gun holsters with shiny, black guns tucked inside of them.

"Royal, come over here," Anatoly ordered, motioning behind the men.

Royal looked over at her friends, realizing that she could not leave them alone, she hesitated.

"Go on," Cory said, nudging her arm.

Royal grabbed Renée's hand and pulled her from behind the counter, where Ivan stood with a sheepish grin watching them scurry to the back of the store behind the Russian strangers that Anatoly had brought with him.

Ivan looked back over at Cory and raised his eyebrow.

"Looks like Royal brought some friends," Ivan said texting someone.

"Evidently," Cory replied nonchalantly.

Ivan put his phone on his hip and yawned. "You know, for fag…you don't squirm much."

"I'm a homosexual, not a punk." Cory answered.

Ivan smiled. "And you're eloquent."

The front door opened quickly and six very large brooding men flooded in to the store, all standing behind Ivan, obviously under his command and ready to demolish the entire place if ordered.

Anatoly did not flinch. He surveyed the room quietly as his men spread out.

"Royal, I had no idea that you had such a large entourage," Ivan said loudly as he moved from the counter to the center of the floor directly across from Anatoly.

"Don't talk to her. Talk to me," Anatoly ordered. "Who are you here for?"

Ivan sighed. "How many times do I have to say it? I'm here for my brother, Dmitry Medlov."

"Well, you're in wrong place," Anatoly was unmoved. His voice only hardened.

"What's the right place?" Ivan asked mockingly.

"You already have information. Don't play me for some kind of fool," Anatoly snapped. "Mr. Medlov will not be happy that you've come here. Not happy at all."

"I'm counting on it." Ivan smirked.

Just then, Dmitry walked in the front door of the shop with the newspaper in his hand, whistling a tune to himself. Mirroring his brother's style in a pair of gray slacks and black t-shirt and flip flops, he looked up stunned. The door chimes rattled as the door closed behind him. Everyone looked over at Dmitry, who looked back with a deadly grimace.

He took off his shades and looked around, eyeing each of the men. The entire room calmed when they saw him, almost stiffening in fear. Their demeanor quickly changed from aggressive to docile.

"What the hell is going on in my store?" he asked, searching for Royal.

"You have…visitors," Anatoly informed his boss. He didn't budge or take his eyes off of the men.

"Obviously," Dmitry said, finally eyeing Royal in the back with Renee looking on confused. He reached out and waved for her.

Royal huffed. Now she was supposed to go back across the room to him? She looked over at Renée and let go of her hand. She knew Dmitry. He was not worried about protecting anyone but her.

Slowly, she inched through the nearly crowded room alone, past the beautiful devil named Ivan and clouds of armed men to get to get to Dmitry, the tallest and most fearful of the entire crowd. Her heels clicked on the ground as she did so. All eyes followed her short silk dress and her long legs until she arrived at Dmitry, who was now visibly fuming.

"Are you alright?" he asked, ignoring everyone else in the room. He took her face in his hands.

"No," Royal said, feeling the tears weld up in her eyes. "They all have guns."

"I know," he said softly.

"In a fucking dress shop," she continued in a strained whisper.

Dmitry looked up from her and stared over at his brother.

"Ivan," he growled, pulling Royal behind him.

"Dmitry," Ivan said, giving a devilish grin. "I see that not much has changed. You still know how to stop a show." He turned to face his brother, but did not move towards him. Even he knew his boundaries.

"I see that you still don't know how to make an entrance," Dmitry said, nodding his head at Anatoly.

He looked at the men all crowded in the store. He did not recognize any of the men with Ivan. They were not the ten men from the file he had received from New York. These were Ivan's personal bodyguards. The thought only angered him more.

"Do I need to say anything?" he asked softly, looking at the men disapprovingly. "Because if I do, it will be *kill, mangle, burn, hang and destroy.*"

There was an uncomfortable silence in the room. Ivan's men appeared suddenly vulnerable to Dmitry and his overbearing demeanor that trumped even his brother's pompous temperament.

"Follow me," Anatoly instructed, turning around and walking out of the back of the store.

All of the men, including Ivan disbursed quickly through the back door following Anatoly. They filed out of the building quietly, but they left Royal shaking in her flip flops. Tears were forming at the corner of her eyes, but she tried to keep them behind her long lashes.

When the last man had gone, she looked up at Dmitry and buried her head in his chest.

"Shh," Dmitry said, kissing the crown of her head. "Now, now shop girl, it's okay."

"That man says that he's your BROTHER, but he came in here strapped like he was ready to kill someone and asking for ME!"

"He's just putting on show."

"Yeah, a horror flick," Renée snapped.

Dmitry rolled his eyes.

"Anatoly had on guns like this is the Wild West. So did the others, I'm sure of it. What in the hell is going on in here? Did I miss something?" She shook her head in disbelief. Tears ran down the sides of her cheeks.

Dmitry tried to calm her. "Nothing is going on," he said, smiling at her innocence. "Russians carry guns, especially Russians with money. And my brother has never known how not to be confrontational. Plus, you must have hit the panic button, *dah*? What did you expect Anatoly to come over here with – a bat? We protect our own."

"From what? Protect yourselves from what, Dmitry?" Royal asked.

Dmitry was quiet. He could see that pacifying her would only make the situation worse. "Can we go in back, please? We need to talk."

Royal wiped her eyes and stormed into the back room.

"They aren't coming back, are they? Renée asked in a cracked voice.

"No. There's no need to be scared," Dmitry said, looking over at Cory, who had a strange unreadable look on his face. "No one is going to let anything happen to you."

He set down his newspaper and checked his buzzing Blackberry on his hip. Then slowly, he made his way to the back office where Royal waited.

"Dmitry, um...who is Kirill?" Royal asked Dmitry as he closed the door. Her hand was propped up on her hip.

"What?" Dmitry looked up with a stone stare on his face. The ice in his eyes seemed to chill her bones. Royal stepped back. She could easily see the resemblance of him and Ivan now.

"Ivan said that he was here to replace Kirill." Royal's voice lowered. "Who is he and why did he have to be replaced by someone like that?"

Dmitry's eyes relaxed and he sighed, tired of the confrontation. "Kirill died last month. If you recall, I went to his funeral. Ivan will be taking over some parts of my company's operations," he said, putting his phone back on his hip in its holster.

"How did he kill himself?" Royal asked, swallowing hard. She knew that she was treading in very unfamiliar territory by asking him questions about his business, but something would not allow her to restrain herself.

Dmitry looked at her. She was shaking, afraid. He knew that there was no need to intimidate her anymore than his brother had already done. Carefully, he tried to explain, making sure to control his growing frustration. "He shot himself in basement," Dmitry said, grabbing for her hand. He pulled her to him gently.

"He also said something about you living by a monk code. What does that mean?"

"It's nothing for you to worry about."

"Then why won't you tell me. Why does it always have to be bits and pieces with you? Answer me!"

"That little shit comes in here and starts babbling like teenager, and suddenly I'm supposed to be the one who has to explain?" Dmitry snapped.

Royal rolled her eyes. "You won't tell me, will you?"

"There is nothing to tell. He's an idiot."

"The point is that you never told me you had a brother."

"I disowned him years ago. There is nothing to tell."

"But if you disowned him, why is he taking Kirill's place?" she snapped, stumping her foot as she did so.

Her quick response made Dmitry pause. She was quicker than he'd given her credit for being.

"I needed someone I could trust to do what Kirill did for me, but I couldn't find anyone...that I could trust. So, I ended up at least with someone who was mildly competent and overwhelmingly predictable. That's the best answer that I can give you."

Royal changed gears. "What did Kirill do for you?"

"He traded in very expensive machinery."

"What kind?" Her eyes narrowed.

"All kinds."

"Uh huh. You know what I find odd?" she asked angrily.

"Whatever you are thinking, stop it. Everything is fine."

"Of course, it's *fine*. There was nearly a gun fight in my store, but everything is just *fine*." She rolled her eyes.

"I'll take care of it," he assured her. His voice was softer now.

"Take care of what? Everything is supposed to be *fine*. Remember?"

"It is."

"You keep saying that, but it's not true. I know it in my gut. You said that you would never lie to me...*just couldn't tell me everything*. But you're lying to me!" Tears ran down her face.

"Royal," Dmitry looked down at the ground. He couldn't find the right words to soothe her.

Royal looked up at him. She clenched her jaw and wiped the tears from her face. "You can't marry me. You can't tell me anything that's worth knowing. You only move with bodyguards. And everything is *fine*? Really? Tell me that I can trust you, Dmitry. Look me in my face, *in my eye* and tell me that I haven't made some big mistake in loving you - a man who is supposed to love me so much but can't even give me a straight answer even when my life is in danger."

Her words cut through him like metal to bone.

"Your life was never in danger. You are overreacting."

"Bullshit."

He raised his brow.

"If you really loved me..." she continued.

Dmitry interrupted. "So now you're questioning my love for you?"

Royal didn't answer him, but she did raise her brow, mimicking him.

"I can understand that you're upset," he explained.

"Can you? You seemed almost pissed that I would even question you about it. I'm just supposed to follow you blindly. Is that it? Well, I won't. I want a fucking answer."

He sighed. "Royal, I've always taken care of you. That hasn't changed, because my brother came in here and acted an ass today. Yes, you can trust me. No, I cannot marry you, and as painful as that sounds it has nothing at all to do with what is going on here at this very moment."

"Another lie," Royal said, under her breath.

"Look, certain parts of my life are not *your* business, like it or not. I didn't hire you to be detective. I hired shop girl. You let me know when that becomes problem for you. And we'll find something else for you to do."

The tears ran freely down Royal's face as his ice cold words destroyed her. She crossed her arms and looked away.

"Oh, I'll let you know."

Dmitry retracted. He could tell that they were headed towards an argument. "If you only knew how much I had to overcome to be with you – you would not…" he stopped himself. He saw that he had wounded her far too deeply. "No, you have not made a mistake in loving me, just in doubting me, which infuriates me so much that I must excuse myself now."

Fuming, Dmitry turned and walked back out of the office leaving Royal there in silence and tears. She did not chase after him. He did not expect her to do so. She was as stubborn as he was, unable to bend to his will.

Cory and Renee watched as the back door flung open, and Dmitry glided to the front entrance, visibly brooding over the concealed argument that had just taken place. He looked as if he could kill someone. Then suddenly he stopped and turned towards them stone faced.

"Close the shop for rest of day," he ordered, looking at Cory.

"Will do," Cory replied.

Then quietly, Dmitry left. The doorbell jingled as the last of the Russians emptied out of Royal's now somewhat disheveled dress shop.

There was a sigh of relief.

Unable to hold back their curiosity or concern, both Cory and Renee ran to the back to check on Royal.

Chapter 10

Dmitry had ordered Anatoly to take Ivan and his men to the basement of the restaurant. They waited there now unarmed for the boss while more of Dmitry's own men flooded into the basement with them.

Anatoly watched them carefully, never speaking a word, only occasionally looking at his Patek watch. He knew what was keeping his father. Royal. The question was had he managed in all of this to keep her. He would know as soon as he arrived, based upon the body count.

There had been many horrifying stories of the great Dmitry Medlov, as cruel as he was beautiful, as cold as he was cunning. The men had whispered about him the entire trip down to Memphis. There were many stories about the infamous crime boss all over the states, the UK and Moscow. But one could easily mistake his kindness for weakness because of his charisma and his ever graceful demeanor.

Then there was his brother, Ivan Medlov. The story in New York and in Moscow was that Dmitry had raised Ivan, but since he was a boy, he had been a hot head. The brothers had fought back and forth over the years about many things.

One night, after a deal went bad because of Ivan's antics, to make a point, Dmitry cut his brother's throat just enough to leave him in the hospital, but promised to finish the job if he ever crossed him again.

Dmitry left New York while Ivan was yet in the hospital and moved to Memphis in search of another new start. The only way that Ivan gained control over the Bronx was because Dmitry left it for him. However, since Dmitry had been away from New York, Ivan had gained the favoritism of the decision makers there and had proven himself to be nearly as formidable.

The door finally opened, and Dmitry stormed in and slammed it behind him. His men looked over at their general, watched the perspiration on his forehead, heard his hurried breath, and watched his twitching eye. He had walked from the boutique. *A sure sign of danger.* It was subtle anger that they knew to worry about, subtle anger like this. A man like Dmitry never was irate. His coldness was only reflected in the manner in which he destroyed.

Dmitry instantly made eye contact with Ivan, who was even quiet now. He walked over to Anatoly and said something under his breath, then walked over to the head of the table where he sat down. He leaned his long body forward under the large light and grinded his teeth together.

"Before I even get to how badly you have already fucked up Ivan, I want to skip to finding out who the hell these men are," he said, placing his elbows on the table and crossing his fingers.

"These are my men," Ivan said, still somewhat smug. He turned around and gave the men a big smile, then turned to his brother again. "Consider them value added."

"As in extra value to me, brother?" Dmitry smiled.

"*Dah.*" Ivan smiled.

Dmitry smirked. "Many of you in this room don't know but my brother is psychopath." He over enunciated the words as he wiped the sweat from his brow. "When he was young man, I had him evaluated by woman I was seeing who was doctor. She told me that men like him have no feelings or remorse. They are very callous creatures."

"That bitch was just upset because I did not find her attractive," Ivan said conversely.

Dmitry sighed. "However, one thing that he does understand is loss of assets. He learned value of dollar much earlier in life than he learned appreciation for human life. So, he would covet an object so much until, he would start to love it, but he could never love person. This was true even in grade school for him."

"Ah…there was one I loved, brother," Ivan corrected softly.

"*Dah*, another psychopath." Their eyes locked. Dmitry smiled and then continued as the men listened on carefully unsure of why the boss was revealing such deep intimate secrets about his only next of kin to them – peons.

"Anyway, I said all that to say that you follow him blindly, and all the way to Memphis not knowing that he does not give damn about you. He never will. He only covets something that it will require you to take from someone else. He will not pay you what you are worth to keep you.

"He does not care if one or all of you are injured just so long as someone can replace you. You are not Vor, so he has no oath to you. This is why he calls you value added. You all have come as a bonus, nearly free of charge to him. And none of you, regardless of whose womb you slid out of, matter here."

Ivan's men looked at Ivan and each other curiously, but did not change their protective stance behind him. Dmitry shook his head and Ivan smirked, not denying any part of what his brother had just divulged.

"Plus, he put you in a very precarious situation. Because you are not Vor, I don't know you. You could be spies, cops…Brighton Beach." Dmitry shrugged his shoulders. "And you come down here and create problem for me with someone that can't be fixed very easily."

Deviously, he looked at Anatoly and hunched his large shoulders. "It is unnerving. My anger is nearly beyond control and someone has to pay." His voice was calm.

"One thing I forgot to tell the men was how you love to give long lectures," Ivan said sarcastically. "Next time, I'll tell them to bring notebooks."

Dmitry stood back up with his hands behind his back and walked midway of the long table and leaned against it. He ignored Ivan's smug comment, understanding that it was his way of dealing with discomfort.

"No smart men would come into their boss' *boss'* place with guns and present a problem unless they were only loyal to the latter. And I can't have that. Can I? My men are only loyal to me. And you have proven that you are only loyal to him. *And* you have proven that you can piss me off quicker than you can tell me your names, which by the way, I don't even know. And don't want to know."

The men started to fidget, realizing the grave error that Ivan had caused them to make. Dmitry's men spread further across the room in attack position. Ivan's men started to step back into the room, while he only rolled his eyes.

"I guess what I'm saying gentlemen," Dmitry pulled his arm from around his back and pointed the gun with the silencer at Ivan, "...is that I don't need value added."

He pulled the trigger slightly away from his brother's face and shot each of the three men in the head quicker than they could start to flee. Their bodies fell quietly as the blood splattered across the walls.

Ivan did not blink. He swallowed hard and a sighed and he looked behind him again. He shook his head in utter disgust. The smug smile was gone.

"I just paid them thousands of dollars. You could have at least given me until next month – until they worked it off," Ivan said hastily. He turned around from the dead bodies pissed. "You have cost me large sum of money, brother." His anger was sincere. His tone much different now. It seemed his loss pained him. "I don't have their account numbers. It will take me weeks to track the money down, if it's not already spent."

Dmitry looked at the bodies and his little brother and sighed. He turned around and looked at his men all staring in bewilderment at the strange turn of events.

"Like I told you…a fucking psychopath," Dmitry said, passing the gun to Anatoly. "You all get rid of the bodies," he said to the men. "Anatoly…Ivan…you both come with me."

Chapter 11

Renee and Cory decided to stay after the store was closed and retired upstairs to Royal's apartment, a place that they had never been invited before, but desperately wanted to see. Royal was happy to have them; having been shaken up so badly, she didn't want to be alone. They followed her upstairs, nudging each other as they got closer. When they reached the large, heavily decorated double doors, they knew that the inside had to be spectacular, because even the entrance was grand in scale.

Taking her shoes off at the front door, Royal invited the two in for a glass of wine.

"Wow, girl! This is so beautiful," Renée said, looking around the elaborately decorated loft that had been recently filled with more gifts from Dmitry's various business trips.

Renee marveled at the large crystal chandelier high above them in the vaulted ceilings reinforced by exposed, lacquered timber and brick in grid patterns. Below the hanging chandelier was a beautiful leather and chenille sectional with a matching oversized leather ottoman in front of a beautiful limestone fireplace. Exquisite bouquets of fresh flowers filled the room along with paintings of beautiful country sides. It looked like a scene from an upscale interior decorator magazine.

"This is so European villa," Cory said, rubbing his hand over the marble-topped tables. "I'm talking really expensive."

"Well, Dmitry has great taste," Royal admitted, admiring the place herself. She was humbled every time that she entered into the apartment, bemused by the fact that it was her home.

"You can make yourself at home in here," Royal said, escorting them.

After taking off their own shoes, they followed Royal to the dinning room hidden behind two stain-glassed doors. The room was painted in a warm khaki color, illuminated by an equally beautiful black tiered iron chandelier that hung from a lower ceiling covered in timber and highlighted with only dim receding lights. The room had no windows, which gave it a cozy intimacy, and it was sprinkled with color in the large area rug, accent chairs and large painting of St. Basil's Cathedral in the Red Square.

Royal pulled out her finest crystal flutes and a bottle of Chateau Petrus that Dmitry had bought her last week when he had come home from a meeting in California. He actually had brought her a case, which is why she hadn't minded sharing one bottle with her friends considering that had all been through a bonding experience downstairs.

She sat down at the round table and plopped comfortably in her plush chair. Pouring hefty glasses, she pushed the flutes around the table to Cory and Renee. This was the first time that anyone besides Dmitry had ever been in her apartment. The company was welcome by Royal, even it if was under the duress of such a hectic and unusual day.

Under the dimming lights of the dinner table and among the 60-rose bouquet in the center of the table that gave off a beautiful aroma, they toasted and drank merrily, recapping every minute of their first encounter with Ivan, the valiant efforts of Anatoly & Cory, and discussing the king of them all, Dmitry.

"Okay, so Cory and I have been talking, and we've come to the conclusion that Dmitry is mafia," Renée said, looking for Cory to chime in. She sipped her wine and nodded her head.

Royal stopped smiling. Her face changed into a grimace.

"You watch too many movies." Royal denied.

"And you are too naive. Did you see what happened downstairs? I nearly pissed my own pants," Renée said, savoring the taste of the thousand dollar bottle of wine.

"I was scared too, but you don't have to get so Hollywood. This is Memphis, for God's sake. Home of Elvis sightings and pig-eating contests. What would the mafia or anyone else for that matter want with Memphis?"

Renee raised her brow. "Well you do have a point…"

"Exactly." Royal got up and went to the kitchen to retrieve a platter of cheese and a handful of grapes. Leaning against the countertop, she held her stomach. She stood there quietly for a moment, praying softly, silently moving her lips with her eyes clothes. Then she took a deep breath, exhaled her troubles and grabbed the tray. She came back and set the food on the table and smiled. "Anybody want some caviar? I've got extra."

"Okay. Well, who has extra caviar sitting around, and bottles of expensive wine in this economy. I don't even have extra containers of milk at home, and that runs me about three dollars each not one thousand," Cory argued.

Royal snapped quickly. "So every one who has any money is now suddenly a criminal, especially a Russian man, right?" she asked defensively. She took a deep breath. "Dmitry has worked hard his entire life. He's made some very wise business decisions, and he's paid his dues. That's why he's wealthy." Her hands shook in frustration and pain.

Cory raised his brow. "Royal, I've never seen Dmitry actually work once since I've been here. He gives orders, but I don't even think he drives his own car."

"What does that have to do with anything?"   Royal snapped.

"Well, I'm sure he worked at some point," Renee added.

"I mean, the abundance of caviar though, Royal?" Cory continued. "He seems to have an abundance of everything. Cars. Businesses. Money."

She ran her fingers through her hair. "He owns a caviar company in Russia. It's like owning a fishing business here in the states…nothing to get all hyped about. And he made his millions over a decade ago. We were all still teenagers then." She looked around for understanding but there was no compassion around the table, at least not for Dmitry.

"Uh huh," Cory said, pouring another glass of wine. "He also has a lot of bodyguards and guns for a restaurateur. It's kind of odd, don't you think?"

"No, I don't," Royal lied as she stood up, unaware of how upset she was becoming. "He's Russian," she ranted. "They protect their own." She could hear his voice as she said it. She sounded like him. She was defending him, even though he had cut her down moments ago downstairs.

Realizing she had stood up, she sat down in her chair and looked down at her hands covered in expensive diamonds and pearls. Suddenly, she wanted to pull off the jewelry and hide it. She was ashamed of it, of him, only she didn't know why. There was nothing left to say. She didn't know anything else.

"The truth of the matter is that I love him. And I know that he would never lie to me. It's not in him," Royal's voice was soft and timid.

"Maybe he's not lying to you, he's just avoiding telling you something that he knows that you know that you already know." Cory reasoned with her.

Royal sighed. "You both are making my head hurt. He pays you above the normal pay grade. He gives you excellent benefits. All he wants is a little loyalty. You're both ready to throw him to the dogs."

Cory looked at Renée and set down his glass. They had obviously gone too far and needed to fix things as best they could before she fired them both and kicked them out.

"Look, we are in no position to talk bad about our boss. He's been great to us, but honey, you have to wonder," he said, sighing. "Well....don't you? You're too smart not to wonder or maybe you're just too scared. Believe me, no one would not understand that. We just love you. We've grown to see how beautiful you are, and we don't want you to get hurt, is all."

"I'm not afraid of Dmitry. I trust him," Royal said, looking at Cory. "So, I don't have to wonder." But the statements that both Cory and Renée made weren't new thoughts for Royal. She wondered about Dmitry and his businesses now more than ever. Only she was far too in love with him to stop now, to leave him or push him away.

∞♥∞

Back upstairs in the elegant ambience of *Mother Russia*, Ivan sat across from Dmitry in a closed private room in the back of the restaurant. Anatoly stood in the far corner, quietly watching and listening as his father and uncle sat at a large table under the light of a Tiffany glass hanging lamps talking quietly.

"Is he your pet?" Ivan asked, referring to Anatoly. He looked over at the young man and blew him a condescending kiss.

"More like protégé," Dmitry said, relaxed in the red leather booth. He looked over at Anatoly and nodded.

"Huh…well, he looks like fag." Ivan turned around in his seat and popped his knuckles. "I don't like to be stared it. It makes me conscious of my overbite," he said, sarcastically. He took a shot of vodka and slammed the shot glass on the table.

"Don't worry about him." Dmitry waved at the waitress, who entered the room quickly and brought their lunch. "Tell me why New York sent you of all people? I thought you had good thing going in Bronx since I left a ton of shit for you. Now, you come here? What for? What are you up to?"

"Kirill was a friend," Ivan said, tasting his brother's legendary borscht. "This is excellent. You were always a great cook. You could do amazing things with the trash we had to eat as kids."

"It's your mother's recipe. Probably the only thing that she ever gave us worth anything." Dmitry watched his young brother eat the food quickly and sloppily. With all the wealth that he and Ivan had acquired over the years, he still had never learned any manners. It was true what they said, all the money in the world couldn't buy a lick of class.

After he had scoffed down the food, Ivan put down his fork, wiped his mouth with the napkin and used the knife to check his teeth. Lighting a cigarette, he waved his sulfuric match out and took a long, needed drag, slowly blowing smoke out of his mouth.

Dmitry watched irritated. Ivan had always been so theatric. Waiting for an answer to his question, he sat up and clasped his hands together. His nostrils flared.

"Dare I even ask about the beautiful black girl at the shop? Are they calling themselves black or African-American these days?" Ivan asked, cocking up one of his long dark eyebrows. A devilish grin crossed his lips.

Anatoly twitched a little in the corner wondering if his father would demand that he shoot Ivan right then. He would enjoy every second of it. Family or not, Anatoly's only thought was to draw first blood.

Dmitry looked at Ivan with a stone stare. "My patience is starting to run very thin with you, brother." He sighed but continued to control his tone.

"Well, we all know what happens when you become impatient," Ivan taunted, tapping his knuckles on the wooden table. "Bodies hit the floor." He sucked his teeth again and smiled.

"Do you think you are immune?" Dmitry asked. "Answer my questions now, before I get…frustrated. Why did they send you?" His square jaw clinched.

"I requested to come here, and I gave up my territory in the Bronx. That rat race was getting old anyway. I wanted to start over here with family," he smirked. "Plus, Kirill was a friend." He made sure to reiterate his point.

Dmitry shrugged his shoulders. "He was coward, and he deserved to die. I should have killed him myself to make point."

"What is your point, brother?"

"You will know if and when I ever have to make it to you, and don't think because you are my blood that I would hesitate for even a minute."

"Oh, I know damned well that you wouldn't. You've proven that. Just answer me why you thought that you had to kill the only family that we've ever really had?"

"And don't ever question my authority. It has its consequences. Not much has changed since we last saw each other, brother. I do not answer to those below me, and I don't play well with others."

"Oh, I remember. I still have this to show for it." He pulled his shirt collar down to show his brother the long knife mark that Dmitry had left many years before only inches from his carotid artery. "Besides, I'm not here for fight. New York said I could leave, start over and take over for Kirill with your blessing, of course. That is all that I'm here for. So many years have passed; I thought that this would be a new start for us."

"A start to do what?"

"Business. What else?"

Dmitry ran his finger down the table, checking for dust. He looked back over at Ivan, wide-eyed and trying desperately to be clever. If he had trusted him, even an inkling, he would have informed him that he did have more family in the form of the young man holding tightly to the nickel-plated Glock in the corner, but the truth of the matter is that he did not trust him at all. And considering there was still a score to settle, evidently now more than ever between the two, maybe it was best for him to keep his long lost brother close and under a watchful eye.

"For now, I let you take his place, but you play by my rules. Don't get creative down here. It's taken me long time to get things where I want them. And if you came here to avenge Kirill or anyone else for that matter, you might as well get up and leave now, while you're still breathing."

"Given that we are still brothers, I feel as though I can say my piece."

"Then say it."

"He came over from Russia with us. He took care of me while you were in prison. He planned your escape, for God's sake," Ivan said, tapping his cigarette. "And you shoot him like he's nothing, when you could have still been rotting in prison for being a thieving, murdering bastard."

Dmitry smirked. "I made it painless. I could have cut him open with the end of broken bottle in front of his family, shot his young daughter and mother, raped his wife *repeatedly*, burned down his house and took his dog," Dmitry said, tasting the borscht and making his point that Ivan wasn't very angelic himself.

"Hey, I liked that dog," Ivan said, smiling. "I still have it. And I didn't shoot Vladimir's granny. She had heart attack from too much commotion."

"You're the real monster, Ivan. I thank God everyday that we have different fathers."

"What did you expect? Our mother was whore," he laughed. "Okay. Okay. I work your plan …this way I can grow."

"Memphis isn't big enough for the two of us, brother, unless you do work my plan. You stay here; you will always play by my rules. You work for me. I give you his share. You take his pay, his territory and his responsibilities." Dmitry leaned closer to him. His voice lowered. "You work the plan, you have good life, live long time, maybe even have family. Hell, you can have Kirill's wife, if you'd like. She is as discerning as a blind, deaf dog in heat. But if you get out of your lane, get greedy, disrespect me one time, I swear to the sweet, precious Mother Mary that I'll kill you myself… and for good this time." Dmitry's words were laced with paralyzing venom. He seethed with anger and disdain, but it was only evident in his tone, his eyes, and the point of his finger to the table.

"I'm not interested in getting out of lane. I just want new start," he said seriously.

"Alright." He stood up. "Anatoly, show him to his new place. Oh…and one more thing, Ivan. I didn't kill your men just because I didn't trust them. I killed them, because you brought them near Royal. Stay away from her, or you'll be next."

Dmitry walked out of the door and in his gentle manner greeted a customer who passed him.

∞♥∞

Royal and her friends had nearly finished the bottle of wine and had moved on to other discussions about various unimportant issues when they heard the front door open and close. Heavy footsteps on the hardwood floors echoed throughout the loft and silenced them all. Royal's heart skipped a beat. Her tyrant was evidently back. He rounded the corner and leaned on the doorway. Cory and Renée sat up in their chairs, a little uncomfortable. Both wondered should they be there.

"Sorry, I didn't know that you had company," Dmitry said, looking at Cory, who shifted in his seat.

"We were just leaving," Renée explained, standing up. "We just wanted to keep her company for a while."

"Please, don't leave on my account," he said, waving her to sit back down.

"It's getting late anyway." Cory stood and pushed up his chair. "Royal, do you mind if I use your restroom?"

"The guest restroom is just down the corridor to your right," she said, barely acknowledging Dmitry.

Dmitry looked down at her, still angry at him from earlier. He knew that he deserved it. None of this had been her fault, but somehow, he had gotten her involved. Running his fingers over the door frame, he sighed and turned away.

When Royal was certain that Dmitry was out of earshot, she turned back to Renée, who was quickly gathering her things. "Thanks for coming over," she said appreciatively.

"You're welcome, girl." Renée reached over and hugged Royal. "Call me if you need anything."

"I will." Royal sighed.

When Cory came out of the bathroom, Royal thanked her friends and saw them out of her house. After making sure that the door was locked, she went to her bedroom, where Dmitry had retired to the bathroom to take a shower.

Frustrated, she picked his clothes up off the floor, folded them, and placed them carefully on the wooden valet. She hated when he threw his clothes on the floor like he had a maid...*over here*.

Turning around to leave, she looked over at him and noticed how solemn he actually was. Something was wrong. He leaned his large frame against the marble and let the water cascade down his long back. The stream looked like a small river as it poured down the valley of rippling muscles. Feeling a tinge of sympathy for him, she walked over to the glass shower door and tapped her index finger on the glass.

Dmitry turned and looked over at her, then pulled open the large door. She stepped away to avoid getting wet, but he reached out with his long drenched arm and pulled her in with him.

"Are you still mad at me?"

"Are you serious? Of course, I am. It just happened like five minutes ago."

"I thought you might give me break for first offense."

"Are you negotiating down your dog house time?"

"Yes."

"Who negotiates how long your girlfriend can stay mad at you?"

"Who doesn't?"

Royal shook her head. He was impossible.

"What do you want to ask me? You have that look like you're thinking crazy ass thoughts." He waited.

"What is going on with you, Dmitry?" she asked, now soaking wet.

"The ghost of Christmas past," he said, pulling the yellow dress over her head.

"What?" she asked, taking off her ruined heels. "See, that's what I'm talking about. Code. That doesn't answer my question. When you speak in code like that I can't…"

"Shh." He put his finger on her lips. "Я так люблю тебя."

"I love you, too." She had only learned a few sentences in Russian since she had started dating Dmitry, and *I love you* was the first.

Pulling Royal to his body, Dmitry reached around her and loosened the clasps on her black bra. It fell to the ground between them on the granite flooring. He leaned over and kissed her bare, satin-like shoulders and held her close, feeling her soft wet skin against his own.

He began to speak slowly in a tongue that she could not understand. "Ya blagadaryu boga chto vstretil tebya," he whispered in her ear. Royal smiled. His voice sounded more even more like silk in his Russian baritone brogue. "Ya palyubil tebya s pervova vzglyada." He continued.

"What does all that mean?" Royal asked, feeling his large hands run up and down her body.

"I thank God that I met you, and…I fell in love with you from the first sight," he said, feeling her small hands moving down his stomach to the large erection nestled in her diaphragm.

"You'd say anything to get out of trouble," Royal whispered.

"Umm...you know I've taken out as much frustration as I can on my men, the rest will have to be taken out on you," he growled, kissing her neck.

"I'm sure it was a slap on the wrist," she huffed, rolling her eyes. "After all, it was *nothing*. Remember?"

"Are we still discussing this?"

"Yes?"

"You think I was lenient?" He stopped and looked at her. The sound of water drowned the room.

"I'm sure you were." Her hands were still wrapped around him. She wore only a condescending stare.

"There is one thing that is constant with me – killing makes me horny." His face was still charming and soft. "Do I feel horny to you?" He pulled her closer to into his engorged body.

"The only thing that you're killing right now is the mood," she said, pulling him closer. "Really, Dmitry. You don't have to act tough for me." She kissed his lips slowly, taking in the smell of his sandalwood soap on his skin.

"Now, you're really in trouble," he said turned on.

Dmitry looked down at her, pleased at how she had grown accustomed to all of his silent commands and equally pleased at how oblivious she was at who he really was. Running his hands down her breasts to her nipples, he watched the goose bump form all over her body. She obediently leaned her neck back where he could better kiss her.

Completely enraged, he ripped her panties by the lace sides violently and tore them from her skin. The water poured over her curly long hair making it stick to her back and cover her breasts; he moved the jet black mane back from her face as he kissed her all over.

Royal gasped, feeling that familiar sensation of floating as he picked her up. She reached up for his mouth and kissed him passionately, tasting vodka and shower water in her mouth, smelling his cologne around them. She wrapped her long legs around him as he leaned her body against the wet marble. Planting his feet firmly, he invaded her slowly and powerfully. She gripped his back with her long nails as the steam crowded the room. Finally, soft moans came from shower.

∞♥∞

Royal could feel herself drifting away as she lay on top of Dmitry's chest. Exhausted, she listened to John Coltrane play *Traneing In* on her IPod system in the dark of the night with only a candelabrum of white candles to illuminate the room. Dmitry rubbed through her hair and looked up at the ceiling. His eyes were fixed on the fan, but his mind was many miles away.

Regardless of where his thoughts were, she savored the feeling of safety when he was near. It was something about his very presence that made her feel a tranquil solace. By far, it was the safest that she had ever felt in her entire life, and she was very grateful to him for it. She ran her fingers down his chest as she felt him breathe – in and out in a slow, rhythmic tone. The only thing that she did regret was how mysterious he still was to her. She only hoped in time that he would open up more and show her the many sides of him that she was certain existed.

"I want you to move in with me to my home," Dmitry said, finally after much thought.

Royal looked up at him curiously. He had been quiet for nearly half an hour, but that was normal for him.

She had learned early that often he was a man of few words. Reaching down, he grabbed her by her waist and pulled her up to him. She sat up on his chest and sighed.

"Because of Ivan?" she assumed.

"No, because it's time," he said quickly.

"Well, it hasn't been that long, Dmitry."

"Long enough." He cupped her bare behind in his large hands. "Have I not proven myself to you in every way a man can?"

"Yeah," Royal said, assuring him of her confidence in their relationship. "But I don't understand why you want me to move in now."

"Trust me," Dmitry said, kissing her lips. "Plus, I get tired of running from place to place. I am not rolling stone. You should be in my bed every morning when I wake up and in my bed every night that I go to bed."

Royal laid her head back down on his chest. "That does sound nice. Okay. When do you want me to move to *Castle Dmitry*?"

"Tomorrow. I will stay with you here tonight."

Royal jerked up again. "Tomorrow? Dmitry?"

He rubbed her back and smiled. "You know, for a woman in love, you don't trust much."

His words shamed her.

"I do trust you. I'm just not stupid. Everything was fine. We were fine just like we were until today when your *mysterious* brother popped up offering sex and brandishing guns with his boys."

Dmitry cringed. "When did he offer you sex?"

"It doesn't matter," she looked away. "That's not the bigger picture here."

"Baby, listen to me. Ivan is very dangerous person. Don't ever trust him. Don't ever get close to him, and don't ever find yourself alone with him."

Royal could see the urgency in his eyes. She knew to take heed to his warning, even though she didn't understand why.

"Why don't you send him away if he's so dangerous?"

"I've thought about it, but he has to be neutralized. Sending him away doesn't work anymore," he sighed. "I've done that. So, you keep friends close and enemies even closer. This is not cliché statement. It is truth."

Royal laid her head back on his chest and closed her eyes.

"Tomorrow it is, then," she said, pulling the comforter over her body.

Chapter 12

The Fall trunk shows and VIP diamond and fur shows had gone extremely well for Royal. She had been interviewed by all the local television stations and showcased by *The Commercial Appeal*, *The Downtowner*, *Skirt Magazine* and the *Memphis Flyer*. All four were highly visible print media that promised her an even bigger market share by Christmas.

Business was doing better than well. *Dmitry's Closet* had more than quadrupled its profits for the second quarter with clients knocking down the door every morning for a private viewing of the newest collections, special orders from Milan and Moscow and consultations with the new *it* girl of the Memphis fashion scene.

Royal was a hot commodity, even more sought after now due to a very popular local blog that did a high profile story on her at her $3.5 million home that she shared with tycoon and sexy business man, Dmitry Medlov.

Since the story broke and all of Memphis had seen pictures of the two relaxing around town in the hottest night clubs, the finest restaurants, the most elite of circles; Royal had become a notorious figure. One reporter wrote,

"It's not just that she's a talented young business woman with a keen eye for fashion, she's also breathtakingly beautiful. The combination creates the desire to spend money to look like Memphis' newest princess, Royal Stone."

Dmitry celebrated their new found success by buying Royal a new X6 BMW, fully loaded in all black and a beautiful Tiffany swing necklace. She had no idea that the platinum chain cost $40,000.

Royal celebrated by purchasing more ad space in the same magazines that tooted her store and increasing her inventory of all things Russian.

She sat reading the newspaper in awe as it boasted about all the celebrity patrons that she was acquiring. Little did they all know that she was on the verge of starving at the first of summer. She closed the newspaper and blew her nose with roll of tissue on the kitchen table. The weather had started to change, and in celebration of that fact, she had acquired a nasty little cold.

Coughing, she made her way across the cold tile floors on her bare feet to the counter to pour another cup of coffee. She sneezed unexpectedly. Quickly trying to cover it, she turned away from the defenseless coffee pot. Germs. Lots and lots of germs. She rubbed her aching head.

Dmitry walked in the kitchen in his silk pajamas bottoms and bare-chested with an empty cup in hand. His nose was red and his high cheek bones rosy. He walked up behind her and wrapped his arms around her silk silver kimono.

"Good morning, love," he said, kissing her neck. "I think you gave me flu. Hopefully not H1N1." He set his black coffee mug in front of her so that she could refill his caffeinated beverage. He coughed a little as he rested at the mesquite-topped table island covered in newspapers.

"No, I think you gave me the flu," Royal said, pouring him another cup of coffee as well as herself. She walked back over to the table with their cups and sat down.

"So, what are we going to do today?" Dmitry asked, picking up the paper that she had discarded. "These people can't get enough of you. This is like the tenth paper that you've been in this quarter." He pulled the paper to his face and began to read quietly.

Suddenly there was a quiet gasp from Royal. He pulled the newspaper down to see her sitting with her hand over her mouth looking directly at him.

"What...what is it?" he asked concerned.

"Look, it's Woodrow Conners." She grabbed the newspaper.

"Who is *Woodrow Conners?*"

She read quickly, placing her fingers on the paper. "It's the guy that I cut with the scissors when I was in foster care." She looked up at him stunned.

"Oh...that guy. What about him? Did they convict him of trying to rape some other teenager?"

"He was murdered...in the bathroom of a club...cut from ear to ear."

Dmitry sighed. "Sounds like karma caught up with him."

Royal was silent.

"You aren't sad, are you?" He sipped his coffee.

"No. It's just weird." She shook her head in disbelief.

"This is Memphis. Someone is killed here all the time - everyday. This is why I tell you to be very careful at shop, not to get too comfortable."

"I know. I know." She sighed.

"Well, you have done your thirty seconds of mourning. I do not want to give that pedophile a minute more of my day."

"You're right." Royal pushed the paper away from her. She redirected. "It's Thanksgiving. I think that we should have a big American dinner together. I won't work from home, and you won't work from the restaurant."

"I don't work."

"Well whatever you do." She leaned over the island and smiled. "Please." She batted her watery eyes and sniffed, unsure if contagious charm had the same affect.

"You want to have this at the restaurant?" He barely looked up from the front page of the paper. "If so, I can call the girls and make them come in to cook."

"No. I was thinking that you and I could have dinner here. I could invite Renée, and you could invite Anatoly. We could watch the football game and have some soul food and have a few beers. You know, celebrate the red, white and blue way."

"Anatoly lives here. How can I invite him to dinner at his own house?"

"You know what I mean." Royal took a sip of her coffee. The hot burn made her aching throat feel better.

"No, I don't."

"I mean that you could insist that he come. If I invite him, I think that he'll say no."

"Why would he say no?"

"I don't' know? I just get that feeling. I think that he thinks I'm a pest."

"He won't say no. You ask him. This will be good communication between you two." Dmitry sneezed. "Shit." He grabbed the tissue and blew his own nose. He continued. "And you're going to fix this *American* meal?"

"Yep. Renée will help me. I'll run to Wal-Mart and pick up anything that I don't' already have. But I' think that we're good."

"You don't have to do this. It's holiday. You're supposed to be getting some rest. Plus, you are sick."

"I want to," Royal said, quickly. She walked over to him and slid between his long legs. Wrapping her arms around him, she gave him a big hug. "You're always doing stuff for me. I want to do something for you for a change. Don't say no."

He groaned a little. "Okay," he said, rubbing her back. He sneezed again and buried his head in her shoulder. "I feel like truck hit me."

∞♥∞

For Dmitry, life was lived through the details. His home or as he affectionately referred to it, their home was a mansion full of perfect, intricate details. The very first time that Royal had been inside it was weeks after their first sexual encounter. Dmitry had persuaded her to spend the night and enjoy a nice dinner, cooked and served by him. The beauty of it stole Royal's heart, as it was supposed to. It was the most perfect date that she had ever been on with a five course meal, great music, expensive wine and passionate love making.

That evening, Dmitry walked her through each room explaining his motivation for his interior choices and sharing the history or the various cultures behind each piece like she was at a museum on a private tour.

The seven-bedroom, five and half bathroom monster of a house was designer's dream. He had chosen a French and Russian theme for the house, complimenting the many tall arched windows, iron chandeliers, limestone and marble floors, exotic tiles, beautiful woodwork and masterful furniture with equally brilliant hues of paint, iron work and paintings.

The house in its entirety blew Royal's mind. It was a testament to his many travels all over the world, his love for Russian culture and his growing dynasty.

The back yard was landscaped with beautiful shrubbery, a large infinity-edged pool and protected by rows and rows of well-pruned trees.

The four-car garage was occupied by his favorite Mercedes-Benz McLaren, a black 7 series BMW, a white
Mazerati GranTursimo that he hardly ever drove and
Royal's truck. The entire property was surrounded by a
brick and rod iron gate and two very non-vicious Dober-
man pinchers that Royal liked to pet whenever they would
come to her.

His masterpiece would not be complete without a maid,
whom Royal opposed having but Dmitry contended was
necessary. Royal made sure to never leave a mess and
always help with the cleaning still to make a point that she
was not a pre Madonna. In all, his fortress was a dream
that now seemed more complete with his Memphis princess.

∞♥∞

Anatoly was outside feeding the dogs, when Royal got
dressed and headed out to look for him. She found him
bent over in the kennel speaking in Russian to the canines.
She was certain that he knew that she was behind him, so
she waited patiently and quietly until he was finished. He
set down the ten-pound bag of Purina and wiped his hands
on his jeans and turned around to face her.

"What's the matter, Royal?" he asked, grabbing his bottle of water off the ground. "You need me to take you
somewhere?"

"Uh…no. Actually, I came out here to see what you
were doing this afternoon."

Anatoly looked at her curiously. "Why?"

"Well, I'm going to cook a homemade American meal
for Dmitry, and Renée is coming over. And I thought that
it would be nice if we all had dinner together."

Anatoly scratched his stubby beard. "I don't know,
I…"

"Please," Royal said, grabbing his hand. "It would mean a lot to me."

"Are you trying to hook me up with black girl in your shop?" he smiled.

"No," Royal laughed. She was taken back by his ability to have a conversation about something normal. "Why? Do you like her?"

"*Net*...no," Anatoly said, shaking his head. "I just want to make sure that this is not love connection."

"No, this is not a love connection. It's just four people getting together for Thanksgiving dinner." Royal tried to close the deal. "So, can I count on you?" Her voice pitched higher. "What do you say? You might have some fun."

Anatoly looked across the back yard as he made his decision. "I say...okay. How bad can you're cooking be, eh?"

"Great!" Royal jumped a little, happy that he accepted her invitation. "Dinner will be at four, so don't run off."

∞♥∞

The fall leaves swept across Cory's feet as he trotted down Union Avenue in a pair of blue Adidas breakaway pants and a University of Memphis pullover. Having the Thanksgiving holiday off, he celebrated by taking his coveted 4-mile run near his midtown apartment. There were dark, low-level clouds blanketing the skies and promise of a heavy afternoon rain. He only hoped that he could finish his errands before the storm began.

Stopping at Smoothie Queen on corner of Union Avenue, he stretched out his legs and went inside to grab a protein shake. A tall, muscular Italian man in a *Best Daddy In the World* t-shirt and a Miami Dolphins baseball cap sat in the corner of the shop reading a *Flex* magazine. He and Cory made eye contact, and the man gave him a nod.

The shop was empty with only a bald, bulging black man in a white apron behind the counter. Cory quickly ordered and made his way over to the table adjacent from the man.

"You got a tail?" the man asked, turning the page of his magazine.

"Nope," Cory said, looking out the window.

"Alright. We've got 15 minutes. Give me an update."

"Umm, let's see." Cory sighed. "Royal is still living in Dmitry's house. From what I can tell, nothing illegal is going on over at the boutique, but I can't be 100% sure because of the locked door that leads to the basement. From what I can tell, Dmitry won't let anyone do business there. The restaurant is where all the big deals pass through, but they clean it for bugs and check for wire taps daily. Dmitry's still first in charge, and Anatoly is still second, but Dmitry's brother Ivan is closing in. There's some real bad blood between the two of them."

The man looked over at Cory and sighed. Closing his magazine, he leaned over across the table; his large muscular forearm was covered in tattoos and a dark tan.

"Hamilton, you aren't telling me anything that I don't already know. Hell, I could get that Intel from my kids. We sent you in to give us the real insight. You gotta find a way to get deeper inside and get in that damned basement."

"Lou, I'm fucking trying," Cory said frustrated. He scratched his head. "I don't want to jeopardize my cover."

"I'm not asking you to do that," Lt. Agosto said, looking around. "Look, you're right. Ivan is definitely making moves. We've got credible sources that say that he moved in a shipment of girls to Memphis within the last week to start up a whore house here. Now, before this, Dmitry never dabbled in human trafficking. He's a guns and drugs type of guy. But if he's changing his inventory…"

"I don't think so," Cory interrupted. "This sounds more like Ivan trying to carve out a new niche for himself."

"Well, we need to divide and conquer. So, I need them to go at each other's throats. Maybe then, we can get one of them to give us something more. Fucking Kirill got popped, and he was our only lead."

"I was close to a confession in the boutique, but they were talking pretty low. They said it was a suicide that happened in the basement, but they didn't' say where."

"Close is no cigar." Agosto patted Cory on the back. "What about Royal? Does she suspect anything yet?"

"No, she's totally clueless. I keep trying to get her to open her eyes, but she doesn't want to. She's in love with him."

"There's no way that it could be a cover?"

"No."

"Look, you're doing a good job, but what I need you to do now is help me figure out how to get the ball rolling between these two. If the blood is as bad as you say it is, it won't take much. We need that to happen."

"They're Vor. I don't think that they'll turn."

"That's what they said about Kirill." Lt. Agosto's voice turned to a whisper. "Look, there's something else," he sighed. "We've got a leak."

"What?" Cory rubbed his forehead. "No, no. Lou, I've got a family, I can't…"

"We'll find out who the bastard is," Agosto tried to calm him. "Someone told Dmitry about Kirill. I just have to figure out whom."

"It could have been a leak with the feds."

"I'm not taking any chances, which is why I wanted to meet you here."

"I see you brought Patton." Cory lifted his brow at the black man standing behind the counter. "Where is the real cashier?"

Lt. Agosto smiled. "This is Patton's wife's store. He *actually* runs it on the weekends. It's no cover. Can you imagine someone trying to hold up this place? They walk in and this motherfucker's got two Glocks under the counter and a bad case of the rages from coming off one of his steroid cycles."

They all laughed. The man behind the counter gave them the finger as he sipped on a protein shake.

"Screw y'all. This shit is natural," Patton said, flexing his 23 inch arms.

"Okay, we really believe that," Agosto said, sarcastically. He turned his attention back to Cory. "You worry about getting me the information, and I'll worry about the leak. Hopefully, we're approaching the end of this soon." Lt. Agosto gave him a small leather satchel. "See if you can place these in the restaurant or the boutique again. Who knows? We might get lucky. Also there's a jump drive in there with the pictures of the girls from the whore house. Memorize their faces just in case they end up at the boutique for clothes or at the restaurant. Alright."

"Alright," Cory said, taking the satchel. "You know, if you want to set them up against each other, you might start by approaching Dmitry about the whorehouse. I'm sure he doesn't know."

"Okay. I'll take your advice on that."

"How's my family?" Cory's face became solemn. He missed his wife and two kids.

"I went by to see them a few days ago. They're doing great. I told Becca that you'd be home really soon. She can't wait. The boys are being themselves. You know, being kids."

"Lou, these men are heavy hitters. If they ever found out about me, they'd go straight for my family."

"They'd have to get through all of us first, man. It ain't gonna happen. Patton has a house full of girls. I've got a family at home too. Ivy's working on our third child, and I don't know what I'd do without them. Look at me; I went from Armani to Gap, because I can buy everybody's stuff at the same place. Trust me. I know how much they mean to you. But we watch out for our own. I've got a car on the house 24-hours a day and tail on kids and your wife when they leave. We know their every move."

"Thanks." Cory finished his shake and slipped on his hood. "Till next week," he said, headed back out into the sprinkling rain.

∞♥∞

Royal's Thanksgiving masterpiece was nearly ready. Renée helped her pull her ham out of the oven and put the garnishes on the plates. Carefully, she carried her dishes to the dining room, where she had taken extra care to make sure everything was as festive as possible.

The men sat obediently in the entertainment room watching a football game and talking to one another. Dmitry could smell the food wafting through the house. There were interesting soul food smells, unlike the ones from his restaurant all around him. His stomach rumbled loudly, but Royal wouldn't let him eat a thing until dinner.

"She's going all out for you," Anatoly said, not taking his eyes off the game.

"Royal is good girl that way." Dmitry looked back behind his chair to make sure that no one was behind him. Then he turned to his son and leaned over. "She saw the newspaper this morning. Conners was in it."

"Did she know that it was you?"

"No. Why would she?" His voice was nearly a whisper. "She thinks that I'm some kind of saint or something."

"I don't know. Maybe you should tell her. She would probably appreciate it – this proves chivalry is not dead, eh?" Anatoly smirked.

"You don't know anything about women. If I told her, she would go insane."

Anatoly ignored his father's concerns about Royal. "I know a thing or two about women."

"Two things...hardly impressive." Dmitry sat back in his seat.

"Do you think that she knows yet about the other thing?" Anatoly whispered.

"No," Dmitry said, looking behind him again. "Enough talk about her. Let's talk about you. Did you give any thought to what I said to you?"

Anatoly sighed. "I'm not meant for college, Papa. I have no desire for it. I enjoy what I do here."

"You really enjoy it?"

"Yes. Don't you?"

Dmitry shrugged. "I've excelled in it, but if I could do it all over again, I would only have my shops."

"You keep shops. I was born a Vor."

Dmitry raised his brow at his son. "Such over exaggerated enthusiasm would be better used on your girlfriend not on your tired, retirement-bound father."

"What is all this talk? Where are you going?" Anatoly sat up in his seat.

"No where, but everyone has to have plan B, *dah*? I have told you this many times."

Anatoly looked at him suspiciously.

Royal walked to edge of the stairwell and smiled at the men. She was finished cooking her first Thanksgiving dinner for her first ever pseudo-family. She wore a large, proud grin and pink apron. Renée stood behind her, awaiting her announcement.

"Gentlemen, dinner is served," Royal said, clapping her hands.

Dmitry and Anatoly turned around in their chairs. That was evidently their queue to head to the dinning room. Dmitry led by turning off the television and making his way with his box of Kleenex up the short stairway to her. He leaned down and kissed her head.

"Show me what you've been up to for half the afternoon," he said, a little excited.

The walnut dining table covered in crystal sat under yet another beautiful Italian-inspired chandelier. Around an extraordinary bouquet of roses was a full meal of dressing and gravy, ham, mixed greens, green beans, sweet potato pudding, warm biscuits, wine and champagne.

Dmitry stood at the head of the table, lost for words and extremely impressed.

Royal could not control her smiles by this point. She looked over at Renée proudly, glad that her new friend had gotten out of the bed and helped her on this very important occasion.

"Dmitry, do you wanna say grace?" she asked, standing beside him.

"Grace?" Dmitry asked, a little confused. No one had asked him that since he was a boy in school.

"*Dah*, grace?" Royal mimicked.

"I'm Catholic. Are you?" Dmitry realized at that very moment that they had never discussed their religion.

"I'm familiar," Royal said, bowing her head. She made the sign on the cross and closed her eyes.

Dmitry looked over at Anatoly, who smirked and followed Royal's lead. He had never heard his father pray aloud.

Dmitry felt a sudden serge of discomfort. Sure, he did it in the privacy of his home, where no one would see and mistake his religion for weakness, but he had not prayed in front of anyone since he was ten when his mother had been beaten badly by a john, who left her on their doorstep covered in blood. He prayed for her then, aloud, so God would hear him and protect him and Ivan, but not since then. She died on those steps.

"Very well," Dmitry said, clearing his voice. He made the sign of the cross and began to pray. There was something strangely normal and liberating about what Royal had asked him to do. He prayed aloud the words that he had whispered near his bed many nights before. He prayed for his son, for Royal, for himself.

"Amen," they all said, a little shook up by his kind words, his soft tone, and his humble actions. Royal wiped her eyes and reached over to give him a kiss.

"Happy Thanksgiving, baby," she said as she pulled the seat out for him.

Chapter 13

Later that evening, after the food had been eaten, the wine bottles emptied and the company had gone, Royal lay relaxed in her favorite tub. It was a classic creation – cast iron, gloss gold enamel on the outside and beautiful gloss white enamel on the inside with beautiful golden brass claw feet. It sat in the middle of the bathroom surrounded by twenty square feet of black marble flooring, accented by two beautiful, petite water basins and a very large shower in the corner, big enough to fit ten people in that doubled also as a steam room. When Dmitry purchased the house, the tub had come with it, but he was too large of a man to ever use it. So it had sat untouched until she moved it.

Dmitry had set candles around their large bathroom to give the area a little ambience. He left her there soaking while he went downstairs to meet with a few of his men, who had stressed on the phone with him the importance of an emergency meeting. As usual, he had apologized for the interruption and promised not to be too long. However, Royal was certain that he might be gone the rest of the night.

She finally got out and wrapped herself in the large terry cloth bathrobe. As she opened the door the bathroom, a peculiar feeling over took Royal. The room became blurry. She leaned against the post of the bed and looked over at the oversized fireplace that Dmitry had lit directly across from their bed. The wood crackled on the fire in the dark room. Silence was all around her. She felt as though she would faint. The heat from bathtub, the many glasses of wine and the heat from the fireplace were trying to overtake her.

Shaking, she lay down in the bed and turned on the plasma flat screen mounted above the fireplace. She crawled to the middle of the king-sized bed and rubbed her hands over face. She had to cool off. Maybe, she was just overheated. Pulling the bulky robe off, she lay down naked, feeling the room spin around her. Her eyes closed.

∞♥∞

Downstairs on the other side of the mansion, seven men sat in Dmitry's private study, near his fireplace in leather seats and drinking out of crystal goblets. They talked over each other, nearly arguing in Russian, back in forth with one another, while Dmitry stood looking out the window and listening. When he had heard enough, he turned around and spoke quietly, calming the men with his voice and his temperate demeanor.

"This issue is no longer up for discussion," Dmitry said quietly.

"The men sent from New York have done their part. It's time to send them back."

"I'm not convinced," Dmitry argued.

"Our men can do the job better," one man argued back. "Unfortunately, they don't even know the routes. These other men have more control over our business than we do. That is absurd."

"Your men?" Dmitry sighed. "I'm not convinced that all of your men are loyal. I know that these ten are. You need to leave here and go and check your men, clean your houses. Someone else is communicating with the police. Until I know who is, I'm going to see that these ten continue to do as they're told."

"Our men have always been loyal," Vladimir, and older man of the counsel said.

"True Vladimir. Your man have. Until I am sure that all men in this camp are as loyal as the ten that are out there right now – none of your men will be allowed to know anymore about the route. It's security for everyone. You should be thankful. It's not like you don't still get your cut."

The men were quiet. Again, another person was talking to police. This had never happened in all the years that they had been in Memphis. Now, at least two incidents had happened in less than six months. They all looked around at each other suspiciously.

"There is another thing to discuss," Vladimir continued.

Dmitry raised his eyebrow.

"We have the opportunity to move into larger investments with local bank in the area. It is failing and needs new investors. They have approached us with offer. However..."

"The key word is *failing*, Vladimir. We don't want to put money into a slow sinking ship."

"We can turn the bank around and take larger control of the business in order to launder our money better."

Dmitry was silent for a minute.

"And they came to us with offer?" Dmitry asked curiously.

"With offer we cannot afford to ignore, Dmitry."

"Ignore it," Dmitry ordered. "If it sounds too good to be true, it probably is. My sources have told me that the FBI is investigating four banks here. They probably pushed one of them to make offer to us in exchange for break for leniency."

"Well, we've discussed the need for new revenue streams. I am just trying to find new ways."

"And we will have our people meet with the accountants to do just that, but they will not be revenue streams with holes."

"I mean no disrespect, Dmitry," another man said. "But you seem scared these days to take any risk that could bring the men money. Has that woman clouded your focus?"

The room became quiet. Dmitry looked at the man and then at Anatoly. The veins in his neck started to show. He scowled like a vicious dog. Even the tailored oxford and sweater vest, the perfect hair cut and clean shaven face could not conceal his savage instinct.

"There has only been one man in ten years who has gone to jail under my watch. How many families can say that? How many times have I protected your ass? I can't even count anymore. You all are allowed to marry and have children. You live in lavish homes and drive luxury cars no different than my own and yet you feel as though you can question me?"

"Not all of us," Vladimir said, pouring himself another glass of scotch.

"My focus has never been *clouded,* but my patience is starting to wear thin. If you get too damned comfortable talking to me, brother, I may be forced to cut out your tongue."

The men silenced. Sensing that Dmitry was near one of his maniac-like episodes, they rested their collective case. It was settled. The men Dmitry called on to make the serge through Tennessee to secure their guns route would remain until further notice. Everyone except Ivan. The man that Dmitry wanted gone the most would be there indefinitely.

Ivan stood up with smirk and excused himself from the group. Anatoly was standing at the door, as he tried to pass.

"I need to use your restroom," he said, reaching for the knob.

Anatoly looked over at Dmitry, who nodded to let him pass.

"It's down the hall to the right," Anatoly said, opening the door but still watching him carefully.

"You know, I'd like to have a little butt boy like you to do whatever I say one day," Ivan said sarcastically. "How much do your services cost? Maybe I can write you check to come work for me? Take for instance now; I need someone to hold my big cock up for me in the restroom. You think you could manage that? It's quite heavy."

"Down the hall, to the right," Anatoly repeated before he closed the door in Ivan's face.

Ivan smirked and looked down the grand hallway illuminated by glass lanterns. He walked down the herringbone limestone floor, hearing his feet echo, looking at the painted wood molding over sage-colored columns and the Russian paintings.

A house fit for a king, he thought to himself as he went inside the restroom. He closed the door and waited there for a minute. Checking his nose hair in the mirror, he turned on the faucet and let the water run. Then, he peeked out of the bathroom to make sure that no one had followed him. Slyly, he stepped out of the bathroom and closed the door, making sure to leave the water running.

Quickly, Ivan headed up the back stairwell to the second floor of the house, memorizing the layout of the home. He checked each door, all left unlocked. Looking in, making note of each room, he made his way down the long hallway to the master bedroom.

When he arrived at it, he looked back. There was a giddy thump of his dark heart. His long hand grasped the crystal doorknob and turned it slowly. He just wanted to see where they slept, where his relentless brother rested. *Even lions had a den.*

The door opened without a sound, and the light from the hallway glittered in over Royal's naked body. He looked on hungry. She was asleep, thus vulnerable. A devilish smile crossed his lips. He opened the door a little more. She was so long, so shapely. His heart began to race. If he only had the time, he would do it now. Do her. But the clock was ticking.

Crossing the threshold, he walked up closer to her. He had to get a better look. Her body slumbered with her back towards the door, still glistening with water. Her long hair fanned the pillow. The brown tips of her swelled breasts sat up invitingly.

He walked up to the bed, hidden in the shadows of the room and stood over her, thinking of what he would do to her soon. For a moment, he was tempted to run his finger down the curve of her body, but he decided against it. If she woke up and screamed, he would have to snap her neck. That would ruin all of his plans. He finally looked over at the clock and crept back out, making sure to close the door behind him.

When Ivan made it near middle way of the hallway, he saw Anatoly approaching. He stopped in his tracks and spread his arms wide.

"This is very, very nice house my brother has, eh?"

Anatoly looked down the hallway at Royal's closed door.

"What the fuck are you doing up here?" Anatoly asked, reaching for his gun.

"Relax. I just wanted to see his property. You know, he's never invited me over. Me. His own brother. It's no harm in looking right?" He walked towards Anatoly with a cocky swagger, a smug grin on his face. "Looking at all that he has acquired has made me realize that I must strive more for more."

"Strive for getting your ass downstairs with the others," Anatoly said, motioning at the back stairwell.

As Ivan headed back to the men, Anatoly went to the master bedroom door and opened it. He saw Royal lying there – still breathing most importantly. Quickly, he closed the door and shook his head in disgust. Ivan had seen her. He was sure of it.

Chapter 14

Dawn emerged from the horizon, casting a small translucent glow into Dmitry's bedroom. Unable to sleep, he laid in the bed looking at the fireplace and listening to the crackling of the embers thinking of all that was required of him this day.

Royal lay curled under him, wrapped in his embrace, asleep and protected. He raised her chin to see her glowing face. She barely moved but smiled as she dreamed. He rubbed her chin softly and kissed her forehead. Finally, carefully, he pulled his large body away from her satin-like naked skin. It was becoming harder and harder to do.

Every morning, when he woke, she was there faithfully with him. Where he used to jump up and seize every day, now, he only longed to be with her – his perfect Royal Flush.

Tucking the silk silver sheets around Royal's body, Dmitry stood naked by the side of the bed watching her sleep. Had he the time, he would wake her in his usual fashion, with soft kisses, massaging her long, voluptuous body, urging her to make love to him so that he could start his day. But she looked so comfortable that he decided to leave her there, unbothered until the alarm sounded for her own day to start.

Turning from Royal, he headed to the shower. As he turned, Royal's eyes opened, and she watched him quietly walk towards the bathroom door. His long, muscular body always fascinated her. She wanted to reach out to him and call him back, but she held her silence.

Instead she took a long deep breath of his pillow that smelled of his cologne and turned back into the softness of the bed to rest.

Royal must have dosed off for quite awhile, because when she awoke again the alarm was sounding. She reached over to the night stand and hit the blaring machine. She laid her head back down on the pillow and watched Dmitry walk towards the bed, fully dressed. He smiled at her, and she sat up a little, covering her body with the sheet.

"Good morning," she said, waving as she clutched the sheets.

"You slept well, *dah*?" Dmitry asked, standing at the foot of the bed, smiling back at her.

"Yep," Royal said, stretching her long body. She yawned. "You're off mighty early."

"There is a lot to do." Dmitry pulled the comforter from the bed and grabbed a hold of the sheet. Pulling it down to him slowly, he watched Royal's body revealed. He swallowed hard as he looked at her.

She lay with her elbows planted firmly into the mattress, her long legs crossed at the ankles and breasts exposed. Dmitry was silent, only talking to her through the sensual look in his eyes. He pulled the cover to the ground and reached out for her ankles. Pulling her body to him, he heard her giggle. He opened her legs and lay in between them, kissing a trail from her ear down to her neck.

"I should brush my teeth," she said, trying to cover her mouth.

"You taste wonderful," he said, pulling her hands away. He could feel her body coming alive with every kiss. She moaned a little, causing a stir in his pants. He kissed her shoulder softly then shifted his focus to her pouty mouth. Sucking at her bottom lip first, he then passionately covered her mouth. She kissed him back, lost in his embrace. Her long hands ran down his chest to his belt and unbuckled his pants. Eagerly, she pulled his pants down grabbing his exposed buttocks. His pants hit the ground, pooled around his ankles. Kicking them off, he crawled fully in the bed over her body and took off his jacket. Now, only in his white button down, he kissed her ankles and her feet as he stood on his knees in front of her.

"I love you," she said sincerely, smiling and looking into his eyes.

"Do you?" he asked.

"I do," she said, shaking her head. "So much."

"I love you, too," he said, running his hand up her long leg. "Lift your thighs," he said, focusing on her body.

He pulled her to his growing erection and entered her softly. Her body arched as he did. She closed her eyes and opened her mouth. Biting her bottom lip, she reached out for him. He moved her hair from her face and kissed her lips again.

"I'm going to be late," he growled, laughing and rolling over in the bed with his hands on her hips.

"Well, you should stop now, before you're late." Royal grabbed his face in her hands as she sat up on his thighs. Her long dark hair wrapped around her like a blanket.

"Not going to happen," Dmitry whispered as he watched her move on top of him. He held her by her wide shapely hips and closed his eyes.

"Open your eyes," Royal demanded. "I love to see your eyes." She adored the ice blue crystals that peered up at her with so much power and resilience. His look was the one thing that continued to devour her long after his touch.

Dmitry opened his eyes and looked at her sensually, his eyes rolling a little. "If I look at you, I may not be as late I as I could be."

Royal laughed. "Open them still."

"Alright," Dmitry sighed. He pushed into her body, holding tightly to her hips and pushing her down against him. Her hands sat atop his chest, her long legs planted beside him. He looked at her in sheer amazement. This creature making love to him was in part his own making.

"One day." He rolled her over and lifted her leg over his shoulder. "One day, I'm going to give you my son." He kissed her lips.

"Anatoly?" she asked, confused.

"No," Dmitry laughed. "I'll give you my second son. Here." He touched her stomach. "What do you think of that?"

"One day, I think that I'd like that," she whispered.

"I'd like that too," he said, kissing her wide inviting mouth again. "But for now, I'll settle for giving you orgasm."

∞♥∞

Dmitry crossed the threshold of his home and closed the large wooden front doors behind him fully dressed in a tweed Burberry jacket, a crisp white Michael Bastian button down, Louis Vuitton jeans and a pair of vintage loafers.

He looked out across his manicured lawn at the foggy, dark overcast. No sun would greet him to do his business today. There was no need for his shades or flip-flops. The weather was changing dramatically covering the city with cold winds, dreary skies and the closest resemblance of climate that he had to Moscow.

Mexican lawn workers dressed in old tattered jeans and red cotton jackets edged Dmitry's massive lawn and cleaned up fallen leaves on his property while one of his men sat on the long porch rubbing the guard dog and watching them carefully. He looked over and nodded at the man, who immediately stood up.

Dmitry never came out the front door. He normally went to the garage through the hallway leading from the kitchen. But today he was surveying -checking out what his staff was doing and how they were doing it. The maid had already cleaned up the food from the night before and had started coffee and breakfast for him when he arrived downstairs to grab his newspaper and check his emails earlier that morning. The grounds crew was doing their job. His man was up and guarding the front of premises. Overall, he was pleased.

"Relax," Dmitry said, smiling at his guard. "I'm just going to my car."

"Yes, sir," the large, graying Russian said, pulling at the dog's chain to walk Dmitry around to the car.

"No need," Dmitry said, opening his jacket just enough for the man to see his gun. "I remember time when I had no bodyguards, just balls and gun." He motioned for the man to sit back down.

Walking along the manicured walkway, Dmitry made his way across the front of the house, to the garage. As the doors rose, he quickly jumped in his Mazarati and pulled out of his driveway.

∞♥∞

Royal watched from the bedroom window as Dmitry pulled out of the gate. She was still naked, wrapped in the sheets that Dmitry had torn from the bed. Her mind was now drifting the to night before, when she had come down the back stairwell in the middle of the night and heard Dmitry speaking in Russian – screaming at Anatoly, screaming at the men that guarded their home with a gun in his hand.

They all stood stiff as board, evidently afraid of the man that she adored. She couldn't make out what he was saying to them, but she could hear that it was not good. She sat near the base of the stairwell as quiet as she possibly could, wrapped in their bed sheet listening – making out some words and completed missing others. The one word that she could understand was IVAN! Once she was sure that no one had seen her, she quickly made her way back up stairs, leaving him to his tirade.

Now she was confused about what to say to him about his brother and her increasingly complicated life. Looking at her Rolex watch, she turned away from the window and went inside of the bathroom to get ready.

After a quick shower, she walked into the large walk-in closet and circled the racks looking for something simple to put on. Even though she had access to every label in Memphis, she still liked understated elegance. Hair in a simple ponytail, she pulled on a black Ralph Lauren turtle-neck, jeans, slipped on a pair of black boots and grabbed her RL Rickey bag.

Her stomach growled as she headed down the main stairwell leading into the front foyer of the house.

Quickly, she headed to the kitchen to grab an apple and found Anatoly sitting quietly looking at CNN on the flat screen mounted on the wall and nursing a cup of coffee and a bowl of corn flakes.

"Hi," she said, trying to smile.

Anatoly looked over at her but did not speak. Evidently, the good feeling of the Thanksgiving dinner the night before had worn off.

Royal walked up to the table and grabbed a green apple out of the bronze bowl. She rubbed it on her pants to make it shine and sighed.

"Is everything alright?" she asked, trying to start a conversation.

Anatoly looked over at her from the television with a smirk on his face. Hunched over his food, he ran his spoon around the edge of the white porcelain bowl.

"Does it have to do with Ivan?" she continued, when he did not answer.

Anatoly still said nothing.

"Don't you think yesterday was a lot more fun. We should communicate more…like normal people." Her words fumbled out. She was treading in new territory by trying to talk to him. He was like a statute most days.

"Everything is fine," he finally said, tired of her whining.

"Now was that so hard?" Royal asked, recognizing progress, even in small increments. "I'm headed to the shop." Turning on her heels, she headed out the back hall to the garage but she stopped at the doorway. "Have a great day, Anatoly," she said, turning around to give it another try.

Anatoly didn't take his eyes off the television. "I will."

∞♥∞

Lt. Agosto and FBI Special Agent Danny Sorrello followed behind Dmitry in an unmarked, unwashed black Dodge Charger as he pulled into the Peabody Hotel valet parking area. Stepping out his conspicuous vehicle, Dmitry stretched and looked around, then proceeded inside to have a meeting with Omar Jackson, a well-known financial advisor.

Agosto turned off his car on the hill of the parking area and got out after Dmitry went inside of the doorway. Sorrello soon followed, putting away his half-eaten Porto-bello mushroom wrap. The two men had been following Dmitry since he pulled out of his driveway to various meetings all over Memphis with some of the most influenti-al bankers in the city. This was the most activity that they had seen in nearly a year. Most of his meetings were out of the city and often out of their joint-task force's reach, especially when he chose to meet in London and Moscow.

"Something big is going down," Sorrello said, closing the passenger door.

"I don't get it. He never meets in broad day light and never this many meetings."

"Reorganizing because of Ivan, I suppose," Sorrello concluded, pulling his leather jacket to ensure that his guns were concealed.

"Let's take a walk inside and visit our old friend," Agos-to suggested, hitting the alarm to the car.

Dmitry had just ordered a nice early evening meal of fresh hearts of palm, Great Hill blue cheese and black truffle casserole, when Agosto and Sorrello interrupted him.

They found him sitting at a small booth on the second level of Chez Phillipe restaurant nestled comfortably in the east wing of the hotel sipping on a glass of wine and reading the newspaper that he had neglected the entire day.

It had taken Agosto and Sorrello showing both badges and one gun to get into the restaurant in their jeans and t-shirts, since Chez Phillipe only allowed a minimum of business casual. Plus, it was only five o'clock and the restaurant had not officially opened to the public.

Dmitry ate alone, as he often preferred to do. The am-biance of the soft music, the strategic low lighting, beautiful rich fabrics and painting, regal French décor and marble columns throughout the fine dinning establishment fit Dmitry just right. Waitresses set down his drinks and picked up the extra placements quickly, but he never took his eyes off the newspaper.

Lt. Agosto skipped the theatrics of making a scene and quietly had a waitress bring both he and Sorrello a chair. Dmitry finally looked up as she set the chairs in front of his table. He placed the newspaper on the white table cloth and sighed.

"If I had known that you were coming, I would have ordered for you." He motioned at the chairs and invited the men to sit. "Please bring these men a bottle of your best wine," he said, sitting up a little from his slouched position.

"You know we're on the job. We can't do that," Sorrello said, countering Dmitry's offer.

"Speak for yourself. Bring me a glass of your best scotch. Keep the wine," Agosto said, looking at Sorrello. He raised his eyebrow and smiled. "What?"

"Nicola, you still are drinking scotch?" Dmitry asked.

"Still doing a lot of the same shit," Agosto smirked.

"You too know each other," Sorrello asked, even though he already knew the answer.

"Yeah, we used to know the same girl," Dmitry chuckled.

"That was way back when you first came to Memphis," Agosto reminisced. He looked over at Sorrello. "She was a Grizzlies dancer, very flexible."

"Really?" Sorrello said, suggestively.

"Only, I can't remember her name now." Dmitry looked at Agosto.

"Me either. It was Karen or Keasha. I don-no...something." Agosto shook his head.

"Miss, please bring him a scotch and water for the other gentleman," Dmitry said to the petite woman still standing by the table waiting with pen and pad. The woman scribbled something and quickly excused herself.

Now alone, the three men convened an impromptu meeting at the dinner table. It was a strange sight to see. Each man was comparable in size and all three overshadowed the small table. They sat trying not to invade the other's space with their overbearing bodies crammed into the little area.

"I can arrange for us to sit somewhere else," Dmitry noted.

"Don't worry about it. We won't take up too much of your day." Sorrello shifted in the chair.

"An innocent man would want to know what this is all about," Agosto said, softly. He looked up at Dmitry under long dark lashes, his brown eyes focused in on his new opponent.

"My question was just about to be, tell what this is all about," Dmitry smirked. He looked back at him with an ice cold stare.

Sorrello let Agosto take the lead considering that he had an established relationship. He watched as Agosto did his magic.

Agosto tapped his fingers on the table before he began contemplating how to convey to Dmitry that he knew more than he actually did. "You're a very hard man to track. You've been all over this city today, burning gas like its water. Hell, I had to run three red lights to keep up with you. I'm surprised that you didn't get a ticket."

Dmitry smiled and took a sip of his wine. "You followed me here to tell me to slow down?"

"Come on, man." Agosto laughed. "I came down here to talk to you man-to-man about some shit going on around town that's got your name all over it."

"Very suspect kinds of things," Sorrello added, eating one of the rolls in the basket on the table. Dmitry motioned at his own mouth, indicating to Sorrello that he had bread crumbs on his chin.

Dmitry looked at Agosto and laughed. "Evidently not suspect enough for you to make an arrest, or I'd be in custody already, old friends or not." Dmitry passed Sorrello a napkin and raised his eyebrow.

Agosto laughed, revealing deep dimples in this well-tanned skin. "Hey. You know me. I keep going until I get my guy."

"Who are you meeting here today?" Sorrello asked interrupting.

"My financial advisor," Dmitry said, completely relaxed. "My stocks are in the toilet, but my off shore investments are doing great. I would like to move around a little capital."

"By off shore, you mean your millions in pharmaceuticals in Switzerland or medical research in Belgium?" Sorrello asked, revealing his inept knowledge of Dmitry's private life and financial investments.

"Both actually," Dmitry answered. "Sounds to me like I should have invited my lawyer, too. This could definitely be considered harassment, gentlemen. "

"Well now, we didn't come here to harass you." Agosto took his drink from the waitress. "We came here to give you a heads up, if you're not actually a criminal."

"I am no criminal." Dmitry confirmed. "Heads up about what?"

"Well, we have received reports that a whore-house full of Russian beauties is being operated in one of your many homes in Memphis, and its being run by your baby brother. What is his name?"

"Ivan?" Dmitry asked, intrigued. This was something new.

"That's his name," Agosto said, smiling at Sorrello. "*Ivan.*"

Dmitry's calm was starting to show a tattering edge. He shifted in his seat a little. "I assure you that I don't deal in whores," he said, cutting his eyes at Agosto. His prominent strong jaw was clinched tightly together.

"That's what I thought. I mean, you've been here for every bit of ten years or more. How many times have the police ever accused you, of all people, of anything? You're a pillar of our community. A charitable, wealthy business man doesn't dabble in human trafficking." His voice was laced with sarcasm.

Agosto slid him a picture of Ivan standing outside of one of his rental properties escorting a group of women inside. He gave Dmitry a smug grin. "So, I keep asking myself, 'what the fuck is this then?'"

Dmitry's eyes snapped to the photo. His breathing slowed down more, to a calm even tone. "Gentlemen, I am afraid that I cannot tell you," Dmitry smiled.

"Mr. Medlov, have you ever heard of a group called the International Law Enforcement Academy in Budapest, Hungary?" Sorrello asked.

"I've heard of it a few times," Dmitry sat back and his seat, still composed.

"Most people haven't. It's a working group that focuses on international crime syndicates like the Eurasian trash that we keep linking to you, and they discuss you pretty often along with a larger Eurasian working group that has been curious about your global operations." Agosto injected.

"*Like I said*, I've heard of it. It's no secret. You can Google it, you know."

"You know, I worked my entire life because of my family's money and my ethnic background as an Italian American to disprove all the rumors and assumptions that because I had a vowel on the end of my name, I had to be mafia."

Agosto and Dmitry locked eyes.

"You didn't like the stereotype, huh?"

"I despise it," Agosto replied. "But you seem to embrace it and meet all of the expectations of the label, man. You don't care that people look at you like you're some sort of animal."

"When you're older, you'll realize that they look at you like that anyway. We are in Memphis, you and I. Sorrello, you too. Though I get the feeling that you are more of a blunt object that Agosto." Dmitry smirked and took a sip of his water. "It's doesn't matter if you have big millions or little millions, Agosto. You're still foreign to this place, still different and everything you do, including race-mixing is wrong. You and I have a lot in common, don't we?"

"No, I don't think that we do."

"All they'd have to do is prove that those women are there involuntarily." Agosto confirmed.

"Well, they are not their involuntarily," Dmitry said calmly.

"You had better hope that no one says otherwise," Agosto spoke under his breath.

"Why are you giving me this heads up?" Dmitry slid the picture back to Agosto, having immediately recognized the property.

"Just want you to get your house in order – that's all,"
Agosto said, drinking the entire glass of scotch. He set the
glass down gently on the table and stood up. "We know
that you are a good guy and couldn't possibly know what's
going on. We just came here to tell you what the rumors
were and to make sure that you had no hand in this." Both
Agosto and Sorrello looked down at Dmitry.

"I assure you that I've had no hand in this. What do I
owe you gentlemen for such a kind gesture?" Dmitry asked,
hands crossed and eyes focused. His voice barely rose.

"Nothing at all. Consider it a gift," Agosto said, putting
his coat back on.

"I will remember this favor," Dmitry said, trying to control the fire coming from under his collar.

The two men left as quickly as they had come, passing a
black man in a nice business suit, whom they were sure was
Omar Jackson, arriving for his meeting with Dmitry. After
they entered back into the hotel lobby, Sorrello looked back
to make sure that no one was following them.

"That is one magnificently cold-hearted bastard up
close," Sorrello said, checking his cigarette patch to make
sure that it was still on his arm. Suddenly, he was craving a
cigarette.

"It's the eyes. They don't even look like their supposed
to be on a human."

"Cause he's not human. So, what do you suppose he's
thinking?"

"Are you kidding? He wants to kill his brother. Put
that tail on him now.   He doesn't even care that we're
following him. He's going straight to Ivan after he finishes
with Omar," Agosto said, sure of himself.

"He didn't flinch once."

"Cause he knows that we don't have shit," Agosto said, hitting the alarm for his car. "It's a shame. All of this work, for all of these years, and we still have nothing."

"I've never seen anything like it."

"Me either. He's one of the best."

"If not the best…"

"Dmitry has run this whole operation without so much as one hiccup for years, but we may have hope now because of his black sheep brother Ivan. As soon as he showed up, shit went south. I just know that he's going to teach him a lesson, though. He knows that we'll barely have a case with these prostitutes, but now, if Ivan slips and gives us something on the gun trafficking, we'll have a stone clad case against the entire organization."

Sorrello spat on the ground. "Fucking Vory."

Chapter 15

Black Friday had been a hit for *Dmitry's Closet*. Royal, Renée and Cory nearly emptied their summer collection as well as their clearance fall items. The boutique had been crowded since it opened early that morning and had kept a constant flow of traffic the entire day. Now, as the night settled in, Cory escorted the last customer to her car while Royal counted down the drawer. Suddenly, the phone rang. Renée answered, listened to the caller and quickly brought the phone over to Royal.

"Who is it," Royal asked, trying not to lose count of the large wad of money in her hand.

"Dmitry," Renée answered, putting the phone to Royal's ear.

"Hello," Royal said, putting the money down.

"I'll be late coming home," Dmitry said, shifting gears in his car. "I've got couple of more things to handle."

"Okay, baby." Royal could since trouble in his voice. "What's wrong?"

"Nothing," Dmitry said quickly.

"Are you sure?"

"*Dah*," Dmitry said, focused on the streets as drove quickly down the winding back path of Main Street to his brother's house.

"Okay," Royal sighed. "I'll see you later then."

"Is everything cool?" Renée asked, as Royal hung up the phone.

"Yeah. He's just *busy*." She looked up as Cory walked back in the front door. "Lock the door," she ordered as she picked up the money again. "I have to hurry up with this. Anatoly will be here in a minute to pick it up."

"Man, we made a killing," Renée said, astonished at the huge wad of money.

"I know, girl. This is only one handful. I've got a ton of credit card receipts, checks…everything."

"Anatoly isn't here yet?" Cory asked, looking for Royal's bodyguard.

"He just called and said that he was on his way." Royal said, counting the money out. "Give me a minute. I just need to make sure that this is right." She counted out the money quickly and bagged it with the receipt. "Damn, that is the most we've made since we opened."

Just then Anatoly came in the back door in a black suit. Everyone watched on amazed. All anyone had ever seen Anatoly wear were jeans and t-shirts. Never a suit. Now, he looked a lot like his father.

Cory looked at him suspiciously as Anatoly passed him. He made his way to the cash register with Royal and walked behind the counter.

"You look nice," she said smiling. "What's the occasion?" She held the bag of money in her hand.

"No occasion." He reached for the bag.

"Bullshit." Royal pulled the bag away. "What gives?"

Anatoly reached over without a smile and scowled at Royal. "Give me bag, woman."

"Tell me what gives," Royal smiled. "You look like a million bucks. I wish that Dmitry could see this. He'd be so proud."

"*Spasiba*," he said, growling. "Now, give me bag."

"Oh, alright," Royal said, finally giving in. He took the bag carefully out of her hand and smiled at little at her. "You really think it looks nice."

"I think you look dreamy," Royal said smiling. "Really."

Remembering himself, Anatoly cleared his voice. "I have to go. Make sure that someone escorts you to car."

"I will. I know the drill," Royal said, waving as he walked off.

"He cleans up good," Renée said, watching him walk away. "I never realized how buff he is."

"I know, right." Cory said, chiming in. "Too bad he's not swinging for the other team."

"You never know," Renée added.

"So, do you want to try on the new stuff that just came in from Milan?" Royal said, quickly changing the subject. It made her incredibly uncomfortable for the two of them to talk about Anatoly. For some reason, she was very protective of him, even though she was sure that he could take care of himself.

"Oh, girl. I almost forgot." Renée said, grabbing her purse. "Let's go."

"I've got some stuff in the back. Let's close up shop here and go upstairs," Royal said, hitting the lights.

When a new shipment of clothes came in, Royal and her staff always played dress up before they put the clothes on the racks. While Renée could barely afford the clothes, even with her fifty percent discount, Royal would seriously look at the clothes and buy the ones she thought were extremely complimentary to her body type. Cory always chimed in with advice on fit and look. While he was not a woman, he was a gay shopkeeper with excellent taste that both ladies valued dearly.

They all went quickly up to Royal's old apartment and set the clothes out on the couch in the living room. Royal poured a glass of wine for each of them and stood by the fireplace laughing as they talked.

"Okay. So, do you want to try on the new Dolce or the new Armani?" Renee asked, salivating at the prospect.

"Um, definitely the Armani for me," Royal said, unbuttoning her shirt. Taking off her shirt and sliding off her jeans, she stood in only g-string panties and a black lace bra. Renée walked over and passed her the black Armani dress.

Cory sat sipping his wine and quietly watching on. There were *some perks* of pretending to be gay, like watching women strip nearly naked in front of him. He sat on the couch watching carefully as Royal slipped her long bare legs into the dress.

Royal was absolutely beautiful. She had gotten undressed in front of him a hundred times, and with every inspection of her body, he'd never seen one flaw. He found her fascinating and breathtaking, and if he weren't married and Dmitry not a cold hearted killer, he would have definitely pursued her.

Renée had slipped and told him once that Royal was virgin before getting with Dmitry, which explained his boss's obsessive behavior and his constant protection of her. The news had hit him like a ton of bricks. It also gave him a new found respect for her. As beautiful as she was, she could have had any man or anything that she wanted long ago, but judging her choice for a first, she would have that anyway.

"Cory, zip me up," Royal ordered backing up to him as he sat looking at her exposed rear end.

After a few sips of wine, he felt like slapping her on the ass and leaning her over the end of the couch. Instead, he stood up behind her and zipped her up slowly, taking in the sweet smell of her perfume and soft fragrance in her hair. Dmitry doesn't deserve you, he thought.

"There you go, girlie," he said, tapping her hip. "Slow down on the Twinkies. You're getting wide."

"You really think so?" Royal asked, touching her hips. "Do I look really wide?"

Cory sat back down and looked at her rear again. "Oh yeah." He took another sip of his wine.

∞♥∞

Bone chilling winds whipped through the riverside as Dmitry pulled up and parked his car in the front of the luxury loft apartments overlooking the Mississippi River on Front Street. He made his way up the long stairwell quickly with long forceful strides.

Arriving at the front door, Dmitry was greeted by two armed men who moved hurriedly to let him in and most importantly move out of his way. He walked in and made them stay outside guarding the door. The loft was empty with loud music blaring from the Bose surround sound. He closed the door and locked it behind him.

Walking softly across the hardwood floors, Dmitry slipped up the stairwell leading towards the music to a half-opened door. He pushed the door open with his index finger. The bedroom was dark, illuminated by large candles and a large king-sized bed under a wall-to-wall window where Ivan lay with three women. One small blonde had straddled his chest and was kissing his mouth. The other small brunette had her back to the blonde and was bent down sucking wildly on his penis. The third woman lay beside the three of them, visibly high and disoriented.

Dmitry walked into the room and closed the door. Instantly, all four looked at him. He took off his coat and rolled up the sleeves to his shirt. He smiled at the women and with a nod, walked up to the bed.

"Dmitry, what the fuck are you doing here?" Ivan asked, pushing the short women off of his body. "Here, you can have one if you like. I knew that Royal must not be too exciting," he laughed. "Good girls never are."

"Speaking of Royal, I heard that you paid her a visit last night while she was a little *indisposed* as well. Figured, I'd return the favor," Dmitry smirked.

Ivan gave a devilish grin and lifted his brow. Utter defiance in his rebellious manner.

Dmitry acted quickly. With the force of all his might, he plunged his fist into Ivan's face, punching him with precision, busting open his mouth and the side of his eye.

Afraid, the women ran quickly to the other side of the room, except for the drunken redhead whom Dmitry threw out of his way as he snatched Ivan up. She fell to the floor and rolled under the bed where she stayed.

"Get your fucking hands off me," Ivan said, trying to push Dmitry. He punched back, but Dmitry penned him down, pulled out the butt of his gun and punched him again in his face. The sound of the gun made a blood wrenching sound. When Ivan finally submitted, stopped moving like a smart victim under a bear's attack, Dmitry stopped. Breathing hard he stepped away and wiped the blood from his face.

His voice was steady and low. "If I ever catch you near her again, I'll kill you." Dmitry said, spitting.

The room was deathly still, music blared from the sound system. Dmitry turned from Ivan's naked, bloody body. He calmed himself. He caged the beast before he could spring forth.

The women screamed as he approached, afraid not only of the bleeding man but of the bloody giant in front of them breathing heavily with the gun in his hand. Their screeching voices irritated Dmitry.

"Shut up you fucking dumb bitches," Dmitry screamed, pointing the gun at them. "Get up and get the fuck out of here." They ran quickly to the door, naked and afraid, down the hall out of his site.

Dmitry turned and looked back at Ivan. "And you, *brother…*"He grinded his teeth. "Get dressed and bring your fucking ass downstairs so that I can talk to you about your little whorehouse experiment." His voice was now calm and virtually quiet.

Bloody, Ivan smiled cunningly and stood up. His naked body mirrored that of his brother, with not as many tattoos but just as many muscles. He grabbed his sheets and wiped the blood out of his face. "So that's what you're angry about?" He spat on the ground.

"The whorehouse? Hell, I'll cut you in. It's not making much yet, but it will." He slipped on a pair of jeans and walked in front of Dmitry, who guided him with the nickel-plated Glock down the stairs.

"I knew you'd be trouble when I laid eyes on you."

"Do you want drink?" Ivan asked, walking into the black kitchen.

"No," Dmitry said, looking at Ivan's home. "You live like shit." He cringed at the urban-like interior with exposed brick, black on black furniture and black appliances.

"You sound like fag. Everyone can't live like king in a big fucking palace," Ivan said, pouring a glass of vodka. "I think you knocked my tooth loose." He rubbed his index finger across his shaky front tooth.

"Good," Dmitry said, putting his gun back in his holster. He sat at the center island on a bar stool and looked at Ivan still bleeding badly.

"How did you find out? I'm so curious."

"It's my city. How did you expect me not to find out?" Dmitry asked.

"I just wanted to prove to you that my plan could be lucrative first."

"You just wanted to find something that you knew would make money fast without the Vory finding out."

Ivan leaned over the island with the icepack to his head. "It had to be a cop who told you, eh? Come on. Tell me."

"I am not without my resources." Dmitry sighed. "Get the girls out of that house tonight. Don't fucking kill them either. Give them few dollars and send them on their way. Burn the house down, just in case there is something incriminating there. Make sure it looks like accident, or I'll make you look like one."

"I get the feeling that you don't like me."

"Really? What gave you that impression?"

"You think that Royal will leave you for me? She probably thinks that you're boring. All you ever do is mope around lamenting because of your pitiful conscious."

Dmitry hit back. "I know of at least one person I'm not sorry for killing."

"Is that all?" Ivan asked irritated. The very mention of *her* got under his skin.

Dmitry knew he had put Ivan in his place. "No that is not all. I'll figure out what I'm going to do with you soon enough. For now, just make sure that you have the usual percentage into me at the next meeting, plus an additional thirty percent for my troubles."

"That's nearly all of it," Ivan scoffed.

"Good idea. Why don't I just take all of it," Dmitry said with his voice rising slightly.

There was a long silence.

"And as far as Royal…" Dmitry shifted in his seat.

"How was I supposed to know that she was in there?"

"You went looking for her?"

"I was checking out the place."

"Stop before you start, Ivan. I know you. You were casing the place and looking for her."

"You have me all wrong," Ivan said, spiting blood into the sink.

"I doubt that very seriously," Dmitry said, looking over at him expressionless. "Less you forget that I was the only father that you've ever known. There are things that I still know about you…like when you're lying to me."

"Well then, you were horrible father."

Dmitry ignored him. "As far as Royal, you consider this your only warning. Any more pursuing her, and I don't even have to tell you what I'll do."

"No, brother. You've made it very clear," Ivan scowled.

"Good." Dmitry stood up and took a deep breath. "No one told you to come here. You just have to accept it for what it is." He grabbed a towel and wiped the blood from his white shirt and slipped back on his tweed jacket. "Don't get up. I'll see myself out."

"Do that," Ivan said, rolling his eyes.

Chapter 16

Instead of Royal's cold getting better, by the day, it was only getting worse. Dmitry had stayed up with her the night before while she coughed and ran a ferocious fever. He had given her everything that he could buy over-the-counter. The results had not been favorable. She only coughed more. Tired and extremely worried, he finally rang his private doctor to come over and take a look at her.

After the doctor prescribed a few antibiotics, Royal was sent back to bed under Dmitry's ever watchful eye. Royal had, of course, contested his decision that she was to stay at home and rest. She had argued that the shop would be open in a couple of hours, and she should go and just hang out upstairs in case anyone needed her. Dmitry had given her a stern look, an even sterner voice and escorted her back upstairs to the bed, where he tucked her in and insisted that she not step foot outside of their home until she was better.

At first, Royal started to fight him on it. But alas she could not. He stood before her, unshaven, in a pair of jeans and a t-shirt from the day before and coughing a little from being exposed to influenza.

Just let him take care of you, she said to herself as he pulled the duvet comforter over her legs. Without a word, he kissed her on her forehead and closed the door behind him, leaving her to watch Wendy Williams on the television and read fashion magazines. She smiled. It was nice to have him pamper her, but it was even nicer to watch her favorite daytime talk show host give the skinny on all the stars.

Barefoot and exhausted, Dmitry made his way back downstairs to his study, where he found his son filing away some papers. Anatoly looked up as his father entered the room but continued with his task. Looking back just to make sure that Royal had not followed him, Dmitry closed the door behind him and sat down in one of the large leather chairs to relax his aching body. He rubbed his temples and sniffled a little.

"Good Morning," Anatoly said, initiating the conversation.

"The sun is not even up yet, so why are you? Were you disturbed by Royal's cackling all night, too?"

Anatoly smirked. "You know. This is first time I've ever seen you take care of anyone except yourself." He slid the last of the files in the drawer and closed it.

Dmitry sighed and looked up at the ceiling. "There is something about her… I cannot explain."

"Maybe it's because she isn't a money grubbing whore like the women before her."

"That could be," Dmitry sat up. "She wanted to go to work today – in the state that she's in."

Anatoly leaned on the corner of his father's desk. "You sound surprised. This is Royal that we're talking about."

Dmitry nodded in agreement.

"I did as you asked," Anatoly said sighing. The conversation quickly changed. Dmitry stopped smiling and sat up in his chair.

"And?"

"There is more than one of these whorehouses. Ivan has more like ten."

"Ten?"

"There is more. Word on the street is that he's trying to negotiate with the Mexicans on an upcoming drug shipment of meth coming up the pipeline, and he's been seen with the owner of the Black Tie strip club. I think that he's pressuring him to sell."

The news definitely bothered Dmitry, but he dared not show it. "Do you know why we have done so well for the last ten years, Anatoly?"

"No. News of our *unorthodox* tactics got around?"

"More than that." There was a twitch in Dmitry's eye. "It's because we found niche, and we did not bother to spread ourselves thin by doing more than the things that we were good at. Each of the original men who came to Memphis from Moscow or New York had strong background in gun running. Some of them had been rebels for legitimate causes in the motherland and others simply criminal minds with a hunger to get rich.

"Now, weapons trafficking is not just about selling to thugs and funding street wars. We have an array of high-end hunters who want untraced quantity, cops who want unmarked reliable guns, rednecks who stockpile for race wars, guns for hire who need professional grade munitions, ex-military who want the weapons they used in Iraq, aficionados who want them in the house for show and tell and heads of organized crime, who need them for protection." Dmitry smiled, as he watched his son soak up the information like a hungry sponge.

"So you cut your market share by not expanding when you clearly had the man power, and this is a good thing?" Anatoly was perplexed. It didn't make much since to him. It never had. He had always wanted his father to expand the empire by selling more than just guns.

"No. This is better than a good thing…it is smart thing. See, you have to know history of a place before you just come in and start to take it over.   Do you know much about Memphis' organized crime families?"

"Elvis, Bar-b-que, Three-Six Mafia rap group. What else is there to know?"

"Much more, son."

"Well, it's four o'clock in the morning. Why don't you explain it to me? I have nowhere to be for hours." He tapped his finger on his watch.

"*Dah.* I tell you all so that you are smarter than the next generation of Vor, and you lead best."

Dmitry motioned at the chair across from him. Anatoly took off his suit jacket and sat down in the comfortable chair to listen to his father. He sat up attentively awaiting the knowledge that only Dmitry could share.

"We came from different market. There was much opportunity when the Soviet Union fell. Those who were in a position to leave did. We went so many places before we came here, but the long and short of the route was Moscow to New York. When we got here, this area already had drugs and whores by the bus loads. Black and whites were shipping cocaine in from Mexico via Texas, heroine from Afghanistan, cooking and shipping meth and crack cocaine here locally and from the southern borders, getting marijuana and prescription drugs from Canada and California and home growing their own whores. We could not add any value to these things. Plus, the relationships were there. People had their supply chains set in stone."

"What about other things?"

"Other things? Chop shops are more risk than return. Pornography doesn't do it for me. We wanted something we could centralize and maintain for this area. Small dollar schemes are for armatures. Plus, we have lucrative businesses all over US and other countries.

"Running numbers and the whole betting machine belongs to the Italians, and they took big hit when the casinos came to Mississippi. So they responded by clinching their unions tighter, increasing their chop shops and construction businesses and cutting into the drug market, which by the way, when we arrived here was basically run by three major drug dealers. One Italian and two blacks had the entire city locked down. Eventually the drug dealers got popped one by one and their investment bankers retired to nice locales in more tropical regions. All of this was due to a war between the blacks and the Italians that nearly lasted five years."

"What started the war?" Anatoly asked.

"The one Italian drug dealer wanted to expand more into areas that were not really the blacks' territory but not really his."

"And the blacks pushed back?"

"You're damned right. It was bloodshed on both the streets and in the police department. That's why Agosto and Brooks were named leads on the mayor's war on drugs. Agosto is Italian, and he's an implant to Memphis straight from Miami. Brooks was a native black with ties directly to the mayor, since both he and his father worked for him.

"This union created by Mayor Henderson was to begin to develop a peace between Italians and blacks in the community. But people were pissed because Agosto and Brooks never once busted any large black or Italian drug dealers. They hit up a middle weight Hispanic drug dealer by the name of Caesar. Agosto ended up killing him in his own bedroom after Brooks was assassinated. When Brooks died, the city went insane on their drug witch hunt. And all sides went scrambling to take over Caesar's territory that was eventually divided by the black and Italians after a truce

was called, but it's still mostly run by a Mexican cartel out of
Mexico City, because there was big transition from crack
cocaine to meth. You know, the economy is bad…"

"So why didn't Vory use that opportunity to move in?"

"Opportunity costs were too high. We had credible Intel from the feds that all parties were being watched carefully. However the ATF did not have a strong presence in the
area. Now the fucking DEA was hopping all over this city.
They had stake out on every corner. So, we opted to stay in
guns, because it was safer. Plus the Hispanics, Blacks and
Italians were shooting each other left and right, and we were
the ones making a killing. Sure we have drug cartels and
money laundering across the US, but we only handle guns
here. A lot of Vory have gotten to the point that they don't
even do business in their home cities. They just run things
from a central base. It's safer that way. It never comes
back on you."

"Yeah. I heard you talking to the men about it. So with
guns, you had neutrality?" Anatoly was much more interested in what market share they already controlled.

"Exactly. Everyone came to us. And we had an understanding with all sides that we would sell to *anyone* with cash
or goods to barter. Since that time because of our supply
chain nationwide, we have amassed so much wealth it
is…ungodly."

"Selling to everyone didn't create a problem for you? I
can't see how it wouldn't."

"At first, it was hard to persuade them. And my old
boss taught us to think through things with our minds
before we resulted to guns. But when I saw that we
couldn't reason with some of the groups, we brought in
enforcers from Israel and Georgia and introduced them to
what the Vory v Zakone was all about. Then people started

to respect our territory. We showed up at people's jobs, at their homes, at their businesses. Then the extortion began and after that, it was almost total submission. They saw that no place was safe or sacred. Hell, once a man was cut from ear to ear outside of the police department. Unfortunately, they never got his cooperation."

"So violence does work." It was one of Anatoly's most effective techniques.

"Sometimes it works, but you will find my old boss' advise very helpful. Only young men like you roll heads. As you get older, the way that people can tell that you are leader is not by what you have to do but what you don't have to do. Anyway, we moved in quickly and knocked the small fish out of pond.

"Most of the Vory that came down here had been to war and back. So, they lived and breathed the takeover. It took us seven months to kill the competition, set up our headquarters and start taking large orders for guns. The death toll was astronomical. But it eventually leveled off once people saw that we weren't after their drugs or whores or their cars or anything else. We just wanted to sell them some quality guns."

"Just like that? Huh?"

"Just like that," Dmitry said, quickly. "Now the importance of our legitimate businesses, which as you know go completely against our original code, is to launder money efficiently. All of us bought real estate, started business, and purchased stock, bonds and CDs. We washed the money clean through our intricate web of family businesses. In less than five years, we made millions on top of millions. Plus, every time the crime rate goes up in Memphis, not only home owners get guns, bad guys do too. So, we sell to everyone. Between the heads of the Memphis Vory, we have four guns shops here, two pawns shops, a shooting range, three restaurants, a tire shop, a beauty salon, a grocery store, six check cashing stores, four liquor stores, over 20 residential properties, an upscale boutique, seven commercial properties, and a fucking partridge in a pear tree. That, my son, keeps our shipments safe and legitimate. We ship guns, but not all of them are illegal. And when some young agent or hard-up cop wants to get hot on our trail, a friendly brother-in-blue gives us the heads up…for a fee, of course."

"So, you've always owned a few cops to give you the inside scoop?"

"They are sometimes hard to find. But yes. A cop was the lead that let me know that Memphis was an untapped oyster for my business eleven years ago. He helped me get started here in exchange for us supplying his own little war against some very unwilling citizens that didn't want to sell their land to a major corporation that needed the land to expand."

"How did you meet him?"

"I was introduced to him while he was on trip to New York looking to acquire some hired help after he made the deal with corporation."

"What happened to the cop? Is he still around?"

"He retired once the land was acquired. Evidently, he got big, big cut from sale of the property because his wife was the land broker."

"Does everyone retire?"

"If you're lucky." Dmitry sighed. "If I am lucky."

"So now we control the flow of guns into the city and out of the city for everyone, even North Memphis where the Hispanic gun traders had settled in and we have ten whore houses." Anatoly didn't see the problem, but would follow his father's lead.

"Do I look like a fucking pimp to you? It's not my style. My mother was whore. She died in my arms on the steps of our home because of a John that both me and my brother knew well. It's not pretty business, and it's not business that has a great return. Munitions on the other hand, we have a lock on."

"So what do we do about your brother's ambitious new businesses?"

Dmitry looked his son in the face and smiled. "Burn it to ground. It's a matter of survival and none of our council has agreed to this new business of his."

"I can see it. You're on the verge of a war with him."

"The verge? My boy, we are battling every day. The biggest battle has just not begun yet."

"Are you going to kill him?"

"I don't know. I don't want to, but I fear that if he continues, as much as I love him, I will."

"You should have me do it." Anatoly said eagerly.

"You do not have your stars yet," Dmitry said absently. He could see that just the mention of that fact defeated Anatoly.

"It is not for lack of trying."

"You have proven yourself. Give me until the next meeting of the high council, and it will be done." Dmitry reached out and tapped his son's knee. "Now, I am going to hit my gym. Class is over. You get some rest."

It was mid-morning when Dmitry opened the door their bedroom carrying a large silver tray with a bowl of chicken noodle soup, a glass of orange juice and a flower. The sun beamed into the room and onto the bed where Royal was curled up under the comforter.

She had dosed off to sleep again, completely drained from her constant coughing and the strong drugs the doctor had given her, but she quickly woke up when she heard his feet walking across the floor. She opened her eyes, looked up at him and saw small circles under his eyes. Maybe she needed to take care of him for a while.

"Are you still running fever?" he asked, setting the food down on the large nightstand beside them.

"I don't think so," she said, touching her own forehead. "I just feel stuffy."

"I'm going to use remedy on you that has worked wonders for me for years." Dmitry passed her the glass of orange juice.

"What would that be?" She stretched out her long legs and moaned.

"First you take hot shower; then you put Vick's vapor rub on your chest."

"Oh, I've done that before. Not for years, but I've done it."

"We do it today," he confirmed. "So eat your food."

Dmitry stood up and walked into the bathroom, where she heard him turn on the jets to the shower. She grabbed the remote, flipped through her channels and suddenly realized that this was the first day in a very long time that she had been home during this hour.

It was quite odd to her, how the sun shined through the blinds so bright and forceful. It was practically begging her to get up and go to work. It was also such a shame to waist a brilliant day of sunlight, even if it was freezing outside. But Dmitry would never let her go. He might, in fact, keep her longer if she pushed him. She huffed at the thought.

Submitting to his relentless will, she grabbed her bowl and spoon and ate just enough of the soup to make her throat feel better then pulled herself out of bed. Shedding out of her heavy University of Memphis pullover and jogging pants, she walked into the bathroom in her panties in bra, where she found Dmitry leaning over the sink shaving.

He looked over at her through the mirror and then motioned for her to get into the water.

"Breathe in fog once you're in there," he said as he tapped his razor against the porcelain bowl. "It will open up your passages."

Running his razor through the stream of water coming out of the faucet, he lifted his neck and let the long four-pronged blade gently glide the length of his lower chin and neck.

Royal took off her panties and bra and placed it in the wicker hamper, and then opened the large, smoked glass door to the box-like glass shower room where water shot from the many jets shot straight into her from every direction. Taking deep breaths as Dmitry instructed, she grabbed a bottle of tea-tree shampoo and washed her hair. The steam enclosed the room, hiding her from Dmitry's view, and the hot water soothed her aching body and her congested chest.

Now cleanly shaven, Dmitry opened the door and dropped his towel. Entering into the shower room, he grabbed the soap and walked up beside her. Running his hands over the knobs, he adjusted his jets to his own temperature and pressure.

Royal eyed him while she rinsed her hair. His large frame towered over her, and even with his wall-like back turned away from her, she could see his magnificent sculpting from every angle. She tilted her head a little to get a better view, but he turned enough to catch her peeking. Rinsing the soap from his face, he pulled her over to him and stood in front of her, hiding her from view.

"You're supposed to be sick" he said smiling.

He knew Royal's devilish look. The cascade of water ran over his body, flattened his normally curly hair. She watched as the water glistened on his wet skin. Instinctively, she ran her hand down the front of his marble chest.

"Then make me feel better," she whispered, moving in closer to his body.

Dmitry ran his hands through her soapy hair and pulled her in front of jets to rinse her off. The water covered her face and caused her to tilt her head back. She could feel the warm water and his large hands on her head rinsing her clean. With her eyes closed, she felt Dmitry's hungry lips meet hers. He kissed her softly, exploring the soft ebb and flow of her lively tongue. She could taste the minty freshness of his toothpaste and feel the warmth of his full lips. He held her face in both of his hands as he bent over to her. She bit his lips playfully and smiled as he pulled her out of the water.

"Come on. I'm going to dry you off before you get worse." He opened the door to the shower and handed her a large towel to dry off.

"But I thought you said that you would make me feel better?" She wrapped the towel around her body and followed him out into the bedroom.

"I never said that, shop girl," he said, going to his large armoire to pull out a clean pair of underwear.

Royal lay back on the bed in her towel, placed her feet on the side rails of the bed and looked at the ceiling fan.

She wasn't sure if she was overheated from the shower or the man. Raising her head, she looked over at him as he slipped on his jogging pants.

"Do you feel ill again?" he asked.

"Just weak."

"In your state, why do you want me to make you feel worse?"

"You won't," she leaned over on her side and watched him walk up the bed.

"I will, and you know it." He crawled in the bed beside her and grabbed the remote.

"Are you going to tease me all day?" she asked, taking her eyes off him and concentrating on the television.

"Are you going to pout all day?"

"I may." She crawled back out of bed to get dressed. When she returned, Dmitry had the bottle of Vick's vapor rub. Rolling her eyes, Royal sat near the opposite edge of the bed in one of his tailor-made dress shirts and checked her cell phone.

Dmitry watched her pouting and laughed a little. Reaching across the bed, he pulled her to him, straddled her over his lap and slipped his hand under her shirt. She watched curiously as his hand landed in between her breasts with a palm full of salve. He rubbed it into her skin softy and tapped her on her nearly exposed behind.

"Lie down and rest," he said.

"But I can feel that you want me," she said, rotating on his growing erection.

"*But* you're sick and you need to get well first." His breathing was growing sporadic watching her seduce him. The swell of her breast was showing slightly at the top of the unbuttoned shirt, and her nipples pressed out against the fine cotton. Had she not been sick, he would have already bedded her but decided against it with her fever rising by the minute. He could feel the heat between her thighs. She needed rest and medicine not what he so desired to give her.

Pouting again, she scooted down in the middle of the bed and put her legs under the cover. As he reached over to kiss her on the forehead, she sneezed.

"Told you," Dmitry said tauntingly.

Cory could not recall a day that Royal did not come into the boutique. She must have either been really sick or Dmitry really insistent. Either way, this gave him the perfect opportunity to get downstairs in the basement. To ensure that he had enough time, he had sent Renée on a run for lunch, office supplies and to drop off a package at the post office. She'd be gone now at least an hour. As soon as she pulled off, he closed the shop and headed to the back office.

Digging into the pocket of his tight and very uncomfortable khakis, he pulled out a small piece of paper with a code. He typed the numbers into the security device and saw the red light turn green. He quickly opened the door and headed down the dark staircase.

Reaching the bottom of the stairs, he ran his hands against the wall until he found the light switch. As he hit it, the large lower room illuminated. It was empty with the exception of a large bed, a standing mirror, a flat screen television mounted on an opposite wall and a dresser. In the far corner of the airy space sat a large surveillance center with monitors all over various establishments of Dmitry's including *Mother Russia*, the boutique and the front and back entrance of his home.

He looked at his watch and realized that he didn't have much time. Pulling open the file cabinet in the corner, he looked for the surveillance footage from the last week. He needed to find out what was going on with Ivan. Maybe these tapes would tell him more about his whereabouts.

Carefully, he placed dated CDs on the table and made copies on the small laptop on top of the desk. He tapped his foot impatiently as the copies were generated to his jump drive. Taking them one by one out of their plastic protective coverings, he slid them into the computer and downloaded the information.

When he finished, he picked up the handful of CDs to take them back to the cabinet and clumsily dropped them on the floor. He huffed under his breath, and then quickly tried to gather them up in his arms. As he stood, he heard footsteps coming down the stairs. His heart began to race.

He grabbed the handle of the file cabinet and dropped the CDs back into their original file. He knew that he did not have a gun. So he looked around for a weapon. Skimming the room, the one thing that stuck out was the bed. He ran over to it and ran his hand under the railing to find what he was looking for...a weapon. Sliding the compact oozy from the Velcro enclosure, he walked up slowly to the door and pointed it.

The final footstep landed on the ground anchored by a large leather loafer. From the shadows, Dmitry stepped out of the doorway and looked over at Cory, who stood with the gun pointed.

"Shit, Dmitry. You scared the shit out of me," Cory exhaled, putting the gun down.

"How did I scare *you*? You're supposed to be cop for Christ's sake," Dmitry smirked, making his way across the room to the surveillance equipment. "Did you find any-thing meaningful?"

"I don't know. I haven't viewed them yet. I'm going to take it back to the apartment and see if there is anything incriminating on them."

"Let's hope that there is," Dmitry said, looking back at Cory. "Why are you wearing those tight-ass pants?"

"Part of the cover," Cory said, going back over to the bed. He pulled a pillowcase off of one of Anatoly's pillows and wiped the gun down then placed it back under the bed where he had found it.

"All gay men don't dress two sizes too small, you know."

"This one does. Where is Royal?"

"Sick."

"Pregnant?"

"No. She has flu." Dmitry sat down in the chair by the desk and sighed. "I'm exhausted. Have you thought of possible *exit strategies* for Ivan?"

"Yeah." Cory put his hands in his pockets. "I've also thought about some possible exit strategies for you, too."

"We'll get to that soon enough." Dmitry waved off the portion of the conversation that he cared nothing about.

"Okay. Well, if I can prove on these tapes that he is up to illegal activity; I can roll this entire investigation over to him. Almost everything that they have on you won't stand in court now. So, if I give them this bone, they'll bite."

Dmitry listened attentively with his hands crossed be-hind his head. Rocking the seat, he weighed his options.

"Get the ammunition, but don't do anything yet. He's my brother and a Vor. We must deal with him on our own."

Cory nodded. "Okay. Well, I have to give them something. This *is* an investigation."

"Give them the fact that you've seen the surveillance room, but it was only a glimpse when the door was open. Give them information regarding the ten whorehouses after I get the deeds out of my name, and I'll work on deciding the rest in the next couple of weeks."

"Yeah, about that. I'm taking a week to go home and be with my wife and kids. Christmas is coming up, and I don't want to miss it with them."

"Of course." Dmitry understood. "I plan to take Royal away for Christmas anyway. Renée can watch the place. How is your mother's cancer doing?"

"Thanks to you, she's in remission. We could have never afforded the treatments otherwise."

"Then our little arrangement is worth it, *dah*?"

"Oh yeah. It's worth it," Cory sighed. "Let's just hope that it continues to run smoothly."

"It will," Dmitry said, turning towards the monitors. "Head back up. We have customers coming in. I'll stay down here and look around a while." He peered at the busy noon traffic at *Mother Russia* and his staff eagerly working. "I'm going to watch them work for a while to ensure that they are actually living up to my standard of customer service."

"Alright," Cory said, leaving Dmitry to his surveillance.

To Cory, Dmitry was a very odd man but in a lot of ways very merciful. Cory had blown his cover the night that Royal had her opening celebration. He had no idea that the building had a basement, because it was not on any of the plans that he and the team had gone over.

That night, seeing that only Royal's car was there and Dmitry was still at the restaurant, and knowing that Royal always closed her door upstairs and never came down until morning, Cory snuck in after hours to comb the boutique's back office for clues.

Anatoly quickly emerged from the basement, gun in hand and held him at gun point until Dmitry arrived. Cory was expecting Dmitry to kill him, but they took him downstairs to the basement and talked to him – asked him what it would take to flip. Cory had just found out his mother was in the third stage of cancer, and as an only child, he could not afford he bills.

Dmitry agreed to pay the doctor bills in full through a doctor that he knew who would classify the project as a *charitable* case. And just like that both of his problems went away. He would live another day and so would his mother. Now that his beloved mother was in remission, Cory felt that he owed Dmitry everything, including the useful Intel that he gave and the protection that he offered through that intelligence.

∞♥∞

After Dmitry left *Mother Russia* later that afternoon, he headed back to his house to check on Royal. He was quite surprised to see that she had listened and stayed at home. He had expected to pull into the garage and find her truck gone, but it was still there, which indicated that she was still sick. Carrying a small red bag, he walked up the long spiral staircase of the main hall to the west wing of his home, where he found Royal in bed watching television.

"Hey," she said, turning off the television with her remote.

"Hi." Dmitry closed the door behind him and walked up to her side of the bed. "Has your fever gone, yet?" He placed his hand on her head.

"Yep," she said, moving his hand. "Did you stop to check on my shop today, since you wouldn't let me leave the house?"

"Everything is fine." He sat on the bed beside her. "I have surprise for you." Handing her the small red bag, he leaned in to kiss her lips.

"What it is?" Royal asked, taking the bag.

A large smiled came across her face as she pulled a small Christmas tree ornament out of the bag.

"Oh, it's so sweet. A figurine of the Red Square." She held it up to the light to look at the intricately detailed work. "Does this mean that you're going to let me put up the Christmas tree now. You know, I've been dying to do it?" She grabbed a napkin and blew her nose.

"Even better that that." He smiled. "I'm going to take you to Moscow for Christmas and New Years."

Royal looked up at him stunned. "Excuse me?"

"Well, you've always said that you wanted to go." Dmitry was confused. Did she not want to?

Royal was quiet for a moment. She moved the comforter from her legs and stood up. "Does this mean that I'll actually see it all? The Red Square? Kremlin? Lenin's Mausoleum and St Basil's Cathedral?" She finally smiled brightly and jumped on top of Dmitry. He caught her in his embrace and kissed her.

"I was hoping that you would be happy."

"I'm thrilled. I've never been anywhere outside of the South. Now, I get to see a new country...I just can't imagine."

"You know why I like doing things for you?" he asked, moving the hair out of her face.

"Why?"

"Because you are the only woman in my life who truly appreciates and deserves it."

"No, that's not why you do it," she said, in a matter of fact tone.

"Really? Then why?"

"Because you love me," she said, kissing his lips and hugging him tight. "And I love you too."

He looked her in her eyes and shook his head. "*Dah*, that's why I do it for you. I love you."

"Does this mean that you're going to make love to me?" she asked with her legs wrapped around his back.

"No," Dmitry laughed. "You're still sick." He tried to pull her off of him. "I don't want you to get any sicker."

"I'm not that sick." She kissed his checks and coughed.

"Ugh! You are, too." He laughed.

"Baby, I can't believe that we're going to Moscow!" She screamed as she wrestled him down to the bed.

Chapter 17

Royal had never been out of the country. She had never been above the ocean, the clouds, so near to the heavens. And above all, she had never been in a luxury private jet. There was a certain amount of prestige that came with such a thing. It was far richer that she could ever describe.

Earlier that morning after a hardy breakfast and a hectic packing session with the maid and Renée to help, she had been escorted in a limo from her house to the private airstrip, where she and her entourage of Russian men, Dmitry and Anatoly included, boarded a swank, LearJet 60 and set out on a trip to a land that she had never seen.

Dmitry and Royal sat in the interior forward leather off-white chairs beside each other looking out of windows and listening to television that played in front of them on the flat screen.

Dmitry was thinking of the tasks that lay ahead upon his landing, and Royal was literally in awe of the beauty of the clouds and the blue sky. The stewardess bent down to Royal and offered her a glass of champagne. She took it happily, inwardly thinking that champagne was a great way to celebrate her new lifestyle. However, when offered, her companion quickly waved the woman away.

Royal looked over at Dmitry, who was completely apathetic of the entire trip. He had traveled the world over and found it the same, wherever he went. It baffled her how a man of such wealth and affluence found her so interesting.

"What are you sighing about?" he asked, taking his eyes of the window. He looked over at her and tilted his head.

"It doesn't move you anymore, does it?" she asked, setting down her glass.

"What?" He looked around.

"Any of this." She kept her voice low, so that the others could not hear them. If they overheard her, it would only prove more how unworthy she truly was.

"It is my life, Royal. You'll get used to it." He leaned over the arm rest to her. "Does it bother you? The way that I live?"

"Hell no," she retorted, and then smiled a little, revealing her perfect white teeth. "It fascinates me. I wake up everyday and pinch myself."

Dmitry liked that. His eyes sparkled. "Then it is all worth it."

"Tell me…how you find me…"

"Yes?"

"Interesting? When you live like this? I just can't understand what I bring to the table that blows your skirt up."

"Sincerity. Genuine sincerity. It's a hard thing to come by when you have money. Plus, you're stunning and smart and hard working and….if you just wanted a compliment, my dear, you should have just said so. This is quite a long way around the bush." They both laughed.

Royal reached out and touched Dmitry's golden bronze face. "You're such a good man."

"I am just a man."

"No. You are so much more than that to me," she said, leaning in to kiss him. Her eyes were bright with conviction. "Do you know that I've never had one meaningful relationship with a man in my entire life? No dad, no brother, no decent boyfriend. But you are, in a way, all of those things."

Dmitry didn't smile. He looked her dead in her eyes and listened carefully.

Royal allowed him to kiss her forehead. It was all that he could do to express his gratification for her honesty.

"Was that too heavy?" she asked, sitting back. "You know how I am. I just…get caught up in the moment sometimes."

Dmitry sighed. "No. We are just very much alike, you and I. For us to have come from such different backgrounds and cultures, we share the same perils."

Royal agreed with Dmitry, but she could count on her hands how many similarities that they shared versus the countless things that she could not relate to him about, mostly surrounding money. No one ever prepared her for this in her many fairy tale stories as a girl. The knight in shining armor showed up, just as the story promised, but there were no details of what happened during the *ever after.* She was completely and utterly clueless. With a shake of her head, she looked back over at Dmitry, who was studying her.

"I like it better when you think out loud," he said, taking her glass and sipping her champagne.

She watched the crystal touch his delicate pink lips. "I just hope that you're the real thing, Dmitry. Because I'm definitely in over my head. And you don't make it any better spoiling me like this." She moved her hair from her face and rested her elbow on the arm rest.

Dmitry looked over at her and raised his eyebrow. "Oh, I am the real thing." He put the crystal flute back on her table and smiled.

∞♥∞

To Royal's surprise and delight, they stopped in New York City before their long trip across the ocean. She had never been to New York but had always dreamt about the opportunity. Now she was in a limo being rushed around the busy city in style. She sat quietly in the limo looking out the window, gawking at the sights while Dmitry talked to Anatoly in Russian.

Dmitry mentioned that the reason for his stop was two-fold. He needed to stop for a quick business meeting and to buy Royal a proper mink coat for the Russian cold. Both errands would be short, because they were blocks from each other in the busy burrow of Manhattan. Instead of sending Royal with Anatoly, Dmitry had taken Royal personally to an upscale shop on Madison Avenue.

The bodyguards stood outside while Royal and Dmitry went inside of the luxury fur gallery, Royal Chie. The innovative Japanese designer Chie Imai's collection was breathtaking. It was internationally recognized for its eco-friendly designs, versatility and high-profile clients.

However, up until now, Royal had only read about the shop. Now, she was in it being shown their finest coats and accessories. She felt like a kid in a candy store. She was allowed to look through the entire new line of furs before making her selection, a chocolate Swakala Coat with Russian Sable Trimming, and matching muffler and ear-muffs.

The sales woman was about to wrap her new gifts, when Dmitry instructed her to dress Royal quickly in the furs immediately so that they could leave for his meeting. With a bow and smile, she was escorted to the fitting area and came back out looking richer than she had ever felt in her life.

As she came out, he was sitting on a chair texting. She walked in front of him and cleared her voice. He looked up at her pleased. Having already paid for the merchandise while she was putting them on, he was ready to go and on schedule. Under his arm, she followed him back out of the shop and into the limo where they ended up at the Wall Street Bath and Spa a short while later.

Instead of going inside the bath house with Dmitry, he insisted that Royal stay in the car. She did so obediently. She preferred it, in fact. It gave her the perfect opportunity to call and tell Renée about her newest gift and her trip thus far.

She wasn't left alone, however. She was accompanied by a driver and a blonde, brick of a man, who Royal concluded was one of Dmitry's men. She had never seen him before, but he was a cookie cutter copy of all of Dmitry's bodyguards – huge, arctic polar bears.

He sat across from her, trying not to look directly at her, but she caught him staring several times. Sliding her shades over her eyes, she tried to ignore the brut while she talked on her cell phone.

Thirty-minutes later, Dmitry returned with Anatoly and his men to the car, and they were back on the jet eating lunch before noon.

∞♥∞

Before dawn of the next day, Royal and her party arrived in Moscow, Russia. Dmitry had been right when he said that she would need a big coat. It was the most bone-chilling winds and rain that she had ever experienced in her life.

Two very large black G550 Mercedes –Benz trucks were awaiting them outside of customs. Once they received their clearance into the country, they were immediately carted off to the Le Royal Méridien National Hotel.

To Royal's amazement, the hotel was directly across from the Kremlin. She stood gazing out the elaborately decorated windows of their presidential suite at the palace in her view. The gold sphere-like tips of the cathedrals caught embers of light that reflected from sun trying to break free from the cloudy day and shined into her room. It was a spectacular sight. She could not take her eyes off the fortress.

The architecture was amazing, and the massive size of the great bricked wall surrounding it was astonishing. It was so remarkable until it held her attention beyond her own control. By far, it was the grandest thing that she had ever encountered, but there was something else very special about the wondrous place – perhaps just the thought that Dmitry was born and raised in the country.

While she basked in the beauty of her view, room attendants quickly put away their things, changed out a few amenities per Royal's request and ran a bath for Dmitry. With all the commotion in the room, she never broke her gaze. Dmitry found her new interest intriguing. He spoke to men in Russian, flipped through his blackberry and gave out orders, but mostly he admired how entranced she had become. She was like a child with a shiny new toy.

Dmitry noticed how Royal seemed to be maturing day-by-day, not that she had been a child when he met her. It was just that he had exposed her to so much so very quickly, until she was forced to elevate herself at a hyper speed. When he first met her, saw her, he knew that she was a diamond in the rough, but even he did not know how beautiful and brightly she would shine once she was groomed.

Royal did not notice that everyone had left the room until she felt Dmitry's hands on her shoulders. She turned around and looked at him.

"It's…mind-blowing," she said, shaking her head. "I've never seen anything like it." She touched the frosted window. "That's the Kremlin? It's huge…massive."

Dmitry massaged her shoulders. "I'll make sure to take you to the Kremlin *later* this week."

"Tomorrow," Royal demanded. "I've got a whole day lined up for myself. I brought gym shoes, jeans, a camera with a butt load of memory and a pea coat." She smiled at him. "What? Why are you looking at me like that?"

"You're such a little tourist. Tomorrow, I actually had other plans, but I'll cancel them, and you and I will spend it touring the entire Red Square and your precious Kremlin. Well, the part that we can get inside. You know the President of Russia lives there."

"Like the White House? Wow. I can't wait until tomorrow then." She reached out and gave him a big hug. "This entire place is like one big dream, Dmitry. I still can't believe that I'm actually here." She released him and turned back towards the window.

Dmitry huffed. "When I was your age, I thought this place was nightmare. I couldn't leave here soon enough. And look at you...you want permanent visa." He wrapped his arms around her waist and kissed her neck.

"That was when you were young. Surely, you miss it now."

"No. I just come here to take care of things I can't take care of anywhere else."

"But it's a part of you?"

"A very big part of me," he confirmed.

"Well, I feel like it's a part of me, as much as you talk about it."

That made Dmitry smile. "You feel that strongly about it, eh?"

"Yes," Royal couldn't control her smile. "It's so different from Memphis."

Dmitry laughed so hard, his voice rattled the room. Her only point of reference was Memphis, yet to look at her, Royal looked like she had traveled the world for years.

He turned Royal around and pulled her to him.

"I will open your little eyes to this big beautiful world soon enough. And you will see that everything is quite different from Memphis. Maybe even, you appreciate it more. Who knows?"

"I appreciate it...when I'm away from it," she said, hanging her arms around his neck. "I don't want to live there forever."

"I'm certain that you will not." Dmitry rubbed his hands through her hair.

"Oh, change of subject. Tomorrow is Christmas Eve. So, I've got to go and get your other gifts while we're out."

"Other gifts?"

"I brought some things with me." She wiggled her nose. She knew how much he enjoyed her gifts.

"What it is? I want to see it now." He gripped her waist in his hands.

"No. You have to wait till Christmas."

"I haven't had Christmas gifts since I was little boy."

"Well, it's a good thing that I'm around, because I've got a great Christmas planned. We're going to have eggnog and Christmas stockings and the whole nine."

"You and your holidays." His thick accent covered his words. "I have to step out for a few hours and take care of some business. So, you'll have the suite to yourself." He pulled away from her and went into the master bedroom to take off his clothes.

"Completely to myself or will that big blonde dude be outside of my door?"

"What? You don't like blondes. Fine. I get you red-head." He laughed.

"Whatever." She pulled her coat off and pulled her hair out of its pony tail. Scratching her head, she went over and sat on the bed in front of him. "Do you think that he'll take me to get something to eat? I'm starving."

"Order in."

"I don't want to. I want to stretch my legs. I've been in a jet for hours."

Dmitry pulled his tie loose and looked at her. "Alright." He began to unbutton his shirt. "He'll take you anywhere you want to go."

Royal stood up on her knees in front of him and started to unbutton his tailor made oxford for him. He ran his hands down her back to her bottom.

They made eye contact.

She raised her eyebrow.

"Are you thinking of cancelling your plans for this afternoon." Her hair sat flirtatiously around her shoulders.

"If I could, I would."

Unbuttoning Dmitry's shirt, she pulled the fine clothing from his body revealing his massive chest. She reached for his belt and pulled him closer. The smell of his cologne danced about her nose. She inhaled his fragrance and bit her lip.

"Can you...cancel?" she asked suggestively.

Dmitry gave a devilish grin and licked his lips. His voice was low and baritone. "If I could, you'd already be screaming and crawling the walls, my dear." He tapped her behind softly, indicating his commitment to his previous engagement.

Sulking, Royal let go of his belt and watched him walk into the large bathroom. He smiled playfully at her and closed the gold double doors behind him. Defeated, she slumped down in the bed. It was highly unlike Dmitry to turn her down. He must have had something very important to do. And what did she have to do?

It was snowing like crazy, the skies were blackened with dark clouds, and she didn't speak much Russian. Maybe the brick wall standing outside of the hotel door wouldn't mind escorting her to the restaurant for something to eat? She sat back up on the bed and slipped on her shoes.

Chapter 18

Morning rays crept through the curtains of the presidential suite, as Royal and Dmitry lay wrapped in each other's arms snuggled comfortably in their king-sized canopy bed. Dmitry snored lightly, and Royal listened to the grandfather clock in the corner tick the seconds away. She had been awake for nearly an hour, tossing moderately under the strain of Dmitry's long arm wrapped protectively around her waist.

Twirling her fingers in her tangled hair, she thought about where she would have her blonde bodyguard Davyd take her today. She had seen many the sites in the last few days, even though Dmitry had cancelled on her repeatedly. He apologized everyday promising also to spend time with her the next, but everyday he left her in Davyd's care. To her surprise, however, Davyd had been quite the tour guide. Plus, he seemed to enjoy doing something other than taking orders from her anally-retentive boyfriend.

Today, she planned on shopping. Dmitry had given her the American Express Black Card and told her to "knock herself out". She was going to do just that. Evropeiski Mall was supposedly the superior shopping experience, and their stores would give her insight on what new things she could bring to *Dmitry's Closet*. Then she would go over to Tverskaya Street, which was filled with hundreds of shops and boutiques, where she would do more shopping, and then dine at the finest restaurant that she could find. She might even buy her bodyguard something nice.

Strangely enough shopping had become a well-proven stress reliever for her. She relished in the idea of seeking out bold statements made with expensive fabrics. Accessorizing with precious gems, bold bags and beautiful shoes made her giddy with excitement and temporarily satisfied some insatiable lust for more that dwelled inside of her. It was bizarre to her that such materialistic things brought her comfort, but they did, especially when she was not receiving ample attention from Dmitry.

Rolling over on her, Dmitry nuzzled his face down in her hair and pulled her closer to him, grunting as he did so. Royal looked over and touched his face. He growled, acknowledging that she was already awake. Sparkling diamonds emerged as the slits of his eyes opened. He gave her a content smile. She turned towards him and slipped her arms around his neck.

"Morning," she whispered.

"Good morning." His deep baritone voice cut through the silence.

"I'm glad that you slept later than normal."

"What time is it?" He raised up a little.

She pulled him back down. "It's early. Don't go yet. I miss you."

"Umm...I miss you too." He kissed her lips.

"Do you have plans today?"

"I have a few meetings."

There was silence.

"When are you going to start our vacation?"

"Soon. Isn't Davyd showing you a good time?"

"Yes, but I want you to show me a good time."

"Name a morning that I haven't."

Royal laughed. "I mean outside of the bedroom."

"Oh...I'll be finished with all of the madness very soon."

"What have you been doing over here?"

Dmitry eyed her curiously. "I've been consolidating some of my businesses."

"How many do you have?"

"Here?"

"Period."

"Many, love."

"Maybe I could help you with some of your businesses if you're having troubles, since I did an okay job with the boutique?" Her eyes were eager with anticipation.

Dmitry smiled and rubbed his hand down the side of her neck.

"Business is good, but thanks for the offer. I may take you up on that one day soon."

"Well, I just wanted you to know that the offer is always there, especially since I'm about to spend up all your money today with your little black card."

Dmitry smirked. "Spend as much as you like. It won't break any of my banks." He looked at his watch and sighed. "I better get up."

"Okay. I'm starving. Will you have breakfast with me before you leave?"

"*Dah*," he said, standing up naked beside the bed and stretching. "Come take shower with me first."

Pulling herself out of the bed, Royal followed Dmitry into the bathroom and closed the doors behind them. She felt his arms wrap around her as she did. He pulled her close to his body.

"Are you ready for that *good time* that we were talking about earlier?" he asked, picking her up off the ground.

She giggled. Of course, she was.

Chapter 19

Dmitry prepared to leave the building with his full entourage for his meeting. They were all in expensive black suits and dress coats, all standing tall and wide, intimidating the onlookers as they passed by quietly.

People whispered as they glided through the building. Mafia. Vory. Medlov. Men moved over to let them pass, and women looked on curiously.

Their footsteps could be heard in cadence down the long marble grand hallway, full of force and retribution for anyone who dared block their paths.

While the others relished the attention and the urgency that came with their presence, Dmitry walked confidently, never really paying attention to all of the attention that was on him. He considered the men's eagerness and their aggressive attitudes to be an attribute of youth, therefore brushing it off.

Instead, he focused on the important meeting that would convene in less than an hour. It was imperative that everything go as well as it had the day before in New York.

The heavy snow storm had picked up and violent winds ripped through the front doors of the hotel as Dmitry passed through them. The force of the winds waved through his heavy wool black coat, through the curls of his hair, straight through his suit to his bones.

Dmitry took in a deep breath, expanding his lungs in the cold, feeling the burn through his chest. He welcomed the cold and the violent weather. It was just a friendly reminder that he was home.

His eyes sparkled like blue diamonds in the snow, the blondness of his hair and the rose embellished hue of his

fair skin blended well in his native terrain. However, there
was nothing more natural to him that the tech nine automatic machine gun in its holster under his coat, the knife in
his pants leg or the Glock in his briefcase.

Many heads of Vory chose to travel light and let their
men carry the real hardware, but Dmitry believed that
leadership started with good examples. He insisted that
every man with him come strapped or not come at all.

Dmitry and Anatoly were loaded in together in the middle of the caravan of Mercedes trucks. Then they all were
carted off to a private summit with heads of the Vory v
Zakone, unsure of what the events might have in store.

Dmitry had not shared with anyone outside of his son,
the purpose of the meeting but insisted that it was most
urgent.

Anatoly sat across from Dmitry, shaved, showered and
suited. The change in his wardrobe had been deliberate and
demanded by his father. Dmitry had come to him a few
weeks ago with a card for a tailor and instructed him to go
there. *No one will ever take you seriously if you don't*, Dmitry said
to him in a low, baritone chastising tone.

That day, Anatoly had gotten rid of most of his favorite
clothes and started to wear tailored suits, made especially
for his body, for his job. Playtime was nearing its end for
Anatoly, and even he knew it.

"If all goes well, this will be the last time that you and I
will travel together," Dmitry said with a small, proud grin.
"To ensure that all is not lost in an ambush, we won't be
allowed."

"You mean there will be no more chauffeuring you
around?" Anatoly asked sarcastically.

"I know that you will miss it," Dmitry said jokingly.
"But I will need a new driver."

"Are you sure that you want to do this?" Anatoly asked, concerned.

"You act as though I'm leaving something that has brought me great joy." Dmitry chuckled a little under his breath then looked over at his son. "I couldn't be surer of anything. Trust me."

"It was your life for so long, though. How can you walk away? If she loves you, she can do so with you as the man you are. To reinvent yourself seems hopeless. It doesn't seem right to give up your life to enhance hers."

Dmitry was quiet for a moment. "My life is back in that hotel now. I'm growing tired of this, Anatoly. Yet, I've worked too hard to just give it over to someone who doesn't deserve it. You are my son. This is your rightful place. You are the rightful heir. It has worked out a lot better than I ever expected it to. Before you came into my life, I was sure that it would end...badly."

Anatoly nodded. "I only hope that I can make you proud."

"You've already done that," Dmitry confirmed.

"You know, for years, I was a snotty-nosed teenager terrorizing these same streets, dreaming about becoming Vory v Zakone, dreaming about meeting you and plotting on ways to make more crumbs." Anatoly looked at his father and smiled. "Now, I may very well be a boss at twenty-one years old. That sounds unbelievable."

"One of the youngest...ever."

"It's a big responsibility."

"Well, I have prepared you well. There is no better tutelage than my own. You remind me of myself, except for your height. You are barely 72 inches. That is extremely short for a Medlov, but your heart is like lion. You are a fighter and a leader. No one can deny this. You won't let them."

"And a killer," Anatoly added. Even he was not without some guilt.

Dmitry looked out the window and sighed. "That is one of the staples of this brotherhood, son. To kill or to be killed. Very few of us are blessed to die of old age."

Dmitry cleared his throat. "It's…how we are born. To worthless women, to lives of crime, famine, darkness. We are bred to be what we are now. You should never feel bad about that. It is the nature of the beast. Besides, no one can ever say that I gave you a silver spoon. You came in and worked as a lowly solider. You had to gain your respect, and you did. Now, these papers in my briefcase confirming your biological DNA link to my own, your loyal work to the Vory v Zakone, the blessing from the New York family and my final stamp of approval will end all doubt that your rightful place is at the head of your father's table."

Anatoly tried hard not to get emotional. Instead he nodded at his father and sat up straighter. He wished that some of the young men, who had made fun of him as a little boy when he told them who his father was but did not believe him, could see him now being escorted through downtown Moscow with Dmitry Medlov, the most feared of the Vory v Zakone in all of Russia.

Anatoly wished more than anything that he could see all their faces when he had stars across his chest. His mother would have died of pride. His younger brother would have wanted nothing more to do with him. His boys…they would have been so jealous – extremely envious of him. But he knew that all of his hopes were in vain. Nothing would ever be the same if he received approval today. He looked over at his father, relaxed and confident, even going before the wolves. How he wanted to be him one day.

There were supposed to be no meetings while Dmitry was away in Russia, and most of the council chose to adhere to his wishes. However, a small group led by Ivan gathered under the cover of night in the back of a small restaurant on the outskirts of Memphis to talk about the future of the Medlov Family without Dmitry as its leader.

Although all the men feared Dmitry, and rightfully so because of his iron hand, some longed to grow their legacy through other means that had been deemed *unstable for the Memphis operations* by the collective council many years before.

Ivan had picked up on this tension in many of the meetings and had provided the men an audience as soon as word reached them that Dmitry would be away for a few weeks. He was great at reading people, especially corrupt people. He had used his intuition on many occasions to capitalize on his own ambitions. This situation was no different. Now, he would use these disloyal bastards to get to his brother.

The rain beat on the building as they drank heavily under receded lights and soft music. Each of the three men, including Ivan, were a still a little leery of what they were attempting to do, even though Dmitry was thousands of miles away.

Each understood the grave consequences of his actions and insisted that at least four of their best men stand post surrounding the building. However, they all knew that should Dmitry come for them, those men would not be enough protection.

"Let's get started," Ivan began as his man closed the door of the private room. "I've spoken with several other men not associated with the Vory v Zakone around Memphis who would be interested in doing business with us. And they have agreed under one condition." He looked around the room at the eyes glued to his mouth and his every word. "The condition being that we eliminate Dmitry and any men who are in agreement with him. That would mean the entire council."

There was an automatic sigh of defeat. The condition was more than a notion for any of them. While it appeared that Dmitry traveled light, the truth of the matter was that he had over 200 men within the region were in allegiance to him. His organizational skills should have been the seventh wonder of the world. In a dangerous business of organized crime where men continuously stabbed each other in the back, Dmitry was no Caesar and no one had ever been strong or bold enough to be his Brutus.

"Dmitry's men are larger in number than our own by thirteen heads if you have forgotten," Nicolai, one of Dmitry's most trusted men said, taking a sip of his strong drink. "What we are proposing is the deliberate overturning of our own leader. To do that would send the wrong message to others who have long been interested in taking over our business. Plus, let us not for get the code. Thieves- in-Law. What we are proposing will cause us to face retaliation by New York and Moscow."

"Not if we do it the right way," Ivan protested. "New York has never been one hundred percent sold on Dmitry's tactics even if Moscow has. However, they have never gotten in the way, because he has always delivered. What we need to prove is that his new love interest is proving to be his Achilles' heel. He is one of the first in the states to amend the code and allow marriage, family and legitimate business, and look what it had done to him...to us. There was a reason that the codes were in place. Who is he to change it? That is reason enough in itself for him to be killed."

"I didn't know that you cared so much about the code," Nicolai said unconvinced. "Didn't *you* have a wife?"

There was a silence in the room. Ivan looked over at the man with a scowl on his dark face. Then he smiled. The deepness of his dimples and the curve of his beautiful face were over powered by the sheer hatred and malice that he carried in his soul.

"Had a wife? Yes, I did. Funny thing happened with us though. Dmitry killed her." Silence over took the room long enough for the clicking of dishes to be heard out in the main area of the restaurant. No one wanted to talk about Ivan's dead wife. Many had heard the rumors, but no one dared utter a word.

"So this is about revenge?" Nicolai pressed the issue. "Because if it is, you need to get in line. Many people want to kill Dmitry because of someone that they've lost. It doesn't mean that they will be avenged, especially by his own captains."

"No. This is about money. And the only way that we make more of it is to cost him and New York a great deal of theirs."

"Are you proposing that we become sloppy in our own business?" Max asked, another of the closest of Dmitry's council.

He had long wished for more money to pay for his mistresses and wife. The multitude of his harem was growing and his cash flowed was dwindling due to the aching recession.   Plus, his jealousy towards Dmitry had only deepened through the years.

Max had asserted to his wife and closest friends on many occasions that it was Dmitry's looks that got him as far as he had gone. Had Dmitry been fat like Max, who had been treated for diabetes, obesity and heart disease for over ten years now, then the story would have been quite different for him.

"I am simply saying it's going to take a sacrifice in our own daily business to get rid of him."

The men were not sold.   In fact, they were more resistant that ever.

"He'll only tighten the reigns.   Our incompetence all of a sudden will send red flags.   He'll cut us down where we stand."   Nicolai was ready to pull away from the table.   He had hoped that Ivan had a better plan than this.   "Please do not tell me that you have brought us down here for some paper thin conspiracy plan that will only land our heads on the chopping block, our families, and our men.   You have to have more than a few adolescent whores in mind and suggestions that we become careless in our finances.   Tell me something more or I walk.   Besides, if Dmitry would kill his brother's wife, God only knows what he would do to us."   He looked at the other men, reminding them of how close to death they were at that very moment.

"We also give him over, limb by limb, to the police," Ivan continued adamantly.

He was unmoved by their fear, unmoved by the mention of his dead wife.   His only goal was to get them in agreement.   Once the plan was laid out and complete, he would kill them too.   He smiled as he thought of it.   A whole new breed of Vory v Zakone would be put in place...all following him.   "There is an ongoing investigation on all of us right now. You. You're family. Your men." He mocked them.

"We're listening," Max said, concerned.   He reached for his friend Nicolai to settle down. Dmitry had always protected them from any real police threat. This was a new development, a reason possibly to validate their new alliance with Ivan.

"I don't have a lot of information right now, but I know that Dmitry was approached by two police officers at the Peabody only weeks ago. They know something and they must be close to producing evidence."

"How can we be sure that they are not his?"

"They are not." Ivan snapped.   He would not give away his sources. "All of us are being watched. Maybe even now. I'm sure that New York would want to end the investigation here and not allow it to end up at their front door. This is how we will couch our ambush to them when they become concerned about their white knight."

"So how do you suggest we give him over? His lawyers will find a way to have him out by night fall should the police, federal or local, pick him up. Plus, he has moles."

"I've set up shop in quite a few places since I've been here. But I made one house very special. It's full of under aged girls, prostituted out for the most depraved sex possible." He licked his lips and grinned like a chess cat. Many of the girls at the house had been used for his own pleasure on tortured nights when he would visit. "It's a cash cow, and the house is in Dmitry's name. No one knows about it. The girls are drugged day and night. The oldest of them is only seventeen. All we need to do is somehow turn this information over to the cops. He'll be faced with hard time. That will give us time to shut down his other operations and set up our own."

"So what are you waiting for?" Max asked. "If this is *all* that we need to do."

"I am waiting for the right time. When he returns, we'll set it up. I'll need your help for that."

"If that doesn't work?" Nicolai asked. "After all, it is his house. We cannot be sure that he doesn't already know that it's there. You underestimate your brother and you definitely underestimate the reach of the Vor…"

"If all else fails, we kill him." Ivan said, rolling his eyes. "No elaborate plan. We just fucking kill him."

"Just kill him?" Nicolai laughed. "How many have tried that? Numerous men. They are all dead. And I am not talking about good deaths. Their body parts are all over this city."

"I am his brother. His blood. If there is a man who knows how to get to him, I do. Plus, he and I have an unsettled score." Ivan took a shot of vodka and wiped his mouth with his sleeve. "Don't shit your pants, ladies. I don't need your help for this. I do it myself, but when I do it, I take his place, his house, his life. I have given you three plans that can go on simultaneously. One of them will work."

"Okay. What for us if you succeed…same percentage? Still there is no reason yet for us to consider joining with you." Nicolai didn't want to change one dictator for another. It was fruitless.

"More. A lot more. There will be less of us to deal with. If I kill him, you kill the remaining council. That shouldn't be too hard to do, considering that they hold on to his every word. They won't know what to do without him. We will usher in a new era for the Medlov family – one where we make all the money." He looked around. His hooded dark eyes gazed over them. "Agreed?"

"Agreed," the men said, looking at each other.

"Good," Ivan chucked. He raised his drink and toasted the men, mocking them inwardly. They were backstabbing, disloyal servants who had no right to be called Vory v Zakone. He would make them pay but not before Dmitry. It was all that he could think of anymore.

He had waited for his big brother to rise just to make his fall harder. The fury showed on his stone face. He looked off in the distance, thinking of his own wife and her bloody, limp body.

Dmitry deserved death, but it would not just be enough for him to suffer. His brother's sins would be revisited upon Royal also. Ivan ached to have her. The revenge would not be complete until he had ravaged her sweet little body in such a way that it would kill Dmitry dead without the use of a weapon.

Chapter 20

Two weeks had passed quickly. This was the last night that Royal would spend in Moscow. Her trip had been the most surreal experience of her existence. Dmitry had finally done as he promised and taken her on a grand private tour of the Red Square, the Kremlin, the Cathedrals, downtown Moscow, great five-star restaurants for fine cuisine, shopping sprees at the best boutiques, a walk in the snow-filled park, and he had topped the vacation off by sending her to a real fashion show.

Gostiny Dvor's atrium was packed the night before New Year's Eve. The 18[th]century architectural gem was filled with fashion aficionados speaking many different languages all at the same time. They huddled together in their packs, smiling, laughing and networking. People wore high fashion by designers that she knew well and some that she had never heard of before.

Waiters and waitresses bounced around the room with food and champagne; a live ban played a hip, Russia techno tune. And Royal had a natural high from simply being there. She tried desperately not to look like a deer in headlights. She only spoke English. Many of the people in the room spoke many languages and had a lot more to talk about than *Memphis*.

The notion was overwhelming to her that somehow even in all of her glamorized clothing, she was poorest woman of culture in the room. However, at that moment, she did not care. She was just excited to be there.

Her black cocktail bag rattled on her arm. It was her cell phone. Reaching into her purse, she was grateful to see that it was Dmitry taking time to give her a call.

"Hello." She moved to the corner to hear him better.

"How is you evening coming along?" he asked, raising his voice to speak above the crowd in her background. He sat across from Anatoly and a few of his men having a quiet dinner in the hotel.

Royal scanned the room. "It's too much."

"Too much?"

"It's amazing." She grabbed a glass off the tray as a waitress passed by. "There are so many people here."

"Are you afraid? Where is Nadia?"

"No, I'm not afraid. She's around here somewhere. I'm fine. Really." She paused. "I'm excited!" She put her digital camera back in its satchel, allowing it to rest from overuse. "I've never in my life been to anything like this. I'm still high on a super adrenaline rush."

"Good." He sat back in his seat and relieved the tension growing in his body at the mere thought of her being uncomfortable. "Are you going to buy something?"

"Yes. A few *somethings* actually. We won't be able to fit all the stuff that I've purchased on the plane. I'll have to mail it back home." She took a sip of her champagne.

"This is not a big deal. Just enjoy yourself. Let someone else deal with the logistics."

"Okay. What are you doing?"

"Having dinner with my son."

"Good. Tell him I said hello."

He smiled. "I will."

"Okay. I'll be back as soon as it's over. Can we spend some time together?" she pleaded.

While the trip had been called a vacation, Dmitry had worked the entire time, going into meeting after meeting with Anatoly.

"I was just about to ask you the same thing. I know that I've been really preoccupied. My apologies."

"It's fine, baby. I've had a ball."

"You're a very understanding woman, Royal."

She blushed. "I try." She saw her escort, Nadia, making her way across the crowded floor to her. "Well, look. I've gotta go, but thanks for calling."

"See you soon," Dmitry said smiling. He closed the cell phone in his hand and looked over at Anatoly. "She said to tell you hello."

Anatoly smirked. "She talks too much."

∞♥∞

While Dmitry did not attend the show, he did introduce her to the wife of a good friend of his who happily escorted Royal to the VIP event. She could barely understand the Russian woman Nadia, but she was very nice. She spoke with a heavy accent, always nodding her head and smiling as she talked. She wore a wedding ring that resembled the hope diamond and donned the finest furs and leather that she had ever seen.

Nadia looked like she could have gotten up from her seat and walked down the catwalk with the other models. No one would have known. She was extremely beautiful and tanned. Royal found that odd. She was tanned in this type of frost-biting weather.

They had seats by the catwalk, where they watched all the skinny, beautiful women prance around in front of them, showcasing the finest in Russian designs by the crafty heiress and teenager Kira Plastinina.

Royal had purchased a few of Plastinina's collections to put in her store a few months ago. She liked Kira's whimsical dresses and bright colors, but she was now sitting at her show, preparing to order off the runway.

After the show, as they were being escorted out of the building by their bodyguards into the cold brisk night, Royal caught a glimpse of an attractive man in a gray wool sailor's coat and a pair of jeans coming towards her.

As he neared closer, Royal realized that it was Dmitry, towering over the others in the crowd like the gentle giant that he was. He smiled when he knew that she had recognized him. He was without bodyguards or an entourage.

She moved away from the car in her long black gown towards him. Nadia's bodyguard quickly reached for her, stopping her from attempting to wander through the crowd. She looked up at the man and pointed over at Dmitry. He quickly released her, apologizing in his native tongue.

"Did you enjoy it?" Dmitry asked, nodding at the bodyguard as Royal walked up to him.

"Yes." Royal looked back over at the man one last time, before she took Dmitry's hand.

"Take Nadia home," Dmitry ordered him. "And Nadia, thank you so much for escorting Royal."

"It was pleasure," she said with a toothy smile. "*Poka!*"

Winking at Royal, she got into the back of the limo.

Royal looked over at the car as it pulled off. "I guess we're walking."

"This will be fine. You have insulation," Dmitry pulled at her coat. He leaned into her, talking under his breath and looking into her eyes. "I just wanted us to begin our private time as soon as possible. Tomorrow, we leave for Memphis, and we'll be stuck on a small plane with ten people for many long hours." His minty breath tickled her nose.

"I know," Royal huffed. "Moscow was starting to grow on me too. *Oh well.*" She hunched her shoulders and smiled. Her eyes sparkled nearly as bright as the diamonds on her ears.

Dmitry motioned away from the crowds of people outside loading into fine cars. "Shall we?" he asked, graciously offering his arm.

Royal wrapped her arm around his large bicep and stayed close as he whisked them through the crowd. They walked towards the lights of their hotel. Their footsteps could be heard on the bricked pavement as they moved further and further from the crowds into the silence of their own company.

Royal walked close to him, under his embrace. She was a little afraid to be out so late alone, having been used to the bodyguards now. But Dmitry walked carefree, unworried with being alone. His solace calmed her.

"Where are we going?" Royal asked.

"Up to the room, so we can get rest for tomorrow. Maybe we can have *nightcap*."

"Are you being a dirty old man," she asked, raising her eyebrow at him, recalling the night before.

"What? I didn't do anything." He smiled at her. "This time, I really do want drink. But I just felt like walking for change." He took a deep breath. "Slow down finally. It's been long time since I could do that, you know."

"I see you have on your Christmas gift," Royal said, observing the nice new leather carrying case for his blackberry.

"*Dah*. This was a very thoughtful gift. *Spasiba*. I love you almost as much as I love my phone." He smiled at her.

"Well, I knew that you needed a new one. You're old one was starting to look bad."

"You know, you always seem to get me the things that I can really use and that I appreciate it."

"Yeah?"

"Yeah," Dmitry repeated. "I am thinking that one day, you might get me a son or even daughter." He looked at her.

"You have your order mixed up. The cart is not supposed to go before the horse." She rolled her eyes.

"You seem sensitive about it tonight."

"I have my reasons." There was silence as they walked.

Dmitry stopped and turned to her. "This expression *horse and cart* refers to marriage right?"

"Right."

"You're very sensitive about that too."

"Most women are."

"*No one* is as sensitive about it as you."

Royal could feel the heat of her skin. How dare he? She tried to stay calm but it was not easy. She took deep breaths and focused on the beauty around her. No reason to ruin the night.

Dmitry observed her anger. He knew her well by now.

"Why are you so sure that you're missing out on something?"

"You wouldn't understand." Tears pricked at her eyes. She held them back.

"Understand? What is there to understand? Tell me."

"Every time I turn around, you're giving me diamonds, and at first, I didn't understand your generosity. But now I think I've finally gotten you figured out. You shower me with all these diamonds for my neck and my ears and my wrist, because you want to take my mind away from the one I really want on my finger."

She turned and started to walk again.

"I'm not avoiding it. I think of it probably more than you do."

"Why would you? You have the milk, no need to buy the cow now?"

"What? What is this about a cow? Horses now cows. I'm confused."

"I'm not playing, Dmitry. It depresses me. It…pisses me off. It makes me feel less than a woman."

Dmitry took her arm and looked into her eyes. "I would never want to make you feel less than a woman. That is not my intention at all, Royal Stone."

"But it *is* your intention to keep me a *kept* woman?"

"By whose standards are you kept. I don't believe in the world's social norms. I live by another set. One that has ruled me since I was a boy."

"And does this society of yours have wives?"

"No."

"That's what I thought. As much as I love you, don't you ever ask yourself if all of this will end? If I can't be your wife, then I can't be in your life forever."

And there it was, Royal's ultimatum.

Dmitry shook his head. It had taken her longer than he had first expected.

"Yes. You can. You belong to me. Tell me that you can't feel it? We have a covenant…you and I. Whether there is a ring on your finger or not, I will always be your husband. You gave me your virginity…I gave you my entire life."

"And I'm grateful. I mean, if it were my place, I'd have already asked you to marry me." She sighed. "But it's not my place, because I'm not the man in this relationship."

"Thank God."

Dmitry smiled. *Clever little girl.* She was determined to get what she wanted. She looked up at him and rolled her eyes.

He reverted back to his previous discussion knowing that it would only irritate her more. "So *cow*, children with you is not out of question?" he asked, holding in a chuckle.

"At this point, I'm damned certain that they are in the picture." Royal had learned not to expect Dmitry's constant questions to go anywhere. Sometimes, he just wanted to know. "I just want to be married first. And if you call me a cow again, I'll climb up your lanky body and kick you in the balls."

He did chuckle that time and put his hand over his groin.

"Whoa, horsey. I hope that we have a whole house full of babies with their *kept* momma. And they can have your last name. I like it more."

Royal was incensed. She snatched her arm away. "You pompous asshole!" Shaking her head, she stormed off. "How I could even wait on baited breath for you to ask is beyond me. I'm an idiot! Just as much of an idiot as you are. We deserve each other. We're both ridiculous!"

Dmitry stopped walking and watched her pout her way down the street.

"Royal. Royal come back," he called after her.

"No!"

"How about now?" he asked, smiling.

"How about now what?"

Royal stopped walking and whipped around. Her heart stopped. Dmitry was on one knee under a street light. His grin was even more devious that ever. He had a look of utter accomplishment on his face.

As she walked closer to him, he took off his gray wool skull cap, revealing his blonde curly locks. He looked up at her, still nearly as tall on one knee as she was standing. His eyes sparkled.

"Hi," he said softly. His dimples created creases in his jaw line.

"Hi," Royal whispered with her hands over her mouth in disbelief. "You really got my goat this time. Didn't you."

"Goats, horses, cows. This is why I love you."

"I love you too."

Dmitry cleared his throat. "Some people do this after dinner in crowded restaurants. I prefer privacy. We are here in the city that I was born, the city that created what I am, whether it's good or bad." He looked around and sighed. "So much has happened in the last few weeks, things that have come to fruition that have completed my legacy. It is time for me to move on with my life. I have worked hard enough, and I want to start this new life with you – the woman that I love, and a woman that is pure but is not all ignorant of the world. No man can ask for more."

Tears ran down Royal's cheeks. No longer cold or afraid, she clung to her coat shaking not from coldness but from shock. She stood in front of him on the sidewalk in the snow looking down at her knight in shining armor.

"Will you be my wife?" Dmitry asked, pulling a small box from his coat and opening it to show a very large solitaire diamond ring. Its simplistic beauty and grandiose size caught her attention instantly, but it was Dmitry's question that captured her. When she did not answer, Dmitry continued. He felt his strength weaning. He wasn't expecting her to say no. He began to stutter. "I… I know that you don't know what I do, what I've done, who I am. If you give me time, I will show you the man that I can be..."

"Yes," Royal said, sticking her left hand out. "Yes, I will marry you."

"Are you sure, because you took minute," he joked.

"Yes," Royal screamed and a laughed. "Yes." She smiled bright as he slid the ring on her finger and picked her up. The luminous d-grade diamond sparkled in the moonlight on her long slender finger.

"Come here," he said, holding her close. They hugged tightly. "You have made me very happy. Now I will have beautiful wife who has promised to give me lots of children and no more lip."

"I love you," she said with her hands around his neck.

"You do?"

"Yes," she looked into his eyes. "I'll always love you."

"I love you too," he said kissing her lips. He scooped her up in his arms and laughed and smiled at her. His deep voice lit up the night. "We're getting married!"

"Yeah!" Royal screamed. She looked at her ring again. "I've gotta get a dress," she said, shaking her head.

Chapter 22

There was severe winter storm circling Memphis. In celebration of the weather, Ivan sat on his rooftop in a lawn chair as the wind and snow beat down on the riverside. With only a black wool sweater and a pair of jeans on, he sat with a silver flask of vodka in the silence of his thoughts, gazing at the blackness of the Mississippi under the heavy winter night skies. Instead of sitting towards the middle of the building, he positioned his flimsy chair on the very edge of the rooftop with his feet propping him safely up on the flat surface. If he dared slip, he would fall to his death, but Ivan did not care. He liked the edge and all that it represented.

He looked down at the quick fall of the snow to the ground below, where cars lined the front of his condo nearly four stories down. His men were inside preparing for a war, and he was outside preparing for his brother's judgment day.

Guns had been shipped and stolen from many miles away in anticipation of what was to come. Many would still not do business with them until Dmitry was dead, but they sent complimentary weapons in hopes that Ivan would be able to do the job. Most doubted he could. Few believed that he would get out of this alive. He took in a deep breath and smiled. The thought of drawing first blood made his heart skip a beat. The gleeful feeling of crushing Dmitry under his boot was a far better rush than any drug could provide. It wouldn't be long. A week at most. Now that he had his plan in action, he just had to make special plans for Royal.

A mocha-colored black man walked out on the rooftop
and interrupted Ivan's silence. He was bald, tall and clean
cut with very dark, prominent features. His large frame was
covered by gray turtleneck and dark jeans. With him, he
carried two large guns in the holsters under his arms. He
coughed a little, hitting his chest as he did so.

"Люди готовы для вас," the man said in a deep baritone, offering Ivan his coat. His deep voice rattled the quiet
snow.

"Препятствуйте им ждать, брат," Ivan scoffed. He
offered his brother-in-arms a drink, but as usual the holy
man would not touch it.

Dorian was an old friend who had flown in from Moscow specifically for Ivan's coo. Before he left, he had
confirmed for Ivan that Dmitry was back in their homeland,
then he had quickly come to Memphis to set up shop.

Dorian was an expatriate of neighboring Sochi, Georgia
with a healthy appetite for building dirty bombs. His father
had been from Africa and his mother a quiet Muslim
woman and native of Sochi. Dorian had been a rebel during
many of the conflicts in Georgia and had since his teenage
years, very much like the Medlov boys, been involved in
organized crime.

Ironically enough, Ivan met Dorian through Dmitry,
but not in an amicable way. Over a decade before, Dmitry
sent Ivan to kill Dorian, but when Ivan arrived in the city of
Tbilisi, Dorian paid him well to allow him to keep his life.
The secret was maintained for a couple of years. And Ivan
thought it was all water under the bridge when they left
permanently to work for the Vory in the states. However,
their scandal was still uncovered.

Dmitry later found out that Dorian was not dead and
discovered the $3.5 million American dollars that Ivan was

paid only after Dmitry came in contact with the man in New York by chance. Small world.

In retaliation of Ivan's willful defiance, there was a bloody fall out between the brothers that landed Ivan in the hospital with his neck cut open and his wife dead. Dorian was smart enough to sneak out of the city and hide away in Thailand until it all blew over. Now, he was back to ensure that Ivan's final stand against his brother had a fighting chance.

"You still prefer to speak Russian brother?" Ivan asked, leaning into the edge a little with his feet.

"I prefer no one language over another," Dorian answered, looking at Ivan play with death under the slick snow.

"I've been forced to speak the language of the natives for so long until I sometimes forget who I am and where I come from. Dmitry wanted to come to the states, but not me," he said with a sigh. "I would like very much to go back to Russia when all of this is over."

"For good?"

"I don't know about all of that, but for a while, *dah.*" He pushed the seat back and stood up. "It's long way down, eh," he said, looking over the edge of the building one last time.

"Yes. So you should not tempt God by pretending that it's not," Dorian said, walking towards the door. "As I said before, the men are waiting on you."

"And as I said before, let them wait," Ivan said, taking another swig of his vodka.

∞♥∞

The limo pulled in front of Dmitry's home at exactly 6:00 p.m. Royal had fallen asleep on Dmitry's arm with her feet stretched across his lap. They were finally alone after many long hours of low chatter on the plane ride. When the driver opened the door, Dmitry rubbed Royal's arm and woke her up. She grabbed her purse and followed Dmitry to the porch, where the bodyguard sat with his dog. Nightfall had set in and the large compound was quiet and still.

"Hey poochie," Royal said, gesturing at the dog, who came over quickly and kissed her hand.

"He's supposed to be a guard dog?" Dmitry asked, shaking his head. "Are you sure that he even bites?"

"Yes, boss. He bites," the man said with a faint grin.

"Good," Dmitry opened the door for Royal.

While Moscow had been beautiful and different, Royal could not explain the joy of walking back into their home. The familiar smell of vanilla and jasmine filled the airy atrium. She looked around in awe and hugged herself quietly. Kicking off her shoes, she headed up the staircase.

"Where are you going," Dmitry asked, looking through the mail on the table.

"To take a bath," she screamed down as she ran up the stairs.

"You're like fish," he said under his breath. "Always in water."

The driver walked behind Dmitry and placed their luggage by the door, tipped his hat and left quietly.

Frustrated with the bulk mail he had been receiving lately, he shuffled through the pile and found a blue envelope with no return address. He picked it up and flipped it around, then slid his long finger between the paper to break the fold. There was a small white note inside the suspicious envelope that simply read in blue pen, "Call me as soon as you read this."

Dmitry took a deep breath and looked up the stairwell. Royal had retreated to her bathroom, where she would surely be for hours. He tore up the small piece of paper and stuffed it deep into his pocket, then made his way to his study, where he closed the door and went to his desk.

The fire crackled in the darkness, illuminating the large room.

He sat down and sighed, then dialed the number slowly. The phone rang twice then picked up immediately.

"Hello." The southern male voice sounded eager.

"How long has your note been sitting on my table?"

"One day," the voice confirmed.

"What is the problem?"

"Your brother is planning to wage a war on you. Two of your council members are in cahoots with him."

"Which ones?"

"Max and Nicolai."

"Impossible."

"Wanna hear the tapes? They met at Ginger's Pub out in Arlington maybe a day after you were gone."

There was silence on the phone.

"Leave Max and Nicolai to me," Dmitry said finally.

"And your brother?"

Dmitry leaned his large arms over on the table and crossed his hands. "Use the information that I've given you, but trust me…you won't need it until after."

"About that," the voice sighed.

"Yes?"

"He's trying to connect you with over ten whore houses here, one of which is selling off teenagers. We don't have proof right now. Can't ever catch anyone in the act, but he said that he'd come in and give testimony against you and proof this week."

"Teenagers?"

"Yep."

"My brother has something else up his sleeve. He would never cooperate truly with the police anymore than I would."

"Well, he's your brother. So, I hope you know him well enough to know what he's up to. You could just put this all on him and have him sent up to prison for a while."

"No. We settle this among the Vory not among you."

"Anyway you want it, chief. We just got word that you've arrived back in Memphis. Cops will be there soon with a no-knock. You better get your house in order."

"Fine. I'll call my lawyer." Dmitry rolled his eyes in aggravation.

"Everything's circumstantial right now. You won't even be held for even 24 hours. We don't have shit really. The houses are yours on paper, but there is no direct connect between you and the girls."

"How could there be? I'm not the one whoring them out; Ivan is. Have they been taken from the house?"

"The few that we could find. They'd been moved and not one of them is talking."

"I'll find out where."

"You don't have time. ETA is less than ten minutes."

"Ten?"

"Yeah, so you best be on your way. Make your calls quick."

Dmitry hung up the phone and reached into his pocket for the waded up paper with the number on it. Quickly, he threw it into the fire.

He had to make several calls before the police arrived. One to Anatoly to gather the council. One to Cory to watch over Royal. One to the head of his henchmen team. One to his lawyer. He wasn't sure that he had enough to time. He picked up the phone and sighed. He had to try.

Chapter 23

When the police arrived to Dmitry's estate in their heavily equipped SUVs and unmarked squad cars with their blue lights flashing, the gate was open for them so that they wouldn't break it down. Regardless of the chaos that he caused, he despised unrest around him.

The police quickly rushed in and pulled around the long drive, parking in front of the large mansion in an over exaggerated convoy.

In anticipation, Dmitry had conveniently opened the front door of his home, turned on all of his exterior lights and was having a cigar out on the front porch with his men when they pulled up.

To the officers' chagrin, the element of surprise had been ruined. Almost as if Dmitry had been tipped off. All of his guards had discarded their guns and stood outside in the front smoking cigarettes, eagerly waiting to be hauled downtown for a quick visit, according to their boss. They complied obediently, having been trained long ago how to deal with the shields.

Dmitry had switched cell phones and dumped his computer files. Everyone had been notified including his attorney.

He was ready for them.

As they came up the porch steps with guns drawn, he raised his hands and looked confused.

"What is this?" he asked as they turned him around against the front door and put the cuffs on him. His rights were read to him. Politely, he did not interrupt. There was no resistance. All the planning and gun power was for nothing.

A man of very muscular build and bo-legs in all-black tactical gear and his face covered in a black mask walked up to Dmitry and noted his cocky smirk.

"Happy New Year," the man said sarcastically.

"Just get this over with," Dmitry said, looking down and eyeing the man. "You all don't have anything on me. I'll be home before morning."

"Did you get the girl?" The masked man turned and asked another officer not far from him.

"I didn't know she was on the list."

The man smiled. "Oh, she's on the list."

Dmitry was suddenly enraged. There was no need to arrest Royal. She didn't know anything. She was supposed to come down from her bath and find them all gone. He would then return later and inform her of the awful mix up.

But that was the masked man's intention. He knew that Royal was unaware, but he wanted her to know. He wanted to talk to her, to get in her head, to turn her from her sanctimonious lover one truth at a time.

The resistance started immediately. Dmitry jerked and pulled one officer down trying to get into the house to warn Royal, but the masked-man clashed against Dmitry's giant frame. Their bodies collided and made a loud thunder. Other officers quickly piled on top of him. He still pummeled through like a linebacker on a scrimmage line. The last tackle took him down at the threshold of his doorway.

He hit the ground hard. The thud rocked the marble floor. With men on top of him and blood in his mouth, they struggled to get him up off the floor. He spit blood and shook off his dizziness. He was still fighting. The large group of men dragged him out to one of the squad cars, pushed him in and hit the roof of the car, signaling to drive him off.

∞♥∞

Relaxed and in a tranquil daze, Royal soaked in the water with her hair up in a bun and the candles lit around her with the music blasting on her IPod.

Her eyes were closed but every once in while, she would lift her hand out of the warm water and look at her engagement ring sparkling in the darkness.

She had never loved diamonds as much as she loved them now. Maybe it was because she had a whole chest of them given as gifts from Dmitry on nearly every occasion. Diamond rings, diamond earrings, diamond watches, diamond necklaces, diamond hair pins. Diamonds. Diamonds. Diamonds.

She hummed a soothing tune under her breath. Life is great, she thought to herself.

At first Royal thought that it was all too good to be true, but it had turned out to be her big break. She had the dream job, the dream fiancé and the dream home. She opened her eyes and grinned at the thought. She had it all.

She was just about to close her eyes again when she noticed a light shining from under the door. Why did Dmitry have a flashlight? She sat up in the tub as the door knob turned slowly.

"Dmitry?" she called out, looking across the bathroom for her towel. Her heart skipped a beat. She could feel the constriction in her chest. Something was not right.

The door flung open and four men barged in the bathroom with their guns pointed in full black tactical gear with their lights on their guns blinding her in a standard two-by-two cover formation. She screamed when she saw them, trying to both cover her body and prepare to be shot.

Launching a bar of soap, she hit one man in the head. Her shrieking cry and vulnerable state made another man almost lower his gun. Almost. He quickly refocused the infrared beam on her wet bosom. She was like a deer in headlights. Tears ran down her face as she screamed for Dmitry, but he never came.

"Someone call the cops!" she screamed, only covered by the bubbles in the water. Her lips quivered.

"FBI, maim," one man said, walking towards the bench where her towel had been placed. He grabbed it and threw it over to her.

Royal was confused. The FBI?

"Well what the hell are you doing in my bathroom?" Royal asked, catching the towel. She was too afraid to stand up and wrap herself, but she was certain that the men would not turn around and give her a chance to cover up. "Dmitry!" she screamed again.

"No need for the screaming, maim. We have a no knock warrant. We need you to get dressed and come with us immediately," the man ordered. His face was completely covered by a black mask only revealing his brown eyes.

Royal looked over at him, breathing hard and shaking. She wiped the water and tears from her face.

"Why? I haven't done anything?"

"Get dressed now, maim." The man signaled for the men to leave the room. He walked slowly out. His footsteps squeaked against the puddles of water now on the floor. He stopped at the door and turned around.

"Do you have something in this bathroom you can put on?"

Royal shook her head quickly. "No, the maid has already cleaned everything up," she sobbed.

"Where are your clothes? I can't allow you to start digging around in these drawers. There could be weapons."

"Weapons?   Who do you people think that we are?" She shook her head.

He did not answer.

"I set my nightclothes out," she said, pointing into the room. "There on the bed. My jeans and my sweater for tomorrow are on the chaise lounge chair." Her voice quivered.

The man walked into the bedroom, grabbed her clothes and her black silk panties and bra and brought them back inside to her.

She reached up and took the clothes, grateful for his compassion. Unable to control his virile instincts, he looked down at her wet naked body in the bathwater. So you're what all the fuss is about, he thought to himself.

"Look, you've got two minutes to get dressed," he said in a low voice. "We'll be right outside. Don't take my kindness for a weakness, Royal."

"I…I won't." She was shocked that he knew her name.

With a nod, he turned on the lights and left her alone in the bathroom.

After getting dressed, Royal was escorted in hand-cuffs by the police officers from her room, down the long staircase and out of her home. Angry and ashamed, she wiped the constant tears from her face and tried to hold her head up.

"Where is Dmitry?" she asked before they put into a black unmarked squad car with tented windows much like the one they had carted Dmitry off in earlier.

"He's already been taken downtown to the federal detention center," the masked man answered.

"Why?"

"Well, we can talk about that once we get you there. For now, let's just get you out of the freezing cold."

∞♥∞

Like something from a movie, the walls were gray; no windows were in the room and single halogen light hung from the ceiling. Dmitry found it typical and theatric.

A tall, Italian man with a bald spot in the top of his head and five o'clock shadow walked into Dmitry's room finally after looking at him through the mirror for a while, looking through is his file and comparing notes to the pictures of the young girls. He closed the door softly, sat down and took a sip of his coffee.

"Remember me from the restaurant?" he asked Dmitry.

Dmitry looked up from the table and smiled. "Sorrello? The sloppy Italiano from the Peabody."

"You remembered?"

"I never forget," he sighing. "Why am I here?"

"We have reason to believe that you have been trafficking underage illegal aliens into the United States for the purpose of soliciting sex for your profit. Here, we call that pimping. We have you connected to several drug dealers in the city, very recently preparing to go into agreement for the shipment of Meth to the Memphis area for distribution. Let's not forget the new chop shops in Binghampton you just purchased, and if that ain't enough, if it ain't illegal, it sure is a shame to have such a pretty girl next door locked in shackles because of your tricky ass," Sorrello said, taking a deep breath.

"You don't have shit," Dmitry said, checking his Rolex. "Chop shops, whored-out kids and meth. What do I look like to you…an Italian? Now, where is my lawyer?"

"You don't want to play ball, huh?"

Dmitry sat up in his seat. "I am an upstanding, tax paying American citizen. I have not done any of the things that

you have just suggested. You have the wrong man, cow-
boy."

"So how do you explain how we got your name?"

"Do not answer that," a short, gray-haired man said,
busting through the door in his tuxedo and overcoat. He
was Olich Slovinky, Dmitry's lawyer.

Dmitry rolled his eyes. "I was just asking about you,"
he said, scooting back from the table. "You're late."

∞♥∞

Agosto watched Royal through the glass very carefully.
Something about her said that she was a victim. Although,
he would not go with his gut yet, he was certain after his
interrogation, she would confirm his suspicions.

Sorrello was surely next door botching his investigation
with his hard-hitting Hollywood tactics. Agosto found him
irritating at most, but this was a joint-task force effort. He
had to put his personal reservations aside for the betterment
of the investigation.

The real work would start in this room, maybe not
through her mouth, but most definitely her eyes. Agosto
knew women. He had been married for three years to a
maniac of wife whom he could not help but impregnate for
the hell of it. He would handle Royal Stone with kid gloves
and get enough to put to Dmitry Medlov to jail where he
belonged.

Royal sat in the lonely, cold room with her head buried
in her arms on the table sobbing softly. When she heard
the door open, she sat up in hopes that Dmitry had come to
collect her, but it was just a cop.

With a nod, he closed the door and walked over to the
seat across from her. He cleared his throat.

"Want some coffee?" he asked, offering her a cup.

"Thanks," Royal took the cup. She wiped the tears from her eyes.

"Are you alright?" Agosto asked.

"No. I was…" Royal began to cry again. "I was in the bath tub when *they* came. Do you know how embarrassing that is?"

"It couldn't be helped. However, I gave you a towel," Agosto said apologetically. "It's more than I would give to most."

Royal looked at him and put the cup down. "What's your name, officer?" she asked with fire in her eyes.

"Nicola."

"*Nicola*, would you ever want your girlfriend to be interrupted like I was?"

"No. My *wife* would freak out." He shook his head. Mrs. Agosto was a firecracker. "She'd kill the messenger."

"Exactly." She pulled her hair from her face and looked away from him.

"But I would never put her in the situation that your Dmitry has put you in."

Royal was silent.

Agosto opened the files and began to place pictures of young women in front of her. She looked down at the pictures of the teenage girls in short dresses, lingerie and some with bruises and scrapes. He did not talk until the last picture was on the table, lined against the others to form a collage.

"Royal, how much do you know about Dmitry?"

Royal looked up from the pictures at Agosto.

"Why?" Tears started to form again.

"Do you ever wonder about where he gets all of his money?"

"His stocks. His businesses."

"His whores?" Agosto added.

"Dmitry is not a pimp," she said, pushing the pictures away. Now, he was just being preposterous.

"No, not *just* a pimp. That is actually a new niche for him *in Memphis*. Although, I think he runs a group out of Eastern Europe that is heavy into the prostitution. You may want to ask him." Agosto pulled another file out.

"Dmitry would never."

"Maybe. He has been tied to money laundering, extortion, drugs trafficking, illegal gambling facilities, nuclear weapons trafficking, precious gems trafficking and a host of other serious crimes globally. We just can't prove it. Everyone who has ever thought about testifying has been murdered. Plus, the way that the Vory v Zakone sets up some of its organized crime syndicate models, you never really can connect the top guys with the soldiers and the ground work."

"Are you insane? Listen to you. Listen to what you are saying." Royal shook her head.

"I know it's hard to believe. He seems like a nice guy. Treats you nice. But who would blame him. Look at you."

"You're lying."

"No, I'm not. There are only a few other people as major as your man in the Eurasian crime community, and he's worked with and for all of them. He is the true meaning of connected."

"If that's true, then why would he be out on the streets, just walking around like a normal person? Why in the hell would he be running a restaurant if he's so major?"

"Many crime families run their illegal businesses out of legitimate business store fronts. Many well-known Russian crime bosses have run them out of restaurants."

"Dmitry is just a normal guy. I would know," she argued as she beat against her chest. "I live with him each and every day. I would know if he wasn't normal." Tears ran into her mouth.

"Would you? What's so normal about Dmitry? You're just used to him, used to his lifestyle. In actuality, everything about him screams mafia. Love blinds people."

"I don't believe you," her voice was hushed.

He passed her a napkin.

"We can't prove that he did this, but you wouldn't want him to confirm this for you." He slid a picture of woman with her neck sliced open, lying on a bedroom floor covered in her own blood.

"Do you know her?"

"No," Royal said, letting the tears drop down on the paper. The sight instantly brought back thoughts of her sister and the man that she had killed as a child. She wanted to throw up.

"That is the late *Mrs.* Ari Medlov." Agosto met her con-fused eyes. He nodded. "Not Dmitry's wife. His sister-in-law, Ivan's wife. She was found in New York like this. No one knows why. Everyone thinks Dmitry did it. What a temper, huh? I've heard that he can be a real son-of-a-bitch. You might want to be very careful with him."

"Why are you showing me all of this? Are you saying that he's a... monster?"

"Haven't you been listening?" Agosto put the pictures away. "He's the worst kind."

"I want a lawyer," she said flabbergasted.

"You have your rights. They were read to you. *I know*, because I did it." Agosto slid a small picture across the table to her. "Do you know this guy?"

She picked it up and shook her head. "Yes," she said, handing it back to him. "That is Anatoly."

"Who is he?"

Royal was about to tell the truth, then she caught herself. Agosto could see it before she began to lie. "He's the butler or something like it. He does everything."

"Even kill?"

"I've never seen anyone killed." She snapped.

"Have you ever heard of the Vory v Zakone then?"

"No."

"He's a member of a very elite organized crime group that has connections globally. Just remember that."

"I don't believe you," Royal said, looking away.

"So, you want to end up like Ari Medlov?"

"No." Royal stood up from the table and walked to the corner. "He's all I have," she said, swallowing hard. "You don't know what that's like."

"To love someone? Of course, I know what that's like, but I don't think that he loves you. He's using you." Agosto stood up and walked over to her with his hands balled in the pockets of his jeans.

He was only inches away from her. She turned and looked up at him. Her face was red, puffy and swollen. But Agosto still thought that she was striking.

"Maybe you should just walk away before it's too late," Agosto quietly urged. "A nice girl like you doesn't deserve to be put through this. Find some new place to start."

Royal listened as he spoke barely above a whisper. She watched his mouth as it moved. She heard his words, but her thoughts were in a different place.

"It's not your fault. You just wanted a job. Just wanted a family. Someone to love you. You just picked the wrong guy. He took advantage of you." They made eye contact. He was working her.

His dark curly hair looked like silk against the contrast of his olive-toned skin. Agosto was a knockout, a little shorter than Dmitry but very well built. His bold Mediterranean features eased her spirit. He wasn't hard to look at or stand by. His cologne wafted up to her nose. He knew his charms worked. He moved closer.

Tears fell down her cheeks.

"If you're trying to get me to turn on him, don't. I won't do it."

"You don't have to turn. Just help us out a little."

"Help you?" She scoffed. "Help you how?"

"What's the code to the basement of your shop?"

"I don't even know that," Royal snapped

"Can you get it?" Agosto asked.

She looked up into his eyes bemused but didn't answer. Agosto almost felt sorry for her situation. He knew that she did not know anything now, but he was certain that if she tried, she could dig far enough to get him what he wanted.

Plus, Agosto found Royal incredibly attractive. Although he was a married man, he was *still* a man. He knew what he saw in the tub - a fresh, ripe woman vulnerable and beautiful.

If he didn't have control, he would have kissed her right then – made her feel what it was like to be truly protected. But he did have control, a wife and a strong desire to keep his job. Instead, he smiled at her and whispered, "Get me the code," as he slipped his business card in the back pocket of her jeans. His finger trailed on the denim.

Just then, Dmitry's attorney barged into the room waving papers and giving directives. The mood instantly changed. Agosto's magical hold on her was broken, and she was suddenly reminded of who waited for her outside of the door. Slovinky demanded in a high-pitched voice that Agosto move away from his client. In a theatric movement, he stood in front of her and wedged his way between the frantic woman and the cop.

Within minutes, Royal was released and followed her balding, frail Jewish lawyer as he and his team led her to Dmitry, who waited eagerly to have his fiancée back.

Keeping his distance, Agosto trailed behind them in a slow-paced walk as they darted down the hall. He wanted to keep his eye on Royal, wanted her to know that he was not afraid of them – not afraid to come after her.

"Are you alright?" Dmitry asked, standing as Royal approached.

"I'm fine," she pulled away from Dmitry's grasp and looked back at Agosto. He smiled as she did, grateful that she would even acknowledge him at all.

The two men made eye contact, but Dmitry was too proud to show his true vulnerability, especially in front of his future wife. He scowled at Agosto.

"Handle him, Slovinky," Dmitry ordered putting a fur coat over Royal's shoulders. "His presence *irritates* me."

"This *is* a fucking detention center. It's sort of his turf," she bit out, walking off from both he and the lawyer.

Dmitry sighed and followed with his lawyers in tow.

Chapter 24

The ride home from the FBI Detention Center was quiet for both Royal and Dmitry. Just like five hours before, the driver pulled into the front driveway of their home and let them out. Only this time they both were very somber.

Anatoly was waiting for them at the door, sitting on the porch clipping his nails while his men patrolled the perimeter. Royal walked up the stairs of the porch behind Dmitry but did not speak. She simply brushed past Anatoly when the door opened and ran upstairs. Dmitry watched her until she was out of his sight, and then followed his son into the study.

"Did you call the council?" Dmitry asked, exhausted.

"*Dah.* Каждое приходит."

"Make sure everyone is there, especially Max and Nicolai."

"Is it true?"

"Yes it's true."

The men went inside to talk, but Dmitry did not want to be long. He had a feeling that Royal was on the verge of breaking. She would not tell him what Agosto had said to her in the room, or from what his lawyer had said to him, why the Agosto was so close to her. Instead, she stared out the window and wiped her teary eyes the entire ride.

"I've taken care of everything that you've asked." Anatoly sat in the chair opposite of his father's desk and crossed his hands. "So, what now?"

"We wait." Dmitry sat down in his chair.

"Is Royal alright?"

It was odd to Dmitry that Anatoly would even ask about her. He never did. He must have seen it too. Dmitry rubbed his temples and tried to control the anger boiling in his chest.

"No. They burst into the bathroom with her naked pointing their guns and pulled her out."

"Naked?"

"No, but the whole time all I could think about was the fact that they were up there with her naked. Did they even give her enough privacy to get dressed or did they stare at her?" He paused in fury.

"Relax, father. I'm sure that they did not." Anatoly tried to calm him. "You know what I find amazing?"

"What?"

"Your brother is plotting to kill you; you face many charges that could have you caged in a jail for life like rat; the council is at each other's throats; we're about to enter into a blood bath, and you are concerned about who has seen the woman upstairs naked."

Dmitry looked over at Anatoly and frowned.

"I don't see problem with this," Dmitry said softly. "If it were not for the woman upstairs, I would have already pulled the knife planted firmly in back out and gutted my brother, Max and Nicolai along with anyone else who I thought was a threat to me."

"Well now, I don't see a problem with that."

They both smiled at each other. Dmitry sat back and sighed, releasing a little pressure.

∞♥∞

After talking to his father, Anatoly left the house quickly, and Dmitry headed upstairs to Royal. As he walked down the corridor to his bedroom, a strange nervousness overtook him, like when he was schoolboy. He frowned at the thought. Had this woman taken possession over him so that he was actually nervous? Such a thing had never happened in all of his adult life.

He walked into the bedroom to find her wildly packing her things. She was trying to leave. She was still crying, but now she was stuffing her Louis Vuitton bags to the brim with clothes. Dmitry instantly noticed that she had taken the engagement ring off and placed it on the night stand.

He walked over and picked up the ring, while she stumped around him, cutting her eyes at him every few minutes.

"Why is this off your hand?" he asked, sitting down on her side of the bed. He smoothed the sheets under his palm.

"Because I accepted it under false pretenses," she snapped, throwing more clothes on the bed.

"I don't think that you did."

Royal stopped. Her eyes were wide and wild. "Do you know what I found out today? The man that I was going to marry is murderer, pimp, mafia…psycho." She started to pack again, violently pulling one of the bags to the bedroom door.

Dmitry watched her as she struggled with the bag.

"I'm not a pimp." His voice was low and calm. He lacked defense.

"Then explain those poor, starving girls."

"They are Ivan's. He's trying to set me up."

"Oh, well that explains everything," she said sarcastically. "And the dead woman with her throat slit? I suppose that she was just part of the set up too?"

He was silent. Agosto *had* said too much.

"And the dead woman?" she asked again. That was the one thing that she hadn't necessarily believed – the only thing. It was far too gruesome to be real. It had been the worst of all the allegations.

She turned around petrified and looked at him. He was still sitting with the ring in his hand looking completely unmoved by the murder of an innocent woman. Yet, there was arrogance about him now that indicated that he had done it but that there was a reason behind it.

"Did you do it?" she asked in a near whisper.

"The question should be *why*…why did I do it?"

She dropped the bag and put her hands over her mouth.

"He said that I would end up like her. Her name was Ari Medlov, you fucking bastard! She was cut from ear to ear. How could you cut her throat like that? What kind of monster are you really?" Tears ran down her cheeks.

"If you would just let me explain."

"What kind of a man kills a woman? You're such a hypocrite. Always acting like you're above it all, when you're right in the thick of it."

"That was a long time ago."

"But you did kill her?"

"Yes, I killed her. But the *why*…"

"Then there is no why! She was a woman, not a man!" she exclaimed. "And you killed her. Now, I'm supposed to just forget it? Ignore it? Have you lost your rabid-ass mind!"

Dmitry walked towards her, but she screamed and darted out of the room. With no shoes on, she ran down the hallway on the marble floors as fast as she could, away from the bedroom. She looked back to see Dmitry come running out of the room behind her.

She screamed again as she made her way to the stairwell. Her heart pounded as she skipped every other step, trying quickly to keep Dmitry from closing the gap with his long stride. She nearly fell at the bottom of the stairwell. Feeling for her keys in her jeans, she headed towards the kitchen. If she could get to the garage, she could get off the property, even if she had to plow down the fence and the bodyguards.

"Someone help me!" she screamed.

She ran through the foyer to the kitchen and could hear Dmitry gaining on her. Suddenly, she felt his arms reach out for her and pull her down. She hit the floor fast, missing a face-on collision with the marble only because instinctively her hands slapped the ground first. She turned around and started to kick him as hard as she could.

"Calm down, Royal," Dmitry ordered, trying to get her to stop screaming.

"Get off of me," she screamed. "I hate you!"

She managed to squirm away from him and jump up. She grabbed a knife off the island bar and pointed at him. Her long hair was now down and flowing freely. Her shirt was torn and her hands shaking.

"Stay away from me, Dmitry," she screamed, taking a jab at him.

"Royal, what the fuck?" Dmitry's eyes were fixed on the knife. "Put that thing away." His voice was still calm and quiet. His continued sensibility frightened Royal even more.

"I *won't* let you kill me!" She was frantic.

"What? I would never harm you." He raised his hands so that she could see. "Look, baby. No guns, no knives. Just me."

"I saw what you did to her," she said crying. "Why?"

"Because the bitch was trying to kill me. She was a ruthless killer. She wasn't like you," he explained.

"You're a liar!" she backed away from him. "Stay away from me, Dmitry." She held the knife sturdy. "I'm warning you. I'm getting out of this place right now, and you're not going to stop me!"

Dmitry looked at the garage door. "I can't let you leave, Royal. It's not safe."

"For who? You?"

"No, for you."

"Bullshit! I don't believe you. I don't believe anything that you say." She shook her head and looked over at the door. How she wanted to just get away.

Dmitry walked closer to her. "I would never hurt you. You have to know that."

The bodyguards heard the commotion and entered the kitchen behind Dmitry. They were astonished to find Royal wielding a knife at their boss. They looked on confused. Dmitry shook his head at them and waved them off.

"Leave," he said firmly. "Now!"

They walked out slowly looking both at Royal and each other. Once they had gone, Dmitry walked closer to her. She kept the knife pointed at him, backing herself into a corner like a scared animal, desperate to defend herself.

Dmitry stretched his arm out to her and opened his hand. In it was Royal's ring.

"I'm the same man that gave you this ring. Please don't let them tear us apart," he pleaded. "Baby, listen to me. Listen. You're all that I have. I can't lose you. I can't live without you."

"The man that gave me this ring is a monster," she said crying. She wiped her eyes. "He's a liar! To think that I actually trusted you."

Dmitry shook his head. It killed him to hear her say the words. The knife would only quicken his suffering. He walked all the way up to her with his dress shirt now torn open revealing his rippled, tattooed chest.

"If you believe that I would ever harm you, go ahead. Kill me now," he said solemnly.

Royal cried, still holding the knife as he approached. He did not realize just how frightened she was of him until he got closer and realized that her entire body was shaking. What did Agosto tell her? *The truth, probably.*

Dmitry's large body completely overshadowed Royal's, dwarfing her existence in the corner. His size, his presence, his past all scared Royal speechless. She thought of the dead bloody woman and her heart nearly stopped. Revving back, she launched the knife into his arm as he reached for her.

"I told you to stay the fuck away from me!"

"Shit!" Dmitry said, grabbing his arm. The knife stuck out of his bicep muscle.

Royal tried to run past him, but he snatched the knife out of one arm and grabbed her with the other. Fighting, she tried to kick away from him, but he picked her up off the ground. He held her against her will close to him and carried her back upstairs. She screamed as he did, begging for help. Grabbing the staircase banister, she tried to hold on, but he ripped her away from it.

The bodyguards stood at the foot of the stairwell downstairs watching on as he took her upstairs passed them. They were all unsure of what he would do to her considering the blood pouring down his arm.

None of them had ever seen Dmitry interact with a woman on this level. No one had ever seen him argue with a woman ever.

Royal screamed as loud as she could and reached out for the men to help her as Dmitry carried her against her will, but they ignored her pleas. As much as they adored her, they knew their orders and their places.

If Dmitry chose to take her upstairs and kill her, it would be none of their business. The most that they would be responsible for was getting rid of the body.

Dmitry carried her crying and kicking to their bedroom again and slammed the door. Setting her down on the ground, he locked the door. As soon as her feet hit the floor, she tried to run to the bathroom. He grabbed her quickly. Upset and scared, she tried to slap him, but he caught her arm.

"Stop it," he said sternly. "Stop it right now. I won't have any more of this. You've gone mad!" He released her.

"I've gone mad?" Royal asked, pointing at herself. "I'm not the one who has…"

"Killed someone?" he interrupted. "I'm not the only *murderer* in this room – just the only one who does not judge."

"I knew at some point you would use *that* against me."

There was silence. He looked down at his arm.

"You killed your own brother's wife? That explains why he's so angry with you. Who would blame him?"

She could not let the subject go even if it meant her own death. She was baffled by the fact that he could keep something like that from her; deceive her with such disregard for her feelings.

"I didn't want to do it," he said, hitting the wall. A small painting fell on the ground and broke apart. Royal jumped, startled by his sudden anger.

"I know that she was my brother's wife. That's what hurts so bad. I had no choice." He tried to explain.

"Then why did you?"

"She came to my bed after I found out about one of Ivan's *many* side deals, and I was tempted by her and angry with him. And so," he rubbed his forehead. "I slept with her."

Royal eyed him as he continued. Even in the middle of talking about a murder, she was mildly jealous of the thought of him being with another woman.

"I had been with her all that night. Then while I was sleeping in my own bed, she tries to kill me with a fucking knife. While I was fighting with her, the knife cut her up pretty bad. I finally put it to her neck thinking that it would calm her down, but she was insane. She pushed against it and spit at me as it sliced her neck."

"You expect me to believe that she helped you kill her."

"It's the truth. No one believes me. She was *insane.*"

"So Ivan hates you for sleeping with his wife and then killing her, and he's the bad guy?"

"Ivan *is* most definitely the bad guy. He sent her to my bed to kill me. Evidently, his love didn't run too deep – not for me – not for her." He confessed it all without any need for probing. "My baby brother. The man that I had raised from a baby. I went after him. I was going to end this family feud for good, but while I was cutting his throat with the same knife Ari had used on me, he swore to me that she had acted alone.

"Normally, I would have finished the job just to be sure, but he was my brother and if there was a slim possibility of it being true, I could not risk it. So, even though I cut him, I took him to hospital. They said that he would be okay. And then I left and I came here. I could barely live with what I had done, even though it wasn't my fault."

"Is that why I'm in trouble? Why you wouldn't marry me?"

"Yes. I am what I am. I held true to my code, because it was all that I had before I had you."

"Besides murders connected to your immediate family, any others I should know about?"

Dmitry was silent and unwilling to answer that question.

So Royal continued. "And the girls aren't yours?"

"No. You know that my mother was prostitute. I would never…"

"And the mafia?"

"In a matter of days, I will no longer be the head of the Vory v Zakone here."

"*Oh my God*, Dmitry," Royal said, shaking her head. "It's true? You're like some Don Corleone?"

"It's overblown, trust me."

Royal was completely flabbergasted, looking at him standing by the door with blood dripping down his arm and ruining the carpet. She had unknowingly hooked up with one of the largest organized crime bosses in the United States. What an idiot, she thought to herself.

Dmitry cleared his throat and shifted a little, trying to ignore the pain. He wanted her to say something, anything that would let him know that she would stay. He raised his eyebrow and sighed.

"I don't want you to leave." His voice was just above a whisper.

"At least you know what you want," Royal crossed her arms. "You've been lying to me for months now, Dmitry. Why should I stay? I don't even know who you really are."

"I never lied to you," he growled.

"Bullshit. You lied!" Royal snapped.

"You'll never know everything about me, Royal. It doesn't work that way."

"If it can't *work that way*, then I don't want to be here."

"I'm not a child. I don't do ultimatums. You won't be able to stomp your feet and get your way. I know that I have spoiled you, but there has to be still some resemblance of common sense inside of your head. Look at the life you lead. Go on, look around." His voice rose. "What did you *think* that I did for a living?"

"What you told me that you did! I trusted you enough to believe your lies," Royal responded, livid.

"I never lied to you."

"Fuck you," Royal said, grabbing her purse. Tears started to form at the corners of her eyes again. "You're so full of it. I don't have to stay here and take this."

"You're not leaving until I'm finished!" Dmitry stood in front of the door. He breathed heavily and grabbed his arm. "Then…go if you must," he shook his head.

His words deflated her. She did not want to go, but she did want the truth, to be able to trust him.

"My life is very complicated, and I don't ever plan to tell everything that I've done. I will not confess my sins at your feet. Neither you nor I could take it." His eyes watered from the pain. "But I will tell you that I love you, and since the day that you said that you'd be mine; I've made plans to spend a quiet, safe life with you. It's just going to take time. I am what I am, Royal. I've kept that away from you for your own good. My kindness to you has been genuine; my love for you has been the same, but there is another side of me."

"Which side reigns supreme?"

"My desire to be rid of this, to live a life with you."

"Can you just walk away from all of *this*?"

"Yes. It's just going to take time."

"How much time, Dmitry? Am I going to have to wait until you're seventy to really have you? I won't kiss the ring, man. I didn't sign up for this." She turned away.

Dmitry tamped his anger. "When have I ever asked you to *wait* on me to do anything? I asked you to marry me, because I want to be with you. But it's good really that you know now. You have sometime to truly make your decision – now that you know. I just want to ensure that my son is left a legacy that is truly worth something regardless of your decision. Believe it or not, other people's lives are at stake here."

"You want Anatoly to live like this?" she asked angrily, turning back around.

"What I want is not important. The point is that he's doing it. He's a man, and I have to make sure that he is taken care of before I go. I owe him that."

"How do I know that you won't go back to living the way that you did before?" She sobbed. "It's not like I would ever really know. I wouldn't know now if the FBI hadn't held me at gun point in the," she kicked the side of the bed in frustration. "…freaking tub. I had lasers on my body for no damned reason at all, like I was a criminal!"

"I give you my word, woman." He walked to her slowly. "Give me a chance to clean things up. All I need is a little time, and we can leave. You told me that you wanted to go to Prague, eh. Remember? Well, let's go. Let's open a restaurant and boutique on a cobblestone street in Prague and grow old together chasing our little children around."

The idea rang in her ears. Happiness. A new start.

"Don't sell me lies, Dmitry. I can't take it," she cried, as he walked closer. She held herself and let the tears fall down her face. "I can't take it. Damn you."

"I know, baby. I would never do that to you." He walked up to her and held her close. Kissing the top of her head, he whispered. "I love you. I love you. I love you."

She cried as she buried her face in his large chest. In pain, he wrapped his arms around her.

"I'm sorry," he whispered. "For everything that I did, I'm sorry."

Royal wiped her face off and tried to stop crying after a minute. Breaking his embrace, she walked to the door and opened it.

"Get out," she said, pointing out the door.

"My first night on the couch?" Dmitry asked.

"You've got like six other bedrooms in this house. I'm sure you'll fit in one."

Dmitry walked to the door where she stood and kissed her on the forehead one more time. "So, you'll stay?"

"I need to think about it," she said, looking up at him.

"*Dah*, that's fair. You think. I'll go stitch up my arm." Dmitry tried to be understanding of everything that she had gone through, plus he knew that she would forgive him. If he didn't know her that well by now, she would have not been in his home. "You want me to have maid come up and unpack for you?"

"No, I'm not sure that there will be a need to," she said, closing the door behind her.

∞♥∞

While trying to tend to his arm, Dmitry drank a six pack of Foster's beer and looked out of the window above the sink at the backyard. Anatoly walked back into the kitchen from the garage and saw his father over the faucet with tweezers, scissors and thread. He sat his keys on the counter and walked over.

"What happened to you?" he asked unmoved.

"Royal," he answered, pulling the thread through his flesh.

He smacked on his gum. "She stab you?"

"*Dah*,"

"Why?"

"She's woman," Dmitry groaned, motioning for Anatoly to give him the antiseptic.

"She found out who you were, didn't she?"

"*Dah*," Dmitry said, pouring the chemical over his wound.

"Well then, you should be glad that she didn't shoot you." Anatoly walked over to the refrigerator and opened the door, chuckling.

Dmitry shook his head. Anatoly did not know the first thing about love. "She's a good girl. She was just very afraid. I can't say that I don't blame her," he explained to his son.

Anatoly sifted through the food to find a container of chilled oysters. Grabbing the small bowl, he closed the door and turned around to look at his father. "Are you sure that you're ready to do this? To give all of this up for woman who is… not even Russian?"

"You look around and see all these things. I look around and see a large fortress, keeping the whole world out. I don't want to live like this anymore. And yes, I know that she's a black woman. I've seen more of her than you have. I know. I don't care about that. I want woman who is going to stand by me, even when it's in her best interest to run. Let's not ever forget where we are from, boy. From the streets, lower even, from the gutters of the streets. We have no room to pass judgment on anyone, especially good people."

"So you're saying that she's worth it?" Anatoly was still not completely convinced. He cracked at his father.

Dmitry shook his head. "Yes, so get busy. I want this transition to happen now."

Dmitry's Closet
291

"The meeting is scheduled for tomorrow. We make the big announcement then."

"What time tomorrow."

"Six on the dot." Anatoly tapped his watch and left the room with his bowl of oysters, headed to the entertainment room to watch television.

Chapter 25

Dmitry decided instead of sleeping in one of the guest rooms to back go to his study. It was his *man cave*, full of reminders of why he had to press forward whenever times were hard. He had done it a hundred times before, slept in the place he worked. Tonight was no different.

Relaxed, his long body sprawled out over on the long leather sofa with his arms elevated on back of the soft wine-colored textile, looking up at the ceiling fan circling above him. The darkness of the room strangely brought him comfort. A world wind of events had taken even him by surprise. And while he had not allowed the feds get under his skin, Royal had. She was quite exceptional at that.

It was the painful tears and the scared stare in her face that disturbed him most. How did she see him now? Would she leave? Would she ever trust him again? He loved her dearly and treasured her like no other woman.

He rubbed his temples and growled. A headache was looming over him. He had worried less about murder than he did about loving her.

With his free hand behind his head, propped up on his waded up, torn shirt, he listened to the crackling of the fireplace and recalled each and every event of the day. Reaching over, he grabbed the crystal container off the table and winced; the wound reminded him of Royal's aching heart and bad temper. He laughed a little. She was such a firecracker. He poured the last of the brandy in a glass and swallowed it quickly. Drinking heavily was not one of his releases, but he needed to numb the pain in his arm and his heart.

Closing his tired eyes, he tried to cast his cares away and sleep for a few hours when suddenly he heard soft footsteps approaching on the marble outside his door. His eyes popped open. Royal.

The door knob twisted slowly, and a light appeared from the hallway. She stepped inside cautiously. Dmitry lifted his head a little as she made eye contact with him. She closed the door behind her and walked towards him. He followed the unintentional sway of her full hips and admired the silhouette of her body under the silk chemise.

"I came to see if you were…okay," she whispered, kneeling before him. His peering eyes sparkled like diamonds at her. Even now, she was in awe of how handsome he was.

Dmitry looked at her for a moment without saying a word. She glowed in the darkness of the room. The fireplace made her look like an angel. Her hair danced about her freely, skin free from make-up and resilient. For a moment, he forgot about the pain.

She took his arm and looked at the dressed wound. "I'm sorry," she said with tears running down her cheeks. "I tried to stay up there as long as I could. Even though you deserved to be brutally stabbed, I still felt bad about it." She fumbled over her words and swallowed hard.

Dmitry grunted then turned his body to sit up on the sofa. His muscular frame flexed as he moved. She stood up and stepped back. Dmitry automatically wondered if she was still afraid of him. The thought bothered him, frustrated him.

"Come here," he said, waving her to him. She moved closer to his body slowly and felt his long arm reach out for her waist and pull her to him. He rested his head on her stomach and rubbed her bottom.

Royal wiped the tears from her eyes and lifted his head where he could see her.

"Will you forgive me...for stabbing you?" she asked.

He laughed a little. "*Dah.*" His deep voice filled the room. "Will you forgive me for being who I am?" His eyes were wide and anxious.

"*Mozhet byt',*" she said in a soft voice.

"Perhaps?" Dmitry smiled. "Well, I guest that's better than *net.*"

"*Dah,*" she said again.

"You know your Russian is very limited for a woman who lives with me."

"I'm sure I'll learn." She nodded.

Dmitry rubbed her back and ran his hand down her leg. He smelled the perfume on her body and signed. "Is this a peace offering?" he asked, pulling her closer.

Royal looked down and rubbed through his hair. "Would you like for it to be?"

"I need it be." He focused on her body.

"I love you still," she whispered.

Dmitry's stare was carnal. Having drunk too much, he forgot his normal carefulness as he reached for the top of her gown with his large hands and tore it off. The fabric ripped as he pulled it away from her soft skin. The act only inflamed him more. His desire for her grew by the moment.

She was stunned at first but did not move. She gasped as he rose over her like a hungry lion. Her naked body was vulnerably exposed. She tried to cover herself with her hands, but he pulled them away, licking his lips as he drank her body in through his eyes. She looked up at him through matched hooded eyes ready to accept whatever he wanted to give. Everything.

He moved her hair from her face, off her milky brown shoulders to see her better. She was his gift from God.

He picked her up in his arms and kissed her mouth, forcing her to shed her civility. Her long legs locked around his waist and closed around his back.

Carrying her to desk, he pushed the contents to the floor, shattering the glass mementos as they hit the ground. Papers floated down to the ground around his feet. She sat back on the desk and rested her elbows on the surface, watching him change from a docile creature to a hunter.

Dmitry leaned over the desk, in between her legs and kissed her lips again, holding her face in his massive hands. She moaned under his touch and the pressure of his body leaning against her.

"Don't ever be afraid of me," he demanded, pulling her to him. Her body jerked. Her long hair fell over on the desk. "Don't ever think that I would hurt you. I would hurt myself first."

She said nothing. He spread her legs further apart with his thighs. Her back arched, and she ran her long nails over his bare skin. Sensually, he kissed down her neck to her collar bone to her aching nipples. Cupping her warm flesh in his mouth, he suckled her.

Biting her lip, she undulated under his body. She wanted him so badly now. Why did he make her wait?

Dmitry breaths became quicker as she came alive before him. Taking both of her large thighs in his hands, he pulled her body closer to his steely erection.

He could feel her long fingers on his pants, forcefully pulling them down. They hit the ground and made a jingle as his belt buckle hit the floor. He stepped out of them quickly and pulled her body to the end of the table.

Lifting her long legs to fit safely on his large shoulders, he pushed deep into her body. There was an immediate, collective sigh. Instinctively, she tried to pull away from the initial sharp strike, but he only gripped the front of her knees tighter and kissed the insides of her legs.

She screamed in unadulterated pleasure, looking at his sculpted forearms, his fatless marble frame and the shining of his Rolex reflecting in the fire light. It was embarrassing to admit how much his power and sex appeal suddenly turned her on.

His tattooed temple pulled back and crashed back into her body, bringing her back to the task at hand. She arched her back and bit her index finger as she absorbed his impact. Pain. Pleasure. Pain. Pleasure. Pleasure. Pleasure.

Dmitry winced from the twinge of his arm and the ecstasy of her eager body. His rhythmic jolts made her bounce on the table. Easing her back and forth with his strong hands, he felt her begin to shiver. She moaned his name, but he would not stop, would not let up. His motions became hypnotic; each caress, kiss and thrust was filled with heart-felt passion that coupled with lusty exhilaration.

Royal's quiet moans soon became loud screams. The shivering became shuddering, and her body convulsed like she was the subject of an exorcism. Still he would not release her. His face was focused, drowned in sweat, mouth open, eyes gleaming like the fire behind them. She eyed him curiously of how long he would continue to punish her. The anger in his face showed that it could be a while, but her body would give out at any moment. When she could not take one more jolt, she reached out for him.

Dmitry allowed her legs to fall to either side of his waist as he leaned over the table to kiss her. She sat up to meet him. His tongue searched her mouth softly, awakening her senses with every taste. She whimpered in his embrace, feeling his large hands search her body, pull and rub at the most tender spots.

Picking her up off the table, he stood up with her on top of him. They looked at each other for the first time as he held her. Royal saw Dmitry, and Dmitry saw Royal. They were no longer strangers, just two people who desired more than anything to be together.

"Hi," she said, biting her lip.

"Hi," he snaked his tongue out the side of his mouth as it watered.

Royal wiped the sweat from his brow affectionately. He had all but destroyed her inside and out. He held her close as he made love to her, never taking his eyes of hers. She hugged him tightly, submitting to his will. He was far too strong of a man to fight and far too good of a lover to stop. He continued for a while, standing in the middle of the floor with her riding him without ever once shifting.

Finally falling to the gravity of the earth, she felt her body against the plush rug. The world shifted. She went from looking at the floor and holding on to his iron grip to catching glimpses of the vaulted ceiling. He laid over her, connected to her inner core, deep inside of her troubled heart.

Her screams started again and were intermingled with Dmitry's deep, masculine groans. Tears formed in her eyes as he continued. He looked at her with tears in his own eyes . In them, there was a glimpse of humility – sorrow for the way that he had deceived her. She had never seen him cry until tonight. It was frightening to her.

In the silence of the room, she held him tight as he moaned and tensed up, releasing himself into her body. His mouth converged on hers in a long, passionate kiss and deep, frustrated sigh. His deep breaths vibrated against her sweaty body. He covered her, hiding her from God and man. She looked up at the ceiling beyond his large arm and smiled. How could she deny him when he loved her beyond words, beyond barriers, beyond life?

Too weak to move, Royal stayed under him shaking until he finally sat up. She breathed free air as he did. On his knees in front of her, he wiped the tears quickly from his face, embarrassed that she had seen him show so much emotion.

He looked down at her with a now expressionless face and then picked her exhausted body up off the ground. She closed her eyes and lay against him nearly asleep. Naked, he carried her in his wounded arms, up to their bedroom.

Chapter 26

Ivan took a drag of his cigarette, while he watched the sun rise above the horizon. Spitting over the balcony, he propped his long leg up on the railing and listened to the local news on the television just inside the patio door.

Although there had been no reports of an arrest of his brother, Ivan's contact told him that Dmitry had been detained by the FBI. However, he suspected that it was not for long enough, so, he and his men had relocated in the middle of the night to a vacant studio apartment downtown. It was right under his brother's nose, but the last place Dmitry would think to look – directly across from the restaurant in view of everything.

Ivan's men were ready to battle and hungry to take over the new territory. They were not skittish like Max and Nicolai's men, and they were not blindly loyal like Dmitry's drones. His men were like him – opportunistic, ready to *carpe diem*. Most of them had no official ties to Vory z Vakone. They had no true understanding of the code, but they were aggressive, moral-less, vile creatures willing to do anything to make a buck.

Ivan preferred them that way, instead of true soldiers. He would have less remorse should he ever have to kill them all – all except Dorian, his only true brother, whom he would never kill. It was a pity that a division such as this had to bring them together and tear he and his real blood apart, but at least he did not walk away empty handed.

Dorian walked out on the patio beside him and took off his acrylic work goggles.

"The payload is ready," Dorian said confidently.

"Then it will happen today," Ivan confirmed. *"Doom's Day."* He smiled.

"Only this is no Normandy," Dorian said yawning. "I suppose I should get some sleep then. I've been up for thirty-six hours."

"After this evening, you can sleep for days. There will be no more threats for either of us."

"Have you decided about the girl?"

"Dah. She'll pay too. She'll pay for Ari." Ivan still said her named with reverence.

"I don't know if it's right. Ari was one of us – a killer, a warrior, part of the resistance in Georgia. This Royal doesn't seem to be a fighter at all."

"Do you say that because she's black, brother? Do you feel some sort of kinship to her?"

Dorian smiled. "No but if I did, I wouldn't have any shame in telling you. I just wonder if going after an innocent won't damn you."

"Innocent?" Ivan huffed. "Why do you think she's innocent?"

"I don't know her. I've only seen the pictures of her, but she doesn't look like she should be involved."

Ivan thumped his cigarette over the balcony and turned to Dorian. "Well if you feel that way, I would suggest that you *not* stick around for the grand finale. It might turn your stomach." He winked at Dorian and went inside.

Dorian sincerely cared for Ivan. He was like his brother, and he sympathized with him for all that he had lost because of their alliance, but it did not stop him from seeing that at times Ivan was evil to the bone. It was because of Ivan's malice that he decided that this favor to him would be his last. He would not have a hand in ravaging a young woman to avenge Ivan's murdering and conniving late wife.

∞♥∞

The sun rose over Dmitry's bedroom and casted a glow over Royal's naked sleeping body. Dmitry on the other hand had not slept since he carried her up to their room many hours before. Instead, he sat across from the bed in a leather-backed chair watching her sleep and thinking of what was surely to come.

Night had receded behind dawn's rising call, and Dmitry still had not moved. It was News Year's Day. He had spent the night before fighting demons of a past that had come back to haunt him at his most inconvenient time, and he still could not determine if he had won. While the beast he called his lust had been tamed, and Royal thoroughly satisfied, he wondered if the good feeling of the previous night would still be there with him when *she* woke.

Without Royal's knowledge, he had planned a very romantic evening for them the night before, but it had been rudely interrupted by a truck full of feds and a very sharp steak knife.

He rubbed his throbbing head and put down the pen and paper that he had used to write up some very important notes for his son and his lawyer to follow in the next coming days. His head was pounding and his mind raced like a pack of wild wolves…such was the life of a crime boss.

As the sun settled on her face, Royal turned suddenly in the bed. Her movements suggested a nightmare. She flinched and jerked as if she were in pain.

Dmitry sat up in the chair with his hands planted firmly on the armrests watching her, wondering if he should shake her awake. She turned violently again, then sat up on her own. Her hair bounced with full body as it nestled around her small frame, her perky full breasts and beautiful skin.

There was a short calm before the storm. Lazily, she made eye contact with Dmitry; then with a jolt, she covered her mouth and jumped out of bed.

He watched her long body stride through the large bathroom double doors and kneel before the toilet. Suddenly, he heard her coughing and her body up heaving the little food that she had eaten the night before.

Dmitry followed her into the bathroom and walked up behind her as she kneeled before the toilet. Lovingly, he bent down and moved her long, wild hair out of the way for her. She held on to both sides of the seat, feeling the cool porcelain on her long fingers while she coughed and gagged. The smell of the toilet water made her even more nauseated. She gagged again.

Dmitry walked over and ran a small hand towel under the faucet and brought it back to her. She took it and wiped her mouth.

"Thank you," she looked away from him.

"What's wrong with you," he asked, helping her up.

"I don't know. Nerves, I guess. You have worried the shit out of me in the last day or two." She sat down on the bench, while he ran her a hot bath. She refused to look at him.

"You're not a nervous woman." Dmitry sat on the edge of the tub. His eyes were critical.

"Could you get my robe, please?" Royal pulled her hair behind her ear and crossed her arms. "I'm freezing."

Dmitry raised his eyebrow at her but did as she asked. He walked into the adjoining closet and retrieved her pink terrycloth robe. Passing it to her, he sat beside her on the bench and ran his hands over his head.

He yawned. "You didn't drink last night," he said, watching her stand up and quickly cover herself.

"Probably something I ate." She went to the sink and grabbed her toothbrush. Her hands were still shaking.

Dmitry scratched his head. "You didn't eat very much last night."

"Well that's probably it then," she snapped.

She turned on the faucet and grabbed the toothpaste. Looking down at the marble countertop, she saw her tears fall from her eyes. She tried quickly to wipe them away. Looking back up into the mirror she saw Dmitry standing behind her. She turned around and looked up at him.

"I may have little firsthand knowledge in this area, but give me some credit, eh?"

She read his face. He knew. There was no need to lie to him.

"I told you the night that you proposed to me that children were not out of the question," she said, allowing the tears to run down her hot cheeks. "I'm sorry for not telling you. I wanted to. The detention center just didn't seem like the right place."

Dmitry scratched his stubby beard and smiled. "How far along are you?" He kissed the crown of her head.

"Two months. I found out right before we left for Moscow. I was going to surprise you last night at midnight with the news." She rolled her eyes. "But you ended up surprising me with your own."

Dmitry walked over to the tub and turned off the water. She looked at his long body as it slumped over at the news. All of that time he asked me for a baby, now he doesn't want it, she thought to herself sadly.

Dmitry took a deep breath and turned around. "I made you fall last night on the floor in the kitchen. I forced you upstairs. I made you scream and cry." His face was distressed. "I could have hurt you and the baby. I couldn't live with myself, if I did. I'm so very sorry."

Royal's face lit up. He did care. She went over to him and slid in between his legs.

"I'm sure that we're fine."

Dmitry grabbed her arm and pulled at her gently. "Please, tell me that you want it, even though you know what I am. Don't kill it. I beg you."

"Now you're being ridiculous. This is *my* child. I would never hurt it, and you know it. We were both orphans in a way, Dmitry. It's up to us to make this right for our own."

He shook his head in disbelief of his initial thoughts and how strong Royal was. "I'm committed to making sure that both of you have the best life that I can provide you."

"I know, Dmitry."

He touched her face. "You just don't know what you mean to me."

"No, but I'm sure in time, you'll show me." There was little enthusiasm in her eyes.

Dmitry sighed. She still didn't trust him, but who could blame her. He had lied to her, deceived her, endangered her and impregnated her. For the life of him, he did not understand why she loved him. Even all the money he gave did not supplement for the pain he had provided for free.

"*Dah*, I'll show you if it's the last thing that I do," he said, hugging her tightly. "Now, let's get you in bed. And I'll go and fix you some breakfast."

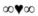

Renée locked the diamond collection in the safe and closed the small vault door. Cory had just informed her that Dmitry had decided overnight to do a complete overhaul of the shop without notice and would have the place closed for at least the next two weeks.

The large clientele list would be extremely disgruntled when they received notice, but Dmitry evidently didn't care.

"And I'm still going to get paid, even though we're *closed*?" Renée inquired.

"That's what Dmitry said. Evidently, Royal is a little under the weather, and Dmitry has hired a contractor to come in and do a big overhaul. He would have told you himself, if you had answered the phone first." He batted his eyes and turned off the lights to the boutique.

"I don't see why he wants to change it. He just opened. Seems like a waist of an investment," Renée continued.

She slipped her cell phone in to her purse and headed for the back door. "Maybe I should stop over and see Royal."

"Not today," Cory insisted as he followed her out of the store. "She's got a doctor's appointments."

"Oh," Renée was disappointed. She had not seen Royal since she left for Russia nearly three weeks prior. "Well, I'll just stop by tomorrow since I'm off *with pay*." She looked at him and raised her eyebrow.

∞♥∞

Sorrello closed the door to the squad car and walked up the steep driveway of Agosto's Central Avenue home. He looked around the property suspiciously, wondering how a young detective could afford such a pricey neighborhood.

Agosto had a stereotypical, luxury southern home, complete with large white plantation-style posts on the front of the house and four very old rocking chairs on the porch; ivy vines grew up and down the sides of the house leading from a well-manicured lawn and garden that was at least a half-acre or more. Patriotic in stature, a large American flag hung from one of the posts, waving in the icy wind.

The dark brick house was three stories tall with huge white shutters on every window facing the front yard. Two large oak trees with swings attached to the large limbs stood on either side of the lawn along with an array of toys that lined the porch.

Sorrello was bemused. Agosto either married into money or was from money. Either way, his style of living far exceeded any lifestyle that Sorrello was used it.

As he stepped on the porch, he heard the dog in the back yard barking. Before he could ring the doorbell, a beautiful black woman in gray business suit with her hair pulled up in a soft ponytail and her neck adorned with pearls opened the stately white door and stood behind the screen door.

"May I help you?" she asked, her silky voice and bright smile warmed Sorrello's freezing body for a moment from the winter weather.

"Yes, maim. I'm Agent Sorrello. I'm here for Agosto, *I think*. Hell, I might be at the wrong address." He took in more of the mansion from door, instantly recognizing the large chandelier a few feet above her.

"No," the woman opened the door. "You're at the right address. He's in the kitchen having breakfast. Are you hungry?" She moved out the doorway and allowed him to come inside.

"No. I just ate some McDonalds." He passed her and came in contact with the fragrance of her Chanel cologne.

"*McDonalds*?" The woman snickered. "Agent Sorrello that is not a hearty southern breakfast. Why don't you come on in and have a seat. I'll fix you a plate, and you can eat with Nicola."

"Well, since you're gonna twist my arm," Sorrello said shocked.

The large diamond ring blinding him on her wedding finger confirmed it. Agosto had never mentioned that his wife was *black*, even after all of the snide remarks that he had made about Royal and Dmitry. He was terribly embarrassed.

Mrs. Agosto escorted Sorrello down the long corridor to the kitchen where Detective Agosto was reading the newspaper and talking to two little boys, who sat in front of him obediently answering their father. He looked up as his wife came through the door. Wiping his mouth with a napkin, he stood up and took off his reading glasses.

"Hey, man," Agosto said, pulling out a chair. "You're early."

"Yeah." Sorrello looked down at the handsome twin boys, who watched him curiously.

"My boys," Agosto confirmed, proudly acknowledging his two-year old sons. "Baby," he looked over at his wife. "Can I get another plate?"

"Sure," she said, going to cupboard.

"I really don't want to be a bother, man," Sorrello insisted.

"No bother. Ivy always cooks too much. It's good to have someone to help me and boys out." He smiled and took the plate from his wife. "Thank, baby."

"Honey, I'm late." She reached in and kissed Agosto's lips quickly. "Boys, put your plates away and let's go."

"Okay," they said in-sync, pulling away from the table and grabbing their small plates.

"Agent Sorrello, it was pleasure to meet you. You'll have to come by again sometime," Mrs. Agosto said, grabbing her briefcase.

"The pleasure's all mine, maim."

Agosto saw them off then returned to the kitchen where Sorrello sat at the table.

"Alright," he said as he made his way back over the counter. "You want some coffee?"

"Yeah, sure," Sorrello said, looking around the large brightly colored kitchen. "How old is this house?"

"Over a hundred years old."

Agosto sat the coffee cup in front of Sorrello. "Ivy made us move into it from down the street when she found out she was pregnant again. *We needed more room.*"

"Pregnant? She doesn't look pregnant."

"She is. Couple months now."

"You guys are a baby factory, huh?"

"Yeah, guess so."

"Well, your place is sure nice."

"Thanks." Agosto smiled.

"Look, it may be a little too late to say, but I'm sorry if I ever said anything to offend you…now that I know that your wife's black…African-American." He stumbled over his words.

"It's cool, man. You didn't know."

Why didn't you ever say anything?"

"You have to learn to pick your battles," Agosto sat down in front of him with his own cup and scratched his stubby beard. "I don't work for the NAACP; I work for the MPD. More often than not, people in this city and on this force are going to have something negative to say about race. You can't always be the verbal advocate. You have to walk the walk."

"I hear that," Sorrello said, ready to move on. "So, have you heard from Royal?"

"No. I gave her my card. Something will pop up. You get anything on the radar from Dmitry."

"My source told me there's going to be a big meeting tonight at the restaurant."

"While it's open?"

"Probably going to close early tonight. I figure we can head down there a little after dusk." Sorrello scooped his spoon into the hot grits, covered in real butter and sprinkled with salt and pepper.

"Is it good?"

Sorrello looked up and smiled. "Does Ivy have a sister?

∞♥∞

The bodyguard at the front of the Medlov complex met Cory at the gate and escorted his little white Jetta Volkswagen to the front of the house. Once he was announced, he was sent down to the solarium to wait on Dmitry, who was still upstairs getting dressed.

Cory had never been to Dmitry's house, and in guests' normal fashion, he was transfixed by its size and architecture. He stood in the large glass room admiring the beautiful flowers and plants and looking out into the vast, finely manicured back yard. With his hands tucked into his pockets, he marveled at what money could buy. Calm. Peace. The ability to forget that a war was waging only feet from your door step.

Cory considered himself to be a good cop in a bad situation. He had chosen his mother's life over his moral obligations and only hoped that in the end, he did not have to pay the ultimate price for his choices. And no matter what, his mother would be alive; that was all that truly mattered. However, looking at the lavish lifestyle of his pseudo-boss, he often wondered if a fifty-grand-a-year job was good enough, when he could clearly make more for his children and his wife working on the other side of the law.

"So, you got my message," Dmitry said, walking into the room, fully dressed in a YSL black suit and tie.

Cory turned quickly from the view. "Yeah. The shop is closed."

Dmitry walked up to Cory with a large envelope in his hand and passed it to him. He stopped and looked at the sun shining through the glass panes.

"Beautiful, isn't it? I never get a chance to come down here anymore, but I've always loved this room. When I bought the home, this was the best selling point for me. I, of course, had to make some alterations and get thicker glass," he tapped his knuckles on the bullet-proof window. "You can never be too safe when you're a gun dealer."

"I've never been in a solarium this damn big in a house." Cory shook his head.

"Well, now you have." Dmitry snapped his fingers and the man standing in the doorway brought Cory a small leather satchel. "Anatoly cannot stay here and watch over Royal because his obligation is to the men, *but you can*. I don't have any weapons in this house outside of the ones that the men carry on them, which are registered for liability reasons with the feds. So, this is a little insurance for me while we are gone today."

Cory looked in the bag to find four Glocks and stocked clips for his use.

"This is a lot of fire power. Are we expecting someone?"

"No. But I'd rather be safe than sorry." Dmitry turned and walked to door with his bodyguards. "She's pregnant, you know." He stopped and looked back, faintly showing a proud smile.

Cory looked up surprised. "Wow. Congrats."

"You have to protect her with your life, Cory, until I can get her out of Memphis for good."

"What's my cover story?"

"You've just come to visit her while the shop is being worked on. Stay by her side until I return."

"I will," Cory committed.

Dmitry nodded his head. "Good. There are guards around the perimeter of the home. No one should disturb you. Should they... use the guns and call me immediately. If I can't get to her, you know what to do."

"Yeah. I know the drill."

"Thank you. You have been most reliable." With that Dmitry walked out of the room, and left Cory alone.

When Cory was sure that Dmitry had gone for good, he curiously opened the large envelope to find bundles of crisp one hundred dollar bills and a note that said, "For your trouble."

Retirement looked closer than expected for him. He nodded his head, feeling a little better about his decision, better about his position in general.

∞♥∞

Dmitry found Royal upstairs in her little office before he left. With the news of the baby and the move, she was anxious to get started on a new business plan for a shop in Prague. The idea of owning a shop in another country scared her senseless and excited her at the same time.

She sat typing away at her computer behind her desk and looking down on the notes that she had written in her notebook hours before.

She looked up when Dmitry walked inside of the room. He was different now, wearing a different face, one she had only learned recently. He was immaculate in his suit, commanding in with his regal looks.

"You look different now that I know what you are," she said absently.

"How?" He walked over to her with a large Louis Vuiton bag in his hand.

"Maybe like Eve saw Adam after she ate the apple," she raised her brow and sighed.

"This is not good analogy. They both ate apple in that parable. You didn't expose anything life altering. That was all me."

"Are you forgetting the baby?"

Dmitry smiled. No, how could he ever forget about the baby.

"What are you doing?" he asked, changing the subject. He could tell that she was still clearly agitated by the entire notion of his true identity.

"Working." Her fingers tapped the keys.

He walked behind the desk, set the bag beside her and placed his large hands on her shoulders. "I have a lot of loose ends to take care of today."

She looked up at him.

"What does that mean, Dmitry?" She finally understood that he spoke in code, therefore requiring direct questioning of his activities.

"I'll be home late."

"Should I be worried?"

"You should never be worried. Haven't I always taken care of you?"

"It's not me that I'm worried about."

"Well I am."

"What's this bag?" She opened in and looked inside. Surprised, Royal looked up at him for an explanation.

"That is just in case, I'm *really* late getting home."

She stared at him quietly with tears in her eyes. "You can't just go off and leave me alone, you know. I don't care how much money is in this damned bag. It won't make a bit of difference if you're dead."

"I don't plan to die, and I don't plan to leave you." He took her face in his hands and kissed her lips gently. "There is a private jet waiting for you in the event that I am...." He looked down at the ground. "There is a new home for you in Prague, a nice shop already purchased. It's on a cobblestone road like I promised."

"What does any of that matter, if I cannot have it with you?"

"I plan to come back to you tonight and every night for the rest of my life, but should my plans change, I need to make sure that my child and my soon-to-be wife are protected and safe. There is enough money for you to make sure that you live well for a thousand lifetimes."

Royal nodded. "You have to find a way to come back to me, Dmitry." Tears fell down her cheeks. "Don't you love me more that you love them?"

"Yes. I do," he whispered. It was the truth, but he felt a strange betrayal to the Vory v Zakone for saying it aloud. It went against every code of the Thieves-In-Law to love and cherish her as much as he did.

"Then just leave with me now. We can get on the plane and go away and no one has to know where we are." Her words were covered in agony. She looked up at him in pain and complete confusion.

"Don't you know if I thought that could be, we would have done it a moon ago. They will only come after us, if I don't do this right. They will come after our child."

They were quiet. Their eyes read each others.

Royal finally gave him a disapproving look.

"Well, what more is there to say?" she asked.

"Say that you love me and that you'll forgive me for this, and you'll be mine forever when I return."

The tears rolled down her neck and onto her t-shirt. "I love you…I forgive you…." She bit her lip. "And when you come back, I'll be yours forever."

"I love you, too." He kissed her hands. "Forever."

Chapter 27

Near five in the afternoon, the sun had already set over Memphis leaving a clear, crisp night with faint stars in the sky. Cars busied the streets of downtown headed home from long days at the towering office buildings. Blinking traffic lights and street lamps lit up the skyline while crowds of people held close to their coats as they marched up and down the sidewalks headed to restaurants, bars and small shops that lined Main Street.

The smell of cooked food drifted from the kitchens of the fine eateries through the alleyways, tempting the homeless who huddled in corners near make-shift burners. Even the sounds of Creole bands, moved by Hurricane Katrina who had subsequently made Memphis their home, could be heard in the near by taverns playing a pretty tune for the happy hour working class. It was a pleasant evening overall. Uneventful and undisturbed.

For Ivan, the tranquility was the calm before the storm. He had been waiting all day, *actually a decade*, for the boom of life and retribution to come calling at his brother's doorstep.

He sat patiently waiting, watching the dials on the clock past slowly, until finally his call came. After he received his full report, Ivan left the balcony and walked into the large, empty living room where the men sat on old, dry rotted furniture loading their weapons. Impatiently, he knocked on the water-stained wall to get their attention. Dust and dirt fell to the ground as his hard knuckles hit the sooty wallpaper. Everyone stopped talking and looked over at him. He was grinning like chess cat with the cell phone in his hand.

"The show starts any minute, gentlemen. So, let's get to our places and prepare give downtown Memphis a grand experience." He sounded like a director about to reveal his grandest production, but he was in fact a cold-blooded killer preparing to terrorize the growing metro.

The men got up and scurried. Many of them chatted up amongst themselves in their native tongue, while Dorian surveyed the outside of *Mother Russia* restaurant with his computers.

"So, they did shut it down," Ivan said, looking at the computer, marveling at the high-resolution clarity of the screen.

"Everything is ready. All you gave to do is say the word," Dorian said, keeping his eyes on the screen, watching for any threat to the operation.

Agosto and Sorrello sat in their car watching *Mother Russia* restaurant from down the street. Eating warm peanuts he had purchased from the Peanut Shop, Sorrello yawned and stretched, tiring of the many stakeouts that they had been on lately.

"Maybe they changed the time?" Sorrello questioned his Intel and looked down at his watch.

"No, they're doing it tonight," Agosto said, tapping the steering wheel anxiously. "I can feel it, you know?" He looked over at Sorrello, who was rubbing the oily residue of the peanuts from his hands onto his jacket.

Agosto shook his head. "You need a wife, man. You're a mess."

"Had one before you were legal to drink, kid."

"Yeah? What happened?"

"The bitch left." He thought about trying to explain but decided not to.

"My bad."

"Ah, forget about it." He scratched his stubbly beard. "I can't say that I blame her. I've spent far too many nights in cars *like this*, doing jobs *like this* instead of being home with my family. And for what?" He sighed. "My daughter is almost fifteen now. And me...I'm just her ATM. She pushes my buttons, and I give her money."

Agosto listened attentively but kept his eyes on the restaurant. "I'm sure that you're more than that. She's just a teenager. That's the way that they are."

"No, I'm her ATM. She told me." Sorrello confirmed. "What about you? The job doesn't affect you and Ivy?"

Nicola smiled revealing his deep dimples. "Like you wouldn't believe." He nodded his head. "But I found a way to keep the peace at home *for the most part*."

"Really?" Sorrello was all ears.

"Yeah. Keep her pregnant." They laughed. "No, I'm just kidding. I...I talk to her. You know. I finally just started to let her in. I'm an open book now. So, she feels better when I'm late coming home at night or when I don't come home at all. She knows that I'm not out chasing ass."

"That's it?"

Agosto took a few of the peanuts from Sorrello.

"And...I...I pamper her?

"Pamper her?" Sorrello smirked.

"Yeah, excessively. This one cop shrink I was seeing after I shot a guy said that if I spent as much energy doing stuff for her that I spent doing for the force, I would be more..." He looked over at Sorrello, who listened with his mouth wide opened. "Never mind."

"No, go on. I've got a girlfriend. It might help. Really."

"Uh…okay…okay. She said I would be more satisfied if I knew that I was putting more work in at home than I was putting in on the force. It would balance itself out when I had to stay away from home."

"Did it?"

"Well, she doesn't make me sleep on the couch, and she acts like its nothing wrong. So, yeah, I guess it does work."

"What kind of pamperin'?"

"Stuff." Agosto laughed and hunched his wide shoulders. "You know…painting her toe nails, washing her hair, cooking her dinner…"

"You sound like a fucking maid."

"It teaches you humility."

"I don't know that I could do that. It sounds *emasculating*."

"Okay. When was the last time a woman asked you to give her a baby?"

Sorrello coughed. "Never."

Agosto laughed. "That's emasculating. My wife…she can't get enough of me. So, I must be doing something right."

Sorrello nodded. "Yeah, but damn. I mean, painting toe nails?"

"She can't reach down that far when she's really pregnant." Agosto explained.

"And she asked you to *give* her a baby?"

Agosto looked over and smiled. "I'm telling you. You start washing a woman's hair and shit, she loses her mind."

∞♥∞

The council had received instruction the night before to meet at *Mother Russia* tonight to discuss "new developments" within the Medlov organization. Rumor had it that they were meeting about Ivan. However, some other people suggested the meeting had to do with Anatoly. Regardless, they all were escorted by their bodyguards after dusk, carted in large black SUVs to the front of the restaurant.

One by one, they filed out of the trucks with hoards of men and were escorted into the building and into a private dining hall secluded in the back of restaurant. They looked around curiously. They were not meeting in the basement? Could it be that there was good news to share?

Nicolai and his men were especially concerned. Had they not shown up, everyone would have known that they were traitors, and the wrath of Dmitry would have not only fallen on them but also their innocent families. It was imperative to come tonight, to state their case, deny any wrong doing and protect their loved ones. Everyone showed up except Ivan.

This was not shocking to Dmitry. He knew is brother well and had decided against meeting in the basement, because he knew it would be ripe for an ambush. He also knew that there were two officers in an unmarked squad car watching their every move. In fact, he had orchestrated this entire event around the fact that those men would be there tonight to witness his brother's revenge and to give him an alibi for what was sure to be a blood bath.

Dmitry knew that many of the men around the table were traitors. Regardless of the familial war going on

between he and his little brother, there would have to be
time to settle the score with the backstabbers who had
gone completely against the code.

Anatoly and his men made sure that the entire
restaurant was secured. The waiters and waitresses had all
been excused for the day. And the men were all alone. It
was time to get down to business.

Dmitry passed the bottles of wine to the men and
looked at his watch. Suspiciously, they all looked around
wondering what would happen to them.

"I brought you here for many reasons, brothers."
Dmitry looked over at Anatoly. "It is ironic that I call
you brothers when in fact my own sibling has not accepted my invitation to dine at my table tonight. But none
the less, we are here like we have been for many years."

"We've heard rumors," one of his council members
said. "Is it true that you were arrested last night?"

"It is very true." Dmitry smiled.

There was a rumbling of voices.

Dmitry raised his hand to silence them. "*However*, I
was released, because they have nothing on me. I am
innocent." His jaw clenched. "Speaking of rumors, I have
also heard them. Other ones." He looked at Nicolai. "It
seems that yet another one of you has decided to go
against me in hopes to overturn our little organization
and take control of everything that I have worked so hard
to build. This constant backstabbing has to stop. It may
be time to re-evaluate *certain* members of the council."

"I'm sick of this shit," one of the loyal council
members said, slamming his crystal goblet on the table.
"Who is the prick?" The vodka splashed against his
hand.

Dmitry smiled. "We'll get to that in due time." His wicked stare swept the room.
"For now, I'd like to talk to you about Anatoly."

The men looked over at the young man, standing in the corner of the room in a black suit, hair clean cut and guns concealed. His eyes sparkled with excitement.

"Come here, Anatoly."

"Yes, Papa," Anatoly responded, stepping forward from the other men who watched on confused.

"Papa?" one of the council men repeated. "He is now...a Vor?"

Dmitry stood up and moved out of his seat at the head of the table. He waived at the seat and had Anatoly sit down. The room became silent. Every eye was on the young man, on his dramatic transformation.

"Anatoly is not only Vor, he is my biological son." Dmitry laid his hand on his son's broad shoulder.

The men looked at Dmitry standing beside Anatoly and soaked in the news. Suspicions put to rest, both father and son smiled at the collective council.

"What is this?" Nicolai snapped. "Now, we're supposed to believe that you actually have a son? You have treated that boy like your slave for years. He would say anything that you wanted him to say. He is your lapdog."

Dmitry threw a piece of paper on the table. It was the DNA report certified by a Russian doctor that they all knew well. 99.999%. It was certified, sealed and signed.

"The resemblance is there," said another council member. "I would not have believed it before."

"*Dah*, it is..." another one agreed.

"So, what does this mean?" Max asked, unmoved by the show.

Dmitry leaned against the table. "The high council of Moscow and New York have approved Anatoly. He is a Vor now. He will no longer be my foot man, my *lap dog*."

"And you want him to sit at the table with this council? There is little room for another," Max said in a matter-of-fact tone.

"No, I don't want him to sit by you. I want him to lead you." Dmitry answered. "Here as my predecessor."

The men shuffled around in their seats.

Dmitry did not speak immediately. Instead, he poured himself a glass of vodka and let them men grumble. He drank quickly. Then quietly placed the glass back on the table.

"Max...Nicolai... I don't think that you have to worry about Anatoly and his new position. You won't be here long."

Anatoly took his gun from its holster and gave it to Dmitry.

"Both of you have been conspiring against me since I left for Russia. I have tapes," he turned towards the rest of the council. "They were planning on Ivan killing me, and they were supposed to kill all of you to usher in a new reign of the Medlov family."

All eyes turned to Max and Nicolai who sat together.

"It's a lie," Nicolai said, denying it all.

"Is it?" Anatoly asked.

"It is," Max said standing up. "I swear to you. You can't believe a thing that Ivan says. True, he did come to us, but we turned him down cold." His voice was trembling.

Nicolai looked at Max, stunned that he had admitted to any part of the discussion.

"Lying *suka*," one of the council spat.

"The tapes don't lie," said Dmitry. He shook his head and grinned deviously at the men. "And neither do I."

"Take them away," Anatoly ordered to his men, who quickly grabbed both men kicking and screaming. They dragged them to the stairwell where they all disappeared behind the large door.

"Remember, it's about what you don't have to do," Dmitry instructed Anatoly.

"He's young," another council member said unconvinced.

"He's loyal," Dmitry said proudly. "He has served you all well as my understudy, and he will serve you still as your leader. He has been approved. He has been steadfast. And gentlemen, he is my choice."

The room became silent again. The men thought to themselves.

"Agreed," one man finally said sighing. "I assume that he will lead under your tutelage or do plan to completely disassociate yourself from all that you have built."

"I will continue to be all that he needs to be, but he is ready. He knows everything there is to know."

"And nothing changes with our percentages?" another asked.

"No," Dmitry said quickly. "Nothing changes period, except that I won't be here in Memphis anymore."

"Where do you plan to go?"

"Away," Dmitry answered. "Prague."

The men looked up. Dmitry waited for the response that he so desired. While he could demand their support, to know that he had their approval and their word to follow his son would mean so much more.

"We were once young men. I think he will do well,"
another councilmember said. "Let's give it a vote. Shall
we?"

∞♥∞

Ivan stood in the living room listening to the entire
conversation taking place in *Mother Russia*. While Cory
had not managed to plant one successful wire, Ivan had
successfully planted many the night before because of
little Tatiana, the barmaid, whom he had been sleeping
with since he arrived in Memphis. It had only taken him
a few dollars and promises of a future together to get her
to bow on her worthless knees and give him whatever he
wanted.

However, he was absolutely flabbergasted now. The
little shit that he despised was his nephew. Ivan swore in
Russian and kicked the table. He should have known. It
should have been apparent to him. Dmitry trusted no
one, but he had allowed the boy to be so close.

Although he would never admit it, there was a strange
solemn void in Ivan's chest now, more so than ever. All
he had ever wanted was a family. And in a way, he had
one through these two men. It was a shame that he
would have to kill them both.

Ivan looked over at Dorian, still breathing hard from
his fit.

"Now," he ordered, turning away from the monitors.

At that moment, Dorian typed in a code on the
laptop and pushed ENTER.

∞♥∞

Agosto and Sorrello watched on carefully, blind for
the most part of what was going on inside the restaurant.
They waited patiently, not knowing what to expect.

Sorrello smacked loudly on his peanuts while Agosto

stared out the window. He listened to the sports commentator report on the game going on over at the FedEx Forum. The home team was winning. That had to be a good sign.

"No movement yet?" Sorrello asked, texting on his cell phone.

"Nope," Agosto growled. "Tonight could be a bust." He got on his radio. "Do you have a visual from your position, Eagle One, over?"

"No movement, over." The voice replied from the radio.

"Come. On," Agosto vented, hitting his steering wheel.

Just as Agosto laid his head back on the cushion of the leather seat and wiped his tired, watering eyes, a loud, earth-shaking boom erupted from the restaurant, following a plume of smoke and fire.

The intensity of the blast knocked the front windshield out of their car. Broken glass and debris flew in meeting them face on.

Car and fire alarms rang out instantly down the street. In a daze, Agosto pulled his head up off the steering wheel and pealed glass from his face. He looked over at Sorrello, who was knocked out. He tried to speak but his throat felt singed. He coughed and wheezed..

"Sorrello." He nudged the unconscious man. "Sorrello!" he finally screamed as he pushed past the pressure on his lungs. He shook the man violently, but Sorrello did not budge. Agosto spit blood out of his mouth and got on his radio.

"Officer needs assistance." He coughed. His head swam in confusion.

"Officers are on the way to your location," a voice responded.

Agosto opened the door of the mangled car slowly and crawled out on his hands. In pain, he lay out on the ground, against the hard, cold concrete and shards of broken glass and stared up at the starry night. He could hear police and fire sirens in the distance. Pulling himself up, he leaned against the car door and gathered himself.

The world moved in slow motion. He could barely hear the people running and screaming past him. He ran his hand over his hair and down his bloody face. He stood up and looked over at the yellow, red flame coming from the front of *Mother Russia* and saw the smoke billowing up above it.

"What the fuck just happened," he asked rhetorically, coughing again.

∞♥∞

The bomb had not been completely successful. While it had blown up the front of the restaurant and had the place set aflame, the center of the restaurant and the back where the men had been seated was only moderately destroyed.

Dmitry pulled himself up off the burning floor and crawled to his son, who had been blown into the wall by the blast. He crawled over several of his men and five of his councilmen who were now dead or unconscious from the blast to Anatoly. He picked the boy up quickly, gathering him in his arms without any effort, then threw a tablecloth over his head. The smoke billowed up and filled the restaurant and large blasts could be heard as flammables exploded throughout the building.

Dmitry knew that he would not be able to save everyone. He kicked and screamed at the men who had

survived to flee for their lives. As he passed through the
corridor to the secret back entrance, he stepped over
Nicolai and Max who had tried to make their way back up
to the surface. Dead or not, he would leave them there to
burn.

Hurrying, he and a few of his men made their way
through the dark smoke. With Anatoly still in his arms,
he kicked open the door that led from the women's
bathroom into the utility closet. It led them into another
dark room that was housed in the neighboring building.
They closed the door behind them and hit the lights. It
was stockpiled with munitions.

Dmitry laid Anatoly on the ground and went to a refrigerator to grab water. He opened the bottles quickly
and poured them over his son's face, wiping the soot
from his burns.

"Anatoly!" Dmitry screamed, shaking him violently.
"Anatoly!"

The young man moved around slowly. His eyelids
fluttered.

"Wake up, boy," his father demanded.

The crystals of Anatoly's eyes emerged from his slits
finally. He looked up at the ceiling and gasped for the
clean air of which his lungs had been deprived. Grabbing
his ribs, he tried to sit up.

"What happened?" he asked, pulling off his jacket.

"We were ambushed."

"Ivan?"

"Who else?" Dmitry stood up, relieved that Anatoly
was seemingly alright. "Can you get about?"

"Yeah, I think so."

"Good, then grab a few guns and follow me. I know
where he's headed. We don't have a lot of time."

∞♥∞

Ivan's men were already in position. The bomb had
done what it was supposed to do. Stun Dmitry's men
before the slaughter. They hit the stairs of the abandoned
apartment building in a single line, guns pointed and
lights shining. Their feet in cadence, they came out of the
front of the building across the trolley tracks and ran
across the street.

Police pulled up, meeting them head on. Blue lights
lined the street with loud sirens blasting. Fire trucks
pulled down onto the fire-blazed cobblestone. Before the
police could respond, they saw the men. Going to their
holsters, shots rang out.

Ivan's men split into two distinct lines, shooting large
high-power automatic weapons. The blasts from their
weapons sparked the dark lane like fireworks.

Police officers ran behind their cars. Shooting came
from both sides; police dodged as the men made their
way into the burning building.

They had one mission. To clean house. Kill Dmitry.
Kill Anatoly.

On top of the roof of the old apartment building was
one sniper. A slender blonde man with a slender nose
and dimple in his chin. He spoke little English and
detested all things American. A Ukrainian gun-for-hire,
he knew the entire routine all too well.

He pulled his black cloak over him and watched
through his infrared as the men made their way across the
street. Slowly, he slipped his finger onto his trigger and
breathed in. As he breathed out, he pulled the trigger and
hit a female police officer in the head. The second shot
hit a male officer in the throat. They dropped quickly,
causing the officers beside them to scatter. He smiled

and pulled the cloak further over him. He would pick them off all night.

The police officers looked at the tops of the building, pointing and calling on their radios for backup. Fear mixed with their adrenaline. Over the doors of their white Dodge Chargers, they shot their futile firearms at the men in black tactical gear and Kevlar.

One man dropped, shot in the leg by a police officer. The one in front of him released a large burst from his shoulder-balanced, rocket-propelled missile launcher directly into the large sea of police cars. Fire and screams erupted. Grabbing the wounded man off the ground, Ivan's team proceeded.

Agosto was on his radio ordering up a SWAT team to the location immediately but knew from experience that he had to get into the top of the building where the sniper was.

After he pulled Sorrello from the car and put him safely in the doorway of a dark building, he fumbled with his keys and opened the trunk, where he retrieved a large bullet-proof vest and gun and ran across the street to a neighboring building by the sniper.

Finding the fire escape, he jumped up and grabbed the cold stairs. They came down with a thud. Looking around, he climbed them carefully. Within minutes, he was at the top of the stairs. Gun pointed, he kicked opened the door and headed up to the roof.

∞♥∞

Dmitry and his men could not hear Ivan's men as they entered the restaurant, but they could see them on the monitors. They came through the flames with masks, shooting everyone who crawled about trying to get out. They were searching for him, determined to find him, even in the flames. He would have stayed and battled it to the death with the cowards, but he had to think of his son. It was his job to protect him now.

Dmitry spoke to the men spoke in Russian. Calmly, they cocked their weapons and checked their gear. He had been smart enough a few years back to purchase bullet-proof vests and jackets. While he never knew if they would come in handy before, he was thankful for them now. He typed in a detonation code into the security pad on the wall and ordered the men out. They had no choice now. The bomb would explode in less than three minutes, finishing what his brother had started.

Quickly, they headed out of the back of the abandoned building and loaded into their cars, barely missing the police, who were headed down the opposite alleyway to cover the rear of *Mother Russia*.

"All is lost," Anatoly said, looking out the window as the bodyguards drove.

"No, all is new," Dmitry assured him. "Head to my house. Ivan is going after Royal next."

"We should get you out of the city, sir," one of the bodyguards suggested.

"Take Anatoly if someone should go. My place is by Royal now." He looked over at Anatoly.

"No. I go with my father," Anatoly said reassuringly.

∞♥∞

Agosto was quiet as he leaped between buildings to surprise the sniper. But the blast from the last explosion helped give him a distraction. It rocked the entire street, burning alive all the people that remained in *Mother Russia* and injuring countless more outside.

The sniper stood up to look in sheer confusion. That was not in their plans. He spoke into his earpiece and began to quickly breakdown his gear.

Hiding behind a large vent, Agosto held his gun close to him as he waited for the man to pack away his gun. The rain started to fall on the already dreadful night. The cold air quickly turned icy slush. How he wished to be anywhere else but here. As he heard the man's footsteps, Agosto stood up and pointed his gun.

"Stop! You're under arrest. Drop your weapon and put your hands in the air!"

Immediately, a police helicopter emerged from the darkness with its lights shining on the rooftop. The wind whirled around the two men as they stood face-to-face. Seeing that he had little alternative and no will to die for Ivan, the sniper smiled and did as Agosto had instructed. Phase two of Ivan's destruction had already begun anyway.

∞♥∞

Royal's stomach turned over and over as she lay in her bed. Something was not right. She could feel it. Without success, she had tried to call and text Dmitry several times, but it went straight to voicemail. Unable to rest, she sat up and turned off her television. Cory was down the hall using the computer. She would have him run down to *Mother Russia* to get her something to eat and indirectly check on Dmitry. She slipped on her house shoes and closed her robe tight.

As she was about to open the door, Cory knocked and came barreling past her.

She smiled. "You were reading my mind. I'm starving. Would you mine..."

"Not now, Royal," Cory ordered. He peaked through her curtains out over the property. "Turn that light off."

"What's wrong," she asked, finally noticing the gun in hand. "Cory, what the hell are you doing with that gun?"

"There's been an...accident." Cory turned to her. "*Mother Russia* was just blown to shit. Dmitry's dead."

"What!?" Royal's heart sank. "Oh my God!"

He cut her off. "No time for that, Royal. Get dressed quickly. I've got to get you and that baby out of here."

"Where will we go?"

"I need to get you to the airport. The plane is waiting for you there to take you to Prague."

"The airport? But…"

He grabbed her shoulders. His virility evident for the first time. "Get dressed." His voice was husky and masculine, completely different from the Cory she had known before.

"I'm not going anywhere with you until you tell me who you are!" She looked into his eyes.

"I don't have time to explain all that to you. If you don't want to die, get dressed!" He released her.

Royal ran to the bathroom with tears in her eyes and grabbed a pair of jeans. She slipped them on without closing the door and grabbed a sweater from the dirty clothes hamper. Not bothering to put on her boots, she slipped back into her house shoes and grabbed her purse.

"Where's your other bag?" Cory asked, looking for the bag full of money Dmitry had given to her earlier that day.

"What other bag?"

"Get the money, Royal. You'll need it. Don't forget your passport."

She ran to the other side of the bed and grabbed the bag. With a look of total disgust, she followed him out in the hallway where two bodyguards waited for them with guns and ammo.

"I guess you were a part of this whole thing," she said accusingly of Cory.

"Not now, Royal. There are more important issues right now, like getting you out of here alive."

She looked around shook her head. *Everything that happens in the dark must at some time come to the light*, her adopted mother used to tell her. Well, the light at the Meldov house was blinding her.

They ran quickly down the hall. She clutched the bag close to her. Her heart pounded as they hit the marble staircase. Guns out, they headed towards the garage.

The men were in front of her and behind her, guarding her from whoever had gotten Dmitry. She couldn't believe it. Someone had killed him. Ivan? Dear God. He had warned her. She cried at the thought. She never even got a chance to say goodbye.

"Their already here!" a man screamed, coming from around the corner shooting.

"Head back!" Cory shouted, grabbing Royal. "Upstairs! Upstairs!"

The men turned and headed back through the corridor. Royal screamed and ducked as Cory pushed her to run. She dropped the heavy bag of money and fled. The hundred dollar bills spilled onto the ground in large, endless bundles and blanketed the stairwell.

Bullets whizzed past her impacting the wall as she ran up the stairs in front of Cory. Adrenaline pumping, she slid into the wall as she took cover. Cory shot back at the men behind him and followed her.

"Run, Royal. Get back to your room!" he screamed. "Get to a phone and call 9-1-1."

She ran as fast as her feet would take her to her room and closed the door. She locked it quickly. Grabbing the phone off the nightstand, she dialed the police.

Time seemed to slow as the phone dialed. She could hear the shots as they got closer. A man screamed. It sounded like Cory? Tears ran down her face. Shaking, she ran into the bathroom and locked the door. Trying to pry open a window, she waited for the operator to answer.

"911. What's your emergency?"

"There are men shooting inside of my house. Someone is trying to kill me!" she said, hearing her bedroom door fly off the hinges. She pushed against the window again, breaking her acrylic nails against the pressure. She cried out in pain and fear.

"Please help me!"

"Police are on the way. Where are you in the house?"

"Third floor. In the master bathroom."

The doorknob turned violently. She pushed back in the corner by the window with Dmitry's razor blade in her hand.

"Hurry," she whispered. "They're going to kill me."

Suddenly, the door was kicked open. Instinctively, she wanted to cover her face but forced herself to meet her attacker head on.

Royal breathed heavily, trying hard to fight the tears that ran freely down her face. She held the razor out – determined not to give up without a fight.

Ivan strolled in the bathroom alone with a large automatic weapon in hand and a clever smile on his face. His size was more intimidating than ever now. He wore a black turtleneck and a pair of black tactical pants that tucked into black steel toe boots. He made eye contact with her and licked his lips.

Royal swallowed hard. She wanted to meet her end with some dignity. Wiping the wet tears from her face, she took a deep breath. Her nostrils flared, she stood up a little straighter.

Ivan walked up to her, biting his lip and looking her over. His gun was no longer pointed. She was not a threat, just his prize. Reaching for her, he felt the sharp razor slice his face. He smiled as he caught her wrist, blood marking her hand.

Slowly, he bent her fingers back and made the blade drop to the ground. She winced in pain as he pushed her back in the corner and put his large hand around her warm neck. Like a rag doll, he picked her up off the ground. Nuzzling his head in her hair as he whispered.

"Do you know how long I have thought about us being *alone* together?" He kissed her cheek. "Hang up the phone, Royal," he said, licking his lips.

She put the phone to her ear, gasping for air. "His name is Ivan Medlov. He killed my fiancé, now he's going to kill me," she cried to the operator before she dropped the phone.

Ivan stomped the phone into rubble as he held her off the ground. "Kill you? What would make you say that?"

Royal couldn't speak. She kicked and struggled to breathe for air.

"Do you have anything smart to say today without your posse to back you up? Go on. Make a joke." He eased her down to the ground so that she could breathe.

She gasped for air and cried. "I know why you're doing this?" she said with tears in her eyes. "But I can't be responsible for Ari."

"What?" Ivan said amused.

"Ari Medlov." She inched down the wall away from him. "It's not my fault. *You* sent her to kill Dmitry. He accidentally killed her. How did all of that become my problem? Why are you after me?"

He smiled deviously. "Don't try to soften me up with reason and bullshit, Royal. You know why I'm here, and it's not to hear you psychoanalyze me."

Royal could see that he was dead set on killing her. She wiped the tears from her face. "You're a fucking psycho. You know that? I guess it drove you crazy when you realized you'd never be half the man you brother is."

"That's what I'm talking about. Don't be a pussy. Don't cry and scream for me to *please let you go*. You know I won't anyway. You can tell me if I'm half the man my brother *was* after I pull my dick from your ass."

Ivan grabbed her by her hair and dragged her out of the bathroom. Kicking and screaming, she tried to bite him and punch him.

"Let go of me, you piece of shit!" She slapped him in his eye as he pushed her. Ivan absorbed the hit and pulled her sweater from her body.

"That's it. Fight. Fight. Fight," he said, grabbing her by her waist and carrying her to the bed. "It's better when you fight, baby," he whispered in her ear. "I can't wait to taste you." She could feel his erection as it prodded against her back. She tried to pull away.

"You rapist!" she screamed fighting back.

He threw her on the bed and dropped the gun. She tried to run, but he caught her by the ankle and pulled her back to him. She kicked him in abdomen and spit at him.

His eyes were wild. He licked her saliva from his cheek and pulled a large knife from his side pocket. The gleam from the blade reflected in her eyes.

"We'll get to exchanging body fluids soon enough, bitch." Reaching back, he slapped her in the mouth.

She fell dazed onto the bed as she felt him pulling her pants off. Trying to hold on, she fought for her panties, but his large hands ripped them away from her skin.

"Dmitry!" she screamed out.

Three black Tahoe trucks pulled into the Medlov estate full of men. Dmitry was the first to emerge. He ran up the stairs of his home into the bullet-riddled front door. He stepped over one of his dead bodyguards and ran up the long, curved staircase straight for his bedroom.

The alarm was blaring, deafening everyone. His heart pounded. Was Royal still alive? What had Ivan done to her and his unborn child?

They heard shots behind them. His men turned and mowed down Ivan's men with merciless AK-47s. Dmitry never looked back. He ducked and continued upstairs. Leaning against the hallway entrance, he looked over the corner to see a couple of men running his way. Pulling a RAP4 hand grenade from his jacket, he pulled the pin and rolled it down the hallway. Shooting it, he stood behind the doorway as the hallway exploded.

Gun pointed, he emerged from the smoke, shooting the injured, bloody men as he passed them. He heard Royal screaming. She was still alive! The bedroom door was open, hanging off its hinges. He ran into room and pointed the gun.

Ivan stood behind Royal with his Glock field knife against her neck. The serrated edge flirted with her life line. He still had a smile on his sweaty face, enjoying every minute of the girl's torture.

Royal was shaking and naked. Her body had small cuts on it that had been carved by Dmitry's insane sibling. She would barely speak, angering Ivan, who wanted more than anything to hear the fear in her sweet, innocent voice.

Ivan rubbed his free hand in her wounds, making her cry out. "She is something else," he said, rubbing her stomach. "She begged me not to fuck her. Told me she was pregnant. What a trip, huh? Looks like the baby got to know Uncle Ivan a little better. We were practically *head* to *head*. By the way, I think it's a girl."

Dmitry pointed the gun at Ivan. His heart raced. If he missed, even an inch, he would kill Royal. All of this would be for nothing.

Royal sobbed. Her long hair wrapped around her and mingled in her salty tears and bloody face.

"This is between you and me, not her," Dmitry said, voice unbelievably calm.

"No, what just happened is more so between your little black bitch and me," he laughed. "It's good man. Really good. I'll give her that."

Dmitry moved closer, trying to get a better shot.

Ivan cut her neck slightly. "Don't do it. I'll slice her open, and I'll enjoy it."

Royal cried again. The pain paralyzed her. Blood trickled down her collar bone onto his large tattooed arm.

Dmitry stopped.

"Okay. I'm not moving. Just don't hurt her."

"I don't know, brother. I had thought about killing her, but I may keep her for a while. Afterwards, I could sell her. Get a few bucks."

Dmitry kept his eyes on Royal. She was starting to fade. She would faint at any moment. Her weak body was only held up by Ivan's strong grip around her waist.

"Royal, stay with me, baby," Dmitry said soothingly. "Don't give up."

Ivan snickered and kissed her head.

"Is this how it felt when you killed my wife?" Ivan asked suddenly. "Did you feel this *empowered* before you slit Ari's throat. It's something, isn't it? The power that women give you over them is *priceless*. You couldn't pay me *not* to kill her."

"Take me, Ivan. Kill me. Just let her go."

"You were already supposed to be dead. I paid all that fucking money to make sure that you burned alive or was shot to death." He shook his head. "Can't find good help these days. Now, I'll have to kill you and her *myself*."

"Start with me," Dmitry said, putting the gun down. "Start with me. Let her go. She's so weak, she can barely stand. She doesn't deserve this."

"Oh but she does. She wants it." Ivan grabbed Royal's breast. "She needs it after being with you." He licked the side of her face.

"I don't have anything. No gun. Please just take the knife from her neck."

Ivan watched his brother for a minute then ran his hand down the side of Royal's body. He enjoyed watching Dmitry in so much pain, having never seen the depths of him before. All he had to do was mention her name, and Dmitry cringed like he had been shot by a thousand bullets. The man who was once made of stone had turned to dust before him.

"Tell him how good it was, Royal," Ivan ordered, pressing the knife against her neck. "Tell him it was the best that you've ever had." He ran his hand down her inner thigh.

Royal closed her eyes. "Only you, Dmitry," she said in a whisper. She felt the knife as it cut into her throat for her disobedience. The taste of iron filled her mouth.

She heard Dmitry as he screamed her name.

"ROYAL!"

Ivan stepped back as Royal's tired, feeble body hit the floor beside the bed. He laughed loud and hearty, enjoying himself immensely.

Dmitry pulled the knife from his side pocket and charged towards his brother, screaming and groaning in agony. Ivan ducked. Catching his brother in the waist, he picked him up and carried him a few feet from Royal's body. Dmitry buried the knife into Ivan shoulder. He tore through the flesh until is stuck in his bone.

The two men fell into the table and slid on the floor.

Dmitry screamed out in pain, pulled Ivan's knife from his leg and rolled over. He was resigned to dying but not before Ivan. Not for what he had done to Royal.

Ivan pulled the long dagger from his shoulder and screamed.

"You fucking rat bastard!" Ivan screamed.

To their feet, they were again, moving around like angry wolves. Their eyes were planted on each other, shoulders hunched, knives pointed.

Dmitry felt the warm blood running down his leg.

Ivan felt the blood gushing from his shoulder.

Dmitry didn't wait. He stepped in and with a swift, stiff arm felt his knife cut Ivan across the chest, long and wide. He moved back out and swung with his balled-up fist, making contact with Ivan's ear. He knocked him off balance, dazing him.

Ivan swung and stuck the knife in Dmitry's chest, then pushed him up against the wall. Blood painted the both of them.

Dmitry screamed and head butted Ivan, then kicked him in the groin. As he bent over, Dmitry kicked him in the stomach and sent him backwards. Pulling the knife out of his own chest, he threw it right into Ivan's chest. There was a minute of shock.

Stunned and dazed, Ivan found the gun. Dmitry ducked beside the bed and pulled Royal's limp body to safety. He covered her, wanting badly to die with her or live with her but do neither without her. Bullets whizzed over the two of them as he held her tight.

Ivan stood up and spit on the ground. He wheezed as his lungs slowly collapsed.

"Son of a ball-headed bitch," he said, coughing up blood. "I'll be damned if I die without taking your selfish, worthless, genocide-fueling ass with me. Trust me. The world will be better for it."

Pointing the gun, he heard shots ring out behind him, through him. His body jolted forward and large bloody holes filled his chest. Sticking his shaking fingers in the wounds, he fell forward on the bed dropping his gun.

Cory and Anatoly stood behind Ivan in the doorway. Anatoly pointed a large chrome Desert Eagle .50AE pistol at his back. He had finally gotten what he most wanted, to kill his murdering bastard of an uncle.

"Hurry, Dmitry. Agosto is on the way. He still thinks you're dead. If you go now, you can get out of here undetected," Cory said, looking down the hall.

Anatoly ran over to help his father, but he stopped by the bed and looked away. "Shit," he said with tears in his eyes. "What did he do to her?"

Dmitry had dressed her wound and was applying pressure to her neck. He finally stood up with Royal's bloody wilted body in his hands.

"Oh no," Cory said, limping towards them, holding his bloody wound from the gun fight.

"Nothing matters anymore," Dmitry said, watching Anatoly grab a sheet and cover her.

Cory walked over and felt her neck. "She's still got a little pulse. We can get her to the emergency room, but we have to go now."

Anatoly touched her arm. "I'll take her to the hospital. You have to go, Papa."

"I have to stay by her side." Dmitry shook his head in despair.

"You have to go." Anatoly knew it was the only choice. "Go, papa."

"The bag is downstairs. The plane is waiting." Cory touched his arm. "There is no more that you can do here. We'll take good care of her."

"She won't live," Dmitry said crying. "She's dead because of me. My wife. My child."

Anatoly took Royal from his father's arms. "Cory take him now, before he goes mad."

Cory guided Dmitry out of the house into the Tahoe and drove off, leaving his son and the woman that he loved behind. The police could be heard in the distance approaching the mansion, and he felt like nothing more than turning himself in for the guilt that he carried in his broken heart.

"I am failure," he said, sitting back in his seat.

"You prevailed," Cory said, passing the police officers.

"I escaped. I am escape artist. That is all."

"Even if you gave yourself up, there is nothing more you can do for Royal. She will live or die without your control."

"Turn back," Dmitry said softly. "Sync up with Anatoly, if he has already headed to hospital."

"Excuse me?"

"Turn back. She will live or die, and I will be there for her as she was for me. The rest of my fate can be determined later."

"If I turn back, you could go to jail, Dmitry, for a very long time."

"I have almost one billion dollars. If I can't get a lawyer who will get me out, what good is my money?"

"Are you sure?"

"I couldn't be surer." Dmitry wiped his tired eyes. "Hurry. Please."

The Thieves' Code

A thief is bound by the Code to:

1. Forsake his relatives--mother, father, brothers, sisters...
2. Not have a family of his own -- no wife, no children; this does not however, preclude him from having a lover.
3. Never, under any circumstances work, no matter how much difficulty this brings. Live only on means gleaned from thievery.
4. Help other thieves -- both by moral and material support, utilizing the commune of thieves.
5. Keep secret information about the whereabouts of accomplices (i.e. dens, districts, hideouts, safe apartments, etc.).
6. In unavoidable situations (if a thief is under investigation) to take the blame for someone else's crime; this buys the other person time of freedom.
7. Demand a convocation of inquiry for the purpose of resolving disputes in the event of a conflict between oneself and other thieves or between thieves.
8. If necessary, participate in such inquiries.
9. Carry out the punishment of the offending thief as decided by the convocation.
10. Not resist carrying out the decision of punishing the offending thief who is found guilty, with punishment determined by the convocation.
11. Have good command of the thieves' jargon ("Fehnay").
12. Not gamble without being able to cover losses.
13. Teach the trade to young beginners.
14. Have, if possible, informants from the rank and file of thieves.
15. Not lose your reasoning ability when using alcohol.
16. Have nothing to do with the authorities (particularly with the ITU [Correctional Labor Authority]), not participate in public activities, nor join any community organizations.
17. Not take weapons from the hands of authorities; not serve in the military.
18. Make good on promises given to other thieves.

Chapter 28

There was complete media frenzy behind the bomb attack on *Mother Russia* and the Medlov compound. Outlets from across the nation stood outside of the gates of Dmitry's home discussing the murder of a young shopkeeper and the attempted assassination of a millionaire of questionable character with alleged ties to the Vory v Zakone by his crime boss brother, Ivan Medlov, who headed the Memphis Medlov Organized Crime Family.

Obviously, the media had it all wrong, which was good for the men who had survived the attack and for his son, who was now the head of the family, but it was not good for his most apparent and haunting dilemma.

For nearly 15 years, Dmitry avoided his name ever making one newspapers regarding his possible connections to the mafia, and now his face was splashed across CNN, MSNBC and Fox News along with newspapers nationwide. He had no choice. He had to leave.

Three months had passed and although the house repaired and the restaurant rebuilt, there were several undercover investigations going on by the MPD, FBI, ICE, DEA and the IRS. Dmitry was embattled, yet none of his worries outweighed the pain he felt for Royal.

He sat in the back of the limo as it escorted him now to the private airstrip, where he had made arrangements to fly to Prague to his new luxury villa that awaited him with a full staff and a newer life.

He also had purchased two large storefronts in the middle of Prague 1 district, where he had already started a new restaurant and an upscale clothing store called *Royal Flush*, just as he had promised her.

A staff had already been picked and both would be open within the week. Besides, he had done everything that he could here. *Dmitry's Closet* and *Mother Russia* belonged to Anatoly now. There was nothing more to fix, no more reason to linger.

"What are you thinking about?" Royal asked, taking off her shades.

Dmitry put his hand on her knee and sighed. "You. This is big move so early in your recovery. I'm not sure that you even need to be out of the bed."

"I'm ready." She rubbed her growing stomach. "I think we both are. This place is just a memory now. It's time to move and time for you to stop treating me like I'm made of glass."

The diamonds sparkled from her neck. Dmitry had purchased a three-million dollar diamond necklace, designed specifically to cover the large knife mark that Ivan had left when he tried to claim her life.

"Prague is a good change. Somewhere new where no one knows me or *you*," she said confidently. "I can feel it. Everything is going to be fine."

Dmitry raised his brow. "They know me, but there is no need to worry. I won't be *boss* in Czech Republic. I'll be shop keeper like you."

"Well, we'll finally have something in common."

The limo stopped on the airstrip and the driver opened the door.

"Mrs. Medlov," he said, offering his hand.

"Umm, I never get tired of hearing that name," Royal said, taking his hand and smiling.

"Good, because you're going to hear it for the rest of your life." Dmitry stepped out after her.

There was not one cloud in the sky, and spring had brought fresh clean air, warm weather and unexplainable beauty. Memphis was wonderful that way, always offering all four seasons in full. Royal would miss that.

As soon as the sun hit Royal's necklace, it lit up the airstrip. Dmitry smiled. No matter where she went for the rest of her days, he would make sure that her lifestyle reflected her name. She would live like a queen. He would see to it.

"Are you sure that you're ready to leave this all behind?" he asked, straightening his linen suit.

He stood beside her taller and more hauntingly beautiful than ever. His blonde hair brandished streaks of new gray. His eyes wore lines beside them where talons of life had clawed at his face in the middle of sleepless nights. But his heart was warm and content. The love he now possessed radiated past the physical and transformed him into something one could only admire.

"Everyone already thinks that I'm dead thanks to Cory and your doctor," Royal said as their bodyguards escorted them. "I might as well start a new life."

He stole a look at his wife. Strong. Beautiful. Resilient. She had stood by him until her end. She had endured the sins of his life with more dignity than even he could, and she had done so at his expense with no blame.

I owe you everything, he thought to himself. It was a recurring though lately. His existence was no longer complete without her.

He grabbed her hand and led her to their private jet.

This was the end of their stories apart and the beginning of their one life together. God only knew what was in store.

Dmitry had been by Royal's side the entire time of her recovery. Every time that she woke, he was there to take care of her – feed her, bathe her, dress her, read to her. Every need had been met. Every promise kept. He did so with little to no sleep. He barely ate. He never stopped worrying.

He paid the coroner, doctors, lawyers, police and the local judges millions to stay out of jail and out of court – to keep his secret of Royal's survival.

All that he cared for was her health. It had been his dedication that kept her and his blooming daughter alive.

And it had been New York and Moscow that had come in to help the transition go smoothly. He had their blessings and therefore their protection. Men came in droves from across the world. They replenished the ranks and worked faithfully under the Medlov Family's newest boss.

Upon her recovery, Dmitry and Royal were married in their home with only Cory and Anatoly to witness a quaint, private ceremony. She could never again call her adopted family or see Renée but the trade was worth it. She wished them all well.

Royal had known no pain after that horrible night with Ivan and no greater pleasure than being married to a man that seemed to live to provide her complete happiness.

For weeks after Ivan's attack, Royal had been displaced. The transfusions, the pain pills, the nightmares overwhelmed her. For weeks, she could feel his large hands on her body, his tongue in her mouth, his scent on her skin. She remembered the thrust of his hips and the cut of his blade. But with her healing, resolve had come.

Ivan's death had been retribution for his crimes against her.

Royal looked up just in time to see Dmitry lean over and kiss her lips softly.

"Let's get the hell out of here, Mrs. Medlov."

She and her entourage boarded and relaxed as the stewardess seated them and prepared the passengers for takeoff.

Quietly, Dmitry sent Anatoly a text. It simply read, *"From a father to a son, thank you."*

Anatoly smiled as he read it. He sped through the streets of Memphis in his father's old Mercedes-Benz with a new lease on life and a new woman in the passenger seat.

"Good Luck, Papa," he texted back. *"I hope that you enjoy your new boring life cooking borscht and chasing brats."*

Dmitry smiled and deleted the text.

"Everything okay, baby?" Royal asked, touching his arm.

"Everything is perfect, sweetheart," he said, grabbing the champagne off the tray as the stewardess passed.

About the Author

Latrivia S. Nelson is an urban fiction and interracial romance author. Her first novel, *Ivy's Twisted Vine* (2008), is the largest interracial novel in its genre. *Dmitry's Closet* is her first urban fiction/interracial romance novel.

Currently, Nelson is working on her next book and pursing her Ph.D. in criminal justice. She lives in the suburbs of Memphis with her husband (Adam) and two children (Tierra & Jordan) and works for The Carter Malone Group, a full-service public relations firm.

www.latrivianelson.com   www.dmitryscloset.com